time and time again

A Collection

ALSO BY TAMARA IRELAND STONE

Every Last Word

time and time again

A Collection

TAMARA IRELAND STONE

Hyperion

Los Angeles   New York

Time Between Us copyright © 2012 by Tamara Ireland Stone
Time After Time copyright © 2013 by Tamara Ireland Stone

Corduroy written by Eddie Vedder, Dave Abbruzzese, Jeff Ament, Stone Gossard and Mike McCready copyright © 1994 by Innocent Bystander, Pickled Fish Music, Scribing C-Ment Songs, Write Treatage Music and Jumpin' Cat Music

If I Could words and music by Trey Anastasio copyright © by Who Is She? Music, Inc. (BMI)

First Bind-Up Edition, June 2017
Time Between Us First Hardcover Edition, October 2012
Time Between Us First Paperback Edition, September 2013
Time After Time First Hardcover Edition, October 2013
Time After Time First Paperback Edition, October 2014

10 9 8 7 6 5 4 3 2 1
FAC-025438-17111
Printed in the United States of America

This book is set in Bell MT, Guadalupe, Type Embellishments/Monotype
Designed by Whitney Manger

Library of Congress Control Number for *Time Between Us*: 2011053368
Library of Congress Control Number for *Time After Time*: 2013018856

ISBN 978-1-4847-8133-3
Visit www.hyperionteens.com

SUSTAINABLE FORESTRY INITIATIVE
Certified Chain of Custody
Promoting Sustainable Forestry
www.sfiprogram.org
SFI-01054
The SFI label applies to the text stock

For Michael, my daring adventure

For Aidan and Lauren, siblings and best friends.
Carriers of my heart.

time between us

Time is the longest distance between two places.

TENNESSEE WILLIAMS

october 2011

san francisco, california

Even from this distance I can see how young he looks. Younger than the first time I saw him.

He and his friends have been skating around Lafayette Park for the last couple of hours, and now they're sprawled across the grass, downing Gatorades and passing around a bag of Doritos.

"Excuse me."

Eight sixteen-year-old heads spin in my direction, looking confused, then curious.

"Are you Bennett?" I ask and wait for him to nod, even though I'm sure it's him. I'd know him anywhere. "Can I speak with you for a moment? In private?"

He knits his eyebrows together, but then he stands up and flips his skateboard over to keep it from rolling down the hill. I catch him looking back at his friends and shrugging as he follows me to the closest bench. He sits at the opposite end, as far away from me as possible.

Everything about him is so similar, so familiar, that I almost scoot over to close the distance, like I would have done so naturally when I was younger. But sixteen years have come between us, and that's enough to keep me on my side of the bench.

"Hi." My voice shakes, and I twist a curly strand of hair around my finger before catching myself and returning my hand to my side, pressing both palms into the wooden slats.

"Ummm . . . Hi?" he says. He studies me through the uncomfortable silence. "I'm sorry, am I supposed to know you or something?"

My instinct is to say yes, but I stop myself, press my lips together, and shake my head instead. He doesn't know me. Not yet. "I'm Anna. Here." I reach into my bag, pull out the sealed white envelope, and smile as I hold it out to him.

He takes the letter and turns it over a few times.

"I thought it would be safer to explain in writing." My next words are the most important. After all my practice, I should have this part perfected, but I think through each word in my head again, just to be sure. "It's too easy for me to say the wrong thing today, and if I do, we may never meet at all."

His head springs up, and he stares at me, wide-eyed. No one's ever said anything like that to him before, and with that one statement, he knows that I'm in on his secret.

"I'd better go." I stand up. "Read that when you're alone, okay?" I leave him on the bench and walk back down the hill.

I keep my eyes glued to a single sailboat skimming across the San Francisco Bay so I won't turn around. After years of agonizing over this moment, I expect to feel relieved, but I don't—I just miss him all over again.

What I just did could change everything, or it could change nothing. But I have to try. I've got nothing to lose. If my plan doesn't work, my life will remain the same: Safe. Comfortable. Perfectly average.

But that wasn't the life I originally chose.

march 1995

1

evanston, illinois

I shake out my arms to get the blood flowing, rock my head back and forth until I hear a little pop, and take a deep breath of early morning air that's so cold it stings on the way down. Still, I muster a silent thanks for the fact that it's warmer than last week. I tighten the neoprene belt that holds my Discman around my waist and turn up the music so Green Day is loud in my ears. And I'm off.

I take the usual series of turns through my neighborhood until I reach the running path that hugs the glassy expanse of Lake Michigan. I twist around the last bend, giving myself a clear view of the route all the way to the Northwestern University track, and I spot the man in the green vest. As we run toward each other, our ponytails—his gray, mine unruly—swing back and forth, and we raise our hands and give each other a little wave. "'Morning," I say as we pass.

The sun is slowly rising over the lake as I turn toward the soccer field, and when my feet connect with the spongy surface of the track, I feel a new burst of energy that makes me pick up the pace. I'm halfway around the loop when the CD shuffles again and the new song transports me back to the coffeehouse the night before. The band was amazing, and when they played those first few notes the whole place exploded, everyone bouncing and head-bobbing in unison as the line that separated us local high schoolers from the transitory college students disappeared completely. I take a quick look around to be sure I'm alone. All I can see is empty row after row of metal bleachers, heavy with a winter's worth of snow that no one's bothered to dust off, so I belt out the chorus.

I'm racing around the curves, legs throbbing, heart pounding, arms pumping. Inhaling arctic air. Exhaling steam. Enjoying my thirty minutes of solitude, when it's just me and my run and my music and my thoughts. When I'm completely alone.

And then I realize I'm not. I see someone in the bleachers, hip-deep in the icy fluff of the third row and impossible to miss. He's just sitting there with his chin resting on his hands, wearing a black parka and a small smile, watching me.

I steal glances at him but continue to run, pretending not to care about his presence in my sanctuary. He looks like a Northwestern student, maybe a freshman, with dark shaggy hair and soft features. He doesn't look threatening, and even if he is, I can outrun him.

But what if I can't?

My mind jumps to the self-defense courses Dad made me take when I started running in the near dark. Knee to the groin. Palm thrust to the nose. But first, you should try to avoid confrontation by simply acknowledging the attacker's presence. Which sounds much easier.

As I come around the bend, I give him a slight nod and a glare that probably conveys a weird mix of fear and tenacity—like I'm daring him to make a move but terrified that he just might. And as I run by, staring him down, I watch his face change. His smile disappears, and now he looks sad and dejected, like I just used those self-defense skills to punch him in the gut.

But as I follow the curve of the track and start heading toward him again, I look up, right in his direction. He gives me a more hesitant smile, but it's warm, like he knows me. Genuine, like he might just be someone worth knowing. And I can't help it. I smile back.

I'm still grinning as I turn the next bend, and without even thinking about it, I flip around midstride to look at him again.

He's gone.

I spin in place while my eyes search the track for him, and then I sprint to the bleachers. At the bottom of the steps, I hesitate for a second, wondering if he was ever there at all, but I gather my courage and trudge up.

He's not there, but he had been. He left proof: the snow

is packed down where he sat, and on the bench below, two depressions show where his feet rested.

And that's when I notice something else.

My own footprints are clearly visible in the powder around me, but where his should have been—leading to and from the bench—I see nothing but a thick layer of untouched snow.

2

I race into the house and take the stairs two at a time. I turn on the shower, peel off my sweat-drenched clothes, and stand naked while I down a glass of water and let the steam fill the bathroom. My reflection in the medicine cabinet mirror fades away behind the thick fog, and when my image becomes completely obscured, I run my palm across the glass, clearing a wet, dotted path in the condensation. I consider my face again. I don't look crazy.

I spend my entire shower wondering if he was real, whom I can tell, and how I might possibly come out of that conversation sounding sane. As I get dressed for school, his face is still creeping into my thoughts, but I do my best to push the whole thing out of my mind and try to convince myself I imagined it. Still, I vow to avoid the track for the rest of the week. I know what I saw.

I shake it off as I zip into my boots and give myself one last check in the full-length mirror. I run my fingers through my curls, scrunch them up in my hands, and shake my head again. Useless.

Throwing my backpack over my shoulder, I force myself to move on to my morning ritual. I stand before the map that decorates the largest wall in my room; I close my eyes, touch it, and open them again. Callao, Peru. Good. I was hoping for someplace warm.

With my travel dreams on his mind, one day last summer Dad spent a secret hour in the garage adhering this giant paper map of the world to a foam-core board. "You can mark all the places you go," he said as he handed me a small box of red pins. I stood there and stared at it—this colorful expanse of paper, with its topographic mountain ranges and changeable shades of blue to depict the various depths of the ocean—and saw a map of the world, but knew it wasn't mine. My world was much, much smaller.

After Dad left the room, I stuck the little red pins into the paper, one by one. My class had visited the state capital last year, so I put a pin in Springfield. We once took a family camping trip to Boundary Waters, so I put one in northeastern Minnesota. We spent a Fourth of July in Grand Rapids, Michigan. My aunt lives in northern Indiana, and we go twice a year. That was it. Four pins.

At first, all I could see was that pathetic little cluster of red near the state of Illinois, but now I view the map the way

Dad intended. Like it's asking me to see every square inch of it with my own eyes, challenging me to make my little world larger and larger, pin by pin.

I give the map one last look and head down the stairs toward the glorious scent coming from the kitchen. I don't even need to hit the landing to know that Dad's standing at the coffeepot pouring out two mugs—one black, for him; one with milk, for me. I grab my cup from his outstretched hand. "Good morning. Mom already gone?"

"She left before you did. Early shift." He watches me take a sip, and then he steals a peek out the kitchen window. "Where did you run today? It's still pretty dark out there." He sounds worried.

"Campus. The usual." There's no way I'm telling him about the guy at the track. "It's freezing, too. That was a tough first mile." I pour myself a bowl of raisin bran and plop down on the stool at the counter. "You're welcome to join me, you know," I say with a grin. I know what's coming next.

He looks at me, eyebrows raised. "Wake me up some morning in June and I'll run with you. Until then, you aren't getting me out of my warm bed for that kind of torture."

"Wuss."

"Yes." He nods and raises his coffee mug in a mock toast. "Yes, I am. Unlike my Annie." He shakes his head. "I created a monster."

Dad turned me into a runner. He had been an Illinois Cross-Country State Finalist in high school. With his glory days behind him, now he's the crazy guy in a professorial sport coat standing at the end of the course, clapping wildly and cheering me on in a booming voice that threatens to take down the forest's most sturdy oaks. It's gotten worse now that the cross-country season has ended and I'm running track, where he's never out of sight and there are no trees to muffle him. Even though he's beyond embarrassing, he's devoted. In return, he's the only one I still allow to call me Annie.

Dad goes back to his paper while I down my coffee and finish my cereal in comfortable quiet. Unlike Mom, who seems compelled to fill silence, Dad lets it stick around like a member of the family. But then the low horn of Emma's car breaks the calm.

Dad drops one side of the newspaper. "There's your Brit."

I give him a peck on the cheek and head outside.

The car is humming in the driveway, and I walk toward it as quickly as I can without banana-peeling on the ice-covered concrete. I let out a little breath of relief when I swing open the door of Emma's shiny new Saab and fall into warm leather.

"'Morning, love," Emma Atkins chirps in her British accent. She throws the gearshift into reverse and flies out of the driveway. "Did you hear?" she blurts out, like the words have been locked up in there for hours and she's finally setting them free.

"Of course not." I look at her and roll my eyes. "Why would I hear anything before you do?"

"New kid starting today. He just moved here from *California*. That could be good, right?" While Emma's seen the world, she hasn't seen much of the States beyond the Midwest. California seems like a fantastic American oddity to her, like frozen custard or a hot dog dipped in cornmeal and impaled on a stick.

"Anything new is good," I say, and when I turn to look at her, I see that she's wearing more than the usual amount of eye shadow, extra accessories, and the uniform miniskirt she had hemmed to make it "mini-er." Clearly the new guy's been heavy on her mind since she woke up this morning. When we stop at the light, I watch her stretch her neck to look into the rearview mirror and blot her lipstick with her fingertip. Not that she needs any extra help. She's English, but she looks more like a Brazilian supermodel with her high, defined cheekbones and dark, sultry eyes. Today I didn't even bother to put on lip gloss, and when we walk into school together, whether Emma's all dolled up for the new guy or not, I know which one of us turns heads.

Even more extraordinary than the extra effort she's taken with her appearance is the fact that she hasn't bothered to put on music. I reach into the glove compartment and start sifting through the pile of CDs, loose and scratching up against each other, until my fingertips feel suede. I unearth the hot pink case I bought Emma for her birthday last year, and start slipping the disks into the little plastic sleeves.

"Hey, why aren't you more excited? This is big news, Anna.

We haven't had a new student since . . ." She trails off as she thumps her fingers on the steering wheel, like she does when she's deep in thought.

I don't even look up from my project as I finish her sentence. "Me."

"Really?"

I shrug and nod. "Yeah. Eighth grade. Zits and braces. Frizzy hair. That horrible plaid Westlake jumper." I wince at the thought of that last one. "New kid. Me."

"Really . . ." She stares out the window and thinks about it, like there's a chance I'm wrong. Then she says, "Huh. I guess so." She reaches over and pinches my cheek. "And see what a good day that turned out to be! Without you, I'd be singing all by myself. Speaking of which, we're going to be at school before you choose one. Here." Emma reaches over and grabs the disk on top. *"Vitalogy.* Perfect."

We've been playing the new Pearl Jam CD practically non-stop for the last three months. She slips it into the stereo and turns up the volume as high as she can without distorting the bass. She looks at me and smiles, moving to the beat as the opening guitar notes of "Corduroy" start out quietly, then build, escalating at a steady rhythm until the car is filled with sound. I lean back into my seat as the drums join in, softly at first, then louder. We hear the last five notes of the intro and that's our cue—we look at each other and sing.

> *The waiting drove me mad. . . .*
> *You're finally here and I'm a mess. . . .*

We sing every word, loud and off-key, but the final minute of the song is instrumental, so that's where we really let go. I air-guitar and bob my head while Emma drums on the steering wheel, her hands flying around and slapping the leather, but as close to "ten and two" as I've ever seen them. As if she were capable of choreographing our arrival, she pulls into her usual parking space just as the last guitar notes fade to black and twists the key in the ignition. "Pearl Jam's coming back to Soldier Field this summer, you know? You should get Freckles to get us tickets."

"Stop calling him that." I stifle a laugh. "His name is Justin. And yeah, he can probably get us tickets. . . ."

She looks at me sideways, eyebrows raised. "*Probably?* Come on, he'll do anything you ask. That boy has it *bad* for you."

"No, he doesn't. I've known him since I was five. We're just friends."

"And is *he* aware of this?"

"Of course he is." My parents and Justin's have all known one another for years, and for most of them, he and I were inseparable. But things have changed. Justin Reilly used to feel like a comfortable pair of sweats, but now he's more like a prom dress. Lovely but itchy.

"Fine, then would you kindly ask your *friend* if he can score us Pearl Jam tickets?" She's just about to get out of the car, but she stops, seeming to have had a new thought. "Wait, what if he can't get them? Then what?"

I stare at her. "Do you want to see Pearl Jam this summer, Em?"

She nods. "Of course."

"And when was the last time you didn't get what you wanted?"

I wait while she thinks about it. Then she shrugs and smiles. "Am I that spoiled?"

"No," I lie. Emma gives me her puppy dog look, and I say, "Sometimes, but I love ya anyway," and that gets a smile.

Emma and I walk from the student lot to the side entrance. Inside, we stamp our feet on the doormat, watching as the heater above us melts the snow on our boots and makes it drip, and for the first time all morning, I have an opening. If I'm going to tell anyone what happened at the track, Emma is the one, and now is the time, but I don't know where to start. How am I supposed to tell my best friend that a guy appeared out of thin air, smiled at me, and disappeared before my eyes, leaving me with nothing more than an impression of his butt and a nagging mystery to solve?

"Em?"

"Yeah?"

"Can I tell you something . . . weird?" I look around to be sure no one can overhear me, because it's one thing to tell your best friend that you may be losing your mind and another thing entirely for the news to catch fire and start making the loop.

"Of course."

We walk toward our lockers and stop, but just as I open my mouth to tell her, Alex Camarian comes around the corner, wearing his basketball jacket and a huge grin, and throws his arm over Emma's shoulder.

He sticks his face between the two of us, and I hear him murmur into her ear, "Good morning, gorgeous."

"Ugh, Alex," Emma says, giving him a small push but still egging him on with a half smile. "Can't you see we're having a conversation? What do you want?"

Before he can answer her question, the first bell rings. "I'll tell you what I want . . ." he says, pulling her to his chest, ". . . if you walk The Donut with me."

Emma looks at me. Then at Alex. Then down the circular hallway dubbed The Donut.

She gives me another glance, this time asking silent permission, and I give her what I think is an encouraging smile as Alex offers her his arm. "May I?" His pseudo-sexy voice is matched by an earnest expression that makes him look like he's trying out for the lead role in a cheesy soap opera, and I watch as she lets him thread his arm through hers and lead her away. She looks back at me with a shrug and a grimace, like she has no choice but to go with him, and mouths the words *Later, okay?*

Maybe Alex's intervention is a sign: if I am seeing disappearing guys, that information may best be kept to myself. I reach into my locker, grab books for my next three classes and a piece of gum for the road, and stand up.

And that's when I spot him. I freeze, staring at him like the apparition he must be. Dean Parker's arm is draped over his shoulders in a fatherly way as he guides him through the hall, past the throng of students, pointing into doorways and calling his attention to the signs on the walls. Directing him to his first class on his first day at his new school.

The new student. The one from California. A guy with dark shaggy hair—and there's no question in my mind, the same guy I saw at the track.

They pass right by me, neither one giving me so much as a glance. I stand there, slack-jawed and pale, as the two of them round the corner out of sight.

3

I'm usually the first one through the door, but today I make it to Spanish just as the fourth-period bell rings. Señor Argotta watches me with this surprised look on his face, like I'm the last person he expects to be late for his class. He waves the bright yellow tardy slip back and forth in front of me as I walk by. *"Hola*, Señorita Greene." He tries to look stern, but he can't hold the expression for more than a second before his face relaxes back into a grin.

"Hola, señor." I race past him with my head bowed at first, but then I turn around and give him an apologetic smile as I collapse in my chair. I remove my spiral notebook from my backpack and dig around for a mint while I contemplate the mystery this day has become.

He's real. And he's *here.*

I can't stanch the flow of questions racing through my head. First: Where has he been all morning? I've walked

The Donut between every class so far and he's nowhere to be found. Second: Why would a high school kid who's new in town be hanging out at a university track at 6:45 a.m. on a Monday? Third: Why did he look at me like he knew me, but pass right by me two hours later like I was a total stranger? Unless . . . maybe he just didn't see me. If I could just find him, I'd know.

Where is he?

Alex flops into the seat next to me, and Argotta picks up the pad of tardy slips and waves it at him with a scolding voice and matching expression. "You're late, Señor Camarian," he says in his thick accent. But within seconds he returns the pad to his desk, and Alex gets the same understanding smile Argotta gave me.

"Sorry, señor," Alex says toward the front of the room, and then he leans across the aisle, well into my space. "*Hola,* Anna." I blink from the glare of his teeth, blinding under the harsh fluorescent lights.

"Hey, Alex."

He opens his mouth to say something else, but before he can verbalize the thought, Argotta clears his throat at the front of the room and begins speaking.

"Attention, please! Today we are welcoming a brand-new student." I look up and my breath catches. "This is Bennett Cooper." Argotta pauses dramatically while the new guy shifts his weight from one leg to the other and adjusts his backpack over his shoulder. "Everyone, please welcome our new amigo and make him feel at home here." Argotta points at a seat behind me and one row over, and the new guy starts walking toward it. "Now, essays, please, everyone."

Twenty sets of curious eyes follow him, settle on him for a moment, and turn their attention to their respective bags to unearth stapled essays on Spain's admission to the European Union. My eyes are among those that look at him, but are also the only pair that can't seem to look away.

Bennett. His name is Bennett.

He's looking down at his desk and playing with the pages of his textbook like he's embarrassed by all the attention, but after a few moments, he slowly raises his head. I watch his gaze land on the door at the far end of the room, move clockwise around the perimeter of the classroom, and come to a sudden stop when he sees me. Because I'm still staring at him.

I don't know how long my face has been frozen like this, but as soon as I realize that he's caught me, the flush creeps up my neck and into my cheeks, and I feel myself do the only thing I can do at this point: I smile. And I wait for it to be returned, with not just any smile, but *that* smile. The one from the track. The one filled with warmth and recognition and . . . interest. But his expression contains none of the above. Instead he shoots me a small, almost shy smile. The kind of smile one might give a total stranger.

I can't possibly look that different in my uniform than I did in running clothes. *Why is he pretending he doesn't recognize me?* I realize I'm still staring at him, and now the tips of my ears are burning and my face has fully ignited. I flip around in my chair and reach down into my backpack, searching for a distraction. My hair starts to tickle my nose, so when I sit back up, I grab a handful of curls, twist it around my finger, and stick my pencil through the middle to hold it in place.

Twenty minutes later, Argotta snaps my attention back to the room when he holds his arms out wide and exclaims, "Let's do four practice groups today, okay?"

I look down at my notebook and discover that its pages are covered with words and phrases and conjugations, which is surprising, because I don't think I've heard a word Argotta's said. He points to Courtney Breslin in the front row and says, "Count us off, señorita! *Por favor.*"

"*Uno.*" And the count-off continues, snaking its way around the room until it comes to me.

"*Cuatro,*" I say, and then I listen. And work hard not to move my head at all. A few minutes later, I hear what I've been waiting for. The voice over my shoulder says, "*Uno.*"

At the end of the count-off, Argotta yells, "Bring your stuff," and we begin moving around the room to our newly assigned sections. I'm in Group Four and Bennett is in Group One— clear across the room—and this is where we will stay for the remainder of the class. As quickly as he appeared behind me, he is now as far away from me as possible; but at least I can study him better from this angle.

His uniform is the same as the rest of the guys': Black pants and a white oxford shirt under a black V-neck sweater. I think he's wearing Doc Martens, but it's hard to tell from here. It's easy to see what's different: his hair. Most guys wear theirs in some conservative, neatly parted style. Others sport ultrashort Caesars or leave it a little long on top but shaved on the sides. But their hair is never *this* long. Bennett's is unkempt, hangs just a little over his eyebrows, and looks like it hasn't seen a brush in days. I can't remember what he was wearing at the track, but the hair . . . That's definitely the same. The hair I remember.

When the bell rings thirty minutes later, everyone stands up and moves for the door, blocking my view. I rise and reach for my backpack, quickly deciding to talk to him on his way to lunch, but all I catch is the blur of his head as he vanishes through the doorway.

When I go through the double doors to the dining hall, I spot him right away. He's sitting alone at a table in the corner, with his back to the floor-to-ceiling windows. I make my way through the salad bar, grab a banana, and fill a large cup with Coke, all while stealing glances in his direction. As it turns out, I'm in no danger of being caught. In the five minutes it takes me to get my food, he doesn't look up once. He just sits in his chair, holding a paperback in one hand while he picks at his food with the other.

Danielle is already planted at our usual table, and as I set my tray down, I steal another quick look in Bennett's direction. He spoons out bites of red Jell-O without looking away from his book.

"Scoping out the new guy already?" Danielle asks.

I look at her with surprise, then panic. "No." I sit down and reach for my drink. "Why?"

"Oh, come on! I've been watching you. I've never seen anyone work a salad bar with her eyes glued on someone twenty feet away. It's impressive. Quite a skill."

The tips of my ears begin to burn. Again.

She laughs and takes a sip of her Coke. "You're talented, Anna, but you're hardly subtle." She moves close and gives my arm a reassuring pat. "Don't worry. He didn't notice. I don't think he's looked away from that book once."

Emma arrives breathless, plops her tray down on the table, and takes her seat. "So . . . what do we think?" She draws out the last word in a higher inflection.

Danielle shrugs and tilts her chair back, balancing on the two back legs and not even attempting restraint as she stares at him across the room. "He looks . . . oblivious. Do you think he knows there are other people in the room?"

"He looks older, or something," Emma chimes in.

I pretend to look around the room before letting my eyes settle on him again. It's not that he looks older—he's actually got a bit of a baby face. Danielle was closer. He looks indifferent, like he doesn't seem to care that he's here—or care that we're all staring, wondering *why* he's here—and that alone makes him even more interesting. At least to me.

"Hmmm . . . I think I'm disappointed." Emma stares straight at him, taking stock of every detail. She turns back to look at us, eyes wide, nose crinkled. "He's definitely not what I was hoping for. He looks like every other guy in this cold, dreary town. No tan. No hot blond surfer hair." She takes a bite of a bread stick. "I shouldn't have gotten my hopes up."

"Maybe that is surfer hair," suggests Danielle. "How do you know what surfer hair looks like?"

"You know, it's long." Emma wiggles her fingers next to her head. "It looks cool. Not like"—she directs her thumb toward Bennett's table—"that mop top of his."

"Come on, you guys. Give him a break." They both turn to me, their professionally shaped brows raised in matching expressions, and stare. "What?" I shrug and take a deep pull on my straw, letting the cold liquid slide down my throat and cool my face.

Emma finally picks up a forkful of salad and directs it toward her mouth, and for a split second, I think I'm off the hook. But then she stops. "Okay, I'll ask." The lettuce and tomatoes hover in front of her. "Why do you care what we think?"

"I don't. It's just . . . You're just being mean."

"We're not being mean!" Emma looks at Danielle. "Are we being mean?"

Danielle shakes her head no. "I didn't think we were being mean."

"We're just observing. Like . . . scientists." She shoots me a smart-ass grin and pops the fork into her mouth.

I let out a sigh and pick at my sandwich. She's right. Why *do* I care what they think? It's not like I know him. And since

I don't seem to be at all familiar to him, I'm starting to wonder if the thing at the track this morning even happened.

Emma and Danielle are watching me intently and exchanging meaningful glances as they eat. Then Emma shoots Danielle her "don't worry, I've got this one" look, turns to me with those soft eyes, and begins to do what she does best: make people tell her things they don't want to tell her. It's like a superpower or something. "Anna?" she sings. "What's going on?"

I look at her like I know this trick, like I'm not about to give in to it, but then I fold. I bury my face in my hands. "It's nothing. It's just weird." I try to say it under my breath, but it comes out loud enough for them to hear. Emma gently pulls my hands away from my face and makes me look at her.

"What's weird?" Then she remembers this morning, and things click. "Wait, like the weird thing you were going to tell me before class?"

I look around the room, checking for anyone else within earshot, and when I turn back again, I find Emma and Danielle leaning in so close to me their cheeks are nearly touching.

I look around the room again before moving in toward them. "Fine." I let out a sigh. "So . . . I was on my run at the Northwestern track this morning. I ran around a couple of times, and all of sudden, I looked up in the bleachers and saw this guy sitting there, watching me. I ignored him at first—I just kept running and he just kept staring at me—but when I came around the bend . . ." I stop and scan the room one more time. "He was gone. And I mean, *gone* gone. He just . . . disappeared." I leave out the part about how he smiled at me.

"Okay, that's definitely weird," Emma says and looks at me wide-eyed. She must see something in my expression that tells her there's more. "And?"

I gesture with my chin toward Bennett's table. "And that's *him*." Out loud, it sounds even weirder than it did in my head.

Emma and Danielle spin in their chairs and take him in again. "Are you sure?" Emma asks without taking her eyes off Bennett.

I look past them, directly at his table. "He looks like the same person. Same build. Definitely the same hair. The weirdest thing was that at the track, he looked at me like he . . . knew me or something. But he doesn't even seem to recognize me now." They're still staring. "Please stop looking at him."

"He's not that bad, I guess," says Danielle.

"Yeah, if you look past the hair he's sorta cute," Emma agrees. But when she turns around again her expression is stern, maternal. "But you know, the track thing is sorta creepy."

I look past them, watching him. If he's noticed the three of us talking about him, sizing him up, he never lets on.

"I know!" Danielle says, and I peek up at her with optimistic eyes. "Go up and ask him."

I roll my eyes at her encouraging smile, but before I can even reply, I hear Emma say, "Good idea." She slaps her palms on the table and pushes herself to standing, with an emphatic "Let's just go get this sorted."

"What? No!" I shove my hair behind my ears. "Please don't. I swear if you go over there, I am not speaking to you."

She stops and turns on her heel. "I'm helping."

I grit my teeth and stare her down. "Emma. Atkins. Seriously; please don't."

Emma walks back to our table. "Look, he was watching you and he creeped you out and now he's acting like it never even happened. I want to know why." She turns and starts back toward him, and before I have time to consider bolting from the room, she reaches his table. Danielle and I watch, frozen and lame, as Emma invades his space with a little wave. They shake hands and exchange a few words before she points back in our direction.

He dog-ears his page and stuffs the book into his backpack, then grabs his tray and follows a beaming Emma to our table. I'd probably get more than detention if I reached out and strangled her upon arrival, but that doesn't stop me from considering it.

"Ladies"—Emma extends her arms toward our guest— "this is Bennett Cooper."

He smiles at the two of us and then looks expectantly back at Emma.

"Take a seat here." She pulls an empty chair out from the table and returns to her own. "So, Bennett, this is Danielle. And this"—she pauses in a pathetic attempt at dramatic effect—"is our track star." She gestures toward me, and Bennett's eyes follow until they rest on mine.

"Cross-country," I correct her.

"Whatever." Emma shrugs at me and turns her attention back to Bennett. "She's a runner." She twists in her chair to face him straight on. "But you already knew that, right?" Her accusatory glare is fierce and unrelenting.

Oh. Dear. God.

He looks at her, then back at me, then back at her. "I'm not sure what you mean."

"Didn't you two see each other at the Northwestern track this morning, Bennett?" she asks, sharp and critical, like a lawyer cross-examining her witness. Emma rests her hand on my shoulder. "She runs there at the crack of dawn. She saw you there. You were watching her."

Yes. Emma is going to die.

"Northwestern?" He furrows his brow and stares at us. Like he's never heard of the university that dominates this town. "I'm sorry, but that's impossible. I just moved here over the weekend. I've barely seen *this* campus, let alone the university." He looks straight at me and smiles—kind and sincere, like he's telling the truth—and even though it's not the same smile, it's much closer to the one he shot me at the track. Close enough to make me all the more certain I've got the right guy. "You must have me confused with someone else."

I don't. I stare at him with nervous anticipation, waiting for him to tell me he's just kidding and reach across the table to give me a friendly punch in the arm. But he just sits there.

Looking at me like this is the first time he's ever seen me. And like maybe I'm nuts. "Are you sure? You were wearing a parka," I finally say.

There it is again. His smile is still tinged with confusion, still lacking any sort of recognition, but it's warm. Sweet. The *same*. "I'm sorry, I don't own a parka," he says. "It wasn't me." I want to believe him, but I can't, and when I look over at Emma, she's still wearing a questioning expression that makes me think she doesn't either.

Still, I decide to let him off the hook, and I try to match the warmth in his eyes. "You just look . . . exactly like him. I guess I was mistaken." I hope my expression is masking my lie. And my embarrassment. I reach across the table. "I'm Anna."

He was already reaching his hand forward to meet mine, but it stops midway. "Anna?" He stares at me in disbelief. "Your name is Anna?"

"Ummm, yes. . . . Should it be something else?" I say, surprised to hear a flirtatious inflection creeping into my voice.

"So now her *name* rings a bell!" Emma says to Danielle, far too loudly.

He's still staring at me, and for just a split second, I see a trace of recognition in his expression that reminds me of the look he gave me at the track this morning. But then he snaps out of it and reaches for my hand again.

"Nice to meet you, Anna." Now his voice sounds forced, his handshake is stiff, and anything that looked like recognition has been replaced by a certain stoniness. He lets my hand go and turns to Emma and Danielle, giving each of them a formal nod. "Nice to meet you, too." He stands and carries his tray to the garbage bin in the middle of the room, and I see him shake his head as he walks out through the double doors and disappears into The Donut.

"Okay, *that* was weird." Emma sighs. "But at least it's done." She brushes her hands together as if she'd just completed a nasty chore.

I know she only wanted to protect me, but that doesn't make me feel any better about looking like an idiot. Words like *beyond awkward* and *mortifying* and *why?* pop into my brain, and I want to turn them into cohesive sentences and spit them out; but I can't think straight. Besides, Emma knows that I'm nothing if not true to my word: I'm no longer speaking to her.

The little bundle of bells that has been hanging on the bookstore door as long as I can remember makes its jingle, and Dad looks up from behind the counter. I lug my backpack over to him and let it land with a thunk.

"What happened to you?" His voice is full of concern.

I left without saying good-bye to Emma and walked two miles through the frozen tundra. My teeth are still chattering, my face is red and chapped from the wind, and there's not a pencil on earth large enough to wrangle my curls into place at this point. "Nothing." I smooth out my hair and distract him with a question. "Has it been slow all day?"

He glances around the empty bookstore my grandfather bought when he retired from teaching at Northwestern fifteen years ago. "Typical March. It'll pick up after finals."

Dad watches as I remove a T-shirt from my bag to change into, then extract textbook after textbook and pile them on the desk. "Good God, how many books can you fit in there? That backpack's like a clown car." He laughs, but I know he's genuinely perplexed by how different my high school experience at Westlake Academy seems from the one he had at Evanston Township.

"You're the one who wanted me to go to that fancy school," I remind him as I wave one of my heftier books in the air.

He grabs it, grimaces like it's far too heavy for him to lift, and lets it crash onto the desk. "You're a rock star." He kisses me on the forehead and heads for the door. "It's supposed to start snowing soon," he says, zipping his parka and wrapping his scarf around his neck. "Give me a call if you want a ride home, okay?"

"It's only three blocks, Dad."

"And I know you're fearless and indestructible, but call me if you change your mind, okay?"

I roll my eyes. "Dad. Three blocks."

He's just about to push the glass door open when I realize that tomorrow morning's walk will be much longer. And colder.

"Hey, Dad." He turns around, one hand resting on the metal bar of the glass door. "I'll take a ride to school in the morning . . . if that's okay?"

"Oh. Does Emma have a doctor's appointment or something?"

"No."

He looks like he's about to ask me what's going on, but he must decide against it, because he just shrugs and says, "Sure," and the little bells jingle behind him.

4

"What am I doing?" I ask out loud as I add a second layer of lip gloss. Staring into the girls' bathroom mirror, I apply a coat of mascara, then roll my eyes at my reflection.

So he's cute. That hardly makes him worth the considerable effort it took me to decide on lip gloss this morning. I'm not a makeup-in-the-bathroom kind of girl, and I feel like I've lost it completely. Yesterday, I thought I was crazy because I was seeing things. I think I prefer that crazy over this one.

As I leave the bathroom and head to fourth period, I start to feel it—the adrenaline rush that I usually associate with the last half mile of a race. I stop outside the classroom for a moment to catch my breath and remind myself to enter the way I planned—looking cool and disinterested. I shake out my arms, rock my head back and forth, and take one last breath before I walk through the door.

I spot Bennett right away. He's reclining in his chair, twisting his pencil back and forth between his fingers. I expect him to look away when we make eye contact, but he doesn't. In fact, his face seems to brighten, like he's happy to see me or something. Then he looks down, still smiling to himself, and starts doodling. He doesn't look up again.

I take my seat and let out the breath I didn't realize I was holding. For something to do, I start extracting my homework from my backpack while everyone else ambles in.

When the bells rings, Argotta throws his arms high in the air and shouts, "Pop quiz!" Thankfully, the chorus of collective groans and the noise of paper being ripped from notebooks drowns out the sound of my heart pounding against my rib cage.

My palms are sweating, and I'm pretty sure the heat from my body alone is about to make my curls frizz up. Without thinking, I sweep my hair back, gather it into a ponytail, twist it around my finger, and hold it in place at the top of my head with one hand while I search through my backpack for a clip. I feel books, a collection of gum wrappers, a roll of Certs, a jewel case, but no clip, no hair band. I look over at the pencil on my desk, which always works in a bind, but I have only one and I need it for the test. My elevated arm is falling asleep and I'm just about to give up when I hear a noise behind me.

"Pssst."

I whirl around, still holding a handful of hair.

Maybe it's because he's leaning so far forward he's practically lying on top of his desk, but he seems so much closer to me right now than he did yesterday. Or perhaps it's not only his physical proximity; it's also the combination of the distance and the expression on his face. His eyes aren't vacant like they were when I stared him down in class yesterday, or confused like they were when my best friend accused him of being a creepy stalker. Today his eyes are soft, like they're smiling completely on their own, and I notice that they're an interesting shade of smoky blue, dotted with little gold flecks that catch and reflect the light. When I finally realize what I am doing—staring into his eyes like a complete moron—I lower my gaze to his mouth to find that it's not only his eyes that are smiling. His mouth is too. Like he's amused. Like he's laughing at me. And that's when I realize I'm missing something.

He points with his chin, attempting to direct my attention away from his face and toward the hand he's been extending in my direction this entire time. The one holding a pencil.

I look at it, and then back at his eyes, puzzled. Then understanding takes over, and I reach forward and take it from him.

Thanks, I mouth.

I turn toward the front of the room, stick the pencil through my hair, and get self-conscious when I realize that in the process I'm revealing the flush creeping up the back of my neck. I take a deep breath and force myself to pay attention to the quiz, which has already begun, but I can't stop the smile creeping onto my face.

He *was* paying attention to me yesterday. He noticed me put my hair up.

It's probably just a plain yellow Dixon Ticonderoga

number two pencil—exactly the same as the one I'm using to complete this ridiculous quiz—but perched in my hair, holding the strands in place, it feels a lot like what we had at the track yesterday: a connection.

Somehow I've managed to go all day without running into Emma. Until now.

I just finished track practice and I'm walking out of the locker room, heading for the student lot and chatting with a few of my teammates, when I see her. She's striding toward her car with her field hockey stick swinging by her side as she moves, and even though I assume she broke into a sweat at some point you'd never know now. Her makeup looks perfect, and her knit cap and gloves match the piping on her warm-up suit. I look down at my sweats. I came straight out of the shower, towel-dried my hair, and piled it under a baseball cap to keep it from freezing on my walk home.

"I'll get the heat going!" she yells when she sees me. After she opens the door and starts the engine, she gets out of the car and relaxes against the hood, waiting for me.

I take a quick look up at the sky and see a mass of dark clouds moving into formation, preparing to send down fury in the form of hard snow. I look down again and see Emma, smiling and beckoning. For just a split second, my resolve melts a little and I picture myself collapsing into the heated seat. I really don't want to walk home. But there is no way, *no way*, I'm letting her off that easy.

I keep walking with the group, straight past her car.

"Anna!" I can hear the shock and hurt in her voice. "Wait." The sound of her tennis shoes padding cautiously behind me closes in and I pick up my pace a little. "Seriously, can't you just stop and talk to me? I'm trying to apologize." My teammates look at me and then at one another. I wave them on and slow down so Emma can catch up.

She grabs me by the shoulder. "I really am sorry." Her remorse looks genuine and her British accent makes her sound so sincere that I'm tempted to throw my arms around her and forgive her without another word. But I haven't forgotten how mortified I felt yesterday, how she made a fool of me. And so instead, I just stare at her.

"I'm sorry," she repeats, and hugs me. I want to hug her back but instead stand rigid.

Her grip loosens, and when she steps back from me I can see how hurt she looks. But then her expression softens and she reaches forward, takes my face in her hands, and squeezes my cheeks in a soft-mittened vise grip. "I was an ass. Please don't be mad at me anymore. I simply can't take it."

I let out a sigh. "That was really uncool." My voice comes out garbled since she's now squeezing so hard my lips are pursed in a fish face.

"I know. But you love me anyway, right?" She wiggles my cheeks. "Right? Just a little?" And that's all it takes. Because I do. When I try not to laugh, my lips must look even funnier, because Emma lets out a snort, and that makes us both crack up.

She finally stops squeezing, but keeps holding my face. "I really am sorry. I just got carried away. I wasn't trying to embarrass you."

I bite my lip. "You did."

"I know."

"Please don't do it again."

"I won't," she says with a smile and a hard shake of her head. She grips my shoulders and air-kisses each of my cheeks. They still feel red from all the squeezing. "Can we get in the car now?" She clenches her jaw and shivers.

When I nod, she leads me to the Saab. She even opens my door and ushers me in before going around to her side and taking her place behind the wheel.

"Where to?" she asks. "Want to grab a coffee?"

"I can't. It's Tuesday."

"Right, family dinner night." She backs out into the nearly empty parking lot. We're silent for a few seconds, and I think she's going to reach over and crank the stereo like she always does, but instead she turns to me. "So, do you still think the new guy was the one watching you at the track?"

I shrug. "I don't know." I start to tell Emma about the pencil, but I stop myself. To someone who already considers him creepy, it might sound weird rather than charming. Come to think of it, perhaps *I* should have found it weird rather than charming. I reach up and touch the top of my head, having forgotten that I'm now wearing a baseball cap and the pencil is tucked safely in my backpack.

"Do you want my opinion?" Emma asks.

"Do I have a choice?"

"No. Stay away from him. I don't know what it is, but there's something . . . off about him."

"Oh, come on. That's just because of the track thing. He made it clear he'd never been to Northwestern. I must have been wrong." I'm not sure why I'm defending him, and I'm still sure I am *not* wrong, but I think I sound pretty convincing.

"What about how he reacted to your name?"

Yeah. That was weird. I shrug.

"Look at you. You think he's cute." She draws out the words as her accent intensifies.

"I don't even know him."

"You don't have to know him to think he's cute."

"Sure I do." I glare at her. "I'm just . . . curious about him, that's all." But if I'm being completely honest, Emma may be right. I exchanged a few meaningless glances and a pencil with him, and that somehow gave him the right to creep into my head and settle there.

The car skids to a stop in front of the house, leaving a two-foot space between my door and the snow-covered sidewalk. Emma turns to face me. "I missed you this morning, by the way."

"Me too." I finally reach over and hug her. I get out of the car and shut the door behind me, and she peels away, kicking up a flurry of dirty snow.

"Grab a knife!" Mom's singsong holler carries from the kitchen into the hallway, over Pavarotti's booming tenor. I follow the tantalizing smell of roasting peppers and onions and see Mom hard at work in the kitchen.

"Hi, honey!" Mom looks up with a smile and returns to her sauce. She's wearing a black apron over her scrubs, and her dark curls—the ones she passed down to me—are piled into a clip on top of her head, though a few loose ringlets have escaped to frame her face. She hums along with the Italian music as she draws a blade through ripe tomatoes. "Can you start slicing the mozzarella?" She uses her knife to point at the ball of slimy white cheese on the counter. "How was school?"

I twist around to watch Mom slide the last of the tomatoes into the stockpot, give them a little stir, and take a seat on one of the bar stools facing me. She rests her elbows on the counter, and I stop cutting to glance up at her. She's waiting for me to tell her everything, because it's Tuesday—the day we cook and I tell her who's dating whom, who's fighting with whom, and who's not quite cutting it on the track. Then I ask her what's going on at the hospital, and even though I imagine it's all fairly mundane, and often a sad place to spend a day, she makes it sound like she works on the set of *ER*, crafting dramatic stories about people who have pulled through even when there seemed to be no hope, and doctors who flirt with nurses, and patients who flirt with doctors. I'm glad she enjoys her job, especially since I know the only reason she went back to work was to help cover my Westlake tuition. It was my parents' idea to send me there, but it takes two salaries to pay for it. Tuesday-night dinner is pretty much all they ask for in return.

"Well?" Her eyes are wide, and she looks like she's about ready to burst. "Go ahead. Tell me about your week so far. Anything juicy?"

I hear myself say, "It's been fine," and I cast my eyes down at my cutting board, run the knife through the mozzarella, and watch it cluster onto the wood. "How about you? How was your day?" I ask in a voice that sounds far too high-pitched, and fake.

I don't look directly at her, but in the periphery I can see her squirm in her seat, like she doesn't know what to do with herself, and the seconds drag on until she speaks again.

"Oh, come on!" she finally says. "It can't be my turn yet." She gets up to check the sauce, hums along with the music again while she gives it a stir, and returns to her spot at the counter. "Come on," she repeats, beaming and practically begging. "There must have been *something* interesting."

I want so much to tell her the truth. Yesterday, someone disappeared right before my eyes. I almost got a tardy slip for the first time in my life. I walked home from school, because, until thirty minutes ago, my best friend and I weren't speaking. And there's a pencil sitting in my backpack that shouldn't feel quite so important. I want to tell her that, so far, nothing about this week has been normal, and that alone is interesting.

Mostly, I want to tell her that there's a guy at the center of all of the excitement, so she can ask me if he's cute and I can blush and nod. Instead, I keep my eyes on the cutting board and say, "I got an A on that anatomy paper you helped me with last week."

She gives me a small, forced smile. "Oh. Well . . . that's good." I can still feel her watching me slice and hoping I'll say more, and I move slowly, waiting for the right amount of time to pass so I can turn the subject back to her. After a few minutes, I hear her start drumming her fingertips on the counter. Finally, when she can no longer stand the silence, she sits up, her back straight. "Okay, I'll go," she says, and she launches into a long story about one of the nurses who got caught kissing an EMT out by the ambulance bay.

Fifteen minutes later, I hear the front door open and close. "I'm home!" Dad yells from the foyer. When he arrives in the kitchen, Mom and I are standing side by side at the counter, layering noodles, sauce, and cheese in a deep casserole dish.

"Hi, Annie." He leans down and kisses the crown of my head.

"Hey, Dad." I lift my cheesy, tomatoey fingers out of the lasagna and give him a little wave.

But before he can take another step, Mom turns around and grabs his face in her sauce-covered hands. "Hi, honey."

Dad takes two steps back, bright red handprints on both cheeks, and we both watch him, eyes wide as we wait to see how he'll react. He just stands there, stunned. Then he shakes his head and gives Mom a peck on her nose. "I'll just go wash up," he says.

"You do that," Mom says with a laugh, and the two of us crack up while we top off our creation with handfuls of shredded cheese. Then the dish goes into the oven, Mom heads for the shower, and I trudge up to my room to start on my homework.

I plop down on my shag rug and open my backpack. In the small zippered compartment in the front, I spot the pencil, right where I left it, now blanketed in gum wrappers. I take it out and run it back and forth between my fingers, just like Bennett was doing this morning as I walked through the door. I close my eyes, picturing the way he smiled as he held it out to me. And I start concocting a plan to return it.

5

Stalling.

There are more details behind my brilliant scheme to return Bennett's pencil, but that's basically what it comes down to—stalling. I intend to dawdle on my way to Spanish so I won't have time to return it before class. Then, when the lunch bell rings, I'll stand up, turn around to block Bennett's path, and give it back to him. If everything goes according to plan, I'll be able to keep him talking all the way to the dining hall.

My heart is racing as I arrive at the door. The bell rings, right on cue, but as I walk into the classroom and pass Señor Argotta, he claps and announces, "Conversation practice! Time to move, everybody!" He bursts out with it like he's declaring a celebration.

No. Not conversation practice. This is the worst of Argotta's clever little group exercises. I've timed my arrival perfectly, but it won't matter if Bennett ends up on the other side of the room again.

Argotta's walking through the rows of desks, breaking us up into pairs, and passing out laminated cards that depict a situation no one would ever find themselves in on a trip to Spain—or anywhere else in the world, for that matter. He gives me my card, and I shut my lids tight, fearing the worst. I open one eye and read: *Partner number one, you are interviewing for a job as a waiter/waitress at one of Madrid's finest restaurants. Partner number two, you are the restaurant owner.* I look over at Alex, my usual partner, and he winks.

Señor Argotta stops and turns back. "Señorita Greene, partner with Señor Cooper, *por favor.*"

What? No. I'm sorry, señor. I cannot partner with Bennett Cooper. All night I've pictured how I'm going to return his pencil. How I'm going to ask him again—when he's not under Emma's and Danielle's scrutiny—if he was at the track on Monday. I'm going to ask him why he seemed to know me then, but now he doesn't. I've pictured the whole discussion, right down to the last detail; but I've never pictured talking with him in *Spanish.*

I consider running for the door. Faking a seizure. I could move across the room and take the open seat across from Señor *Kestler,* as if I've misunderstood Argotta's accent. But it's too late. Bennett has heard the instructions just as plainly as I have, and now he's eyeing me with this "don't worry, I won't bite" look. He lifts his chin like he's commanding me to stand up, and when I do, he turns my desk around to face his.

"Hi," I say when we're both settled again.

"Hi. Anna, right?" Bennett looks completely relaxed, and the act of verbalizing my name doesn't seem to cause the odd reaction it did in the dining hall two days ago.

"Yeah." I look down at the table, trying not to look at his eyes for fear of getting trapped in there again. "Bennett, right?"

He nods.

"Do you ever go by 'Ben'?" Where did *that* come from? Oh, God.

He grins. "No. Just . . . Bennett."

And here comes the flush. I wonder if he is as curious to know what I look like without a red face as I am to see him with a haircut. "Thanks for the loan." As I pass him the pencil, I can feel all my questions just sitting there, waiting for me to launch them one by one, but I can't seem to find my voice now that he's sitting here across from me.

"Any time," he says as he sets it in the long groove at the top of the wooden desk. The pencil must have magnetic properties, because it seems to be pulling both of us into it. "So, what's our assignment today?" he asks as he leans forward, and I swallow the questions down.

"I'm afraid it's a tough one." I reach over, bridging the gap between our two desks, and set the card down with the words facing him.

He picks it up, and a grin gradually spreads over his face. "Oh, this should be easy." He leans forward, like he has a secret. "I've interviewed for several waiter jobs in Madrid before."

"Really?"

"No." He smiles. "I'm kidding."

I laugh too loud. "Well, good." I take a deep breath to steady my nerves and press my palms flat on the desk to keep my hands from shaking. I move in toward him and say, "I have no idea how to hire someone in this country or any other one." I take the card from his desk and lean back, trying to look comfortable. "So," I begin in my most practiced Spanish diction, "tell me about your experience as a waiter, Señor Cooper."

Bennett launches into a lengthy description of his work at various fictitious restaurants throughout Spain. In perfectly crafted sentences, he describes his expertise with a crumb scraper. He explains how he can talk any customer into getting the special of the day instead of the dish they really wanted. He can handle ten tables at once, including large parties, and he always overtips the bussers. He says it all with a straight face and the smallest trace of a glint in his eye.

I understand his Spanish, but I have to work to hear the words he says. He speaks beautifully. His voice is steady and strong, the cadence is balanced, and I'm completely transfixed, pulled into the richness of his voice. He tells about another fictitious job in a restaurant in Seville called *El Mesero Mejor.* The Best Waiter.

By the end he has me smiling. Laughing. And more than a little bit in awe. He concludes in his perfectly confident Spanish: "So you see, I am a perfect waiter for your restaurant." I'm not sure how much time passes between the completion of this sentence and his next word: "Well?" He raises his eyebrows and waits for my reply.

When I realize he's caught me staring again, I bite my lip and wait for the flush to spread over my face, but this time, nothing happens. I go with it. "You're hired," I say with a shrug.

"Wow? Just like that?" he says in English. "You're an easy manager."

I try to think of a clever response, but my mind is blank. "Your Spanish is really good," I say instead.

"I did a study abroad program in Barcelona last summer."

I smile when I think about living in Barcelona with a local family. "I'd love to do that. It must have been fun to *live* there. To really get into another culture."

"It was pretty incredible." He rests his forearms on the desk. "How about you? Have you been to Spain?"

"No," I say under my breath. "I haven't been . . . anywhere. I work at my family's bookstore, and I spend a lot of time in the travel section. That's about as close to the rest of the world as I get."

"I'm surprised to hear that." He leans in even closer, like he's got a secret to divulge. "This is only my third day here, but it seems like a fairly well-traveled bunch."

"It is." I shrug again. "I'm just not . . . part of that particular bunch."

"So, you work in a bookstore." It's a statement, not a question. "And read travel books."

I look at him and try to think how to respond. I'm long past the point of being embarrassed by the fact that I'm the poorest kid in this incredibly wealthy high school, but he doesn't need to rub it in. "Something like that. I take it you travel a lot."

"Me?" He looks down at the table. "Yeah. You could definitely say that. . . ." He trails off and seems to be suppressing a smile. "I love traveling." My expression must show my confusion, because his face gets serious as he clarifies. "Yes. I travel a lot. . . . As much as I can."

"Lucky you." The words sound bitter as they leave my mouth, and I immediately wish I could pull them back.

"I'm sorry. Was that rude? I didn't mean it to be."

"No." It's not his fault I've barely left the state. "You weren't rude."

"Look, anyone who wants to travel can find a way to do it. You just have to get creative."

Señor Argotta suddenly turns the corner, coming within earshot, and Bennett switches back to Spanish. He looks me right in the eye. "You know what they say, *La vida es una aventura atrevida o no es nada.*" He looks out of the corner of his eye, thinking. "I can't remember who said that."

I laugh under my breath.

"What?" Bennett's smiling along with me, even though he has no idea why I'm so amused.

"Helen Keller," I whisper, picturing the poster that hung on the wall in Miss Waters's English class back in seventh grade, its white sailboat fighting against the current in the foreground and the quote *Life is either a daring adventure or nothing* in block letters below.

"She probably didn't say it in Spanish, then."

I try to stifle my laugh but it's hopeless. "No, probably not." We're both still smiling and watching each other, but I break the connection when I look up to be sure Argotta can't hear us speaking English. He's clear across the room, kneeling down next to another team and helping them through a translation. When I look back at Bennett, I discover that his eyes haven't left me.

"Well, whatever language it's in," I say, "I have to agree with her. I, for one, am ready for a *lot* more adventure and a lot less nothing."

His smile fades, and he looks at me with a serious expression. I think he's about to say something significant, but he presses his lips together. I watch him, waiting him out, until it's clear that he's planning to stay silent.

"Were you going to say something?" I finally ask.

He gives me a little grin. "Yeah . . . actually . . ." But then the bell rings. "Never mind," he says rising and heading for the door. "I'll see you later, okay?"

I watch him walk across the room and out into the hallway. When I look down at the desk I see the pencil, still sitting in the groove, right where he put it. I twist my hair and hold it against the back of my head with one hand while I stick the pencil in place with the other.

See you later. That's what he said three days ago—*See you later.* But I didn't see him later at all. He wasn't in the dining hall, I didn't run into him in The Donut, and he wasn't in the student lot.

He was in Spanish on Thursday and Friday—and I'm certain he was watching the door for me both days, because the minute I walked in he looked down at his desk. But there was no satisfied grin when he saw me, no smile on his face as he doodled—and he didn't look up again before I took my seat. Each day, I'd tried to return the pencil, but he bolted for the door in perfect synchronization with the bell. And it was as if our conversation had never even happened.

6

The storm that starts on Saturday morning rains out my track meet, keeps me awake all night, and doesn't let up until afternoon. I walk to the bookstore in a daze, and when I manage to make it to the corner without breaking anything, I decide to reward myself with a latte. Even with the stop, I have fifteen minutes to kill before my shift, so I head into the record store.

"Anna!" Justin yells over the loud, steady backbeat of music coming from the ceiling, godlike and omnipresent. He walks out from behind the counter and pulls me in for a hug. "I was hoping you'd come by this weekend."

"Hey, buddy," I say, and silently scold myself for calling him that. It's probably worse than calling him Freckles, but words like *buddy* or *pal* or some other brotherly sounding term seem to pop out of my mouth whenever I see him. He pulls back and looks at me, and even though it's only for a brief flash, it's there. A twinge, like I just insulted him.

"What's this?" I ask, pointing up at the music.

He leans in close to me. "I scored." He looks around the store to be sure no one's listening—and no one is, since we're the only ones here. "The drummer from Nirvana just cut a demo, and Elliot let me borrow it." I don't know who Elliot is, but I imagine he's someone important at Northwestern's student-run radio station, where Justin has been interning for the last three months. While I dream of visiting far-off places, he dreams of moving into a high-rise dorm just down the street so he can major in broadcasting and spend his college years as a DJ for the station's legendary *The Rock Show*.

"Do you want to borrow it?" he asks as he steps even closer to me.

"No, really, that's—" I'm shaking my head, but it doesn't matter. He's already walking away, and when he ducks down behind the counter, the music stops. He comes back carrying the CD. "Here, take it. Tell me what you think."

"Really?"

"Absolutely. Just bring it back sometime next week."

"Thank you. That is so cool of you," I say as I press it to my chest.

"I think you'll like it."

"I'm sure I will. You know I trust you completely." I look up and find him watching me, and that's when I feel it. Him wanting to kiss me.

"Any other new stuff?" I try to turn his attention toward the rest of the new releases on the wire rack.

"Not there." He shoots me a smile and gestures for me to follow him to his usual spot behind the counter. Then he disappears and pops up again, placing a jewel case on the counter between us. The paper cover is painted in watercolors: blues and reds and greens, all swirling in interesting patterns and fading off at the sides. Like any watercolor, it's unique. One of a kind. Still, it matches all the others on my shelf in my bedroom.

"A new running mix!" I pick it up, flip it over, and read the track names. "You have no idea. I'm so tired of skipping through tracks on my CDs. I always run best to yours."

"I have to say, I outdid myself this time." He smiles and blushes, and I watch how the hue makes his freckles disappear. He's kind like no other guy I know, and I wish for a moment that I could think of him as more than a friend.

"I'm sure you did." And there it is again. In his mind, this is the moment in the movie where I leap over the counter and rip the buttons off his shirt. Instead, I look at my watch. Three fifty-nine. "Shoot." I gesture across the street toward the bookstore. "I've got to run and release my dad from duty. Do you need any books?" I hold up my new CDs. "You know the deal—one for one."

He nods. "Actually, I wanted to ask you some—" Justin trails off and we both turn our attention to the front door, watching as a girl in sorority letters walks in, comes straight to the counter, and stands next to me, waiting. Justin shoots me an annoyed look. "Never mind. I'll just try to come by the bookstore later."

Once my back is turned, I let out a sigh of relief and silently thank the Tri-Delt for buying me a bit more time.

Time seems to have slowed to a crawl. Northwestern students come in and look around, then leave. Mothers come in with their toddlers in tow, browsing the Book Club Recommendations table while their kids destroy the picture-book section. I scan credit cards, adjust books into place until all the bindings are even and the newer books are displayed with prominence, and read the Michelin guide to the Côte d'Azur. At 8:50, I total the day's sales, zip the cash into the green vinyl envelope, and lock it in the safe in the back room. I flip the sign on the front door to CLOSED and click the dead bolt in place.

The coffeehouse is already packed. Finals week at Northwestern has just ended, and no one's studying tonight. In fact, most look haggard and worn, like they've been celebrating since Friday afternoon.

As I walk by, I casually look in the window to see if I can spot Justin with his radio-station friends. He seemed so eager to talk to me earlier, but he never came by the bookstore tonight.

I keep walking, and round the corner to my dark and quiet block. I see a sudden movement in the park across the street and I slow my pace, squinting into the darkness. It's hard to see any details, but there's definitely someone there, and I narrow my eyes again until I make out the shape of a person, doubled over on the park bench, rocking back and forth. I step onto the grass to get a closer look. I gasp, because even from this distance, I'm pretty sure I know who it is.

My feet seem to move toward him on their own, and when I'm within earshot, I whisper, "Bennett? Is that you?" There's no response, but now I'm close enough to make out the sound of groaning, low and weak. "Bennett?" I take small steps, moving in a little closer. "Are you okay?"

"Go away," he grunts. He tries to raise his head, but it drops farther into his lap, and he rubs his temples, making that guttural sound again. I realize he's saying something, so I bend in closer. "I can't leave," he's whimpering. "I've got to find her." He's rocking and moaning and repeating the words, and I'm watching and shaking and starting to freak out.

Suddenly, he stops moving and his eyes find me. He seems surprised to see me standing next to him. "Anna?"

"Yeah, it's me. I'm going to go get you some help. Stay here, I'll be right back."

"No!" He says the single word with force, but it's tinged with agony, and I know there's no way that I can handle this alone.

"Bennett, you need help." I pivot on my heel to leave.

"No." He reaches out and grabs my wrist. "Please. Don't. Go." I stop cold and whirl around. It looks like it's taking all his strength for him to lift his head. "It's . . ." He takes another deep breath. "It's easing up now." But I don't believe him. In spite of the temperature and the frozen bench he's planted on, sweat is beading up on his forehead and running down his cheeks. He looks like me after a sprint, concentrating on each inhale and exhale. "Please. Just. Sit."

I look around the pitch-black park, drop my backpack on the ground by his feet, and kneel down beside it. I can't bring myself to sit on that cold bench.

"I'll be okay." He rubs his temples again and slowly raises his head. His voice sounds a little stronger now. "It's a migraine," he says between breaths. "I get them when . . ." His voice trails off. "Just sit with me, Anna? Please?" I look back toward the coffeehouse.

I start to lean forward to rub his back like my mom would, like a friend who knows him much better than I do might, but I catch my hands and force them to my sides. For the next five minutes, the only sound between us is his labored breath.

"Keep breathing." It's the only thing I can think to say, even though I realize it's not helpful.

Finally, he sits up a little straighter. "Do me a favor?" He hasn't even told me what it is and I'm already nodding. "Don't tell anyone about this."

"I won't." I shake my head and watch the sweat still dripping down his cheeks. "But can I please go get you some water? I'll be fast."

He doesn't say yes, but at least this time he doesn't argue. Before he changes his mind and stops me, I stand up, leaving my backpack at his feet, and sprint back to the coffeehouse. The girl behind the counter gives me a cup of ice water, and I run back to the bench.

"Here you—" I start to say, but my words hang in the air. My backpack is still on the frozen ground, but Bennett is gone.

Bennett's not in Spanish on Monday. Or on Tuesday. I'm starting to lose my mind with worry, but Ms. Dawson in Administration is less concerned.

"Can I just get his phone number?" I beg. "I just want to be sure he's okay." I use my most responsible voice, but it doesn't have the desired effect.

True to my word to Bennett, I've omitted large sections of the story I told her—like the park, the sweat beading up on his face, and the fact that he was moaning about needing to find someone. I'm not sure which part of "Don't tell anyone about this" Bennett wanted me to keep under wraps, but I hope it didn't include the migraine, because I can't think of any reason to be asking about his personal information without disclosing that part.

"I know you just want to help, Miss Greene, but you know I can't release another student's confidential information. I'm sorry." Her tone is patronizing and not at all apologetic. "I'm sure he'll be here tomorrow."

How the hell do you know? I want to say, but instead I mumble, "Thanks," and shuffle out the door. I never should have left him there. All he wanted me to do was sit with him, and instead I left him alone on a bench in a dark deserted park, sweating and panting.

I head into the locker room and change, but as I listen to the team chatter, I start to dread the idea of running in a circle on an overcrowded track. I duck out before anyone notices and make my way to the abandoned and frozen cross-country course instead. And as I run, I try to listen to the sounds of the wind and the woods, the rhythm of my feet sloshing through the mucky trail, but all I hear is his voice in my head: *Just sit with me, Anna? Please?* I feel horrible.

As it turns out, Ms. Dawson was wrong. Bennett isn't at school on Wednesday. Or on Thursday. By Friday afternoon, as I'm walking The Donut between fifth and sixth—and freaking out about facing the entire weekend without knowing what's happened to him—the solution hits me out of nowhere. It's my only option.

I rush to Emma's locker and wait, but she doesn't show. When the bell rings, I pull out my spiral notebook and scribble, *I need to talk to you.* Folding the paper into a small square, I feed it through one of the vents and sprint to class.

After the bell rings again, I race back to Emma's locker

and find her there, reading my note. "I need your help, Em," I blurt out. "Do you think you can get something from the office for me?"

"Probably."

"I need Bennett Cooper's phone number. I asked Dawson and she wouldn't give it to me. But she likes when you come into the office and talk about your auction-party planning, so maybe she'll tell you." She starts to say something, but I stop her. "Please don't ask why I need it."

Emma presses her lips together and raises her eyebrows. She stares at me and does that *tell-me-everything* superpower thing.

"Look. I ran into him last Sunday night, and he was . . . sick. Now he hasn't been here all week. I just want to be sure he's okay." I'm standing there, bracing myself against her locker and preparing for the inquisition, when she breaks into a huge grin.

"You wanna shag Shaggy!" She laughs as I look around wildly to see if anyone's heard her. "Come on, just say it. You like this guy, don't you?" We stare at each other. I don't reply. She repeats herself. "Don't you?"

I let out the breath that's been constricting my chest. "I'm just worried about him."

She stares at me with big eyes.

"Okay, maybe."

She grins. "See. You did it. The first step is admitting you're powerless," she says, bastardizing the first of AA's Twelve Steps. "Let me see what I can do. I'll meet you at the car after school."

"How are you going to get it?"

"I don't know yet. I'll think of something."

An hour later, in the warmth of the Saab, Emma is euphoric, boasting about her skills in crafty manipulation.

"I really can't take any credit for the first thing that happened. That was absolute luck," she says as she whips the car out of the parking space. "Get this. I walked in and Dawson's on the phone—with Argotta, I assume—saying she needs this week's Spanish work so she can take it to Bennett Cooper's house tonight." Butterflies come to life in my stomach at the sound of his name. Someone, please shoot me. "So I offered to take his homework to him."

"She gave you his homework?"

"No. She said she couldn't do that—it wasn't allowed. *Not even for you, Miss Atkins.*" She mimics Dawson's voice to a tee.

"So you didn't get it?"

"Of course I got it."

"Great. Where is it?"

"I'm getting to that part." She turns in to the street and the driver she cuts off lays on the horn. "So I start asking her questions about the auction—so she thinks that's why I came in, right?—and Dawson starts telling me about this great cabin in Wisconsin that the Allens own. . . ."

"Oh, please. You're killing me. Get to the point."

"Okay, okay. So we're talking about the auction, and Señor Argotta comes in and drops a stack of papers on the counter. She thanks him, he leaves, she goes to the monitor—now she's telling me about some antique photos someone else is donating to auction off—grabs a Post-it, writes down the address, and sticks it on the pile."

"And?"

She pauses for dramatic effect. "Two-eight-two Greenwood."

"What about the phone number?"

She flips around to face me. "Are you kidding? No *Thanks, Emma?* No *You're amazing, Emma?*" She brings her attention back to the road, shaking her head.

"I just wanted to call—"

"Well, she didn't write down his phone number, and I couldn't see the screen. But don't you see? I got the better of the two!"

"But now I have to go there!" I wince at the thought.

She shoots me that satisfied smile she wears when she gets her way. "Exactly."

⁓

I can't believe I'm doing this.

I peek out from behind the tall hedge again and stare at the house. Impressive. Two, maybe even three, stories. Tudor style. A carriage house out back, if I'm assessing accurately from this distance and the three times I've walked past the house, chickened out, and hidden behind shrubbery.

Why am I doing this?

I let out a heavy sigh as I move from behind the bushes, walk toward the house again—this time with a determined stride—and turn onto the recently shoveled walkway. It's only 5:30, but it's almost completely dark, and I'm shaking as

I climb the steps. When I reach the top, I pick up the lion's-head door knocker and take a deep breath before I bring it down.

I wait.

There's no answer.

I knock again, tightening my coat against the wind, and glad I've traded my tights and skirt for jeans.

Just as I turn to leave, I hear footsteps. "Who's there?" asks an elderly-sounding woman from the other side of the door.

"I'm sorry. Never mind." I back away and head for the steps. "I think I have the wrong house."

The dead bolt makes a heavy *thunk* and the door opens slowly. She's older but not elderly, and striking, with long gray hair and smoky blue eyes. She's wearing a red silk scarf over her dark, loose-hanging clothes, and smiling at me with a curious expression.

"Hi." She opens the door, wide and welcoming.

"Hi. I'm looking for someone named Bennett, but I'm so sorry. I think I have the wrong address." I start to turn away again.

"No, you don't; Bennett's here. Come on in and warm up." She moves back to make room for me in the entryway.

"I'm Maggie." She holds out her hand.

"Anna." I shake it, still wondering who she is.

"You must be a friend from school."

"Yes." I'm not sure I qualify as a friend, but it's the simplest answer. "I'm sorry to impose, ma'am." Yes. I'm an idiot for coming here. And I'm just now realizing this.

"No imposition, dear." She gestures toward the room on the other side of a wide arch. "Have a seat, and I'll go up and get him."

I peek inside as she turns and starts up the staircase. The living room, with its massive windows, is beautiful, tastefully decorated with dark antique furniture that makes it even more welcoming than I expected it would be. The fire is warm and creates a soft glow.

Instead of sitting on the couch, I walk around, taking a closer look at the room. The wall surrounding the fireplace is lined from top to bottom with dark-stained bookcases filled with a collection of classics that puts the bookstore's section to shame. With the exception of a large black-and-white portrait of Maggie and her husband on their wedding day, framed photos of a little girl—dark hair, bangs cut straight across her forehead—take up every available surface. Some include her mother. A few feature both parents. It's hard to miss the framed snapshot in the center of the mantel: the same little girl, sitting in a chair and smiling up at the camera, clutching a tiny baby with a tuft of dark hair.

"Those are my grandchildren," says a quiet voice behind me, and I jump. I hadn't heard her return. "That's Brooke. She's two. And that's my new grandson." She runs her finger across the glass.

"They're really cute," I say.

She returns the photo to its shelf and picks up another one. "This is my daughter." She points to a photo of a woman with the same little girl on her lap.

"Do they live here in Illinois?"

"No. San Francisco." She lets out a sad sigh. "I keep trying to get them to move back home, but her husband's job keeps them in California. I haven't even met the new baby yet."

Suddenly, I have the strange sensation that we're no longer alone. I glance over my shoulder and find Bennett standing in the archway, watching us. His hair is stringy, his skin is masked by patchy stubble, and the heavy circles under his bloodshot eyes make him look as if he hasn't slept in days. The vacant expression on his face ups the severity.

"What are you doing here?" His voice is tight, and he blinks involuntarily, like his eyes are adjusting to what little light there is in the room.

Maggie jumps in before I can find my voice. "I was just showing your friend photos of my new grandson, Bennett." She turns back to me. "Can you believe that? I've never met anyone with the first name Bennett, and now I know two of them!" She shakes her head at the impossibility.

I look back and forth between them, confused. Bennett winces.

"Do you two want some tea?" Maggie says, seemingly unaware of the tension that's hanging around us. "I was just about to make some."

"No," Bennett answers before I can, shifting his weight back and forth.

Maggie ignores him and looks at me, her eyes still innocent and questioning. "Anna?"

"No, thank you, Mrs.—"

She rests her hand on my shoulder. "Call me Maggie, dear. Maggie's just fine."

I return her smile. "Thank you, Maggie."

Bennett gestures for me to follow him, and we leave Maggie alone to make her tea. We climb the staircase in silence and continue down a dark hallway. Like the living room, its walls are lined with photos, but these are more dated.

His bedroom is nearly dark, insufficiently lit by a small lamp that barely brightens the wooden desk. Coffee cups and empty plastic water bottles are scattered everywhere. Books and papers are strewn all over the floor and across the surface of his twin bed. The antique furniture is beautiful, but hardly reflects the tastes of a high school boy. He looks out of place in the sea of mahogany.

He reaches over my shoulder to shut the bedroom door, and the proximity makes my heart race. Until I realize that he smells like sweat and dirty socks. My face must show something that looks like disgust, because he drops his gaze and takes a step backward. "I wasn't expecting company."

"It's okay . . . I'll just . . . I'm sorry. I'm interrupting you, aren't I?" He doesn't give any hint that he's accepting my apology. He also doesn't clear space for me to sit down on any available surface, so I stand, awkward and nervous, leaning against the doorframe.

"I'm sorry about my grandmother," he says, so quietly I have to strain to hear him.

I'm confused. "Your grandmother? Maggie is your grandmother?"

"She has Alzheimer's." He looks past my eyes and studies the door as if considering his next words. "In her mind, I'm— I'm like an infant."

"Really?" I play back the conversation in the living room. "But . . . the pictures stop seventeen years ago. . . ."

He nods. There's a long, uncomfortable pause, and I feel bad for bringing the pictures up. "They just upset her. We had to take them away."

"So, who does she think *you* are?"

"After my grandfather died, money was tight and she was lonely, so she started to rent this room out to Northwestern students." He makes a dismissive gesture and stares down at the floor. "I guess she thinks . . ." He trails off, and the room goes silent.

He looks horrible. His skin is sallow, and his red eyes are half closed. "Are you okay? You look tired."

He stares at me, and when he finally talks, he doesn't answer my question. Instead, he draws his eyebrows together as he asks one of his own. "What are you doing here?"

The way he asks the question makes me even more nervous. "I haven't seen you since last Sunday night in the park. When you were . . . you know . . ." I wait a moment for a response, and when none comes, I blurt out the rest. "You didn't show up at school this week, and I got worried, I guess, and I . . . I just wanted to make sure you were okay." I reach behind me for the doorknob. "And now I know you're alive. Which is . . . you know . . . really great. So I'll just go now." It hits me like a shot that a phone call would have been much more appropriate, and I want to kill Emma. What was I thinking, showing up at this guy's house like I *know* him?

"Sunday." He squints past me. "That's right. I forgot about that."

I let go of the knob and stare at him. Forgot? How could he have forgotten?

"Are you sure you're okay, Bennett?"

"Yes. I'm fine. I just . . ." He looks worried. No. Panicked. "How did you find me, anyway?"

I feel my hands start to shake. "I got your address from the office." It's true. There's no sense in bringing Emma into this if I don't need to.

"Someone in the office just *gave* you my address?"

"No. It was on a Post-it." Also true.

He looks at me, confused, and he opens his mouth to speak. But suddenly, all the color leaves his face. He wobbles a bit, feeling for the wall as he steadies himself.

I reach forward and grab his arm. "Are you okay?"

He tries to talk, but nothing comes out. He draws in a few labored breaths.

"I'll go get your grandmother." I start to release his arm, but he reaches out and grabs me by the wrist, just like he did in the park.

"No! Don't!" It sounds like he's trying to shout but he can only manage a whisper. He lets my arm go and starts steadily exhaling. "I mean . . . that's okay." He takes a slow, deep breath. "I just need to lie down."

"Are you sure?"

He opens the door. "You need to go." He takes a deep breath. "Now."

"But, I can—"

"No. Now. Please."

I fold my arms across my chest. "You can't make me leave you like this—not again."

His eyes are cold and frightening as they bore into mine. "This is my house. And I'm telling you to leave. Right now."

As soon as I'm in the hallway, the door slams shut behind me, so hard I can't help wondering if he has just collapsed against it. I take a few steps back and stand there watching it and wondering what to do. I step forward again with my arm raised, prepared to knock. But I stop myself. I back away again. And I turn and walk slowly through the hall and back down the staircase.

I stop at the foyer to pull my coat off the hook. As I fasten the buttons, I run through what I'm going to say to his grandmother. *I think he's sick again* or *I think you should check on him.* But I think of his firm *no* and the *don't,* and against my better judgment, I decide I need to hold on a little tighter to his secret this time. So I peek into the kitchen, tell Maggie it was a pleasure to meet her, and assure her that she doesn't need to get up—I can let myself out.

8

"Oh, good, you're here." Like the bells that have just announced my arrival, Dad is way too chipper for me in my current state of mind. "Do you mind if I take off?"

Mind? God, no. Please go so I can pace through the empty bookstore and wonder if I've just left Bennett dying alone in his messy antique bedroom. "That's why I'm here," I say, trying to make my voice as light as his.

"Thanks. Your mom has already called twice, wondering when I'll be home. She might be a little too excited about this party."

He looks handsome. I reach up and adjust his tie.

"We'll be at the Chicago History Museum. We should be home by midnight, but don't wait up. You know how your mother and her friends can talk."

"Go. Have fun." I grab his shoulders and pivot him toward the front door.

He takes a few steps forward, then stops and turns back. "Thanks again for working on a Friday night. We didn't interrupt your social life, did we?"

"Sadly, no."

As soon as Dad's gone, I walk around the store, straightening books and thinking about the look on Bennett's face. When I walk past the front door, I pause, tempted to turn the BACK IN TEN MINUTES sign around and sprint to his house. When I pass the back room, I have the urge to go to the phone and call Emma so I can tell her everything that just happened. When I pass the window and see the police car parked down the street in front of the coffeehouse, I want to run down there and send them over to 282 Greenwood. But I don't do any of these things. Instead I march over to the children's area and grab the denim beanbag chair, drag it over to the travel section, and plop down with Lonely Planet's guide to Moscow.

I'm crouching down on the floor of the back room, spinning the dial on the safe, when the bells jingle. I lean on my hands and see someone in a wool cap holding a black coat standing at the front counter.

"Sorry—we're closing!" I yell. I select the last of the three numbers, pull up on the heavy steel handle, and throw the vinyl cash bag inside.

I'm looking down at my watch as I walk back toward the counter. "Sorry, we close at—"

Bennett turns around to face me, and a small smile moves slowly across his face.

I stop in my tracks. "Hi." I can't imagine I'm doing a very good job of hiding my surprise. He already looks much better than he did just three hours earlier. The dark circles are gone, and his eyes are no longer bloodshot. He looks different, relaxed, in dark brown chinos and a light blue sweater that does something sort of magical to his eyes. And I can't help noticing that he smells shower fresh. He looks better, but still tired.

"Hi, Anna."

"You're okay?" I'm so relieved that I want to run over and hug him.

"Yeah. I'm okay." He smiles. "So . . ." His eyes move around the store. "This is where you work?"

I nod.

"It's nice." He takes a few steps toward me and leans against the counter. "I'm glad you're here. I wasn't sure if you worked on Friday nights."

"I don't. My parents went to a party in the city." I don't know what to say. I walk to the counter and mirror his pose.

"Hey, I wanted to apologize. I didn't mean to be so rude earlier."

"It's okay."

"No, it's not. It was really nice of you to come over." His expression is soft, his voice kind, and any trace of annoyance is gone from his eyes.

"I should have called—or something—instead."

"No, I shouldn't have left the park that night. I didn't

remember you were there until you told me." He looks at me like he's trying to figure out what I'm thinking, gauging where to go next. "Anyway, thanks for helping me. I'm sorry I didn't say that earlier."

"You're welcome."

His eyes stay locked on mine, and he smiles even wider. "Can I make it up to you?"

"Make it up to me?"

"How about a coffee?"

"Coffee?"

"Yeah. Coffee. Unless"—his eyes circle the empty store— "you're busy."

I feel my forehead wrinkle. "Are you sure you're well enough for coffee?"

He shrugs. Nods. "Actually, it helps my migraines. Come on. It's the least I can do after kicking you out of my house."

While he stands there, waiting for my answer, I think about Emma's words in The Donut earlier today. *Just say it,* she insisted. *You like this guy, don't you?* I don't feel like I know him well enough for it to be true, but it is.

"Okay. Sure." Maybe by the time we've finished our coffee I'll know him better. Maybe I'll even have answers to all the questions he keeps adding to the pile.

I walk around the store, shutting off lights as I go, and flipping the sign from OPEN to CLOSED. As I'm locking the dead bolt, Bennett lifts my backpack off my shoulder and throws it over his own.

We walk in silence to the end of the block. I can hear the noise from the coffeehouse growing louder as we get closer, and smell the aroma as it floats up through the frozen air and disappears into the clouds above. As soon as we walk in, I notice a group just leaving, and we weave through the crowded tables and collapse on the crushed-velvet sofa in the corner.

"What can I get you?"

"A lot of explanation." I reach down to pull my wallet out of my backpack. "And a latte, please."

"I've got it." He touches my hand, and I silently chastise myself for the shiver it creates. He leaves and returns with two small, froth-filled, glass mugs, each with a chocolate-dipped biscotti balancing on the rim.

He sets them down on the table and returns to his spot on the couch. I look at him expectantly. "Big talks require biscotti," he says. Now I let him have a smile.

He picks up his mug and breaks through the froth with his Italian cookie, and after a few dunks, he pops it in his mouth and chews. When I realize I'm staring at him, I turn my attention to my own cup. The coffee is warm and soothing.

"So. Where should I start?" He dunks his cookie while he looks at me. "I guess Sunday night. The park? I have to admit, my memory's foggy in some spots, but I take it I told you about the migraines?"

I feel my face soften with concern, and I nod again.

"I honestly don't know what happened. I was walking around town, and I felt a headache coming on. Before I could even process what was happening, it just hit me—" He takes another bite and a sip before continuing, "Anyway, I'm not sure how long I sat there in that park before you found me. All I remember is trying to get home."

"I would have helped you. Why didn't you just wait for me to get back?" I look down at my mug and take another sip. When I look up again, I find him watching me.

"I left as soon as I could walk again." He pauses, searching the air for something I can't see, then looks back at my eyes. "I'm sorry. I don't remember why you left."

"I ran back to the coffeehouse to get you some water."

He nods, like it's all coming back to him. "I'm sorry, I didn't mean to take off on you. I just wasn't thinking straight." He shakes his head as if casting off the memory of that night.

I've never been that out of it, but I can see how it would be disorienting. "And you've been sick all week?"

"On and off. I planned to go to school on Thursday, but I felt another headache coming on when I woke up, and I was worried that it might happen again. It would have been embarrassing to pass out on my second week at school." I'm surprised to hear that he cares what any of us think. "And now I have a ton of homework to catch up on this weekend. A woman from the school came by with all of my assignments after you left."

"Ms. Dawson."

"That's who I thought you were. I guess that's why I was so surprised to see you."

"Surprised?" I raise an eyebrow. "Is that what you call that?"

He drapes his arm over the back of the sofa. "I'm really sorry I made you leave earlier tonight."

He's smiling and leaning, and I find myself doing the same. "That's okay."

"You just kind of . . . threw me."

"I threw you?"

He looks down, then back up again, and shoots me a bashful grin. "I looked horrible. A beautiful girl shows up at my door, and I'm in sweats, smelly, and looking like I hadn't slept in a month." His eyes never leave mine. "I shouldn't have been so rude."

"Don't worry about it." I smile.

"Thanks for not telling Maggie. I don't want her to worry."

"Sure." He's still staring at me, and with all the tension in the air, I latch on to the change of subject. "Your grandmother seems nice," I say. I watch his face light up.

"Yeah, she's great."

"So, you moved from San Francisco to live with her?"

"For now. I'm only here for a month, you know, while my parents are in Europe."

"Oh," I say. My head falls forward as my heart sinks. "I didn't know that." I guess that explains why he hasn't bothered to meet anyone.

"Yeah, well . . . I feel like I can tell you the truth. Can you keep a secret?" He waits for my nod. "It's not just that my parents are traveling."

"Oh?" I take another bite and chew. I hope he knows that means he should continue talking.

"I was supposed to go with them, but I made a mistake," he says. "I blew it pretty big. My parents understand, but let's just say Evanston is the best place for me to be right now. Taking care of Maggie is much better than spending a month with them—or in reform school." The huge grin on his face makes me think that's supposed to be a joke.

"And?" I ask.

"And what?"

"And you aren't going to tell me what you did to deserve this frozen version of hell?"

He shakes his head and gives me a dismissive little laugh. "Trust me, you don't want to know."

"Oh, come on, it can't be that bad. You didn't kill anyone." I stop in mid-dunk and look at him. "Did you?"

He swirls the coffee in his mug, looking into it for answers, as if there were tea leaves inside. "No, I didn't kill anyone. But someone . . . disappeared. And it was my fault."

I picture him on that frozen park bench, rocking back and forth and mumbling about needing to find someone. I start to tell him what I heard and to ask him what it means, but I look at his face and something tells me not to. When the silence continues, I press him for more information. "That doesn't give me much of a secret. Is that really all you're going to tell me?"

"For now." His face brightens as he asks, "So, how long have you lived in Evanston?"

I stare at him. "We're going there now?" I ask.

"We're going there now," he says.

I decide to let him off the hook for the time being but give him a look that signals that he has more explaining to do. I sigh. "All my life. Same house my dad grew up in. Same house my grandfather grew up in."

"Wow." He looks at me with what I think at first are soft, understanding eyes; then I realize what's really behind his expression: sympathy. Like I'm a hobbit who's never left the Shire.

"Yeah." I feel small. "Wow."

He leans in even closer, filling what's left of the space between us, looking like he's genuinely interested in my pathetically simple life. "Do you ever feel . . . trapped?"

I want to tell him about my map and my plans to travel the world, but as the words start to form in my head I realize they sound as pitiful as his stare. Yes, I'm trapped for now, but I won't be forever. Still, deep down, I can feel the reality I live to ignore percolating to the surface: I can dream all I want. It's more likely that I'll be here when I'm old and gray, rocking and knitting on my porch when I'm not at the bookstore I own and run with the help of my grandchildren, who think I'm a crazy old bat because I refuse to go near the Travel section. Trapped doesn't even begin to cover it.

"Every day," I say.

"I can't imagine being in one place that long." I shrink back away from him, but he props his head against his hand and fills the space I've just created. "I've traveled everywhere. I've seen more than most people get to see in a lifetime." This isn't helping. He must realize that, because he suddenly shifts gears. "But you have something I've never had." His expression softens and he looks almost sad. "Deep roots. A history of a place. You've watched the kids you knew in kindergarten grow up right before your eyes. Aside from my parents and my sister, I feel like everyone I know is somehow"—he pauses to search for the right word—"temporary."

It's my turn to look sympathetic. I've known Justin longer than I've known my other friends, but I can't imagine thinking of any of them as temporary.

"Don't tell me you're going to Northwestern." He keeps smiling, so I just keep talking, like I've been injected with truth serum.

"God, no. At least, I hope not. I'll apply, because everyone does, but it's definitely my last choice." I tell him about running and my plans for a scholarship, and he looks at me like he's hanging on every word, and I can't, for the life of me, figure out why. But his eyes are wide with interest, and this time, when I picture my map, I decide I can tell him. "There's also the other plan," I say, "the one my parents don't know about."

He smiles excitedly. "I get a secret too?"

"Yeah, except, see, I'm actually planning to tell you the whole thing," I say, and that makes him grin so wide his eyes narrow into little slits. "I'm thinking of taking a year off after graduation to travel. I know I'll go to college, but I feel like I have this one window after high school, you know, to see the world." I look down at the sofa. "But of course, my parents would never approve of this plan."

"Why can't you travel after college?"

Of course he'd have to ask. I've seen where he lives. "I'll need to go straight to work to pay off my student loans," I explain. "Even if I get a cross-country scholarship and financial aid or whatever, I won't get a full ride." His smile encourages me to continue. "I guess I'm afraid that if I don't go soon, I never will, and I just . . . need to."

He's staring at me. I can't tell what he's thinking.

"What?" I ask.

"You're interesting." His mouth curves into a half smile. *And beautiful,* I want to add. *Earlier, you said I was beautiful.* "I had a feeling you'd be interesting." He watches me, and I hope he can't tell that my stomach has started doing those damn flip-flops again.

And as I stare back at him, I realize that over the last hour I've let myself forget all the little—and big—things that have haunted me for the last two weeks. How he disappeared into thin air at the track that day and then denied it. How strangely he reacted the first time he heard my name. How I found him in the park that night. Even that bizarre trip to his grandmother's house just hours ago. I don't see what he's learning about me that's so interesting, but I know I'm a little too fascinated by everything I don't know about him. I just want to complete this puzzle, but the most important pieces keep dropping on the floor, landing upside down and just out of reach.

But the questions disappear again when he reaches forward and slowly traces the line of my jaw to my chin. I close my eyes as his thumb slides toward my mouth and brushes my lower lip, and I can feel myself moving in closer, like I'm being pulled into the gravity that surrounds him. He starts to kiss me, and I close my eyes and take a little breath as I wait for the touch of his lips.

But the kiss never comes. Instead, I feel him pause. His breath travels past my cheek, and the words *I'm sorry* fill my ear in a whisper.

"About what?" I murmur.

"This." He sighs. "I'm sorry. I can't—"

"What about daring adventures?" I hope he can hear the smile in my voice.

I feel him laugh into my neck and he sighs again. "I'm afraid I'm already on one. A different one." I pull back to see his eyes, and wonder why he looks sad. He rubs my cheek with his thumb and pulls away from me.

He looks at his watch. "I should really get back to Maggie. Can I walk you home?"

I sink back into the chair, confused. Dejected. "That's okay. It's just a few blocks."

"I'd feel terrible if something happened to you."

"If I went missing?" I ask sarcastically. "Yeah, it sounds like you have that effect on people." I'm still close enough to see how his face falls, and then hardens.

"Thanks." He scoots backward, and the part of me that's upset he didn't kiss me feels satisfied. "I'll be right back." He walks toward the bathroom, leaving me alone on the couch to berate myself.

"Bennett, I'm so sorry," I say as soon as he returns. "I was trying to be funny."

He bends forward and picks my backpack up off the floor. "It's okay. Don't worry about it." We maneuver into our bulky jackets and walk in silence past the couches and tables and out into the street. We walk side by side, but there's a visible gap between us. We hardly say a word for the next three blocks, and I can't help noticing that the Bennett I just spent the last hour talking to isn't anything like the one who's now walking me home.

"This is mine," I say when we arrive at my house. I watch as Bennett looks up at our nineteenth-century Craftsman, with its flaking yellow paint and wraparound porch that serves as its only exterior asset. The kitchen light is on, but there's no activity inside, and my parents won't be home for hours. "Do you want to—"

"No." He cuts me off, his voice sharp. He sets my backpack on the ground by my feet. "Look, you were right . . . about what you said back there." His voice is softer now, but it's almost like he's forcing it to sound that way.

"Oh, come on. I was kidding." I try to get him to lighten up, but he stuffs his hands into his pockets and refuses to look at me. I didn't think my comment was that insulting, but it was enough to send him into the bathroom as one person and emerge as a completely different one. The first one was just about to kiss me. This one can't wait to get away.

"You don't know anything about me."

I step closer and give him a flirty smile, hoping I can bring back the Bennett from the coffeehouse. "I know two of your secrets." Something about that near-kiss in the coffeehouse makes me feel brave enough to reach forward and grab on to the lapels of his wool coat. "That's got to be good for something. Isn't it?"

He moves in close to me, just like he did on the couch, but this time his face is tight and he stops far short of my lips. He reaches up and grabs hold of my wrists to remove them from his lapels, and I reflexively loosen my grip. His expression turns even colder.

I can't believe my comment has offended him so much. "What's wrong with you?"

He takes a big step backward. "Listen. This is *not* going to happen again. Do you understand, Anna? This," he says, motioning back and forth between us, "is not going to happen this time."

"I have no idea what you're talking about! What do you mean 'this time'?"

"Nothing." He crosses his arms tight across his body and stares right into my eyes. "Look. I'll be here for another two weeks, and only because I don't have a choice. Then I'll leave and you'll never see me again. So please, go back to your life." He turns on his heel and I watch him march off through the snow.

april

9

Thirty-five days. Bennett's been in town for thirty-five days, which, by my definition of a calendar month, means he should have left town four or five days ago. Yet when I walk into Spanish each day, he's still here. We've barely spoken since the night in the coffeehouse three weeks ago, and he never looks at me; if our eyes do accidentally connect, he gives me a perfunctory smile, and I avert my gaze. But everything about that night still haunts me, and I can't quite figure out how he's still managing to turn my world upside down while simultaneously allowing it to stay exactly the same.

"I have news!" Argotta sings, beaming and spreading his arms wide. He glances around the room, holding all of us hostage with his words, and we stare at him as he walks back to his desk and sits on the edge of it. "How many of you have heard about my Annual Travel Challenge?"

A few of us raise our hands. "Good," he says. "Well, this

year, even *you* will be surprised. Because this year, I have a really big, very exciting reward."

He hops down off the desk and pulls on a long tab marked MEXICO. The giant, color-coded map of the country unrolls from its home in the ceiling. "But first, let me tell you about the assignment. Each of you will be planning a fabulous two-week vacation in Mexico. You must depart from our lovely O'Hare International Airport, but you can land anywhere you like. From there, you must create an itinerary that will allow you to see as many Mexican destinations as you can in fourteen days. The person who creates the most logical, interesting, and cost-effective travel plan will win the challenge."

He walks forward to the front of the room and stops. "Sound good?" Twenty heads nod in unison. "Great. Travel plans are due next Monday—a week from today." He turns his back to the class and erases the whiteboard.

The room is silent. We look around at one another. Finally, Alex clears his throat and raises his hand.

Argotta spins around and throws his arms up in the air. "Oh, wait a minute!" He walks back and forth in front of the class, grinning. "I bet," he says slowly, drawing out each word, "you want to know what you get if you win, right?" He stands there at the front of the room nodding and smiling while we nod back at him. Alex lowers his arm.

"Of course, of course." He paces his words to build tension in the room. "I have this friend, you see, who works for one of the major airlines." I bet he's practiced this all morning in front of the bathroom mirror. "I told this very good friend about my Annual Travel Challenge, and he thought it was such a great idea he arranged for his company to donate a five-hundred-dollar travel voucher to the winner."

We all look around the room at one another. I can't help looking at Bennett and when I do, he gives me an obligatory grin and shifts his gaze to the window.

"So, what do you think?" Argotta searches the room. "Could anyone here put a five-hundred-dollar voucher to good use?"

Sure, everyone here could use it. But I'm the only one who thinks it can change my life.

<hr />

I sit cross-legged on the carpet in front of the shelf marked with the word *Mexico* and scan the book spines. The store is empty and, given the storm that's been raging outside all afternoon, likely to stay that way. Which is perfect, since I have a vacation to plan.

I pull *Let's Go Mexico* from its home on the shelf, and place three more thick books on top of it.

I thumb through the pocket-size Michelin Green Guide and remove a slim book that opens into a giant road map. Pretty soon, I have a stack of guides, each valuable to the planning effort in at least one way. I pull out my spiral notebook and stare at the stack. And decide I need a latte.

I pull on my coat, hang the BACK IN TEN MINUTES sign on the door, and lock the dead bolt behind me. It's only six, but it's pitch-black outside, and if it weren't for the calendar, no one would know that there should be grass on the ground and leaves on all of these bare wooden sticks. We're two months away from summer vacation, but it's snowing hard. Again.

I buy my latte, take it back to the store, return to my spot in the travel section, and start dividing the books on the carpet into smaller stacks. I know what I want: A balanced combination of archaeological sites and beaches, where I can run on sand and swim in a real ocean. I draw a line down the center of the paper and begin my list.

The left column quickly fills with archeological sites: the Mayan ruins in Tulum, Chichén Itzá, and Uxmal. The right column, as it turns out, is more challenging. Cancún has the Great Mayan Reef, so that has to be on the list, but I'm not sure if I want to include better-known destinations like Los Cabos, Acapulco, Cozumel. They all look pretty, so I add them, along with small question marks in the margin.

The hail is pounding against the window, and one of the branches of the giant oak outside keeps scraping against the pane. I've stopped jumping every time it happens, but it's still unnerving. I try to ignore it and let Mazatlán's quaint village squares and the open-air pottery and ceramics markets of Guadalajara take me away from the snow and wind.

But when I hear the noise again, I stand up, peer around the bookcase, and creep toward the window. The storm is still whipping the tree around, but the branch that was screeching against the glass is now limp and broken, dangling silently over the sidewalk below. Then I hear a sound behind me, and I spin in place. This time it's not coming from the street at all—it's coming from the back room, and it's not the sound of the storm—it's a voice. I hold my breath and listen.

My heart's racing as I move to the phone at the counter. "Who's there?" I yell toward the back room while I pick up the receiver and dial 911 with trembling hands. I stand completely still and listen, watching the back door as I wait for someone to pick up. "Answer!" I whisper into the receiver.

Suddenly, the front door bursts open, and I whip my head around in the opposite direction as the bells jingle without their usual pleasant ring. I put the phone back on the cradle and rush toward the door. "Hi!" My voice is shaking. I rest my palm on my chest, like that will help steady the pounding, and try to act as if everything were normal. "Can I help you?"

He looks past me, searching the store, and then over his shoulder at the street. Just as I'm about to ask him if he'll help me check out the noise I heard in the back room, he pulls the door closed so hard the bells slam against the glass and rolls his hat down to cover his face. Then he locks the dead bolt.

"Cash." His voice is deep through the wool, but my attention is on the shiny metal knife he pulls from his baggy jeans. He points it straight at me. "Now."

It's hard to gesture toward the front desk when my limbs are shaking so badly. "Over there. It's not locked. Take it all." It's hard to speak, too.

Before I can move farther away, he pulls me toward him, presses the knife to my throat, and pushes me past the register. "The safe!" he yells into my ear as he tightens his grip.

"In the back—" The words come out wobbly, but I stick to the plan Dad laid out when I first started working here.

"The combination is nine–fifteen–thirty-three. We don't have an alarm. I won't call the police. Just take the cash and leave."

I calculate in my head. The register might have fifty dollars in it, if even that. The safe would have closer to a thousand.

He pulls me around to the register, opens the drawer, and releases his grip on me for just a moment while he dumps the cash into his bag. He grabs me again and pushes me to the back room, while I keep my gaze on the floor and try not to think about the cold steel of the blade on my neck or his heavy breath in my ear. "Move!"

I feel a wave of nausea pass through me.

I figure that's why I'm seeing things.

I narrow my eyes so I can focus on the movement near the bookshelves. I'm somehow certain I saw it, even though I know it's impossible. The store was empty, the door locked.

I squint over the tops of the bookshelves and see a dark patch of hair moving toward the aisle. I jerk my head up to get a better view, but stop when I feel the cold blade tight against my throat. When we reach the back room, the man removes the knife from my neck and shoves me inside, and I land hard on the floor in front of the safe.

"Open it," he orders. I spin the dial—right, left, right—and pull down on the heavy handle. The door opens wide, and he pushes me away.

That's when I see the movement again, slowly emerging from the shadows at an angle where only I can see him, and I watch, stunned, as Bennett puts his finger to his lips. There's no way the two of us could ever overpower a man with a blade and a fierce sense of desperation, but my first feeling even so is one of relief.

He moves out of my direct line of vision but I can see him from the corner of my eye, creeping with careful steps toward me. I stay silent and still.

And while the thief is distracted by the contents of the safe, three things happen, so fast and overlapping that they seem to take place simultaneously. Bennett disappears completely, and suddenly he's kneeling next to me on the floor. He grabs my hands and closes his eyes, and I must follow suit, because when I open them, the store is gone. The robber and his knife are gone. And Bennett and I are in the exact same positions—him kneeling, me sitting, still holding each other's hands—only now we're next to a tree in the park around the corner, the wind throwing snow violently around us.

10

Bennett releases my hands and holds my face instead, and I hear him say the words, but it's like he's far away, muffled. "You're okay, Anna. Breathe and don't talk. Just listen carefully and do what I say. I'll explain everything, but right now I need you to listen to me."

I nod, wide-eyed and blank.

"First, I need you to run to the coffeehouse. Order me an espresso and two big glasses of tap water without ice, and sit down and wait for me." He looks into my eyes. "You can do this, Anna. I need you. Can you trust me?"

I nod again.

"Okay, run. Don't talk to anyone, just order the coffee and water and sit down."

I turn and run to the coffeehouse.

I'm trembling so hard I can barely get the words out, but

the barista is kind and offers to carry my drinks to a table for me. I lead him to the couch by the window and collapse.

The sirens grow louder and louder until two police cars skid to a stop in front of the bookstore. I can't make out much from this angle, but I see their headlights shining on the building, and I watch the cops draw their guns and creep toward the entrance. They quickly disappear from view, and I press my forehead to the glass to try to see what's going on. I'm waiting for them to reappear when I feel a weight next to me.

Bennett falls forward, his elbows on his knees, his fingertips gripping each side of his head. He lets out a small groan between heavy, labored breaths, just like the night in the park.

Without even letting myself question it this time, I begin rubbing his back. "What can I do?"

"Water . . ."

I leave one hand on his back and give him the water glass with the other. He lifts his head and empties it in three giant gulps. "More . . ."

After the second glass, his breathing becomes more regular.

He looks up at me and smiles. "Hey, you're still here." He reaches for the shot of espresso and throws the hot liquid down his throat. I stare at him. I want to say something, but I can't, because every time I take a small breath, my own body seems to shoot it right back out. I try a deep inhalation, the kind I know will slow my heartbeat and get my limbs to stop shaking, but my lungs won't cooperate. *What the hell just happened?*

I don't realize that I'm staring at him until he wiggles his fingers in front of my face and says, "You're in shock." He holds up one of the empty glasses, waves toward the barista, and gestures toward me.

"Drink this," he says. I take the glass with both hands, since I can't trust my shaking limbs to pull off a task as complicated as lifting a cup to my lips. Bennett speaks in measured breaths. "I need you to listen to me, Anna. We have to go talk to the police in a couple of minutes—they've probably called your parents, and I'm sure they'll be looking for you." He grabs my shoulders and pivots me around to face him. "I promise, I'll tell you everything that just happened, but for now I need you to stick to a story. Can you do that?"

I finish my water and nod.

"Good. Keep the first part true: The man stormed into the store and he forced you to open the safe. But then say this: when he wasn't looking, you saw a break and you ran out the back door into the alley. I saw you there and stopped to help. We waited down the street and returned once we saw the police had arrived." He lifts my chin. "Can you do this?"

I nod again, eyes wide.

"Don't worry. I'll do the talking. Just stick to the story." I can't seem to do anything but nod.

We head toward the window to look out at the last two remaining police cars parked outside, their lights swirling. I stand in the store, mute, while Bennett explains what happened. The officer captures every detail of the break-in and my escape through the back door in his black leather–bound notebook. I listen, still nodding, but I know that Bennett's lying, because I'm well aware of what happened. I did *not* run into him in the alley. *How did he get into the store? How did we get out?*

The officer reviews his notes. "Stay here," he says. "I'll be right back."

I'm surprised to hear my own voice say, "Officer?" He stops and turns to face me. "Did you catch him?"

"Yeah. We caught him when he had some trouble with the lock on the back door. This long winter seems to be making some people pretty desperate. But don't worry, he won't be going anywhere for a while." He turns again to walk away.

"Officer?" I repeat and he turns back to me. "How did you get here in time?" Bennett puts his arm around my shoulders and gives me a light squeeze as the cop flips through some of the pages in his notebook.

"Looks like it was an anonymous tip. Someone called and reported a robbery in progress." He looks up at me with a sympathetic smile. "One of your neighbors must have seen him break in. You have a guardian angel, young lady."

Dad bursts through the door with Mom on his heels. Bennett must have stepped back from my side, because suddenly there's room for both of them to surround me, enveloping my body in two familiar sets of arms. "Anna . . ." Mom says, hysterical, stroking my hair and stopping every so often to kiss my forehead. "I'm so sorry," Dad whispers repeatedly while he rubs our backs.

We all hear the officer clear his throat, and we look up.

"Excuse me. I'm sorry to interrupt, but I need you and your daughter to come down to the station to press charges." The police station is the last place I want to be. What I want is a hot cup of coffee and an hour alone with Bennett.

I look at my dad and ask, "Can we have a minute first?" I point to Bennett. It's the first time my parents notice him standing there, but now he has their full attention.

"Hi, Mr. Greene, Mrs. Greene." He offers his hand to Dad first, then reaches toward Mom. "I'm Bennett Cooper."

"Bennett is a . . . friend. From school. He's been helping me since—" My voice trails off when I see Mom's face become contorted. But it relaxes and she smiles after I lie to her about the details, just as Bennett told me to.

"Well, thank you, Bennett." She shakes his hand and keeps her other arm around me as her eyes dart between us. "I'm not sure what you were doing walking around in a snowstorm, but I guess it was a lucky coincidence." She looks at me sideways and raises her eyebrows. I just shrug.

"Can we just have a minute?" I repeat to Dad.

"Keep it to five," Dad says, looking at his watch.

I lead Bennett to the Self-Help section and we're finally alone again, if only for a few minutes.

"So . . ." I look at him, my expression serious. "I take it this is the big secret?"

"Yeah." He laughs under his breath. "Pretty much." He reaches over and grabs both of my hands in his. His hands are warm and soft. "I have a lot to tell you."

"Good."

"Are you sure you want to hear it?"

I nod.

"Think you can angle to stay home from school tomorrow?"

I look at my watch. It's only eight thirty, but it feels closer to midnight. By the time I'm home from the police station, it may be that late. "I think my parents would be cool with that, under the circumstances."

"I'll come over at ten a.m. We'll go somewhere we can talk."

I look at him for answers I don't want to wait until tomorrow to hear.

He leans close and whispers, "Are you afraid of what I can do?"

I look around the room, toward the police and my parents, and back at Bennett. I'm not afraid, although I suspect I should be. Right now, I'm just happy to be alive. And to see that the pieces of this puzzle that Bennett has been since the day I met him are finally starting to fit together, snapping into place and forming an image I may someday comprehend. "No," I say. "Not even close."

11

My room is still dark, but I sense that it's morning. I roll over and stretch and steal a glance at the digital clock radio on my nightstand. Nine fifteen. I can't remember the last time I slept past seven, especially on a school day.

Then everything that happened last night comes rushing back, and it hits me—Bennett will be here in forty-five minutes.

I leap out of bed, pull on my sweats, and bound down the stairs. I haven't eaten anything since lunch yesterday, which explains why I'm starving. I find a note on the counter by the toaster:

> *A—*
>
> *Glad you're sleeping in. Dad's at the bookstore and I'm at work. Call if you need <u>anything</u>. We'll both be home by 5. Relax. And please, no running today.*
>
> > *XO,*
> >
> > *Mom*

I grab a bowl from the cupboard and fill it to the top with cereal. I'm eating so fast I can't really taste anything, but the cornflakes and milk are filling the uncomfortable void in my stomach. All of a sudden, I start to feel nauseated again. I had a knife at my neck. I was in danger, and in an instant, I wasn't.

Bennett can disappear. And reappear. He can make other people disappear and reappear. He has a secret talent, I'm the only one who knows about it, and today he's going to tell me everything.

I shower and wash my hair, and as I'm drying off, I reach for the body oil that smells like vanilla and makes my skin soft. I apply a little mascara and some lip gloss, and dart to my closet to find something to wear.

When the doorbell rings, I fly down the stairs and land with a thunk in the foyer. I take a deep breath and fling the door open. "Hi." I'm beyond giddy.

"Hi." He looks confused. "God, you look . . . actually . . . excited to see me. You do remember what happened last night, don't you?"

I smile at him. "You saved my life. And today, I'm going to find out how you did it." He still looks confused. "You *are* still going to tell me how you did it, aren't you?"

He raises his eyebrows. "Do I have to tell you from the porch?"

"No. God, I'm sorry. Come in." I step back to give him room and close the door as he looks at me with a relieved smile. I hang his coat on a hook and he follows me into the kitchen. "Coffee?" I ask, but I don't wait for the answer before I begin pouring. I hand him an oversize mug with a picture of the Northwestern Arch on one side, and we sit opposite each other on the kitchen bar stools. It's silent as he sips his coffee, and I watch, perched on my seat and ready for him to disappear into thin air again at any moment. He doesn't appear to be going anywhere, but he does look a little bit terrified.

"Are you okay?" I'm holding my coffee cup, but I haven't even had a sip yet, so it can't be the caffeine that's making me twitchy, ready to burst out of my skin.

"Yeah." He shifts on the stool, plays nervously with the handle of his mug. "I'm just not sure where to start."

I give him an encouraging look. "Start from the beginning."

"You have to know you are, literally, the first person I've ever told." He stops and looks at me, like he's expecting some kind of reaction. "My parents know, my sister knows, but I never *told* them. They sort of found out by accident. But that's it—my family, and now you." I nod so he'll continue. "I honestly had no intention of telling anyone else. If last night hadn't happened—"

I get it. He barely knows me, and there are probably countless other people with whom he'd prefer to share this precious secret. But I'm not about to let him off the hook. I can't. Not now. "You can trust me. This is your secret, not mine. I won't tell anyone."

"Thanks," he mutters, and then he's quiet again. "The thing is . . . you don't know how big this is. I don't want to freak you out."

I rest my elbows on the kitchen counter and look at him. "I promise I will not freak out." He narrows his eyes, as if to say that I shouldn't be making this promise. "I will try very hard not to freak out," I revise.

He leans forward, elbows on the countertop. Those smoky blue eyes are striking, especially in contrast with his skin and that hair of his. He looks adorable like this, all nervous and jittery.

"Look, Anna. This—" he says, motioning back and forth between us like he did that night on the sidewalk, the night he almost kissed me in the coffeehouse. "This is a really bad idea."

"Probably," I agree.

He laughs and shakes his head, like he's kicking himself for giving in to me. "I'll make you a deal. When I've told you everything, you can decide what to think, and if it's all too much, I'll totally understand. I'll go back to being the transient weirdo, and you can go back to your friends and your life."

"Or?"

"Or . . . you'll think it's all very interesting. And maybe a little exciting. And somehow that will offset the fact that I'm a complete freak of nature."

"You're not a freak. And besides, I've already seen what you can do, Bennett, and it's huge. If that didn't scare me, I can't imagine what else you could do or say to change the way I feel about you." Crap. I didn't mean to say that last part. I pull back from him so I can see his expression.

He doesn't look fazed at all, though, and I think I may have even made him happy. "That's good to hear. But you only know part of it."

I let out a nervous laugh. "How much more is there?"

"More." He stares at me. Then he pushes back from the counter and stands up. He takes his mug to the coffee machine, tops it off, and drops in two ice cubes from the dispenser in the freezer door. "Where do you keep your water glasses?" He's all business, like a salesman preparing to demonstrate a miraculous new cleaning product.

"That cabinet there," I say, gesturing, "to the right of the sink."

He pulls out two matching glasses and fills them with cold tap water. He sets the glasses and the cup on the counter and comes back around to sit on the stool.

"Okay." He takes a deep breath. "I want you to sit here and watch. I'm going to go away, but I'll be back in one minute." He checks his watch. "Are you ready?"

"Yes." I nod and try not to look anxious.

He looks at me for a moment and smiles. Then he closes his eyes. And I watch him become transparent—I can see through him to the photograph of my parents and me on the wall behind his translucent frame—and he's like that for less than a second before he's gone. The stool is empty. I walk around to his side of the counter and touch the surface.

Yep. He has disappeared completely.

I feel my breathing become shallow as I wait for what seems like more than a minute, never taking my eyes off the stool, and suddenly he's back. Exactly where he had been. Opaque and solid as he is supposed to be. As if it had never happened. But it did.

He gulps down both glasses of water, then chugs the coffee.

"Do you need anything?"

He shakes his head no, looking down at the tiles.

"Where did you go?"

"My room. I counted to sixty and came back." He looks up and watches me with a tentative expression as he weighs my reaction.

"What's with the water and the coffee?" I remember the specificity of his requests last night at the coffeehouse, the water bottles and coffee mugs strewn around his room that night I visited him uninvited.

"Traveling makes me dehydrated, and caffeine helps with the migraines. I don't usually experience pain when I travel *to* a location. It's the returning that kills me."

"Like the night in the park."

"Exactly."

"Okay, so you can disappear and reappear? That's it?"

"You make me sound like a third-rate magician." He laughs. "That's not enough for you?"

"Of course," I say nervously. "I just meant—"

"I'm kidding." He gets serious again. "Actually, that's just the first thing."

"The first thing?"

"Yeah. I told you. There's more."

I look at him. "How much more?"

"Two." He shrugs. "Two more."

"Wait a minute," I say. "The fact that you can disappear is the first of *three* things?"

He nods. "I told you. I won't explain everything today, but I'll tell you . . . a lot."

"What? You don't think I can take it?" My heart starts beating fast as I question my own question. Or maybe it's just that Bennett's face is so close to mine.

"If anyone can take it, you can. But it's still a lot of information to process." He looks at me like he's waiting for me to argue with him. Which I'm considering. "Look, today I'll tell you how I got you out of the bookstore last night. And eventually I'll tell you the rest. Trust me on the baby-steps thing, okay?"

He looks determined. Like arguing with him won't pay off anyway. "Okay." I straighten up in my chair and give him my full attention. Which takes zero effort. "I'm ready. Start from the beginning."

Bennett matches my posture, sitting straight up in his chair too, like we've discovered a cure for this magnitude of nervousness. He takes a couple of deep breaths to prepare, and then he begins.

"One night, when I was ten, I was in my bed reading this book on Greek mythology—I was really into gods and myths when I was a kid—and I thought how cool it would be if I could go there. So I sat up in bed, *Star Wars* pajamas and all, and I tried to 'will' myself there. I closed my eyes and pictured ancient Greece and repeated the date over and over again. And . . . well, nothing happened. But I started thinking about the next best thing, and it got me thinking: picturing the rows and rows of mythology books at my school library. So I closed my eyes, pictured the library, and focused. And the room felt cold—a lot colder than my bedroom—and when I opened my eyes I was standing in front of a metal bookshelf. That's when I kinda freaked out. It was dark, and everyone was gone, and I took off running for these big steel doors that led outside. But I stopped. Forced myself to calm down. I closed my eyes, pictured my bedroom, and focused. When I opened them, I was back home."

He reaches for his coffee and takes a deep sip, and I just sit there hanging on every word, watching his mouth pucker against the rim of the mug and his tongue lick the residue from his lips.

He rests his coffee cup back on the counter, and I force myself to look at his eyes instead of his mouth. "Wait. You actually *went* to your school? In the middle of the night?"

He nods. "I did it a few more times again that week, staying close to home—the park, the movie theater, the grocery store. I never stayed more than a minute or so. Eventually, I started interacting with people to be sure they could see and hear me, and they could. I was *really* there."

"What about the migraines?" I ask.

"I didn't have them in the beginning—it wasn't painful at all. The big problem back then was that I had no idea how to tell my parents. I was terrified they'd take me to doctors or just straight to a mental ward."

I can't imagine keeping that kind of secret from my parents. Not at sixteen, let alone ten.

"When I was twelve, I decided to find out what happened to me when I left. I set our video camera on a tripod, pressed record, and focused my mind on a seat in the back of the theater just down the street. I sat there and timed myself with my stopwatch, waited exactly ten minutes, and returned. The video shows me sitting in my room with my eyes closed; then I disappear, and the film continues, taping an empty chair. Ten minutes later, I reappear."

He stops and looks at me, then continues. "A few weeks after that, my parents found out. My mom woke up in the middle of the night and found my bed empty. She combed the house, and when she couldn't find me, she decided to call the police. She'd already pushed nine and one when I reappeared before her eyes. Scared the crap out of her." He smiles at the memory. "I told them everything that night. Showed them the video."

He stops again. "How are you doing with this?"

"It's sinking in." At least, I think it's sinking in. I can feel my head nodding, so I must comprehend it at some level. "So, what did your parents do when they found out?"

He rolls his shoulders backward and gives his arms a little shake. "Mom freaked out. She still hasn't gotten over it. She wants me to see doctors and psychiatrists—anyone who can 'fix' me—even though I'm not allowed to tell them what's 'wrong' with me. But my dad . . . Now, Dad loves it. He thinks I could be, like, some comic-book hero or something. And he sees that I have total control over it, so he doesn't worry, but he's gotten a little pushy." He looks down at the counter. "Anyway, they see it differently, so when my parents aren't fighting with me about my 'gift,' they're fighting with each other about it."

I feel sad for him. "You saved my life last night. Tell your parents about that."

"Last night was fun." His eyes light up with excitement. "I've always worried about doing so many sequential hops, but last night I did a bunch in a row without getting the headache until the very end. I'm thinking it has something to do with the adrenaline—" He stops short. "But it was so stupid. If the migraine had hit me when I moved from the bookcase to your side, that guy could have killed you."

"But it didn't happen that way."

He closes his eyes tight, then opens them and looks at me. His voice is sincere, regretful. "I didn't think first, Anna. I just saw you in trouble and I reacted. I can't do that. I have to plan and calculate so I don't . . . screw anything up."

I just grin at him. "Well, if it's all the same to you, I'm going to be grateful anyway."

He smiles and watches me, but I'm not sure what he's looking for.

"What?" I ask.

"What would you think about taking this conversation somewhere else?"

"You want to go out in that?" I point toward the kitchen window at the snow and hail, still falling hard and adding inches to the thick blanket that buried the lawn during last night's storm. The driveway is nowhere to be seen.

"I was actually picturing someplace warmer. Someplace . . . tropical." My expression must show that I'm still confused, so he just comes right out and asks, "Do you want to try it?"

"I can go with you?" I guess I should have put the pieces together faster; even as I'm saying the words I'm aware of how dense I sound.

He nods and a huge grin spreads across his face. "If it's too soon, I totally understand."

"No, no . . . I'm just—" I stammer. "Will it hurt?"

"My sister gets stomachaches. My mom's never tried it, but my dad isn't affected in either direction. Technically, you've already been the third person to travel with me." I flash on the park last night and remember how queasy my stomach felt, but I don't want him to change his mind, so I keep it to myself. "This will be a bit of an experiment."

"I can handle that. I think." I let out a nervous laugh. "How long will we be gone? What if my dad comes home?"

Bennett explains that he plans to return us back to this exact spot, just a minute after we leave. "But while we're gone," he tells me, "time will continue as usual for everyone here. You might want to call your dad, just so he doesn't worry if he comes home before we do." I'm not sure I fully comprehend it all, but I dial the bookstore anyway and explain that I'm awake and feeling good, and Dad sounds relieved. While I talk, I watch Bennett fluttering around the kitchen, filling and refilling coffee cups and water glasses.

"Ready?" he asks after I hang up, and I smile and nod, mostly to convince myself that I am. Bennett walks over to the kitchen window where I'm standing and takes both of my hands in his. His are warm, strong, and for some inexplicable reason I feel safe, even though I'm completely terrified.

"Close your eyes," he commands, and I do, smiling in the seconds before my stomach begins to contort. My intestines feel like they're being twisted, kneaded from the inside, and while it isn't painful, it certainly isn't pleasant, either. Just as I feel the nausea, I see a bright light through my eyelids that forces me to shut them more tightly. Then I feel warmth on my face and a hot breeze that lifts my hair away from my forehead.

He squeezes my hands. "You can open your eyes. We're here."

12

We're standing exactly as we had been back in the kitchen, facing each other and holding both hands. Only, when I look down, my feet are in sand.

I squint against the sunlight and look past him at the bright blue-green water that stretches out as far I can see. The cove is small; I can look in both directions and see its entire length. Giant boulders hold back the tranquil, turquoise bay until it meets the sea, and high, jagged rocks reach for the sky, like bookends holding the white sand between them firmly in place. I turn around and look behind me to find nothing but a dense collection of trees. There is no one here. Not anywhere.

Bennett's watching me. He's still holding my hands, which is a good thing, because I'm pretty sure I've stopped breathing. "I know, it's a lame cliché. A secluded beach on a deserted island—" He stops short and looks at me. "Anna? Are you okay?"

I can't take my eyes off the view. This can't be real. "Where are we?" I must drop his hands, because now I'm walking away from him, like I'm being pulled by force toward the water.

His voice follows me. "It's one of my favorite places in the world . . . Ko Tao. It's a tiny island in Thailand. You can only get here by boat, and there's no pier. You actually have to wade through—"

"No way." I stop and turn around to look at him. "We're in Thailand? Right now . . . we're in Thailand?"

"Welcome to Thailand." He smiles and spreads his arms wide.

"I'm in Thailand." Repetition may help it sink in. My feet move toward the water, expansive and sparkling before me. It's like a mirage in a cartoon that looks refreshing and beautiful until one of the characters leans forward in disbelief, and the moment their fingertip touches the water it's enveloped in sand and disappears from sight. I'm so prepared for that same phenomenon that I'm surprised when I kneel down, touch my fingertip to the water, and feel the wetness of the ocean.

I can feel him watching me as I look around, spinning slowly in place, taking in every square inch of this island. Every palm tree. Every boulder. Every wave. Every shell. I can feel the expression on my face. My eyes are wide and my mouth is open and my forehead's all scrunched up, and I think I must look ridiculous, until I look over at Bennett. He's got a smile on his face, this look of wonder, like he's the one who's awestruck. I close my eyes and inhale . . . everything.

"You okay?"

I nod.

"Good. Come on." Bennett takes my hand and we walk along the shore. The water runs over our feet and washes back out again, and we squish through the sand until we pass the giant boulders. Bennett leads me up a slope to a secluded patch of sand that's warm and dry, and I take my sweater off so there's nothing between my skin and the hot sand but my T-shirt. I lie back and melt.

"This is much better than my kitchen," I say to the sky, and then I look over at him.

He's stretched out in the sand, propped up on his elbow and watching me with a satisfied grin, and I roll onto my side and mirror his pose. We each have one hand occupied, holding up our heads, but neither one of us seem to know what to do with the other one. I don't know if it's the physical warmth of the sand or how good he looks in his thin T-shirt and jeans, but all I want to do is reach over and rest my free hand on the small bit of skin peeking out between the two. I picture him pulling me into a kiss and rolling around in the sand like we've just been dropped into a photo shoot for some cheesy designer cologne. But then I remember the night he walked me home after coffee and I summoned up the nerve to grab the lapels of his coat, only to find myself standing alone and rejected in the snow. I can't bring myself to touch him, so I bring my fingertip to the sand and start making little circles there instead. "So . . ." I say, "Thailand."

He shoots me a confident smile.

I watch him for a moment, wondering why he was so worried about bringing me here. Who wouldn't want to have a small part in something so impossible? So magical? "I don't get it. What's not to like?"

When he smiles at me I can tell I've just passed whatever test I'm supposed to pass to get to the next level, like he's got a mental list with an empty box next to the words *teleported to deserted island / didn't freak out.* Check.

But I know he still has more to tell me. Two more things, in fact. I should probably just sit here in the sand and enjoy the view, but I can't. I need answers.

"How did you know I needed help last night?"

"I didn't. I came by to get a book on Mexico. For Argotta's travel assignment."

I'm confused about a lot of things that happened last night, but I'm certain I was alone when the thug with the knife came in. "No way. You weren't in the store."

He reaches forward and my heart starts racing with the idea of him touching me, but instead he grabs a fistful of sand and lets it fall through his fingers. "Are you sure you want to hear this part?"

I stare at him, and finally I nod.

"The robbery didn't happen exactly the way you remember it." When all the sand has fallen from his grasp, he brushes his palm against his jeans and looks at me to gauge my reaction.

I just raise my eyebrows and wait.

"I came into the bookstore. You and I talked about Mexico. Then the guy burst through the door."

"No way. I remember that. I was definitely alone—"

He cuts me off. "Let me explain. The way you remember it, you *were* alone. But that's not the way it was the first time."

"The *first* time?"

"The first time I was in the bookstore. We were talking about our travel plans. When the door blew open, you got up off the floor to help the man you thought was a customer, and he grabbed you. But he didn't see me. I had time to disappear."

I flash on the trick Bennett just showed me—God, how long ago was that? Fifteen minutes or so?—where he was sitting on my bar stool one second, vanishing into thin air the next, and reappearing right where he left a minute later. Even if he disappeared last night, that doesn't explain how I went from having a knife to my throat to standing underneath an elm tree during a blizzard.

"I disappeared from the bookstore, went back five minutes earlier, reappeared in the back room, and called nine-one-one from your phone."

The voice. The sound from the back of the store. "I heard you. . . ." The details are coming back in bits and pieces, but they still don't make any sense. What does he mean by *the first time*? "Wait a minute. Did you just say you went back? Five minutes earlier?"

He nods. "Yeah. I went back."

"In *time*?"

He tilts his head up and smiles shyly. "I . . . do that too."

"You went *back* in time. And *changed* what happened?"

He's wearing a sheepish grin, like he's sorry, but he just can't help it. "It's, like, a do-over."

"So, why didn't you just tell me someone was about to rob the store? Or, like, lock the dead bolt before he came in?" I don't mean to sound ungrateful, but I can't help thinking it would have been nice not to have a knife to my neck in the first place.

"I don't do that," he says. "I don't *stop* events from happening, but I'll change smaller things, little details that might affect the outcome. If I'd stopped the robbery entirely—and I've never done anything like that, so I'm not even sure I could have—something even more horrible could have happened. That guy might have robbed someone else at knifepoint but not gotten caught. He might have seen you walking home a couple of hours later and . . ." His voice trails off and he's silent for a moment. "Anyway, I just make it a rule not to change the big stuff."

"So you couldn't *stop* the robbery. But you could go back five minutes *earlier*?"

He nods. "Technically, I shouldn't have even done that, but yeah."

"And call nine-one-one from the phone in the back room."

He nods again.

"Why didn't the police come?"

"They did, just not fast enough. After I called, I snuck out and hid behind a bookcase. By the time he got you back to the safe, I decided I couldn't wait for the cops anymore. I had to get you out of there on my own. Just in case."

Suddenly everything hits me: Bennett doesn't just disappear and reappear in different places, he can travel backward through *time*? I want to appear brave, unflappable, and worthy of hearing the next thing, but I can't quite wrap my head around it all.

"I take it this is the second thing?"

He nods. "Part of it."

"*Part* of it?" My eyes widen. I lie back in the sand and stare up at the sky.

"You okay?" he asks. I feel my head make a little divot in the sand when I nod. But he's right—this is a lot to process. I throw my arm over my eyes to block out the sun, and we just lie there in silence for a few minutes. One arm is over my eyes, and the other is resting in the sand between us. Suddenly I feel the tickle of warm granules slipping across the surface of my arm and slowly piling into my open palm, and I look up to find Bennett leaning over me, watching the sand trickle from his hand into mine. "See," he says with a grin, "I told you I could freak you out."

"I'm not freaked out."

"Yeah," he says with a nervous laugh, "you are *definitely* freaked out."

I prop myself up on my elbows, ruining his little sand-pile, and look at him. Then I look around at this beautiful setting—palm trees and white sand and turquoise water—this postcard he's just magically inserted the two of us into, and I start to understand how implausible the whole thing really is. It should have taken at least two planes, a boat, and more than thirty hours to get here from Chicago. I should be many time zones away, and it should be dark. I should be complaining about the windchill factor, not enjoying this warm little breeze on my skin. Above all, I should be in AP World History. I look back at Bennett and give him a sincere smile. "Thank you for bringing me here."

He looks relieved. "You're welcome."

"What you can do is . . ." Every word that comes to mind sounds inadequate, but I finally settle on *amazing*.

"Thanks." I haven't heard the rest of the second thing, but I can tell I'm baby-stepping my way toward it.

"Look, I know I can't give you all the answers you want, but at least for today, I can give you that daring adventure." He stands up and brushes the sand off his jeans, then holds his hand out to me.

"You know, I've never been in an ocean before." I try to make my voice light and flirty, like this isn't weird at all.

"I know. You told me last night. You were trying to figure out which beaches to add to your travel plan so you could do your morning run on the sand and swim in the ocean."

Okay, that's weird. "And I assume you had a suggestion."

"La Paz," he says matter-of-factly. Yes, this *is* weird. And I'm not crazy about the fact that we've had a conversation I can't remember. But I don't have time to be irritated, because he wraps his arms across his chest, grabs the bottom of his T-shirt, and lifts it over his head. His arms are more muscular than I'd pictured them and his chest is perfect and I think my jaw just dropped.

He reaches his leg forward and, with his big toe, draws a line in the sand in front of us.

"It's not La Paz, but there's sand and water." He beams and leans forward in a racing stance. "Take your mark, Greene."

I'm not sure if he expects me to strip down to my bra and underwear, but the thought alone brings heat to my face that has nothing to do with the temperature here. I look down at my bare feet, my jeans. I wonder how transparent my gray T-shirt will become. But when I look out to the water and squeeze the sand between my toes, I decide I don't care. Laughing, I lean into my lunge.

"Get set." He turns to me with a sly smile. "Go!" he yells, and we bolt forward, running as fast as we can until the sand turns darker and colder and wetter and eventually the waves carry us away from the warm beach.

I swim out into the current. I dive under. I feel the waves lap against my body as I push myself against them. When I look to my side, I find Bennett there, his arms cutting through the water as he starts to dive again, and I follow him under, letting the water burn my eyes. Letting the taste of salt fill my mouth. Enjoying every minute of every stinging sensation. And wanting it never to end.

Four hours later, we return home to find that one minute has passed. Steam rises from the coffee mugs. The water is still ice cold. And I'm about to throw up.

"You don't look so good." Bennett leads me to the living

room couch and instructs me to lie down. A voice that sounds far away says, "I'll get you some crackers," and in the distance I hear cabinets creaking open and shut. He comes back carrying a giant box of saltines.

He sits on the edge of the sofa, rubbing his temples, and looks down at me. "Interesting." He's watching me with a fascinated stare, like I'm a glob of unidentifiable goo in a petri dish. "It hits me in the head, and you and Brooke in the stomach."

I see a white cracker coming toward me but I can't even take it, and I cover my mouth and close my eyes to keep the room from spinning. *Please, God*, I beg in my head. *Please don't let me throw up in front of him. Please. Just this one thing.* And I'm not sure if it's time passing or the work of a higher power, but after a few horrible minutes the feeling washes away and I can open my eyes again. He's still here. Still looking guilty and still holding that little cracker. This time I take it, nibble on the corner, and then try a larger bite.

"I'm so sorry," he says, but I stare at him, confused, and even though my mouth is full I try to talk. "What did you say?" he asks. He looks so worried.

I swallow hard. "Worth it." I give him a weak smile and grab another cracker. I eat a few more and sit up when he offers me a glass of water and orders me to take small sips. The room comes into clearer focus.

I run my fingernail up my pant leg and bring it back to examine the caked, wet sand. We're home, back in the cold snow, and I'm wet and covered with sand from a Thai island. "No way." My energy is starting to return. I laugh, shaking my head in disbelief. "This is so cool." I look over at Bennett and find that his pants look the same.

I stand up, feeling just a little bit closer to normal again, and he follows me up the stairs to my parents' room. I dig out an old pair of sweats and a T-shirt from my dad's dresser, pass him the folded pile, and show him where the bathroom is.

When I'm alone in my room, I peel my clothes away from my skin. I take off my shirt and shake out my hair, watching in awe as sand flies though the air and sprinkles itself across my bedspread, and I can't help giggling. I pull on a pair of tight-fitting black sweats and a sweatshirt from some 10K race I ran last year, and go back to sit on the bed. I run my palm across the granules and think about Ko Tao. About the heat of the sun and the salt of the ocean, and suddenly I'm so grateful for every last speck of sand—on my bed, on my carpet, in my hair, glued to my clothes—because they're the only tangible things I have to remember this day by.

"Where should I put these?" Bennett's voice shocks me back to reality, and I turn around to find him standing in my doorway, looking adorable in Dad's Chicago Marathon sweatshirt.

I gather my sandy clothes up from the floor and meet him at the doorway. "I'll take them," I say, as I add his pile to mine.

He gently grabs my arm as I walk past him. "Hey . . . you okay? You looked sad for a minute there."

"No, not at all." I laugh it off. "I was just wishing I had a souvenir, like a postcard or something. It was silly. I'll be right back." I float down the stairway, my feet barely touching the wood.

I've left Evanston.

I've left the *country*.

I put the pile of sandy clothes on top of the dryer and walk into the kitchen to grab a plastic bag.

And Bennett's in my bedroom.

I return to the laundry room, looking up the staircase as I pass.

Bennett just closed his eyes, held my hands, and took me to Thailand.

I scrape our clothing, collecting as much sand as I can inside the little bag, and zip it shut.

And now we're back. And he's in my *bedroom*?

I throw the clothes into the washing machine and stand there holding the bag of sand, listening to the water fill the drum, and thinking back to last night. I remember the expression on Bennett's face as we stood in the bookstore's Self-Help section, his voice quivering as he asked me the question. *Are you afraid of what I can do?* I wasn't then. Am I now?

I'm not afraid of the fact that he can disappear and reappear. I'm not even afraid of the fact that he can travel back in time. I'm not afraid of what he can do. I *love* what he can do. But there's more I don't know, and the moment I have the thought I feel a knot form deep in my stomach. I *am* afraid— I'm afraid of whatever's next. Whatever it is that might make me question whether or not I want to know him, even after we have spent the afternoon swimming in a sea so salty we were literally buoyant. Whatever it is, it can't be bad enough to make me not want this daring adventure. And I picture him, alone in my bedroom, and suddenly I can't wait to see him again. With the bag of sand tightly in my grasp, I run up the steps, taking them two at a time.

13

Bennett is standing in front of the wall of built-in shelving, examining my trophies and racing numbers. "Wow. How many races have you been in?"

"Eighty-seven." I cross the room and drop the bagful of sand on my nightstand. It makes a little sound as it hits the surface and I'm happy for this confirmation that it's real.

Bennett walks around the room, analyzing each trophy and photo. "This is incredible. You're really good."

"You sound surprised."

"No." He looks me in the eye and I feel my breath catch in my throat. "I'm impressed. Not surprised."

He turns his attention from the trophies to what's in between them: my CDs. He paces past the shelves, running his finger along the plastic spines of the jewel cases until he finds one, pulls it out, examines the cover, and then returns it to its alphabetized home. I lean back against my desk and watch him check out Blink-182, *Cheshire Cat.* Bush, *Sixteen Stone.* The Smashing Pumpkins, *Siamese Dream.*

"This is quite a collection."

It probably looks like I've spent all my bookstore earnings on CDs. "My dad and the owner of the record store across the street are good friends. We swap books for music. It's pretty much for my benefit."

He removes a few more cases and pauses, letting his fingertip rest on one of the mixes. "What are these?" He removes one of the twenty or so cases painted in Justin's trademark watercolor swirls.

"Running mixes. My friend, Justin, makes them for me. His dad owns the record store."

He nods and turns away again before I can see the look on his face. While he continues examining my music collection, I press play and then shuffle on the stereo, and the lyrics to "Walk on the Ocean" start up immediately.

> *We spotted the ocean*
> *At the head of the trail*

"Hey, I've seen these guys," he says without looking away from the bookshelves. "At a little club in Santa Barbara. They were pretty good."

"You've seen them live?" I heard him the first time, but I have to say something, because my chest feels heavy as I stand here, picturing secluded Ko Tao, and listening to the song tell a story about traveling to a faraway ocean, stepping on stones, and coming home without any pictures to prove it.

"It's sort of a hobby."

"Who else have you seen?"

He shrugs and gestures toward the shelves. "Just about everyone here." As if the exotic world destinations weren't enough.

"Really?" My eyes wander to the bulletin board above my desk, where my lonely Pearl Jam stub is pinned, and I sigh. Even the things I'd treasured a couple of days ago look pathetic and trivial when I see them through his eyes.

He follows my eyes to the desk, then walks over and examines the stub. "No way."

"What?"

He shakes his head hard, like he's trying to dismiss a thought he doesn't want to have. "Nothing. I've got this giant bowl of ticket stubs—" He holds his arms out wide to demonstrate the size of the bowl and confirm my assumption. He probably can't believe I've only been to one concert.

And that's when he spots the map. Now I really feel insignificant.

He walks over to get a closer look, and stands there, arms crossed, serious, examining it like it's a piece in an art gallery. I cover my eyes in embarrassment and force myself to go and stand by his side.

"My dad made it for me. It's supposed to mark all my travels." I flash back to the night we sat in the coffeehouse when I told him about my plans to see the world someday, and I steal a sideways glance at his face. I wonder what he's thinking. No,

I *know* what he's thinking. Like the lone ticket stub, the four little pins on my map must make a pretty sad statement, especially to someone who has never known limits. "As you can see, I'm off to a fine start."

But he just looks at the map and says, "It's fantastic." After a long pause, he steps backward so he can take it all in. "See, now, I've never been to any of these places." I laugh. "I'm serious," he adds. Right. Like he wasn't making fun of me.

I hold my palms flat like a balancing scale and lift them up and down like I'm weighing the destinations. "Let's see. It's a Tuesday. Should I go canoeing on Boundary Waters or rafting on the Amazon? The Amazon or *Boundary Waters*?" I stress the last destination like it's the more interesting and exotic of the two. "It's okay, Bennett. You don't have to pretend to think it's 'fantastic.'" I look past him instead of into his eyes. "To tell you the truth, the map used to make me a little sad. I guess sometimes it still does."

He steps in to close the distance that separates us, and I think I stop breathing when I feel the warmth of his skin next to mine. The oversize sweatshirt doesn't show off his body the way his T-shirt did, but that doesn't keep me from picturing the strong shoulders underneath, the way his arms cut through the water, and the way he pulled his body out of the surf. "Why does it make you sad?"

As I look at him, my chest is tight with the feeling of holding back what I really want to say. "Four pins," I finally squeak, as I shoot him a fake smile and try not to look like I care quite so much. We stare at each other but say nothing.

Then Bennett reaches past me into the clear plastic container of pins and takes one by the sharp silver point. He holds it up. The tiny round red tip looks enormous in the small space between us.

"Five," he says, extending his hand.

I reach out to take the pin from his fingers and stare at it, pressing my lips together so I won't cry. "I don't even know where it is," I finally say with an embarrassed laugh.

"Right there." His voice is kind, not at all condescending, as he points to an unmarked speck in the Gulf of Thailand.

I consider the dot on the map, not much larger than the tip of the pin itself, and wonder how something so tiny could mark the most extraordinary four hours of my life. Then I look at Bennett, dressed in my dad's sweats, his shaggy hair still peppered with sand. His expression is sweet and soft and, if it's possible, even more grateful than mine. He gave me this gift today, but I can't help feeling like I gave him one too.

I consider the pin once again and step forward to meet the map. I'm still fighting back happy, overwhelmed tears as I reach out, hands shaking, and press it firmly into the tiny island of Ko Tao.

⌒

I make grilled-cheese sandwiches and we sit on the couch, eating and trying to think of something to say. He's not starting in on the rest of his secrets, and we're way beyond small talk, so I turn on the TV and flip channels just for something to do, but there isn't much to watch at two thirty on a weekday.

Not that Bennett seems to care; he finds the commercials far more amusing than the actual shows, but refuses to tell me why. More important, he doesn't seem at all concerned that our day's running out, and he still hasn't told me everything. I still don't even know the rest of the *second* thing.

I lift the remote with a dramatic gesture, stare at him, and click the power off. The room goes silent, and he turns to me. "I'm ready for the rest of the second thing."

"Haven't you had enough for one day?"

I shake my head.

"Okay." He sits back against the cushions again and twists to face me. He props his arm up on the back of the couch, and for a moment, it's as if we're back in the coffeehouse, telling each other our secrets. He gives me a little grin, and the small, insignificant gesture makes me want to lean over and kiss him to get it over with. But I'm afraid if I do, I'll never hear the rest.

He takes a deep breath. "I can go anywhere in the world, but *when* I travel is . . . restricted. I can go into other *times*, but only within certain dates." He stares at me like he's waiting for me to react, and when I don't, he opens his mouth to continue.

"Wait." I hold my finger up in front of me and listen.

"What?" he asks.

I hear a car door slam. Mom or Dad would have come in through the garage, so it can only be one person. "Emma," I say in a panic. I'm not ready for Bennett to leave, but I'm also not prepared to explain why he is sitting in my living room.

"Don't worry. I'll go." He grabs my hand and gives it a little shake. "I'll see you tomorrow," he says. I watch as his hand, still holding mine, becomes transparent. Then it's gone with the rest of him. I wonder if I'll ever get used to this.

She knocks hard on the front door and then rings the doorbell for good measure.

"Coming!" I yell as I slide the two plates and their leftover grilled-cheese passengers under the couch and inspect the room for other signs that I haven't spent the day alone. When I open the door, Emma practically falls through it. "Oh, my God!" she yells as she drops her backpack on the floor and wraps her arms around me. "I heard what happened last night! Are you okay?"

Last night? The robbery? Was that *last* night?

"I'm fine," I hear myself say over the deafening thump of my own heartbeat.

"I've been trying to get here since I heard, but Dawson caught me trying to leave campus, and I couldn't escape after that!" Her voice is high-pitched and dramatic. "I've been so worried. Are you seriously okay? Do you want to talk about it?" She plops down in the exact spot Bennett was just sitting in.

"Not really," I huff. But I can tell from Emma's eager eyes that the protective side of her needs to know I'm okay and the gossipy side can't help wanting to hear every detail. Since I can't tell her that I spent the day on a Thai beach and I'm not sure I'm ready to tell her about Bennett, I figure I might as well give her what she wants. "It all happened so fast."

14

"No." I use the firmest voice I can muster this early in the morning. "You're not serious?"

"Afraid I can't keep up?" Dad's dressed in his winter gear, stretching into an almost comical runner's lunge against the refrigerator, like I imagine he did in the olden days.

"No." I cover my eyes. "Listen, I'll stick to the streets. I'll stay off campus. *Seriously,*" I beg, pointing toward the kitchen window, "I don't need a babysitter. The sun will be up in a few minutes. I'll be fine." The last word comes out in a whine, and I feel like the ten-year-old he seems to think I've reverted into. This overprotective parent thing had better pass quickly.

"Ignore me." He takes a long drink of water from his sport bottle and lunges to the side. "You don't have to talk to me or even look at me, but I'll be right behind you, kiddo." Evidently there's no convincing a father of his daughter's safety when she's just been robbed at knifepoint.

"No, it's okay. We'll run together." I set my Discman on the hallway table, already mourning its absence. I need my music to help get my head straight before I see Bennett at school.

Dad follows me out the door and we run side by side toward the lake. In unison, we wave to the man in the green vest with the gray ponytail. We run around the track four times, through campus and past the clock tower as it chimes seven. I race him the last half mile to our lawn, which turns out to be a mistake, because now he can't catch his breath.

"Are you sure you're okay?" I keep asking.

He's red and blotchy, but he nods and forces a smile anyway. "Just. Fine," he pants. "Why. Do you. Ask?"

"You overdid it." I scold him—just like I know Mom will when he can't move tomorrow. I stretch into a lunge next to him. "What, are you going to drive me to school now, too?"

"Nope. I trust Emma with that duty."

"Clearly you've never seen her drive." I finish my stretch, shake out my legs, and run toward the steps.

"Hey, Annie," Dad calls, and I stop and turn around. I rest my hands on my hips while he tries to keep from having a heart attack.

"Invite Bennett over to dinner. Your mother and I want to meet him. Properly."

I glare down at him from the porch. "Dad. We're not even *close* to that." The mere fact that he'd ask is mortifying.

He gives me his best stern-parent voice. "Okay, but if this is serious, we want to meet him."

⁓

"'Morning, love." Emma chirps out her usual greeting and pinches my cheek. "My brave little friend." I don't feel brave. I feel nervous about seeing Bennett. I feel guilty about not telling Emma about him yesterday. I feel tired, because I have barely slept.

She slams the gearshift into reverse and backs out of the driveway. Dad's standing at the kitchen window, staring out at us with a look of mild panic on his face, and I give him a little shrug as we tear away from the house.

"Em," I begin, "if I tell you something, do you promise not to get mad?"

She shoots me an irritated look. "Now, see—I don't understand why people ask that question. How can I promise I won't get mad if I don't know what you're going to tell me?" The look on her face makes me think this might fall into her Stupid Americans category. "Just spill it."

I spit the words out quickly, before I can change my mind. "I didn't tell you the whole story yesterday, about the robbery." I take her back through the high points, but I don't tell her the whole truth. How can I? Even if I hadn't promised Bennett I'd keep his secret, she'd never believe me. Instead, I include the story Bennett crafted for me, including the part where I take off out the back door and run into him. Then I tell her he skipped school yesterday to spend it with me.

"What?!" She swerves dramatically, nearly hitting a parked car. "Crap! Okay, I'm good. I'm good." She looks at me again. "You spent the *day* together."

I smile, picturing the look on Bennett's face when he drew the line in the sand with his toe and challenged me to race him into the ocean. In my head, I watch the slow-motion video of his body floating on the turquoise water and his arms cutting through white-tipped waves.

Yes, we spent the day together.

And I can't tell my best friend about the best parts.

"He was worried about me." The words come out as squeaks, but Emma doesn't seem to notice.

"Now that I think about it, I didn't see him in English Lit—"

The little movie in my head comes to a halt.

"Great. I didn't think about that. Everyone in Spanish knows we were both absent yesterday." I wonder if Courtney has already started speculating aloud.

"Oh, don't you go trying to change the subject. Go back to telling me all about how you two *made out* in your empty house all day." She raises an eyebrow and turns her attention back to the road, waiting me out as only Emma can.

"Hardly. He didn't even kiss me." I can hear the disappointment in my own voice. "We talked. We listened to CDs. We ate lunch. He—" I almost say the word *disappeared*, but I catch myself. "He took off just before you got there."

"And why didn't you tell me any of this yesterday?"

"My dad came home."

She grimaces and rolls her eyes. Here it comes. "Oh, of course. Say, do you have a phone? I do. I have a phone. It's great for telling your best friend the biggest news of your life when you can't do it in person." I don't even have time to squeeze out an apology.

We pull up to a red light and she turns to face me. "What are you doing, Anna?" She sounds like my mom when I'm not washing the dishes the right way, or stuffing way too many clothes in the dryer. "Didn't he tell you that he's, you know, *leaving*?" She stresses the last word like it alone is enough to make me know better.

"Yeah." I can't say anything else. I don't need her to tell me that I'm crazy for walking into this thing with Bennett, whatever it is.

"And it's worth the inevitable heartbreak?" she asks. "For a brief fling you know is going to end?"

Not a brief fling. A daring adventure.

"Yeah, Em. To me it is."

She bites her lower lip hard. "This isn't going to end well."

I study the all-weather floor mats. She's right, and I know it. But the truth is, I couldn't stop now, even if I wanted to. I've spent the whole night thinking about how it will end, but right now, there's only one thing I want to think about: there will be a middle.

"I like him, okay? There. I said it. I really like him." I look right into her eyes. "I know it's probably a mistake, but please, just . . . let me enjoy this?"

We stare at each other.

"Green light." I gesture with my thumb toward the windshield.

She keeps staring at me. She doesn't press on the accelerator, but she nods, and I know that means she'll be on her best behavior. At least for today. When the driver behind us lays on the horn, Emma finally pulls into the intersection. We're silent for the next two blocks, but I know what she's thinking.

"So, while we're coming clean and all, there's something I wanted to tell you yesterday, too." Okay, maybe I don't know what she was thinking. I stare at her and wait for her to continue. "Your friend from the record store, Justin, sort of asked me out."

"Justin? *My* Justin?" As soon as the possessive leaves my mouth, I wish I could pull it back in. Bennett's little do-over trick would come in handy in moments like these, when my foot is stuck firmly in my mouth and all I want to do is go back in time for *one* minute so I can say the right thing instead. "I'm sorry, I just meant—" I don't even know what I meant. "It's just . . . I'm usually with you when he's around, and I've never picked up on . . ." I really should just shut up now, before I say what I'm thinking: *But I always thought he liked* me?

"Well, not always. You know, I stop in the record store sometimes after I drop you off at work." No. I didn't know that. "A few weeks ago, we started talking about music. He knows a lot about music." Yes. This I do know. I've known Justin since I was five. "And then he asked me out for coffee, and we went out to dinner the night before last."

"You went out to dinner?" I ask. "You and Justin had coffee and then went out to *dinner*? Why didn't you tell me any of this, like—I don't know—last week? Yesterday?" But I feel a little guilty when I remember that I never told her about the night I hung out in the coffeehouse with Bennett. It was just too weird, especially when nothing ever came of it.

She gives me an apologetic look and a guilty shrug. "He said he tried to talk to you about me once, when he was first thinking about asking me out, but . . ." Emma trails off, and I flash back to that day in the record store last month. He'd wanted to ask me about something, and I'd avoided him because I'd thought he was trying to ask me out. Now I feel like an idiot on two fronts: first, because I read him wrong, and second, because he and my best friend have been talking about me, bonding over my lameness. "I know he's your friend," Emma continues. "And you know, I always thought he liked you, but—" She likes Justin? Emma and Justin? It doesn't even sound right. "Anyway. I really didn't think anything would ever come of it. I mean, I thought he was nice, but I didn't think we'd hit it off or anything."

"But you did."

"Yeah, I guess we did."

And now it's quiet. I can't remember a time when Emma's car was this silent for this long. A few blocks later, she finally talks again. "We're going to spend the day in the city together on Saturday." She keeps her eyes on the road and tries to play it cool, but she breaks into a huge grin.

"That's great, Em."

"You sure?" She turns to me. "You *are* okay with all of this, right? I mean, especially now."

It's weird, but yeah, I'm okay with it. I have no right not be. "Of course I am," I say, but I feel a little pang of sadness, too because it's Justin. It's Emma. And Justin. *My* friends. Before I can stop myself, I wonder how this will change my friendship with them, if they'll wind up liking each other more than they like me, and which one I'll have to stop talking to if this whole thing doesn't work out. And most selfishly, if Justin will still make me running mixes.

Emma lets out a dramatic sigh. "Good. As long as you're cool with it." She brightens again as she changes the subject back to me. "So—you and Bennett," she begins with a little teasing tone in her voice. "What happens at school today?"

I let a nervous laugh escape. "I have absolutely no idea."

She turns in to the student lot and makes a beeline for her usual spot. "Well, you're about to find out," she sings, and I follow her gaze to find Bennett, standing there on the lawn, waiting for me. I feel sick.

"Oh. My. God." Emma snorts as she throws the gearshift into park. "What did you *do* to that boy? Just look at him." Bennett has gotten a haircut. It's still a bit long for my taste, but he looks crisp and clean in his uniform and nothing short of gorgeous—although after yesterday, it's hard not to picture him in his thin T-shirt and those jeans that rested so perfectly on his hips. And that's when I remember that his clothes are still in my dryer, and I panic for a moment until I realize it's not laundry day. "He's adorable!" Emma gives him a flirty little wave and I slap her hand down.

"Oh, please; you're just saying that to be nice." I'm grateful for the change of heart, even though I know it's fake.

Emma turns and looks at me. "I don't say anything just to be nice, love. Even to you."

"Fine. Then please continue to act like a loyal friend and don't embarrass me." I'm still struggling with the butterflies in my stomach and the latch on the door when Emma gets out of the car and pokes her head back in to say, "Ahhh, it's going to be a *good* day."

She slams the door behind her and struts up the small incline toward Bennett, abandoning all concern about my future heartbreak. "Well, hello!" I hear her say as I scramble to join them before Emma has the chance to talk too much.

"I know!" I can hear her say in a voice as exaggerated as her smile. "I don't think we've talked since your first day here, have we?"

When I reach the two of them, Bennett turns his attention to me. God, he looks cute. "Hey," he says. His smile is so warm I think the snow has just started to melt around his feet.

"Hi."

"So, Bennett, I noticed you weren't in Lit yesterday," Emma says, and he takes his eyes away from mine to look back at her. "Were you sick?" She stares him down, and I shoot her a warning glare.

"No. I spent the day with Anna," he replies, and then he looks straight at me again. We used to be strangers because he insisted on it. Today, we're standing here like friends because he decided he could trust me with a secret so large, so implausible, I wouldn't have believed it if I hadn't seen it with my own eyes.

"Oh. Well." She looks at him, then at me, and then back at him. She reaches up and musses his hair. "Don't cut too much more, or I'll need to find you a new nickname, Shaggy. See you at lunch, Anna." She starts to walk away but pivots on her heel and turns back to us. "Speaking of lunch, will you be joining us today?"

"Yes," he says, still looking at me, and I grin.

"Shaggy?" he asks when Emma's out of earshot. "Is that the best she can do?"

I roll my eyes and look up at the top of Bennett's head and smile. "When did you manage to cut your hair, anyway?"

He shrugs.

I look around to be sure no one's listening. "You traveled?" I ask.

He moves even closer to me and whispers in my ear, "No. I went to Supercuts."

I crack up.

People keep staring at us—walking by, watching us, whispering to each other.

Bennett says, "I just wanted to be sure you're okay. You know, after . . ."

"Anna!" Three of my cross-country teammates burst in on us, cut Bennett off without even looking at him, and start talking over each other. "Oh, my God! I heard about the robbery!

Are you okay?" They all have the same look of concern on their faces.

The robbery. That's why everyone's staring. Of course, a fellow student's being held at knifepoint would make the Westlake grapevine.

"Yeah, thanks, guys. I'm fine."

They all express their relief and we chat for a few more seconds before they each give me a quick hug and rush off. Bennett and I watch as one of them skids on the ice and nearly plows into the rosebushes.

"Anyway, I just wanted to be sure you were okay . . . with everything."

"Yeah." I smile. "I'm okay. But I still want to hear the rest." I wait for him to say something but he doesn't.

"You will."

"We should probably get to class," I say, at the exact same time he says, "I have something for you."

"You do?"

He reaches into his backpack, pulls out a piece of paper, and gives it to me. I let out a gasp when I realize what it is. What he did to get it. I look down at the postcard from Ko Tao and smile at the photo. "You went back? For this?"

He shrugs and gives me a sheepish grin. "You needed a souvenir." The bell rings in the distance, making us both officially tardy. "I'd better get to class. I'll see you at lunch." He turns to walk away, but I call out, "Bennett." He turns around to face me again.

"Yeah?"

"I still have your clothes." That doesn't come out the way I planned, and I quickly look around to be sure no one has overheard me.

His mouth turns up into a satisfied grin. "Good. I guess I'll have to come by and get them."

⌒

Argotta asks me to stay after class, and I reluctantly send Bennett off to the dining hall alone. Argotta asks if I'm okay and goes over some things from yesterday's class, and five minutes later, I walk into the dining hall to find Bennett planted at our usual table with Emma and Danielle. He looks like he's holding his own.

"You're just in time," Emma says as I set my tray on the table. "Bennett was just telling us all about himself." She turns to me and says, "He's not really into sports, you know?" She shrugs and takes a bite of her sandwich.

"Well, like I said, skateboarding *is* actually a sport," Bennett says.

"Oh, I guess it could be. But it's really more of a mode of transportation, isn't it? I meant, you know, school sports. Football. Basketball. Baseball. Lacrosse. Hockey. Those types of sports."

"Team sports."

"Well, no, you could swim, I suppose. Or play tennis. Those are sports too."

"Or, you could skate," he says calmly. I can see the wheels in Emma's head turning as she attempts to land on the perfect retort. She glances at me sideways, and I give her a warning look, reminding her with my eyes of the promises she made me this morning: To be nice. To not embarrass me.

"Sure. You could skateboard, I guess." Emma looks back at me for confirmation that she has said the right thing, and I give her a grateful smile. And silently will her to stop talking. She looks back at Bennett. "So, what other hobbies do you have?"

So now it's a hobby. I just look at him, the boy who doesn't need a sport or a hobby, because what he can do counts for more than either one in my book. Bennett looks ready to jump back into the skateboarding-as-a-sport debate, so I answer for him.

"He travels," I say, and all three of them look at me. "He's been everywhere. Haven't you?"

They turn their attention back to Bennett, and he shrugs like it's no big deal. I sit back and listen as the three of them spend the rest of lunch talking in animated tones about the places they've seen. I've been on this side of the conversation before, but this time, I don't feel left out. Instead, I'm completely captivated, mentally taking notes, and wondering which of these beautiful-sounding destinations Bennett might take me to next.

15

Emma pulls up in front of the bookstore to drop me off, and before she even has the car in park, her head whips around in the direction of the record store across the street.

Okay, this is already a little weird.

"Are you going over there?" I ask as I open my door and step out onto the curb. I lean back in to hear her answer.

"No, not today. Today he should wonder if I'm going to pop in, and then, you know, miss me a little bit when I don't."

I roll my eyes. I don't think that's Justin's style, but then I realize, since I completely missed his attraction to my best friend, maybe I don't know much about Justin's style after all. "Okay, Em. See you in the morning."

"Bye, love," she says, and I watch her drive off.

The bells on the bookstore door give their standard jingle, but an unexpected chill goes through me when I hear them today. I usually associate them with happy memories, like coming in on a Saturday morning to help my grandfather stock the shelves, or the first time Dad gave me my own set of keys and let me lock up for the night. I've spent the last two days being grateful that the intruder was caught before he could take any of our money, but until now, it hadn't occurred to me that he robbed me of my bells.

"Hey, Annie." Dad's at the counter, punching numbers into the calculator, and making a small stack of the day's receipts.

I plant a kiss on his cheek. "Hi, Dad." He pecks my cheek in return and goes back to the accounting. Neither of us acknowledges that the store is different today, but I know we both feel it.

"I'm going to run to the bank and make the deposit," he says without looking at me. "From now on, I don't want you to do the night drop. I'll take care of it." I liked making the night drop. I watch as Dad collects all the receipts and staples them together, and stuffs the cash from the register into the zippered pouch. "I made arrangements to have an alarm system installed this weekend. It sounds pretty fancy. It even has a remote control, so you can just press a button from anywhere in the store and it will call the police immediately."

I look at him sideways. "Which is great, as long as you're carrying the remote."

"Well, yeah, I suppose." He laughs. "That's a little intense, isn't it?"

"No, not at all. We can get matching leather belts, with little holsters." I reach into my make-believe holster, quick-draw my invisible remote, and point it at him. He does the same.

"You know, I was thinking," Dad begins.

"Uh-oh."

"I was thinking that maybe it's time I hired a Northwestern student to help in the store. You're busier now, training for State. And finals are coming up soon—"

"In a month."

"Before you know it, you'll be dealing with college applications—"

"In six months."

"And even though I haven't met him properly, you seem to have a boyfriend now."

"I do not have a boyfriend."

"And you have better things to do than sit in this musty old store every other night, don't you think? It would be a great job for a college student."

"No, it wouldn't, because it's already a great job for me. Thanks, Dad, but I'm fine. I like working here." Besides, I've got to make money for my travel fund somehow, and it might as well be here.

He pulls me into a hug. "Are you sure?"

"Positive," I say, but my voice is muffled by his wool sweater.

He finally lets me go, pulls on his coat, and grabs the bag of cash. He's no sooner out the door than the bells jingle again.

I look up and see Bennett walking right toward me.

"Hi."

"Hi," he says to me.

We stand there awkwardly shifting our weight between our

feet and trying to think of something to say.

"I'm glad you came by." I wring my hands. "I wanted to thank you again for the postcard. That was really sweet."

"Sure." I watch *his* face get red and am grateful that it's not about me, for a change. "I got one for myself, too. To remember the day." He looks as nervous as I am. Which somehow makes me feel a lot better. "Anyway, I just came by to say hi and to get that book. On Mexico. For Argotta's class."

"Oh, right, sure."

He follows me over to the Travel section and I run my finger along the bindings, stopping to extract my favorites. After I've removed a good selection of six or seven, I sit down cross-legged on the Berber carpet and lean back against the shelves.

"Sit." I gesture for Bennett to join me, and he mirrors me on the floor. I reach into the pile of books and I hold up the first one. "This one sucks. Hardly any pictures." I put it down, starting a new pile on the floor, and pick up another. Suddenly I feel a strange sense of déjà vu. "Whoa."

"What?"

I look at him for a minute. "Did we sit like this the other night? Before the robbery and your do-over thingy?"

"Yeah. Pretty much exactly." He smiles. Then he looks surprised. "What? Do you remember it?"

"I don't know. Maybe not."

He picks a book out of the pile and holds it up. "This one's fine for budget travel, but that's not really what we're after." He grins as he puts it on top of the one with hardly any pictures.

It sounds like something I'd say.

He grabs another. "This one has high-end hotels and restaurants, so it's a little too pricey for us. But the pictures are nice."

Yeah. That's true. And this is kind of freaking me out.

He picks up another book, and when he opens his mouth—presumably to repeat more of my words—I interrupt him and say, "Why don't you just tell me which one I recommended?"

He leans over me, reaches back into the shelves, and removes a book. "Excuse me." He brushes up against my arm and returns to his spot on the floor, but closer. So close our knees are touching. "This one's your favorite."

I nod.

"Best details. Vivid photos. Recommendations for budget hotels, but not, like, hostels or anything. And it has recommendations for three-day tours, five-day tours, and longer stays, so we can just put them togeth—"

"I want to hear the rest of the second thing."

He looks at me for a moment. "Where did I—"

"You can do over minor details in the past to affect the outcome, but you can't erase an entire event. You can travel to any place in the world *and* into other times, but only within certain dates."

He looks at me like he's surprised that I remember his words so exactly, but how could I not? They spent the night tossing and turning in bed with me.

"Right." He smiles a little. "I can only travel within my own lifetime. I can't go back before the day I was born, or even one second beyond the current date. The first time I tried it, it worked, but, well, things went wrong. I've tried a thousand times since, but nothing happens."

I picture a timeline in my head that starts at the year he was born and continues on until today. "So, you can't travel before 1978 or after today?"

He reaches down to one of the Mexico travel guides and starts playing with the pages like it's one of those little flip books, studiously avoiding my gaze. "No. I can go further into the future than that."

"But I thought you couldn't—then how—" I'm not getting this. And he's not helping much. "Okay, let me ask it this way: How far beyond 1995 have you gone?"

He inhales sharply. He doesn't look at me. "Two thousand and twelve."

"But isn't that 'beyond your lifetime'?"

But he's looking at me like it's not, and I feel a knot in the pit of my stomach.

He raises his eyebrows, like he's just waiting for me to catch on. "Wait . . . when were you born?"

I think a full minute passes before I get my answer. At least it feels that way.

"March 6. 1995."

I just stare at him. "That was last month."

"Yeah. I know."

"March 6, 1995?"

"Yes."

That's when it hits me. The photos in his grandmother's living room. The framed pictures of her daughter holding a baby. Named Bennett.

"No way." He's still not looking up at me. "The pictures on Maggie's mantel." I don't even realize I've said it out loud, but I must have, because he finally looks up and nods.

"Maggie's your grandmother."

He nods again.

"And the 'real you' is . . ." I can't bring myself to say the words: *an infant*. "In San Francisco." That's the reason there aren't any older pictures of Bennett on Maggie's wall.

"Well, I'm the 'real' me." He holds his arm out and hits it to prove that it's solid. Then he looks at me. "But, yeah. In 2012 I'm seventeen. In 1995, technically, I'm . . . not."

I picture a completely different timeline. One that *starts* in 1995 and ends in 2012.

"What about the . . . other you? The one in the pictures."

"I'm still in San Francisco, probably lying in a crib, staring up at a mobile or something." I cringe and he looks at me sideways, but I shake it off and try not to look like the Baby Bennett thing isn't weirding me out. I must look confused instead, because he clarifies. "I can be in two different places in the same time, just not in the same place at the same time."

"What happens if you are? In the same place at the same time?"

"Well, I never let it happen accidentally. But if I do it on purpose, the *younger* me disappears and I take his place, just like I did at the robbery the other night. Then it's a do-over."

I look down at the books and play with the pages. "You lied to me about your grandmother being sick?"

"Not exactly. She *does* have Alzheimer's, she just . . . doesn't have it in 1995."

"And why does she think you're a Northwestern student?" This time I look up at him.

He sighs. "That's what I told her when I applied for the room."

He's still pressing my hand to his arm, but I pull it away so I can fidget with a string that's pulling loose from the carpet while I try not to hyperventilate.

He can go forward from 1995, because everything from this point on is his future.

He lives with a woman who has no idea he's her grandson.

He's not supposed to be here in 1995.

"This is your past," I say.

"Yes."

"How long have you stayed anywhere in the past?" I close my eyes again. I can't look at him.

"Thirty-six days," I hear him whisper.

"And when was that?"

There's a pause. "Tomorrow will be thirty-seven days."

I close my eyes. I don't think I'm handling this well.

And I still haven't heard everything. I don't know who he was mumbling about in the park that night, or how he got here, or where he came from, or what he's doing in Evanston, or why he was only supposed to be here for a month but he's still here.

I finally open my eyes and take him in.

I'm sixteen years older than him. But I'm not.

He's one year older than me. But he's not.

He looks me straight in the eye. "Look. I know this is weird. And even now that you know the rest of the second thing, you still only know two out of the three." He glances up at the ceiling and it's quiet for a moment before he looks at me again.

"The point is that I'm not supposed to be here, Anna. Not in Evanston. Not in 1995. I'm not supposed to know you, or Emma, or Maggie. I'm not supposed to go to this school, or do this homework, or hang out in your coffeehouse." He takes my hands in his like he's about to transport me somewhere, but we don't leave the room—we just move a lot closer to each other. "I don't stay anywhere. I visit. I observe. I leave. I don't *ever* stay."

I'm not sure what I'm supposed to do with this information. Tell him to leave? Tell him to stay? But I don't have time to consider any other alternatives, because he scoots in closer and brings his hands to my face, and I fall back into the bookcase as he kisses me with this intensity—like he *wants* to be here, and if he kisses me just long enough, deeply enough, none of what he just said will actually be true. And as much as I know it's *all* true and that it's incredibly stupid to feel this way about someone who doesn't belong here—who, when he leaves, will hardly be a plane ride away—my hands leave the Berber carpet, find his back, and pull him toward me until I'm flat against the shelves. Because he's here now. And because I'm pretty certain I don't want this to stop. Ever.

Then he pulls away. "I'm so sorry."

"It's okay," I say as I try to catch my breath.

"No. It's *not* okay. This isn't how I planned it—I shouldn't have made it more complicated than it already is." He stands up and combs his fingers through his hair. "I've gotta go. I'm so sorry."

"Bennett." I try to smile at him—try not to look like everything that just happened doesn't have me slightly freaked out—but he won't even look at me. "It's okay. Bennett, please don't go."

But he's already out the door, leaving me alone with the rest of the second thing and the words he said just before he kissed me: "I don't *ever* stay."

16

"Hey, Anna! Wait up!" Courtney slams her locker and starts walking with me. "Did you finish your plan yet?"

"No, not yet." We smash in close to each other as we squeeze past a group of kids huddled around a locker and then we spread out again. "I'm working on it. How's yours coming along?"

"Good. I was just thinking last night I should probably add some ruins or something, you know—something educational." She looks at me like she's waiting for me to agree, so I nod. "But the beaches just look *amazing.* I swear I could spend the whole time just pancaked on different patches of sand."

"Just do beaches, then."

"Are you doing beaches?"

"Some." I have no idea what I'm doing. Last night, I tried to get beyond the pathetic two-column list I started in the bookstore last Tuesday, but I spent most of the night distracted by a time traveler who visits but never stays. An incredible, beautiful boy with eyes I can never seem to get out of my head, a body I never want to be more than two feet away from, and hands that can take me anywhere I want to go at the speed of thought. The same boy who isn't supposed to be here in 1995, but sat on the floor of my bookstore last night like there was nowhere else in the world he'd rather be and kissed me like there was no one else in the world he'd rather kiss. The boy with secrets, who still has one more to tell.

"Where else are you going?" she asks innocently, like we're not in the same competition to win the same five-hundred-dollar travel voucher.

I bring myself back to the hallway and try to think of what to say. "I've got a bunch of—" I begin, but I lose my train of thought again, because there's Bennett, leaning against the locker bank in front of Argotta's room, looking sweet and shaggy and gorgeous and clearly waiting for me. I try to keep pace with Courtney despite the new gear my heart has just leaped into.

"What? Ruins? I knew it. You're doing ruins. I should do—" I don't hear anything else after that, and when we finally reach Bennett, I come to a stop. My heart, on the other hand, speeds up even more.

"Hi," he says as he shoots me this incredible smile, and Courtney practically disappears from my side while I try not to look quite so happy to see him.

"Hi." Great, and now my hands are shaking.

Courtney's still here after all, and I see her look around

like she's trying to figure out where all the electricity is coming from. She looks back and forth between the two of us as a weird little smile forms on her lips. "Oh . . . interesting," she says and heads into the classroom with a mocking "Excuse me."

"Can we talk?" Bennett asks.

I peek around the door and into the classroom. "Spanish is about to start."

"I know. Come on." He leads me out the doors toward the side of the building and to a pathway obscured by overgrown plants and shrubs, and I hear the bell ring in the distance. We climb the slope to a clump of trees near the top of the ridge and stop at the base of the largest one. Bennett sits down and pats the ground next to him. Once I'm sitting, I know exactly where we are; the floor-to-ceiling glass wall of the dining hall is hard to miss, and even from here I can clearly see our table.

"So, I just wanted to say I'm sorry again . . . about last night." He reaches down for a pebble and plays with it nervously, rubbing it back and forth between his fingers. Then he looks up at me with a sad expression I've never seen on his face. "It's just—I've wanted to kiss you so many times." I lean in closer, hoping my proximity will help make this another one of those times, but he leans back with a sigh and rests against the tree trunk. "I told myself I had to hold back, because I knew starting something wouldn't be fair to you. I didn't want to complicate it. You know? I wanted to tell you everything and let you decide how you felt about it. About me."

"I know how I feel," I say as I close the gap he created between us a moment ago and muster a brave face. "But in that case, I guess you'd better tell me the rest—so I can decide." I give him an encouraging smile so he knows I'm ready to hear it. And I am, even though I also know it involves a girl. It was more than a month ago, but that doesn't mean I've forgotten how he looked the night I found him in the park, rocking back and forth on the bench and mumbling that he had to find her. How he told me in the coffeehouse that someone disappeared and it was his fault.

"I lost my sister." My eyes grow wide. "Brooke and I go to concerts. It's sort of our thing."

Brooke. I hadn't thought about the little girl with the dark hair and the bangs, holding her baby brother in a picture frame perched on Maggie's mantel. His sister. Who is two. Or nineteen.

"It's become a kind of hobby. I research bands I like and find the earliest shows I can travel to. Well, Brooke's the one who always travels with me."

He's struggling to talk. Apparently, telling me how he went back in time to save my life and that he didn't really belong here in 1995 were just ways of warming himself up for the hardest one. Brooke's a big deal.

"Remember how I told you I could only travel within my own lifetime?"

I let out a nervous laugh. "Yeah, I haven't forgotten that part."

"Well, if I try to travel earlier, it doesn't work. I close my eyes and picture the date, and . . . well . . . nothing happens. But Brooke wanted me to take her to this one show, so she convinced me to try it. It was a total experiment. Neither one of us really thought it would work." He smiles at the memory. "We held hands, closed our eyes, and I pictured the location and a date in 1994. And—"

"It worked?"

"Yeah, but only for a few minutes. I was there, and then I wasn't. I got knocked back to San Francisco."

"Knocked *back*?"

He shrugs, like it's a minor inconvenience he has to tolerate. "I usually have total control over where and when I go, but if I push the limits, it's like time *rights* everything. I get sent back where I'm supposed to be."

"But if you traveled there with Brooke, why did you get knocked back and she didn't?"

"I couldn't stay because I didn't *exist* in March 1994."

I stare at him, waiting for the rest.

"Brooke did. She was born in '93."

"Whoa. Seriously?" I ask, and he nods. "Where were you taking her?"

"March 10, 1994. Chicago Stadium." He looks me in the eyes and asks, "Does the date sound familiar?"

I think about it. March tenth. Last year. March tenth. I have no idea what he's talking about.

"The ticket stub," he says. "On your bulletin board. Pearl Jam. It wasn't a particularly epic show or anything. She just wanted to see them play stuff from *Ten* and *Vs.*"

"No way." I say the same two words I heard him say when he saw the ticket stub upstairs. "I was there. With Emma. We were *there*."

"Probably a lot longer than I was. I didn't even have enough time to buy a T-shirt."

I think I'm supposed to laugh along with him, but I'm still staring at him in disbelief. "How will you get her back?"

"I'm not entirely sure yet. At first, I just assumed that if I went back as far as I could—to March 6, 1995—Brooke would have lived out the year and been waiting for me at Maggie's. But she wasn't there and clearly hadn't been. So now I have to wait and see; either she'll 'catch up' to March 1995 and hopefully know I'm here, or time will right itself and she'll get knocked back home to 2012 . . . or, I guess, somewhere else between now and then."

"God, she must be terrified." I picture her roaming the streets, lost in time and looking for shelter.

"I know Brooke, and I'm sure she freaked out a little at first, but she's got plenty of money with her, more than enough to get by. I think she'll be fine. But my mom's a mess, and wow, is she pissed at me. Though maybe my screwup proved she's right and I can't handle this little *gift* of mine."

I have no idea what to say.

"Anyway, I returned alone at a total loss and had to break the news that it could take a while. My mom insisted I come back and stay here until I found Brooke. I explained I could be gone for weeks or more, so she made excuses to people at home and had me bring my dad to Evanston to enroll me in her old school." I can hear the bitterness in his voice. "So, here I am. I go back home every once in a while to check in."

The migraines. The rocking. The murmuring: *I've got to find her. I can't leave yet.* It's all making sense. "You were coming back from San Francisco."

"Yeah. It happened a bunch of times in those first two weeks. I would just disappear from Evanston and reappear in my bedroom back in 2012, so I'd close my eyes and force myself to come back here. In fact, that night you came to Maggie's, I'd just returned. And that's why I kicked you out, because I thought I was about to be knocked back. But I wasn't. It hurt like hell, but I kept myself here, and I haven't been knocked back since." I remember my visit, the coffee cups and water bottles strewn across his room, how he stared me down in Maggie's living room. No wonder he acted so weird when he found me in his house, chatting with his grandmother and staring at a photo of him and his two-year-old sister. No wonder he made me leave.

"So you're only here until Brooke comes back." He nods, and I feel sick. But I've known it all along—deep down in a part of me I keep choosing to ignore—that when I learn his secret, I'll also learn why he can't stay.

"We should get back to class." He grabs my hands, and without even thinking, I close my eyes. But we don't move. The wind is still cold on my face when he says, "Anna." I open my eyes again and see him looking at me. "We're not supposed to know each other. I want us to, but there's a lot at stake for you in this—more than I think you even understand yet."

I think I nod. I'm not sure, but I feel him reach forward and softly brush my eyelids closed. He grabs my hand again, and I feel a twist deep in my gut.

When I open my eyes, we're standing on the path lined with overgrown shrubs and my stomach is contorting. He reaches into his backpack, and pulls out a little bag of saltines, and I immediately start nibbling. Then he pulls out a bottle of water, unscrews the cap, and downs it without stopping. He puts the empty water bottle back in his pack and leads me through the doors and into the hallway. He stops at the exact spot we'd been standing in earlier. I peek inside the room and see Courtney taking her seat.

"Well, you know all my secrets now."

I nod and look around the hallway. We're back.

"So, promise me you'll think about it, okay? And ask me more questions."

Questions. I have plenty of those. What I need is time alone with him, with nowhere we need to be and no reason to stop talking until I understand what the hell he means when he says I need to think about what's "at stake" for me.

He turns to walk into the classroom and I grab his arm. "Hey, when can we talk again?" I'm not about to sit around all weekend wondering when I might bump into him.

"Soon." He gives me a smile. Then he walks into the class-room and I follow him, lost in my thoughts but still taking in the details of the room. Argotta's perched at his usual spot in the front of the room, leaning against his desk. Alex and his too-white teeth are already in the seat across from mine. And

Courtney's in the first seat in the first row, shooting meaningful glances at Bennett and me. Just as the bell rings, she gives me a little wink.

⁓

"Wanna hear the buzz?" Emma asks as she slides her tray onto the table and sits down.

Danielle tosses her hair and turns to look at her. "There's buzz?" Her eyes are so wide they look like they might just pop out and roll across the table. "Who's the buzz about?"

"Anna . . ." Emma purrs. "And Bennett . . ."

"If you follow that with anything about sitting in a tree, I'm leaving." I lean back in my chair and bite into my apple. I don't really want to be the subject of "buzz," but I'm grateful for something else to think about besides do-overs and getting knocked back and a nineteen-year-old girl who's trapped in time.

I turn around in my seat and find Bennett making his way through the lunch line, filling his cup with Coke. Emma follows my gaze and then shoots me a sly grin. "People are talking. Don't you want to know what they're saying before he gets here?"

"Nope." I look uninterested, because I am. "Not really."

"It's *good*," she presses in a high-pitched voice that sounds like she might break into song.

"Don't *care*," I sing back and take another bite.

"I hear he lives with his grandmother," Danielle pipes up, and I stop chewing. Emma and I turn to look at her. Then

Emma looks back at me. "He does?" She wrinkles her nose. I can't tell if she's put off by this new information or just irked that someone else heard it before she did.

My head spins toward Danielle. "How do you know that?" I ask, but I stop and force a grin instead, hoping to cover up how defensive I just sounded.

"Julia Shepherd told me."

"Oh. Julia?" My tone is light and casual now, but only because I'm working hard to make it sound that way. I take another bite of my apple to emphasize how little this topic matters to me. "How does Julia know?"

Danielle touches her palms together in prayer position and bends her head to meet her fingertips. "The Donut keeps no secrets." She laughs and takes a bite of her sandwich.

"Clever."

"So, does he?" Emma asks.

I wipe all traces of irritation from my face and say with a voice calm and steady, like it's no big deal, "Yeah. Her name's Maggie. He takes care of her."

"Oh, that's sweet," says Danielle, and I shoot her an appreciative grin.

"Where are his parents?" Emma whispers as she watches him across the room. "Weren't they supposed to be back by now?"

I wish she'd drop this, because I suddenly realize that I don't know his cover story. He told me his parents were in Europe, but that was before I knew where they *really* were.

I have no idea what he's told the school about his family, but I'm certain he didn't leave emergency contact information for people who live in 2012.

I twist around in my chair again and see him coming right toward us. "Ask him," I say, gesturing in his direction. I hope he has a good answer.

"Hey," Bennett says, sliding his tray onto the table.

"Hey," Emma and Danielle say in unison, with far too much enthusiasm.

At least the two of them have the decency to let him take a couple of bites before they start the inquisition. Then Emma raises her eyebrows at Danielle. Game on.

"So, Bennett." Danielle rests her arms on the table. "I hear you live with your grandmother."

Bennett takes a sip of his Coke, looking unfazed by the fact that she's in his personal space, and nods. "My parents are in Europe, and I'm living with her while they're gone."

"Right," Emma says. "In fact, I thought you were just going to be here for a month. Did they decide to stay longer or something?"

"Yeah. Now I'm not sure how long I'm going to be here."

I think about Brooke and wonder where she is, what she's doing right now. Selfishly hoping she's having the time of her life and won't be returning to 2012 any time soon.

"My dad's working on a big project in Geneva," Bennett says.

I smile and roll my eyes at him, and he gives me a wink.

They all talk about how beautiful Geneva is.

"So," I ask at the first break in the discussion, "how's the auction coming along?"

That's more like it. Bennett and I sit back and watch Emma and Danielle talk over each other with excited intonations and an impressive host of superlatives like *coolest* and *most stellar.* He keeps shooting me little glances while they're talking, like he's trying to guess what I'm thinking, but that's impossible; *I* don't even know what I'm thinking. I'm sure it will hit me at some point, but for now, all I know is that he's sitting here like he belongs.

When the bell rings, Emma and Danielle stand up and start walking to the trash cans while they continue their conversation. Bennett and I follow them, and his arm brushes against mine as he whispers, "So, what are you doing tomorrow?" I don't think he notices that Emma and Danielle have instantly stopped talking.

"Tomorrow night?"

"No. Tomorrow. All day." He smiles at me and adds, "Unless that's too much of me?"

I don't have a meet. And the idea of too much Bennett is impossible to comprehend. I beam. "No. I mean, I don't have plans."

"Great. Can I pick you up at eight?"

"In the morning?"

"Yes."

Danielle lets a giggle escape and Emma elbows her.

"Where are we going?"

"It's a surprise."

I light up again. Or maybe I'm still lit up. I can't really tell.

"Oh, and wear your running clothes."

"Why?"

"Part of the surprise. Excuse me." He nudges past Emma, dumps his trash in the garbage can, and strides out into The Donut. No one speaks until he's left the room.

Then Emma turns to me and squeals, "Okay, that was cute!"

"Yeah, but what's with the running clothes?" Danielle asks.

Emma empties her tray and brings her hand to her hip. "Isn't it obvious? He's going to drive you to the track and make you run while he watches from the bleachers." She cracks up at her own joke.

"Shut up!" I punch her hard in the shoulder but laugh right along with her.

"Yeah, he's cute," Danielle decides.

"He is," Emma agrees. "I'm still watching him," she says, like she's a member of British Intelligence, "but I admit, that boy *is* growing on me."

"And it's sweet that he takes care of his grandma," Danielle adds.

Emma looks at me as if she's just had an epiphany. "Ha! Now we *both* have dates tomorrow! Sunday morning. Coffeehouse. We'll compare."

17

At precisely eight a.m., a blue SUV pulls into the driveway and I slam the window shut and bound down the stairs. For the hundredth time, I wonder where Bennett's taking me. I was sort of hoping our next trip would magically transport us to Paris, but all night I've been studying my map for locations that might require athletic attire for visitors. The Swiss Alps? Machu Picchu? Borneo? It doesn't really matter where we go, but the running-clothes part does have me stumped.

Dad beats me to the door and shakes Bennett's hand while he shoots me a chiding glare, and I know he's already eager for me to get home so he can lay into me about not having introduced them properly. He gives Bennett the lecture about driving carefully and having me home before curfew, and as we're walking toward the door he stares at me and mouths the word *dinner.* I nod and close the door behind us.

"This is your car?"

Bennett holds open the door of the shiny new Jeep Grand Cherokee and waits for me to climb in. It figures. Like everyone else I know, he drives something far too nice for a high school kid.

"It's Maggie's." The inside is immaculate and has that new-car smell. He closes my door, walks around to his side, climbs in, and turns the key in the ignition. The car starts with a purr.

"Are you ready?" he asks, still sitting in the driveway. He leans back against the leather, head cocked to one side, watching me as I study him for clues.

"Of course. Where are we going?"

"Road trip." He clicks his seat belt into place and grins at me.

"We're driving? How far?"

"A little over three hours each way." He looks over his shoulder and backs out of the driveway.

"To go . . . where, exactly?"

He raises his eyebrows and gives me a sinister look. "Still a surprise."

"Do I need to bring anything?"

He scans me from top to bottom. I'm dressed in my long running pants, running shoes, and a fleece zip-up. All as instructed. "Nope. You're perfect."

"Okay. So why drive so far when we can, just, you know . . ." I make a weird gesture, as if I know the universal sign for time travel.

"Ah, look who's getting spoiled!" He navigates through the

neighborhood toward the interstate, heading north. "First, driving gives us plenty of time to talk. Second, I haven't been outside Evanston since I got here. And third, well, I wanted to do something normal for you."

"Normal."

"You know. That has nothing to do with my weird little talent."

I settle into the seat and try not to look disappointed.

We talk and listen to music, and three hours and twenty minutes later we pull into Devil's Lake State Park. I know this because the sign tells me so and not because Bennett has given me any information along the way. He pulls into a parking spot, and we get out and walk around to the back of the car. He clicks open the hatch. Inside are two overstuffed red backpacks, and I feel myself take a step back, confused by the neoprene, Velcro, and shiny pieces of metal that hang from the external loops.

"What is that?" I gesture toward one of the packs.

"That, Anna, is a backpack."

"Yes, I can see that, thank you. What's it for?"

"It's for you."

"What's *in* it?"

"Well, you have the lunch. And the shoes. And the harnesses. I have the rest of the equipment."

"The equipment."

"Ropes, carabiners—"

"You've brought me all the way out here to kill me and bury me?"

"Nope, you'll love this. Trust me."

"Love what, exactly?"

"Rock climbing."

I don't have the heart to tell him that, while I consider myself to be particularly brave and up for most challenges, I tend to avoid sports that require one's feet to leave the solidity of the earth. Like parachuting. And bungee jumping. And rock climbing.

He gives me a pat on the back like I'm an old chum. "You're athletic. You'll love this." He grips my shoulders, turns me around, and lifts the pack onto my back. He heaves the second pack over his shoulders, pulls on the straps to tighten it, and reaches up to shut the rear window. He's a little too chipper as he grabs my hand and leads me to the trail, and I try again not to look disappointed that I won't be drinking a café au lait on the banks of the Seine.

We walk in silence along a peaceful trail, and a half a mile later arrive at some spot deemed by Bennett to be "perfect." To me it looks a lot like a very, very tall rock. And if I'm not mistaken, we're about to scale it.

"Stay here," he says as he opens both of our packs and begins to sort the gear. I watch him change his shoes, strap a thick harness around his waist, and throw a rolled-up bundle of rope over his shoulders. "I'll be right back." And with that, he's off, pulling himself up the sheer face of the rock with what looks like minimal effort. It doesn't take long for him to reach the top, pull himself over the shelf, and disappear from sight. He's gone for a few minutes and I start to wonder if he's left me here.

"Are you okay up there?" I yell.

His face pops up from above the rock. "Great. I'll be right down. Stand back."

I follow his instructions, taking a few more steps than he probably intended, and two thick, white ropes appear from the top of the rock and land a few feet in front of me. Then he's on them, sliding down and bouncing off the rock as he descends. He's all happy and shiny when he hits the bottom.

"Are you ready?"

"No."

"Here, start by putting on your shoes." He reaches into my pack and pulls out a pair of funny-looking red shoes with thin rubber soles and pointy toes.

"Classy." I turn the shoes over. They look brand-new. "Did you buy these for me?"

He smiles. "A little gift."

"How do you know what size I wear?" I slide my foot inside. It fits perfectly.

He shrugs, reaches into my pack again, and pulls out a second, smaller harness, also presumably for me. He takes out a small bag and clips it to the belt. "This is your chalk."

"Chalk." I stand up. The elf shoes feel funny.

"To help your grip," he explains as he holds the harness open for me to step into. He tightens it around my waist and then picks up one end of the rope, wraps his arms around me, and starts fiddling with something on the back of the belt. He smells good.

I look up at the sheer wall. "No amount of chalk is going to help me climb that thing."

"Follow me. Chicken." He picks up the other end of the rope, feeds it through some metal contraption, and clips it onto his harness. "This is a belay device. It keeps you connected to me." I'm still not sure about the climbing, but the last part makes me smile. "All I want you to do right now is learn to trust the device. To trust me and know that you aren't going to fall." He leads me to a part of the rock that has lots of grooves and deep cracks. He calls it a great "beginner's rock" and shows me where to place my feet and hands for the first few moves he expects me to make.

"I'm not sure about this," I admit.

"Why not?" He looks genuinely let down by my apprehensiveness. "You're safe. What's going to happen?"

"Well, for starters, you could disappear into thin air while I am halfway up that rock."

"Never happen."

"Okay, but unlike most people, you could actually vanish."

"It won't happen." That damned grin of his shouldn't put me at ease, but it does.

"You're just mean." I laugh and move toward the rock, dipping my fingers into the chalk bag.

"So, the first thing you want to do is check to be sure I have you securely on the rope. You say, 'I'm ready to climb.'"

"'I'm ready to climb?'"

"And I say, 'On belay.' Then you say, 'Climbing.'"

"Climbing," I say, annoyed.

"Climb on." He's far too cheery.

I lift my right leg up into the grove the way he showed me, reaching up and pulling myself into the spot. I can feel my butt jutting out at an awkward angle, so I find a new hold and pull myself into it.

"I knew it. You're a natural!"

I look for another crack and grip it. It feels like a puzzle, finding just the right hold for my hands and an equally strong foothold at just the right distance.

"Okay, stop for a second."

But I'm just getting the hang of this. "Why?"

"Let go completely, like you're falling."

But I'm not. "Just . . . let go?"

"Yeah. Push yourself away from the rock and let go."

I take a deep breath. Push myself away from the rock. Let go.

I suck in my breath sharply as I swing backward. Hang. Dangle.

"I just want you to feel that. I have you. Right now you're only about ten feet off the ground. But when you're higher, that's exactly how it would feel if you missed your hold, or needed a break, okay?"

"Okay." I do feel safe, even though this sensation is so strange.

"So just swing yourself back to the rock when you're ready and say, 'Climbing.'"

I do as I'm told.

"Climb on," I hear from below.

I continue to look for the right places for my hands and feet, maneuvering into them and surprising myself when I don't fall. I don't look down. I don't even want to. I'm focused on solving this puzzle of a rock, figuring out how to crack the code that will get me to the top, and without my expecting it to be there, there's sunlight. And sky.

I pull myself up and throw my arms in the air, Rocky Balboa style, as I dance back and forth at the summit.

As it turns out, getting down is scarier.

Bennett yells instructions from below, telling me how to maneuver myself back onto the face of the rock, and where to plant my feet.

"I don't hold the rope?" I shout, without looking down.

"No, just plant your feet on the rock and lean way back. I know it feels weird, but I've got you. Just let your arms relax."

I can't seem to let anything relax.

"What if I fall?"

"You won't. Anna, let go of the rope, or you'll flip around." I force my arms to hang by my sides. "Trust me," he says, and I close my eyes and let him lower me.

It's all I can do to keep my feet in front of me, my legs parallel with the earth below, but I manage to get the rhythm, and soon I'm back on solid ground.

"You were amazing!" Bennett says as he throws his arms around me. "How was it?"

"Good." I'm euphoric, though my arms are still a little shaky. "That was actually really cool."

"I knew you'd love it." He loosens his grip on me and I start to move away from him, but then I feel his hands leave my shoulders and move down, pausing at the harness so he can untie the rope. He's so close I can feel the rise and fall of his breath, and it's all I can do to stand still while his fingers work to untangle the knot behind me. A minute later, the rope falls to the ground and his hands leave the belt and settle on the small of my back. He pulls me to him and kisses me, and I feel my adrenaline pumping even harder. He smiles and says, "My turn."

Somehow I manage to respond. "What?"

"Ready to learn to belay?"

"Really? You trust me to hold you?"

"Absolutely." He steps back and I miss his hands the minute they leave me. He opens the metal carabiner, unclips it from his harness, and clips it onto mine.

He takes his place on the rock. "Climbing," he says.

And I reply: "Climb on."

18

By the time I've reached the top of the ridge for the ninth time, my forearms are shaking. I take a deep breath, pull myself up onto the shelf, and kick my leg up onto the surface. I push myself into a standing position and look around at treetops that go on for miles, interrupted only by the bright blue lake in the middle. I smile down at him, awestruck and victorious.

"Stay there," he shouts from the ground as he throws his backpack over his shoulders and free-climbs the rock face in half the time it took me to climb it using the rope. He dusts himself off at the top.

"Hungry?" He sits down, unzips the pack, and removes a bunch of plastic bags and four bottles of Gatorade. "I wasn't sure what you'd like. Turkey and Swiss or roast beef and Cheddar?"

"Gatorade." I reach forward, parched, and thrilled to see the bright yellow bottles, and I open the lid and gulp. Out of the corner of my eye, I watch Bennett do the same, and when he's finished, he reclines against a tall rock and closes his eyes.

The sun is high now, and even though it's still cool outside, the surface of the rock is warm. It really is the perfect day for this, and I sit down next to him and reach for the turkey and Swiss. I'm suddenly famished, and I guess he must be too, because even though we stop and smile at each other a few times, neither us of us speaks as we polish off our sandwiches.

"So," I finally say. "Rock climbing."

"Good date?"

"Unexpected."

"Disappointed?"

I look around again at the painting-like scene. "No way." A trip to Wisconsin may not do much to expand my midwestern clump of pins, but at least, I think, as I look around the forest with the sunlight gleaming through the branches and the rock formations piercing the sky, unlike Ko Tao, I can always come back here when he's gone. When I'm missing him, like I already know I will be.

I've been thinking about it all night, now that I know everything. He's from a time seventeen years from now. He can travel anywhere in the world just by thinking about it. He lost his sister, and when he finds her, he'll have to leave 1995 and return to 2012. And apparently, all of this means something important to me, but I can't figure out what. But he's here now, and he wants to be with me. And even though the first part makes me feel a little bit queasy, the last part leaves me smiling to myself. I look at him.

Bennett pats the surface of the rock in front of him, and I scoot over and settle in, rest my elbows on his knees, and let my head fall forward. A groan escapes my mouth as he squeezes my shoulders. My muscles are ridiculously sore.

"So, how did you get into rock climbing?" I have a million questions for him, but this one is the easiest to ask.

He presses his thumbs into the base of my neck, and I breathe into the pressure until I feel the muscles release. "There's a little coastal town in Southern Thailand called Krabi." I can't see his face, but I can hear the smile in his voice. "Railay Beach is known for its rock formations, but I didn't know that until I ran into some backpackers who told me about it. They took me on my first climb, and I've been hooked ever since."

His hands move with a slow, coordinated rhythm up my back until they reach my shoulders again. I open my eyes just in time to see him reach forward, grab a piece of my hair, and twist it around his finger. Then he unrolls it, gives it a gentle pull, and lets go, and I feel the curls spring back into place. "How does your hair do this?"

"What? Look like a mess of miniature Slinkys?" He's so close I can feel his breath on the back of my neck, and I grimace at the thought that my hair must smell more like sweat than vanilla-scented shampoo.

"I've been sitting behind you in Spanish for the last month, wishing I could to do this." He pulls down on another bunch of curls and laughs when they bounce right back where they belong. "How about you? How you did start running?"

I turn my head so I can see his face, and he lets the curls fall from his grasp. "Oh, no, you don't."

"What?"

"I thought I'd get to ask all the questions today. You told me to keep them coming." I lean back into his chest and rest my head on his shoulder. My head rises and falls with the gentle rhythm of his breath, and when he softly brushes my hair off my forehead, I let out a sigh and sink further into him. "Besides, you're far more interesting than I am."

"That's not true." I feel him start to play with my hair again.

"Fine," I say, "we'll take turns. One for one. But ten bucks says you're going to run out of questions first." I lift my hand in his direction and he shakes it.

"Deal," he says.

"And I'm going first." I smile up at him. "What do you miss most about home?"

He doesn't skip a beat. "My cell phone."

"Come on, I'm serious." I wait for him to laugh, but he doesn't. "Seriously? You miss a phone?"

"What did you think I would say?"

"I don't know. I guess I was expecting you to say your family."

"Families seem pretty much the same. You haven't seen a twenty-first-century cell phone."

"What's so special about your phone?"

"Lots of things. But I can't tell you about them."

"Well, that's no fun," I say as I let out a little laugh. "What good are you if you can't tell me about the future?"

"I'm good for lots of things," he says as his fingers leave my hair, settle behind my ear for a moment, and then slide their way down to my collarbone. I close my eyes and try to match my breathing to his as he traces. "Besides, I've got to leave you some surprises. You do like surprises, don't you?"

"I'd better. You're certainly full of them." I inhale deeply and try to concentrate on my questions. "So what are you saying, I'll never see the future? Never see where you really live?"

He softly makes the sound of a game-show buzzer. "That's another question. It's my turn."

"Come on. . . ."

"Hey, you're the one who made the deal. One for one," he says. I let out an exasperated sigh. "Where were you when you heard about Kurt Cobain's suicide?"

"Hmmm. Wow." It's been a while, but I remember the day well. "That was almost exactly a year ago. I went to Emma's after school, and we were up in her room listening to the radio, and the DJ announced that he shot himself. So we pulled out every Nirvana CD she had and listened to them back to back."

His fingers linger on my shoulder for a moment, then slide down my arm.

"That week was weird," I continue. "People were crying, like . . . really crying, like they knew him or something. I didn't get that so much. Anyway, the whole thing was really sad." He's running his thumb back and forth against the back of my hand and when I look down I realize that I'm doing the same thing to his. "Where were you?"

I feel him shrug. "That was in 1994," he says, and for a moment, I don't get it. But then I do.

"Wow." I stop rubbing his hand. "Okay, that's kind of creepy."

"Sorry."

"And I can't believe I wasted a question."

He brushes my hair to one side and kisses the back of my neck. "I'll tell you what; I'll give you that one," he says with a whispery breath near the back of my ear. I squirm a little.

"Stop it. You're making me forget my questions."

"Good. I want that ten-spot," he kisses my neck again and I lose my train of thought entirely. "You wanted to know if I'd take you into your own future."

"*Mmmhmmm.*"

"I can't. Well, technically, I guess I could, but I've never done anything like that before and I have no idea what would happen if I did."

"Why? Are you afraid I don't exist in 2012 or something?"

"No, that's definitely not what I'm worried about. But I can only travel back and forth within the time I've already lived, and you just haven't lived beyond this moment yet. I'll take you anywhere in the world you want to go, but never before or after this exact date."

"Really?"

He rests his chin in the crook of my neck and nods. I guess I can live with that. I've never needed to leave this date or time, only this place.

"Besides you can't know what happens in your future. That would take all the fun out of it." He kisses my shoulder. "So, tell me about Emma."

"Emma?"

"Yeah. Tell me about her. How did you two become friends?"

I feel the corners of my mouth turn up at the memory. "I met her my first day at Westlake." I look at Bennett and he raises an eyebrow, asking for more.

I let out a little laugh. "Mom wanted me to make a good impression, so she made me wear the jumper." I grimace and shudder as I picture the uniform. "We used to have this ugly plaid dress that was one of the approved options but no one *ever* wore. And she made me put on *tights* and wear this lace ribbon as a headband. It was, like a hundred and six degrees outside, and all day long, all I wanted to do was change into shorts and a T-shirt. I was hot and itchy and my hair was out to here." I hold my hands up to the side of my head, and he laughs. "But then this girl bounced right up to me after sixth period—all cheekbones and braces—and asked if I wanted to hang out with her after school. And even though I really wanted to go home and change, I said yes. And that was just kind of it. Emma has been my best friend ever since."

When I look back at Bennett I can't help picturing the place I'll be tomorrow, sitting in the coffeehouse and telling Emma every single thing about this day. I'm definitely winning for best date.

"Tell me about your family," I say, officially changing the subject back to him.

He lets out a heavy sigh. "There's not much to tell. My mom's a little . . . difficult to talk to. If I ask her about something that happened in the news, the conversation eventually leads to doctors. If I ask her about the weather, the conversation eventually leads to doctors. I don't ever ask her about scientific advancements, because that immediately leads to doctors. She thinks I'm broken. She just wants a normal kid."

I pull his arms tight around my waist and start tracing his palm with my fingertip. His hands are dry after climbing, and the lines are filled with dirty chalk dust.

"Now Dad thinks I'm some kind of magical creature. After he discovered what I could do, he wouldn't leave me alone. He spent the first year researching all the catastrophes that took place between 1995 and the present day, and created this massive document that listed each event—and every smaller event leading up to it—so I could go back and prevent it."

"Did you?"

"No. I mean, I don't think I should change things that happen just because I *can*. You've heard of the butterfly effect, right? One small change can have a massive impact on something else. I don't even think I could manage that massive a do-over." He's quiet for a while, and I lean into his chest and listen to the silence. "Eventually, he found a way to use my gift for another kind of good. *His* good."

190

I keep tracing the lines in his palm, because that seems to keep him talking.

"We didn't have much money when Brooke and I were little. I mean, we had a decent apartment and everything, but my mom was a bit spoiled, I guess, growing up here in Maggie's monstrosity of a house. And Dad hated his job—he worked in a bank downtown; I don't even know what he did—but he was always in a bad mood, and the two of them always fought.

"Then Dad had his big idea. He went back to his research, this time focusing on companies and the positive trajectory of their stock."

"What?" I stop tracing and turn to look at him. "You didn't."

"I did. I'd travel back to each date he listed, a week or so before a major company event, and when I arrived I'd send my dad a letter with a stock tip. He'd buy. The stock would sky-rocket. I'd go back and send him another message to tell him when to sell. And Dad had a new job."

"Isn't that illegal?"

"Not technically. Insider trading laws say you can't buy or sell based on nonpublic information. The information we used was always public."

I give him an incredulous look.

"Okay, it's definitely sketchy. But hey, it's kept them off my back . . . until recently, at least. Brooke and I got to travel and see all the live music we wanted. Mom got the fancy life she expected, and Dad got to feel like he gave it to her. Everyone's happy, no one's getting hurt."

"I take it your dad made some good money."

"Well, the economy has had its ups and lots of downs, but if you know exactly where to invest—"

"You could make a lot?" I guess.

"Sure. Millions, even."

"Millions?"

"Well, we didn't mean to."

"Oh, sure," I say with a laugh. "As long as you didn't mean to." He's an accidental time traveler *and* an accidental millionaire. "So, how do you have access to this money?"

"That's another question."

"I know."

He shakes his head but smiles as he gives in to me. "Cash. For this particular trip, lots of it, minted pre-1995, and hidden in my room at Maggie's."

"And Brooke?

"Backpack. Loaded with cash." He pulls his hand out of mine and grabs my chin so I have to face him. Then he kisses my nose. "That's it, I'm cutting you off now. My turn."

As much as I've loved reclining against him, I'm tired of twisting my neck to see his face. I sit cross-legged and spin around in place, scoot in closer, and rest my knees on his legs.

"Hi."

"Hi." He smiles, but as I watch him, his expression goes from playful to serious. "You know, I meant what I said the other day. The fact that I'm here . . ." His voice trails off, and he gets quiet for a minute. "It impacts you more than it does me."

I don't like this turn toward the heavy, so I copy his

game-show-buzzer sound. "Please phrase your statement in the form of a question."

"Do you understand what all of this means for you?"

"No." And I know I'm supposed to care, but I don't, not right now. I don't want to think about what he can do and where he can go and when he might leave, because at this moment we're both in the exact same place at the exact same time. Right now I just want to kiss him.

He brings his hands to my waist. "It's like my dad's list of world events. I could go back and change a bunch of little things that would likely change the outcome, and my life wouldn't be *any* different as a result. But other people's lives would be. And maybe they'd be better. But maybe they'd be worse. My being here with you *right now* is a change. Not for me—for you. You exist in 2012, just like I do, in a future that doesn't include me. Just knowing me here in 1995, where I don't belong—"

"Will be fun," I interrupt.

"Will change your whole life."

"Maybe for the better."

"Maybe. Maybe not."

"Well, I already know you, Bennett. What choice do I have?"

"Remember what I said at your house that first day—that I would tell you everything, but I'd let you choose."

I wrap my arms around his neck and kiss him. "Yes. Let's hear my choices."

He inhales sharply. "First choice: I can go back to being the strange new kid at school, keeping my distance from everyone until Brooke returns and I can go home again. You and I can say hi in the halls, and maybe we'll exchange little glances now and then, like people who share a secret do. But that's it. Your life from this point on won't be any different."

"No way." I kiss him again. "What's the other choice?"

He smiles. "Second choice: I spend the time I have here with you, and we'll hang out like normal people and travel the world like abnormal ones. When Brooke returns, I'll go back home, but then I'll come back here. And I guess I'll keep coming back until you decide you're sick of me." He pulls back to get a better look at my expression.

It seemed pretty easy up until this point, but now that he's forcing me to really think about it, I can see how enormous this decision is. Two futures: the safe but mundane life I know so well, or one filled with adventure but constant uncertainty. He'll take me around the world, but he'll leave. There will be times when we're together, and times when we're separated—not just by miles, but also by almost two decades. Every rational part of my being tells me to take the safe route, as unappealing as it sounds. But then I look into his eyes and I'm somehow confident in my decision. Still, there's one more thing I need to understand.

"I don't get it. Why would you uproot your life just to be with me?"

"Because you—" He stops. Takes a breath. Starts over. "I liked your sense of adventure. I thought it would be fun to take you somewhere you'd never go otherwise. But now it's more than that. Now I just want to know you." His words have my heart racing again, and I close my eyes and take a deep breath. When I open them, he's still looking at me.

"Didn't you once say something about this being a really bad idea?"

He laughs under his breath. "Yeah. I think I did."

"You were right, you know."

"Told you."

"Still, I'm choosing option two."

"Are you sure?"

"Yes."

His face breaks into a huge grin and he pulls me tighter and kisses me, warm and sweet and long and slow and never-ending, and I know this is what I want.

And I know I need to invite him over for dinner, because there's no question. This is serious.

⁓

We continue trading questions the entire way home, and as we pull in to the driveway, I feel like I've achieved the impossible: I actually know Bennett Cooper. As he puts the Jeep in park, I look up at my house and feel my chest constrict. I've been with him for nearly eleven hours, and I'm still not ready for him to leave.

He turns the car off and leans over to kiss me, but I reach up and put my finger to his lips. "Wait. I have another question." He stops midway and waits for me to continue. "Why were you watching me at the Northwestern track the day you started at Westlake?"

"That again?" He settles back into his seat.

"Well, yeah. You haven't answered me yet."

"I have. I didn't know what you were talking about the day Emma assaulted me in the lunchroom, and I still have no idea what you're talking about."

"It really wasn't you?"

"Look, you know everything there is to know about me. And I'm telling you, I wasn't there that day. I still haven't been to Northwestern. Certainly not at six thirty a.m. in sub-thirty-degree weather. That's your twisted thing, not mine." He laughs lightly, and I want to believe him. Everything about his words and the look on his face says that I should. After all, he's right—there's no reason for him to lie to me now that I know everything.

"Since I've answered that one before—multiple times, in fact—you get one more question."

I'm ready to go back to our comfortable question-and-answer session, so I smile and think of another: "Where is your favorite place in the world?"

He smiles from ear to ear and his eyes shine as he starts to speak. "Easy. Vernazza. It's a small fishing village on the northwestern coast of Italy, in the Cinque Terre, and you have to arrive by train—well, at least most people do. It's the most amazing little village. Narrow, cobblestoned streets. Colorful boats lining the harbor. Row after row of tiny, brightly painted houses built straight into the hillside. It's spectacular."

His eyes fall on my lips and he leans forward and this time I close my eyes and wait for him. "You'll love it there," he says, and as we kiss, the little village comes to life with the two of us in it.

⁓

"I'm home!" I yell in the general direction of the living room, and I start heading up the stairs in an exhausted little daze. My forearms are sore, and my hips hurt, and I have blisters from my new little elf shoes. I can't wait to get into the shower and then into bed and drift off to sleep with nothing but thoughts of Bennett to keep me company.

"Annie, can you come here?" Dad calls, and I turn around and drag myself toward the sound of his voice. Just as I turn the corner and enter the kitchen, I see Mom and Dad push their chairs away from the table and start walking toward me.

Here it comes. "What's up?" I ask, steeling myself for a lecture about spending the day with a boy they don't even know. But as they get closer, I can see that Mom's been crying.

"What?" I repeat, looking back and forth between the two of them. "What's going on?"

"It's Justin . . ." Mom pulls me into a hug, but I resist, stepping back from her.

"What do you mean? What about Justin?"

Mom starts crying again, so Dad jumps in. "Sweetie, he's been in a car accident. I guess it happened earlier today, but we just found out about it an hour ago."

"A car accident? Are you sure?"

Mom tries to pull herself together, rushing to wipe the tears from her cheeks. "We don't have much information yet, honey. I guess he was on his way into the city and someone ran a red light. The Reillys are at the hospital now, and I'm sure he'd want to see you—we've just been waiting for you to get home so we could all go over there together."

"Why was Justin going to the city? He doesn't even have a car."

Then it hits me.

"Oh, my God. He was with Emma."

19

Dad's driving, Mom's in the passenger seat, and I'm in back. No one's said a single word for the last fifteen miles.

We're taking the same route that Emma always takes into the city, so I'm searching out the window for leftover flares. Or tiny balls of tempered glass. Or pieces of red plastic taillight. Something to indicate where they were when their date took a turn for the worse. I can't find a thing.

When we reach the hospital, Dad drops us off at the main entrance and goes to look for parking. It doesn't take Mom and me long to locate Justin's parents. When we enter the waiting room, they stand up, eyes all red and puffy, and thank us for coming. Mrs. Reilly explains what happened, and even though I'm standing right next to her, her words fade in and out of my head and I process only the pertinent details. The accident happened just after two. They didn't get here until four thirty. The girl's parents arrived just after it happened, which is a good thing, since she's in much worse shape. They're up on the seventh floor in the ICU. She's out of surgery now, but her condition is still considered critical. Justin will be fine, but they're keeping him overnight for observation.

I must have found a chair, because I'm now sitting in one. I watch Mom—who looks like she's moving in slow motion—pull Mrs. Reilly toward her and whisper something into her ear.

Mrs. Reilly's voice rises an octave when she asks, "Who? Who's Emma?!" Strangers turn to look in her direction, relieved, I imagine, for any activity that distracts them from whatever reason they're sitting in the ER on a Saturday night.

"The girl who was with Justin today. That's Emma, Anna's best friend from school." Justin. Emma. And Justin. Emma and Justin. I can't breathe. This can't be happening.

Mom talks with Mrs. Reilly in low, hushed tones designed for me not to hear. It doesn't matter. Everyone sounds far away, anyway.

After a few minutes, Mom gets up and comes over to sit next to me. "Sweetie." She rubs my back in small circles. It feels so familiar, even though it's been years since she traced the invisible pattern that used to make me drop right off to sleep. "Justin is going to be okay, but the other car collided with the driver's side, so Emma got the brunt of the impact. The Reillys had been trying to find out who Justin was out with, but no one would tell them anything, and I guess Emma's parents have been with her in the ICU all afternoon.

"If this was Northwestern Memorial, I'd be staff, but

here—" I can hear the frustration in her voice. She hates that she has no clout. "Stay here. I'll go upstairs and see what I can find out."

I haven't said a word since we left the house, but now I find my voice. "No." I stand up. "I'm coming with you."

⌒⌒

Emma looks small and frail against the while sheets. Her eyes are closed, and the skin underneath them—all the way down to her trademark cheekbones—bulges, black and shiny. Red marks speckle the left side of her face, indicating—as her parents explained when they prepared me to see her—where the doctors had to dig the glass out of her skin. There's a clear plastic tube running up her nose, and even given all the rest of the damage, I think that would piss her off the most.

As bad as she looks on the outside, that was all fairly easy to fix. The real mutilation is invisible. Her spleen ruptured on impact and had to be removed, but it took the surgical team two hours to find the source of the internal bleeding. There's a small skull fracture that they say should heal by itself, but they will need to run an MRI before they can determine whether there was any permanent brain damage. When her internal injuries are healed, she'll have to have her left shoulder reconstructed. She has three broken ribs, but at least they didn't puncture her lungs. The doctors delivered that last part as "the good news."

The other car hit them going fifty miles per hour, just as she and Justin reached the middle of the intersection. "A

T-bone collision," Mrs. Atkins called it. Emma probably never even saw it coming, she had said. No, I'm quite sure she didn't.

I sit next to Emma on the bed and cradle her soft and perfectly manicured hand in mine, still caked with chalk dust, with dirt still wedged under my fingernails. The accident happened around two o'clock. While I was reclining against Bennett, laughing and cuddling and kissing him, my best friend was being ripped apart by metal and glass, transported by a speeding ambulance, and then torn apart all over again so that she could be reassembled. It took me six hours to find out. Another hour to get to the hospital. And yet another to get here to her hand. Eight hours.

The whirs and thumps and beeps of all the machines are inescapable in the tiny room. I want to unplug them, one at a time, and give her the peaceful silence she deserves, but then I remember she might not be here without them, so instead of being annoyed, I try to find their musical qualities. *Thump-beep. Thump-beep-whir. Thump-beep.*

We sit like this, Emma silent because she can't speak, and me silent because I can't think of anything to say. I think I'm supposed to talk to her. To let her know I'm here. But every time I open my mouth to say something, I can't quite get the words out.

I hear the door slide open and my jaw drops. Justin is standing there in a hospital gown, bruised and bandaged, unable to move his head because of the blue plastic brace wrapped tightly around his neck. His hair is matted and speckled with something that looks like blood. His wrist is in a cast.

"Justin." I rest Emma's hand on the sheets and run to him. I stop short, afraid to hurt him, so I'm grateful when he reaches out to hug me first. The scratches on his face and body may be superficial, but they make him look like a porcelain doll that's been dropped on the floor and put back together. I'm pretty sure the glue's not yet dry.

"Are you okay?" I grip a spot on his arm that doesn't look damaged, but he sucks in a breath and I recoil as if he were hot to the touch. "I'm so sorry."

"It's okay," Justin says. He gives me a wobbly half hug. "How is she?"

I just shake my head.

I watch his face fall as the information sinks in, then follow his gaze across the room to Emma. I'm pretty sure we're both thinking the same thing. He's okay. She's not. Justin walks over to where I was sitting on the bed and takes my spot. He picks up her hand and strokes the back of it with his thumb.

"You know, you're supposed to be home writing about me in your diary right now," he says. I can see him smiling at her, and I watch her face to see if she'll return it, but she doesn't. She's too far away. But that doesn't keep him from talking. "I had a bunch of great jokes lined up. I read the newspaper this morning so we could talk about current events. I'm telling you, you would've been hooked. Now look at me." He glances at his chest. "I ripped my best sweater."

He keeps smiling at her. Talking to her like I should have but couldn't.

"She was looking for a CD." He's still looking at her, but I know the comment is meant for me, so I sit down on the opposite side of the bed and take her other hand in mine. I watch Justin's face contort. "We were talking about this British indie band that we like and she asked me to find her CD case on the floor." I picture the hot pink suede case I gave her for her birthday last year and my stomach lurches. I was always putting all her CDs in that case. I should have left them loose, piled up in the glove compartment and on the floor where she had them. I shouldn't have given her that case in the first place. "She started to flip through it and . . ." He trails off.

I just squeeze her hand. There's nothing more to say, because our shared silence confirms what I already know. She wasn't paying attention—the accident was her fault. And she crashed holding on to my gift, which shouldn't make me feel so responsible, but it does.

There's a knock on the door, and it slides open before we can react. The nurse pokes her head in. "I'm sorry, kids. That's all the time I can give you." Her voice is just loud enough to be heard over the machines. "I wasn't even supposed to let you in," she says, like we're about to argue with her. "Family only." We know. She's told us this three times since Mom pulled whatever strings she pulled to score us these ten far-too-short minutes.

I squeeze Emma's hand again, reach forward, and run my finger across her unstitched cheekbone. "I'll be back tomorrow," I say into her ear. I walk to the door and wait for Justin.

He brushes her hair back and kisses her forehead. "I'll see you tomorrow too." He stands up, looking around the bleak and sterile room. "And I'll bring you some music. Maybe that will help."

At first, I think he means that the music will help drown out the incessant beeps. But as I watch him watch her, I think he may mean that the music will help bring her back from wherever she is right now.

⁓

Emma doesn't look any better on Sunday, but the room is cheerier. Enormous bouquets of bright flowers hide all the sterile surfaces, cards have been taped to an empty wall, and a collection of Mylar balloons with *Get Well* written on them in fancy script decorate the corner over by the small window. "Ten minutes," the ICU nurse tells us flatly, "just to keep her company until her parents come back from lunch. You're not supposed to be in here." She looks behind her to be sure no one's watching and then draws the curtain and closes the door.

Justin hasn't been home yet, but his mom has brought in this enormous boom box and a series of CDs as he instructed. Now he comes around to the side of Emma's bed, plugs it into the wall by the monitors, and pops open a CD case. It's one of his homemade mixes, though I can't help noticing that there are no watercolor swirls on this one. He presses play, and the sounds of the machines are instantly masked, their *whir-thump-beep* pattern fading into the background as accompaniment to the music. I take a seat on the bed next to Emma and watch her, wishing I could talk to her, the way Justin did yesterday, but every time I open my mouth I feel awkward.

He's watching me. "Do you want me to leave for a bit?" That would be even worse. I'll have no reason *not* to talk to her, but I still won't be able to.

"No," I say.

He walks around to the other side of the bed and lifts her other hand in his, and we just sit like that. Our ten minutes pass, then twenty, but the nurse never returns to kick us out, so the two of us just stay put. I'm silent, watching her chest move up and down. Justin is silent, too, mesmerized by the glowing red blips on the monitor. The music does help make this horrible room feel less sterile, but that's about all it's doing. Emma is still far away.

The Atkinses return, and I look over at Justin. He was discharged a half hour ago, and his parents are still downstairs, filling out paperwork. He looks exhausted, like he can barely keep his eyes open.

"You wanna get some air?" I ask, and after some thought, he finally nods. I leave all my things inside so I have an excuse to get back into Emma's room.

Once we're in the hallway, Justin leans against the wall. "This sucks." He starts to rub his forehead, forgetting about his stitches. "Ow. Damn it."

I lead him to the elevator. "You should go home, Justin. Go rest. Come back tomorrow when you're feeling better." I wish I could say Emma wouldn't be here tomorrow, but we both know she will.

The elevator takes us to the bottom floor and we follow the

signs to the courtyard. We walk around for a few minutes, but it's windy and freezing and it doesn't take us long to get the requisite air and decide to go back inside and find Justin's parents. We locate the registration office easily, and Justin's parents are still sitting there, waiting for the clerk to finalize his discharge papers. Mrs. Reilly assures us that they'll be a while, so the two of us go in search of the cafeteria.

When we're sitting, drinking the worst coffee I've ever tasted, and taking turns picking at a stale doughnut, I say, "So . . . you and Emma."

Justin looks at me with a guilty smile.

"What?"

"Nothing." He picks off a piece of the doughnut and stares out the window. "I'm so sorry. I should have told you about us. I don't like keeping secrets from you, Anna. But I guess the whole thing just seemed a little . . . weird. I've known you my whole life, and—" His voice trails off and he brings the Styrofoam cup to his lips again, takes a sip, and looks right at me. "I should have told you."

"Yeah. You should have." I smile so he knows I'm not angry. "Really. It's okay. Emma told me. And besides, you're my friend. Emma's my friend. This is good."

"So, you're cool with us going out?"

I decide not to tell him that I still can't put their two names together in my head without a question mark showing up. "Definitely. I'm definitely cool with it."

We both look down at the table. He starts tracing the

design of the Formica with his fingertip, and I push my doughnut crumbs into a little pile.

"Tell me about your date. It was obviously going well, until—" I immediately wish I could take back that last part, but Justin doesn't seem affected.

He smiles down at the table. "It was a really good day. We went out to dinner once before, you know, and had coffee one other time, and that was nice, but it was fun to just be together at her house. See her room and her stuff. And just hang."

He stares out the window behind me. "We had the most amazing talk about . . ." He trails off, but his mouth turns up in a small smile.

"About?"

He shakes his head and looks at me again. "Never mind. . . . Anyway. She's very cool."

I rest my chin in my hand and smile at him. "You really like her, don't you?" I ask, and he nods. He leans back and crosses his arms.

"Yeah. I admit, I didn't expect to, and I wasn't even totally sure until yesterday. But yeah, I really do. She sort of surprised me, I guess." I don't know if Emma feels the same way about him, but for his part, he sure looks hooked. Apparently, some guys really *do* make CDs for girls who are only friends.

"She surprised me too," I say, and I find myself repeating the words I said to Bennett on the rock yesterday, describing Emma's cheekbones and braces and how kind she was to the frizzy-haired new kid. And I smile as I picture her now. Or rather, the way she was until yesterday. Same cheekbones, but no more braces. No more awkward stilts for legs. Just gorgeous, funny, charming Emma, who wins over everyone she meets—even a jock-nerd like me and a skeptic like Justin. I suddenly realize we're looking at each other with matching sad expressions, like we're both wondering what we're doing here, talking about her like this.

Justin breaks the awkward silence. "So-o-o-o . . ." he says, drawing out the word. "Better topic: How was *your* date?"

The question makes me flash back to yesterday, and I feel a grin start to form as I think about Bennett and me, curled up on a rock exchanging questions and stories and kisses and chalk dust. But then I'm overcome with guilt. I can't smile while Emma lies unconscious six floors above me. "It was good."

I keep my emotions in check as I tell Justin about rock climbing and how it felt to reach the top and look out at the view. I tell him how Bennett and I talked and talked, about music and running, about traveling and our families. And suddenly it hits me. I'm supposed to be in the coffeehouse right now trading date stories with Emma, not in a sterile hospital cafeteria talking with Justin. I get quiet and start staring past him, fixing my eyes on the vending machine at the far side of the room. "Sounds fun," I hear him say, but his voice sounds quiet and far away. We both look off in opposite directions, and neither one of us speaks again for a long time.

"What time is your mom coming to get you?" he finally asks.

"Six." I look down at my watch. It's only three.

"I should go find my parents, but I can stay here and catch a ride home with you if you want. I don't want to leave you alone." He looks sincere but exhausted. It's clearly taking all his energy just to stay awake.

"I'm okay. It'll be good for me to have some time alone with her."

He stares at me. "Okay. As long as you're sure." He reaches across the table and grabs my hands to give them a comforting squeeze.

I give him a weak smile. "I'm positive." I sound so certain, lying to him like this. But I'm doing it for him. If he didn't look so tired and pained, I'd say what I really want to say. That right now, as we sit here like this, Justin seems exactly like the person he used to be—my comfortable friend who gives me music and makes me laugh and is the one person I can talk to about anything—and all I want is to have him hug me tight and tell me everything's going to be okay, because if he did, I might just believe him.

20

After Justin leaves, Danielle stops by, and the two of us get caught trying to sneak back into Emma's room. The nurse is just about to kick us out when Emma's mom shows up and convinces her to let us stay. But Danielle can't take it for long; ten minutes later, she still can't bring herself to walk all the way back into the room and Mrs. Atkins finally wraps her arm around her shoulder and suggests she come back tomorrow instead. Danielle says she will be back in the morning, since she has no intention of going to school anyway.

Emma's mom and I spend the next three hours making small talk and staring out the window, and when the clock finally strikes six, I can't help feeling relieved. I give Emma an exhausted kiss on the forehead and hug her mom good-bye.

I'm heading to the waiting room to meet Mom when I hear the faraway *ding* of the elevator. I round the corner and literally collide with someone, and we both step back, muttering apologies until we each realize who the other is.

"There you are," he says at the exact same time I say, "What are you doing here?"

"Looking for you." Bennett's face is all scrunched up with concern. "Why didn't you tell me about Emma?"

I don't have an answer. It probably should have occurred to me to call him and tell him, but it just didn't. I can only shrug as he pulls me to him and asks me if I'm okay. I nod against his chest.

I think at this point I'm supposed to cry. If there were ever a good time, this would be it—with me all nestled into him like this, his head resting on mine and his hand on my back—but I can't. Instead I tell him about the tubes and the machines and the stitches, the doctors and the rehabilitation she'll have to endure when she comes to. That she looks awful, like someone I don't know. And that I feel horrible for saying so.

The elevator dings again, and this time Mom steps out. She looks surprised to see me curled in the arms of a boy she's seen exactly one time and whom I've never mentioned on a Tuesday family-dinner night. "Well, hi."

"Hi, Mom," I say nervously. "You remember Bennett . . . from that night . . . at the bookstore."

She nods and extends her hand. "Yes. Hi, Bennett." She keeps shaking his hand and staring at him. I'm waiting for her to give him her signature smile—her nurse smile—the one that makes people warm up to her so quickly, but she doesn't.

Even though there's nothing cold about the look on her face, there's no warmth there, either, and when she finally drops his hand, Bennett looks a little relieved. She turns away from him and looks at me. "How's Emma?"

I shrug. "The same. Her mom's with her now."

"I'm going to go check on her and see if I can do anything to help. Do you want to come?"

I can't even imagine walking into that room again. "I've been here all day, Mom. Do you mind if maybe . . . Bennett takes me home?"

She whirls around to face him again, her expression full of worry as she looks him up and down. "How's your driving?"

"Good. I'm very careful." She still seems concerned, so he adds, "I'll be *especially* careful."

"It's really windy."

"I'll drive slowly, Mrs. Greene."

"Okay, then." She pulls me to her and gives me a big hug and a kiss on the forehead. "I'll see you at home, Anna." But instead of heading toward Emma's room, she lingers for another moment. "You know, Bennett, Anna's father told me that she was supposed to have you over for dinner so we could get to know you a bit. Has she invited you yet?"

He looks at me, then back at her. "Not yet, Mrs. Greene. But I'm sure—"

"How's Tuesday?"

"Tuesday?" Bennett looks at me. I cover my face with my hand. "Tuesday's great," I hear him say.

"Excellent. We'll see you then." Mom kisses me on the forehead again before turning and disappearing down the hall.

In the elevator, Bennett looks at me. "Dinner." He nods. "Tuesday."

"Sorry about that."

"No. It's good. I like family dinners." The elevator stops and we hold hands and walk toward the lot. "Actually, I can't remember the last time I had a family dinner. We're not too big on them."

"We just have Tuesday. We close the store early so Dad and I can get home, and Mom never takes a shift. She insists on one night a week, and that's Tuesday."

Bennett opens the door on my side of the car, and I slide in. We're alone again, back in the Jeep, just like we were at this exact same time last night. But now we're driving in the opposite direction and there's no laughing or punching each other across the console. No question-and-answer game.

"You okay?" Bennett keeps asking in a whisper and I keep nodding, untruthfully.

The streetlights and traffic signals pass by in a slow-motion blur, like Bennett's driving far below the speed limit. Mom must have terrified him. Or perhaps it's me—maybe every-thing is moving in slow motion.

"They were alone." I finally say to the passenger-side win-dow. "Justin was alone for four hours before his parents got there. Emma was alone for two." I run my finger across the glass and stare out into the dark. "I don't know why that part's bothering me so much, but I just keep picturing them in separate parts of the hospital, surrounded by total strangers. Maybe that's what happens, you know—maybe your parents have to wait outside—but how could they just leave them all alone like that?"

"They knew everyone was on the way."

"Did they?" I ask, and Bennett reaches over the console and grabs my hand.

We're silent for a few moments, until I finally say what I'm really thinking. "I wasn't there."

He looks over at me.

"It took me *eight hours* to get there."

"It's okay, Anna. You got there as fast as you could."

He squeezes my hand in his, and even though there's really nothing he can say to make me feel better, his grip is somehow reassuring. I look down at our fingers intertwined, resting on the console—his nails still a little dirty from yesterday's climb—and remember how I traced the grooves in his palm while I happily reclined against his chest. His hands feel so normal that sometimes it's easy to forget how extraordinary they are.

"Oh, my God." I recoil from him. "Pull over."

"Why? What's wrong?"

"Pull. Over." I'm shaking and feeling stupid and having a hard time believing I didn't think of this earlier.

Bennett turns in to a residential street and puts the car in park. He stares out the windshield, and that's the moment I realize that I might not have thought of it before, but he certainly did. He knows exactly what I'm about to ask, because even if I've briefly forgotten about the ability Bennett Cooper possesses, he never does.

"Do it over." I twist in the seat to face him. "Bennett. Please. Do it over. Do the day over."

"I can't." He won't look at me.

"You can. You can fix this. Take us back before the accident. We'll stop her from driving. We'll fix it! Bennett?"

He gets out of the car and slams the door, leaving me trembling in the passenger seat. The headlights illuminate the fury on his face as he slams his fists hard on the hood, and I jump. He paces back and forth, then turns his back to me and leans against the front of the car. I watch his shoulders rise and fall. I think I'm supposed to regret asking, but I don't.

After a while he comes back to the car, opens the door, and gets in. He's calmer now, but he's still shaking with rage. He grips the steering wheel so hard his knuckles turn white.

"Please don't ever ask me to do that again."

"Look, I understand all your rules." I stress the word *your* and hope he hears my point. "I get your butterfly-effect thing and your superstition about affecting the future—"

"It's not *my* butterfly-effect thing. It's *the* butterfly effect, and it's a major concept in chaos theory, which has *nothing* to do with superstition. A small change in one part of a complex system can have large effects somewhere else—I didn't come up with this stuff, Anna."

"Okay, I get it. But you can make little changes, right? Affect small details? How is this any different from what you do for your parents? What you did last Friday before Spanish? What you did that night in the bookstore, when you changed what could have been a *horrible* future for me—it might have been the *end* of me—but it wasn't, because you intervened. And look . . ." I put my arms out to my sides and gesture around the car. "Nothing terrible happened. We're still here. No butterfly mayhem."

"It's not that simple. Eventually *something* has to backfire. I just *can't* do it over."

I stare at him, willing him to look at me, and he finally does. "Can't or won't?"

"Won't."

"Why not?"

"Look, I shouldn't have done either of those do-overs, Anna, but they were different. I went back five minutes, an hour, I didn't go back a whole *day*. I didn't stop the guy from holding you at knifepoint or attempting to rob the store, I just got you out and got the cops there sooner. And that day in school, we still went to class, and it was like that hour just never happened. They were minor little changes. But stopping the car accident entirely? That's erasing a major event."

"Sorry, I don't get the difference."

"Yeah? Well, neither does my dad." He bites his lip hard and turns to look out the window. "Look, it's a slippery slope—I affect one bad thing that happened to one innocent person, and suddenly it's up to me to keep every plane that's ever crashed from taking off and be the one-man-early-warning-system for every natural disaster. Until something even more catastrophic happens *because* of what I did to prevent the last tragedy. This is *my* ability, and *I* don't think that's what I'm supposed to do with it. I'm supposed to observe. *Not* change the future. Period. I'm already breaking all the rules just by being here."

"They're not *the* rules, they're *your* rules. And how do you know your rules are right? Maybe you're *supposed* to test them."

"I'm not." He stares me down. "And if you recall, Anna, the last time I tested the rules for a girl, it didn't turn out so well. For *her.*"

He has a point, but still, I'm not giving up. I can't. Not when my best friend has spent the past day being sliced open and reconstructed, with parts of her missing, other parts now held together by string. She may be a crappy driver, but she deserves a future. "Well, this isn't about me. And it shouldn't be about you."

He looks at me with sad eyes, and I know he wants to help her. To help me. To be the hero, even though he doesn't think he's supposed to be. "It's not about me, Anna. It's about . . . everyone involved. I can't. I'm sorry, but it's just too dangerous."

"Will you at least think about it?" I give him a small smile and hope he'll smile back, but he doesn't. He just puts the car in drive and makes a U-turn.

"No. Don't ask again."

21

"Travel plans, *por favor.*" I twist around to take the stack of plans as they're passed forward to me. One has a laminated cover. Another one is spiral-bound. Mine—which I'd planned to staple—is still handwritten on individual pieces of notebook paper, wedged in a travel book, and stuffed in my backpack. I won't be turning mine in today, but apparently I'm not the only one who's blown the assignment.

Bennett's chair is empty. When he pulled up to my house last night, I got out, slammed the door without saying good-bye, and walked into the house without looking back. Once I was out of sight, I looked through the kitchen window for a minute or so, long enough to watch him lay his head on the steering wheel before smacking it and peeling out of the driveway.

Argotta gives a lecture today but doesn't make us converse, and when the bell rings at the end of class, I linger and wait for the room to clear. Then I stand up, stop at his desk, and wait for him to look up at me. "How am I going to like your plan, Señorita Greene?" he asks as he pats the stack of travel itineraries.

"You'll love my plan, señor. But it's not done."

I expect him to look at me like I've let him down, but instead he gives me an understanding smile, stands up, and walks around to the front of his desk. I tell him about Emma's accident on Saturday (he's heard), and I remind him about the robbery last Monday (which makes him look sad), and I emphasize that I'm not one to make excuses, but it's been one hell of a strange week (he agrees).

"I'd like to announce the winner soon. Do you think you can have it done by Thursday?" he asks. I nod. "If you need more time, just let me know. We can announce the winner next week instead."

"*Gracias,*" I say. I amble out of the room and into The Donut, drop my books off at my locker, and walk into the dining hall. I take one look at our empty table and decide I'm not hungry.

Mom drops me off at the hospital. I lug my backpack into Emma's room, plant myself in the chair, and start working on my travel plan. Thirty minutes later, the nurse comes in to check Emma's chart. She looks at me with a sympathetic smile and leaves the room.

I look over at the bed. Emma's just lying there, looking

far away and isolated, so I grab my copy of *Lonely Planet: Yucatán* and settle in next to her on the bed. I open the book and start reading to myself about "sugary beaches" and "scandalous nightlife" and "pork slow-cooked in banana leaves." And then I get to the shopping. Now, this is something she'd love.

I start talking, just whispering at first. "This place sounds incredible, Em. Listen to this: 'Shoppers will appreciate the handicrafts found on the peninsula. . . . exquisite silver ornaments that reflect the filigree technique introduced by the Spanish, wonderful models of galleons carved from mahogany, and panama hats so tightly woven that they can hold water.' Doesn't that sound amazing?"

I look down at Emma's still features and wait for a reaction. I speak a little louder. "You know, you look really good in hats. If I win Argotta's travel challenge, I'm going to go to Mexico and bring you back a hat." I consult my travel guide again. "Oh, and get this, they make some of the world's best hammocks, too." I look down at her. "Maybe I'll get you a hammock. What do you think? Do you want a hat or a hammock?" I look for a reaction. Any reaction. There's no movement. "I'll just get you both."

I go back to reading, scanning the pages for another section she might like. I'm just about to start telling her about the "famous cuisine" when I notice that there's a drop of something on the page. Then another. Then another. I bring my hands to my face and find that my cheeks are wet, and the tears are falling in a steady stream, faster than I can stop them—on the pages, on the sheets, on Emma's hand. I look at her face, at all the tubes, and my chest feels tight.

"I'm sorry, Emma," I whisper as I lay myself over her right arm, the only part of her that I know isn't stitched or internally wounded, and I finally let myself cry because she's not supposed to be here. She made one small mistake. One tiny little move that changed everything. Would we be sitting here like this right now if just *one* thing about her day had been different? What if Emma and Justin had decided to go somewhere else, like the movies or the mall? What if they had left ten minutes earlier? Or ten minutes later? Or if Emma had committed to a single CD before she left the driveway? What if she had come to a full stop at every stop sign, slowing her progress to that intersection? What if the driver of the other car had forgotten something, run back into the house, and left three minutes later? What if I hadn't insisted that her CDs live in that stupid case? What if, if, if, if, *if*? If any little detail had been different—just one single detail—Emma and I would have spent yesterday in the coffeehouse, sipping lattes and comparing our dates.

He just needs to change *one* little thing. He's the only one who can make things right, and he's too afraid to do it.

I kiss Emma on the cheek. "I have to leave now, Em," I whisper in her ear, "but I'll be back. I'm going to go fix this and make it right, and after I do, you won't remember any of this."

22

Mom shoots me an impressed look as she pulls up in front of Bennett's house. "Wow. Nice digs."

"It's his grandmother's," I say, but I'm pretty sure the one his dad bought with their stock market "luck" is equally impressive. "I'll be home later, okay? Thanks for picking me up. And tell Dad I said thanks for taking my shift today." I shut the car door and walk across the snowy grass, because the walkway hasn't been salted and it's looking a little slippery. I knock.

Bennett opens the door and I blurt out, "I just spent the afternoon with Emma." He looks nervously back into the house and finally closes the door behind him and joins me on the porch.

"How is she?" At least he has the decency to sound concerned.

"The same. Critical condition. No better than yesterday."

"Give it some time, Anna. She'll be better."

"And you know this how? Because you've seen her in the future and know she's happy without her spleen?"

"Technically, you don't need a spleen."

"That wasn't my point."

"I know it wasn't."

"How can you live with yourself, knowing you could fix this and not even bothering to try?"

He grabs my arm hard and leads me away from the door.

"Ow. You're hurting me."

He lets up on the pressure.

"How can I *live* with myself?" he whispers, checking around for eavesdroppers. "Are you kidding? This is killing me, Anna. I want to try—trust me, I do—but what if I can't change it? What if I make it worse? What if the accident happens anyway, no matter what I do? What if I change the wrong thing and it ends up ruining her whole life? Or mine? Or yours?"

"I don't know! Nobody knows! But how can you have this gift and not use it to find out? Maybe you try to do it over and the accident happens anyway and Emma lands in the hospital and nothing changes. But at least you'll know you tried—"

"That's my point! I'm not *supposed* to try. I'm not saying it's fair, or right, but what if this was—"

"Don't you dare say something lame, like 'supposed to happen,' because this was *not* supposed to happen. She is *not* supposed to be there."

"How do you know?"

"What?"

"How do you know that the accident wasn't supposed to happen?" he asks. I feel my face turn red with fury. "Look, I know no one wanted this to happen, but it did. Maybe she's *supposed* to be in the hospital and wake up. Maybe she's *supposed* to heal and go through physical therapy and fight for something important for the first time in her pink-bubblegum life. Maybe she's *supposed* to get better and learn to drive more slowly." I glare at him. I head for the stairs, but he grabs my arm again. "Anna, I'm not saying it's right. Or that I agree with it. I'm just saying that it happened. And whether it was supposed to or not, it's not my place to change it just because I *can.*"

I've heard the words before, but there's something new in his voice. "Wait. Is that what you saw?" I stare at him. "Did you go see her in the future, Bennett? Does she get better? Is that what happens?"

He shakes his head, and I feel his grip on my arm loosen, and I can't tell if I'm right or not, because he's just staring at me, like he doesn't know what to say next. And neither do I, because whether he saw her future or not, I still can't let Emma lie on that sterile bed with those loud machines, just because this might be part of some grand plan to make her a safer driver or a better human being.

I try a different tack. "Look, you don't have to stop the accident itself. You just have to bring us back in time by"—I'm quiet as I do the math in my head—"forty-six hours." I look at my watch. "Forty-seven if we have to stand here in the cold talking about this for another hour."

"That's still playing God."

I cross my arms. It's silent while we wait each other out like we're in a Mexican standoff. Or a third grade staring contest.

"I have homework." I turn for the stairs and this time he lets me go. I'm almost at the bottom when I hear his voice.

"Anna."

I stop in midstep and whirl around. "What?"

"That's not enough."

"What do you mean? What's not enough?"

"Forty-six hours. That's not enough." I feel a lightness in my chest, like I'm taking the first full breath after being held underwater. He's been thinking about it. No, he's not only been thinking about it, he's been doing the math.

He lets out a groan and I know what it means: he's about to do something he doesn't want to do. Minutes pass while I stand there and wait for him to make the next move; then he finally speaks: "Come inside. I want to show you something."

23

Bennett's room looks cleaner than it did the last time I was here. His desk is neat, with nothing but a cup full of pens and a textbook, splayed open. Bennett grabs a tattered red notebook and undoes the rubber band that holds it closed. He flops down on the bed and gestures for me to join him as he opens it to a page near the end. Every available surface is covered with ink. I bend my head closer and take in the dates, times, and mathematical symbols, the complex equations that stretch across both pages.

"I have to be really precise." How long has he been working on this? All night? All day? "I have to find the perfect moment for us to arrive."

He points down at the calculations. "Like I said, forty-six hours isn't enough—that would bring us to two o'clock on Saturday, and we were in Wisconsin, almost three hours away." He points to a timeline that stretches across the page.

"We have to be together, and it can't be while we were in the car, because we can't be moving. So we would have to go back to the morning, right about the time I picked you up."

"Okay. Let's go." I sit up and open my hands on my lap, but he doesn't take them.

"Slow down, Speedy, there's more." He turns the page. "Here's the thing: As soon as we get within range of our other selves, they'll disappear. So we need to go back to the exact moment we were in the car, in your driveway, but before I put the car in reverse." I think back to the morning. How long did we sit there? It must have been just seconds. Just long enough for us to put our seat belts on and for me to ask where we were going. Then we left. He points down at the page. "I think we need to land at about seven minutes after eight."

"Okay." I don't rush him this time.

"But I can't screw this up." He sits up next to me. "I want to test it first. We're going to go back five minutes and land in the hallway just outside my bedroom. By the time I open the door, the two of us will be gone, and we'll replace them." He walks over to his desk and returns with a little sandwich bag of saltines. He leaves them on the bed. "Those are for you, in case you need them when we get back."

"Thanks." I stand up and hold my hands out to him. This time he takes them.

"Just because we're testing this doesn't mean we're going to do it for real," he says. "I'm still not sure I can go through with this."

"Okay."

"You ready?"

I nod.

"Close your eyes," he says.

I do. And when I open them, I'm in the hall, staring at his mother's high school graduation photo. I look to my left and find him there, nervously watching for Maggie. "You okay?" he asks.

"Yeah." My stomach's churning, but before I think too much about it, Bennett grabs my hand with one of his and twists the knob of his bedroom door with the other. He peeks in, then opens the door wide and pulls me inside. It's empty.

I grab my stomach and head straight for the bed, but the saltine-filled Baggie isn't there. "Where are the crackers?"

"Shoot. I forgot." Bennett crosses the room, reaches into his backpack, and returns, holding the bag. "Well, at least we know it worked."

I don't get it. "You do? How?"

"The crackers aren't on the bed because I hadn't put them there yet."

"Okay, wow." I grab the crackers and start nibbling slowly, again hoping I don't throw up in his bedroom.

Bennett recrosses the room and grabs the two red back-packs off the floor—the same ones that just yesterday were decorated with ropes and carabiners, and held shoes and sandwiches and plastic bottles of Gatorade. Today, they look much lighter.

"Stay here, okay? I'll be right back." He leaves the room and returns a few minutes later with heavier-looking packs.

Another full bag of saltines.

Two Starbucks Frappuccinos.

Two bottled waters.

He goes to his desk, takes something from the top drawer, and walks over to the armoire. Removing everything inside, he makes a tall pile of photo albums, scrapbooks, old Westlake yearbooks, and several boxes of loose photographs. When it's empty, he reaches inside and pulls out a wad of bills.

"How much cash is that?" I ask.

He's all business. "A thousand dollars each, in case we get separated. Here." The bundle lands in my backpack with a thud.

While he puts everything back in the armoire, I think about Brooke and her backpack of cash. "Have you and Brooke ever done a do-over?"

He shakes his head. "No. Not that Brooke hasn't tried." He talks while he puts the books and photos back where they belong. "There was the time she failed her History final and almost didn't graduate. The time my dad caught her smoking. A really bad prom date named Steve." He closes the door and walks back to his desk. "Man, now that I think about it, you two have far too much in common. I'm terrified for the day you finally meet."

I feel my face brighten at the thought. "I'll get to meet her?"

He shrugs. "Sure. Once she's home I'll bring her back here to meet you. We always come back to see Maggie anyway."

"Really? You come back here to see Maggie?"

"Yeah. All the time." He nudges me with his shoulder. "I don't mean to be rude, but any chance I can tell you about it later? After I'm done changing the course of history and all?" He gives me a teasing smile.

"Yeah. Of course."

"Thanks." Then he's back to business. "We're going to land at 8:07, just next to the shrubs on the side of your house. Wait for my signal; then run to the car."

"Got it."

He offers me my backpack and I throw it over my shoulders while he does the same with his.

"Oh, and don't let go of my hands—even though it will be hard to move quickly that way. No matter what happens, we need to be sure we stay together." His command reminds me of our rock climbing date, when he introduced the belay device and told me it kept me connected to him.

He grabs my hands. I look right into his eyes. I've never seen him look scared before.

"Bennett?"

"Yeah?"

"Will I . . . remember everything from Saturday?" I don't want to forget the anticipation of our drive, the exhilaration of climbing, or the view from the top. I want to remember the moment when we pulled into the driveway back home and I felt like I finally knew him.

"You'll remember both days—"

I interrupt him. "But how? I don't remember anything at the bookstore before you left and came back."

"That's because you weren't with me. This time you'll remember both versions, just like I do. Now, close your eyes."

But I can't. I'm getting nervous now, and I'm sure he can feel my hands shaking in his. "Are you sure we should do this?" I ask.

"You're kidding, right?" He humphs and looks at me with a puzzled expression. "No, I'm not *sure*. I'm testing fate. I'm messing around with *time*."

I bite my lip, picture Emma, and feel my conviction return. "Thank you," I say. It's not enough, but it's all I've got.

His grip is tighter than usual. "Close your eyes."

I open them to the somewhat familiar sight of our side yard. It's not like I'm over here much, but the chipping yellow paint verifies that we've landed at Bennett's intended location. On the other side of the window above us, Dad has probably just sat down to finish his coffee and read the *Sun-Times*.

"Ready?" Bennett asks.

I nod.

"Go!"

We race from the shrubs into the driveway, pulling each other along like we're in some strange Fourth of July event wedged in between the three-legged race and the egg toss.

The car is empty. We've done it. I start to let out a relieved laugh until I realize the car is moving backward down the driveway, picking up speed. Bennett pulls me toward his side of the car; we work together to lift the door handle, and it rises, but nothing else happens.

He swears under his breath. "It's locked!"

I look up at the kitchen window, my heart racing at the thought of Dad's seeing this, but thankfully, no one's there.

Bennett and I run alongside the car until it reaches the end of the driveway, then watch as it rolls across the street, slows when it reaches a snowbank, and comes to rest against a tree. The wheels spin on the ice.

This time when I look up at the window, I see Dad standing there, watching us. He disappears from sight and reappears when the front door flies open.

"What the hell—?" He runs across the lawn and stops when he reaches us. Bennett and I drop our hands. "What the hell?" he repeats.

"Hi, Dad."

"Annie?" He's looking back and forth from me to Bennett and I have to remind myself that this moment is completely different from the one in his mind. As far as Dad's concerned, the three of us were just standing in our foyer, and he has just shaken Bennett's hand and told me to invite him over for dinner. And now we're standing in the middle of the street.

"Dad, Bennett's coming over for dinner on Tuesday, okay?" I say, and then I just start laughing, loud and hard, and I can't seem to stop. Dad's looking at me like I've lost it completely.

Bennett's trying not to look at me at all. "Any chance you have a slim jim, Mr. Greene?"

This gets me laughing even harder, and I can tell Bennett's trying to keep a straight face.

Dad cups his hands against the glass and looks into the driver's window. "How on earth did you lock your keys in a car that's in *reverse*?"

I have no idea how Bennett's going to answer this, but at least the mystery is keeping Dad from noticing that we're wearing backpacks and completely different clothes. I start laughing again.

"I was starting the car and . . . I thought I felt a flat tire, so I—we went to check it out, and I guess the car was in reverse, and when the doors shut I guess they . . . locked automatically." He leans over to Dad. "I think I'm a little nervous today, sir."

Dad stares at Bennett, and then shoots me a questioning look.

Now I'm laughing so hard I have to walk around to the back of the car so I don't make Bennett lose it too. He's doing so much better than I am. I lean against the back of the SUV, trying to breathe, but when I peek in through the back window, I let out a gasp.

When Bennett opened the hatch in the parking lot at Devil's Lake, I saw two red backpacks overstuffed with climbing gear. Now those same packs are on our backs, and when I peer through the window, I see piles of ropes and colorful metal climbing equipment. Two harnesses. The new shoes Bennett bought me, lying on top of the heap next to the plastic bags of food and four bottles of Gatorade. We went back, but all the gear has stayed right where it was fifty-two hours ago.

Some things may remain the same, but this whole day is clearly about to change.

24

I'm glad we're not in a hurry, because it takes forty-five minutes for the tow truck to get here, two minutes to get the car door open, and twenty minutes for Bennett to sign the paperwork and get the guy to stop making fun of him. But once we're in the car driving toward Emma's, I think we both feel a little giddy.

He just did something he'd never done before, and I got to be there for it. I know Bennett's still waiting for the dark hands of time to snatch us up and throw us back where we belong, but I can't help being caught up in the moment. If my stomach hurt, I didn't even notice.

"Hey, how's your head?" I ask.

Bennett rubs it with his fingertips. "Fine, actually. I didn't even think about that."

"Maybe it *is* the adrenaline, like you thought."

We pull up to Emma's house and find the Saab sitting in

the driveway. No broken glass. No broken taillights. No dents. No blood.

"She's here! She's okay!" I bound out of the car and run to the door. When Emma opens it, I throw my arms around her. She's wearing a bathrobe and slippers, her hair's up high in a ponytail, and she doesn't have a stitch of makeup on—which is perfect, because this way I can see her skin, smooth and unblemished, free of road rash and deep purple bruises. She shrieks when she notices Bennett standing behind me on the porch.

"Bloody hell!" She pulls away from me and tightens her robe. "What are you doing here?"

I don't know how to answer her. I was so caught up in the do-over, I hadn't planned what to do when we got here. "Well . . ." I begin. I point back to Bennett, who is looking down and playing with a button on his coat. "We have a date today. And I know you and Justin have a date today, so we thought we could, you know, combine our dates."

"Combine our dates?"

"Yeah. We thought it would be fun!"

"Fun?"

I look at Bennett. "Would you give us a minute alone?" He nods and returns to his car, which buys me a few seconds to improvise. I turn back to her. "I'm a little nervous, Em. I don't know, I just feel like everything would be better if you were there. You and Justin."

"You don't need me to—"

"I do! Please. Let's just go together. It'll be fun," I repeat.

"Fine. Justin's coming here first; we'll be at the coffeehouse by eleven. Meet us there." She starts to close the door.

I look back at the Saab in the driveway, and know that no matter what happens today, it has to stay parked right where it is.

I stick my foot in the door so it can't shut. "Let's let Bennett drive. His car's nice and roomy." Nice and roomy? When did my mom get here? I take my foot back out of the door and start down the front steps. "We'll pick you up in an hour and a half," I call behind me. "Justin can meet us there."

I practically skip down the driveway, thinking about how healthy she looks. When I catch Bennett watching me through the windshield, I think he looks a bit proud of himself.

⁓

Emma walks into the coffeehouse to meet Justin while Bennett and I wait in the car, and when she points at us through the window, we both give a little wave. Justin looks confused by our presence, but, like Emma, perfectly healthy and unblemished otherwise. No neck brace. No cuts. And as he walks to the car, he looks strong, not at all like someone who was in a T-bone collision.

"Keep cool," Bennett reminds me. And that's enough to keep me from jumping out and running to hug Justin.

"So," Bennett says when everyone's buckled in, "we don't want to change your plans. What were you going to do today?"

Justin replies, "We were going to check out this record store in the city."

Emma adds, "I thought we'd go to the Art Institute."

"Perfect," Bennett says. "Music and art it is." I turn toward the backseat to shoot the two of them an enthusiastic grin, and I catch them exchanging awkward glances.

By the time I've turned to face the front again, Bennett's pulling up near the elevated train station. "Okay if we take the El?'"

"The El?" Emma asks.

"Yeah. It's better for the environment."

"The environment?" Emma asks skeptically as she scrunches up her nose at the train tracks and the grimy-looking staircase that leads to them. "No, really, let's drive. It's so much easier. I know all the great parking places."

"This will be more fun," Bennett says, and he gets out of the car and shuts the door behind him before she has a chance to say anything else. The rest of us get out, and I grab his hand and laugh under my breath. I've never seen Emma get "Emma'd" before.

We start the day at Reckless Records, deemed by Justin the most amazing music store of all time. First, we all take off in separate directions. Then we reconnect as the couples we are. And even, once, as the couples we aren't: Justin and me, looking through the ska titles, and Bennett and Emma chatting about the bands in the Classic Rock section.

"Hey," Justin says in a whisper. He looks around to be sure

we are out of earshot of the others. "I'm so sorry I didn't tell you"—he gestures across the room—"about Emma and me. I don't like keeping secrets from you, but . . . it just seemed a little . . . weird. But I've known you my whole life, and . . . I should have told you." I smile, remembering when he spoke almost the exact same words in the hospital cafeteria.

"That's okay, Justin. Emma told me. It's good. I'm happy for you guys."

He bumps me with his shoulder. "Cool. Thanks. In that case, can you give us a little time alone at some point? Your boy Bennett's making me nervous, and I'm forgetting all my best material. I have some good jokes lined up. Oh, and what do you think of this sweater?"

I stand on my tiptoes and muss his hair. "It's perfect." Justin smiles, and I watch his freckles disappear as the flush takes over.

We spend the rest of the afternoon browsing through shops. We eat lunch in a crowded restaurant. We make sure that by two p.m.—the time of the accident—we're in the safest location Bennett can think of: the third floor of the Art Institute. The hour comes and goes. We take the El back to the Evanston station and pile into Bennett's car again, and because no one's ready to go home yet, we drive to the closest theater and decide to see whatever movie is playing next. It turns out to be *While You Were Sleeping*, which wouldn't have been my first choice, given that it centers on the story of a man who falls onto the El tracks and spends weeks in a coma.

It's ten o'clock when Bennett pulls in to my driveway: Two

hours later than it was the last time we returned from our date. For a moment, I hesitate, picturing Mom and Dad inside, sitting at the kitchen table, waiting for me so they can break the news about Justin.

"Will you come in with me? Just to be sure—you know—it's all different."

He nods, and we walk into the house. It's quiet. I can tell right away that Mom and Dad aren't at the table, and I let out a sigh of relief. Bennett follows me as I lead him through the dark kitchen and toward the sound coming from the living room. When we turn the corner, we find my parents, dressed in sweats and cuddled up on the couch, watching a movie. There's a fire going in the fireplace.

"Hi," they say in unison. Mom shoots Dad a knowing smile that seems meant for my benefit.

"I see you told her about the car," I say to Dad. I smile and look over at Bennett. He hides his eyes behind his hand.

"Are you sure you can make it here for dinner on Tuesday, Bennett?" Mom looks up at him wearing her huge smile—her nurse smile—and Bennett melts like everyone else does when she puts it on. "Because, you know, we'd be happy to drive over and get you if that's easier." She looks at Dad again. "We know how complicated it can all be with the keys, gearshifts, locks . . ." She laughs, and I can't help joining in. Dad buries his face in her shoulder and cracks up.

"Not one of my finer moments." Bennett's still hiding behind his hand. He slides it down to reveal his eyes and laughs along with the rest of us.

"It's okay. We like that around here, Bennett," Dad says. "Now we have something we'll never let you live down."

Bennett looks at the three of us and smiles. "Awesome."

And for the first time since we began the second version of our day date, Bennett looks like he's starting to relax and accept what I knew was true at 8:08 this morning. Our do-over has been a success. Emma and Justin are safe. Nothing bad has happened. And Bennett can do a lot more than he thought he could.

25

"I've had the most incredible week!" Señor Argotta announces after the bell rings and we've all taken our seats. Bennett and I look at each other and grin. I'm not sure what made Argotta's week so "incredible," but I'm pretty sure we can top it.

"I've had the unique opportunity to travel through Mexico on twenty different routes. It was exhilarating! All of them were just fantastic!" He paces around the room, and we stare at him with rapt attention. "But three trips," he continues, "three trips stood out. I'd like to share these with you and see if I can get your help deciding who should go home today with this." He reaches into his jacket pocket and pulls out a folded strip of paper. "A five-hundred-dollar travel voucher." He snaps it taut a few times and sticks it on the whiteboard with a magnet.

I turn around to steal another quick glance at Bennett. At first, I thought working with him on our travel plans would be cheating, but all it took was a smile and a latte to convince me otherwise. On Sunday afternoon, the day after we completed our successful do-over, Bennett showed up for my shift at the bookstore and we sat in our spot on the floor, pulling books from the shelves and reading descriptions aloud. And four hours later, we had mapped two circuitous routes, each different enough to keep Señor Argotta from thinking we'd collaborated, and overlapping only once, in the little beach town of La Paz.

Now, Señor Argotta flips the light off and the projector on, and the screen lights up with a colorful map of Mexico. The route is highlighted in yellow marker, and each destination is marked with circled letters that correspond to points in the written itineraries. This isn't my map. Or Bennett's.

"This first plan comes courtesy of Courtney Breslin." The highlighted route circles the perimeter of the country, avoiding the interior entirely. "You can tell from this plan that this unusually long winter has caught up with Señorita Breslin. She's after some serious beach time."

Everyone in the room laughs.

"At first glance, this looks like she's missing out on a lot of the country. But I chose this one because—even though she selects a few high-tourist destinations—she also found some wonderful secret beach gems." He tapes her map to the whiteboard at the front of the room. "Let's call this one *Hora de Playa.*"

When he clicks the button on his remote again, my map appears. I feel my shoulders tense up. "Señorita Greene has a little of both—some beaches, some ruins—but it's well-paced.

Too often, people plan a trip and try to cover too much ground. They're trying so hard to be sure they don't miss anything that they overschedule themselves. In my opinion, that's how you miss out on all the good parts of a country. I like all three of the trips I chose because they don't try to get everything in. They all save time for surprises. Spontaneous decisions. Señorita Greene's trip is aggressive, but she's left room for mystery! For impulsiveness!" He walks to the front of the room. "I call this one *La Aventura*!"

Atrevida. He left out the daring part, so I add under my breath: *"La Aventura Atrevida."*

"Our final travel plan is from Señor Camarian." Alex and I steal a glance at each other at the same moment, and we both look surprised. "Señor Camarian is interested in archaeology and Mayan culture. He avoids the tourist spots altogether. He flies into Cancún, but gets out as quickly as possible. He is the only person who found one of my favorite spots, the Kohunlich ruins, which show more of the influence of Mexico's neighbors in Belize." He turns to Alex. "Go there at dusk, when the howler monkeys come out. It's eerie. And *fantastico.*" He walks to the front of the room again and tapes Alex's map to the whiteboard. *"El Camino Menos Viajado."* The Road Less Traveled.

He walks over and switches on the light. "I have to tell you, I enjoyed my side of this assignment. You found some places that I've always loved, and others that I'd never even heard of. I was extremely impressed, and now, my friends, I am terribly homesick." He sighs, smiles again, and says, "So, do you want to know who won?"

I already know. Alex has clearly won. I don't have monkeys, howler or otherwise.

Argotta paces back and forth across the front of the room, letting the tension build. "These were all great trips, but there was one that was the best-paced, most well-rounded plan. If I were going to see the country for the first time, it would be the trip I would choose." He walks to the whiteboard and gestures dramatically in front of the three maps. "And the winner is," he says, pulling my map off the wall and holding it up high, *"La Aventura."*

The class claps as the bell rings.

I walk to Argotta's desk to collect my winnings. Bennett walks past me and tells me he'll meet me in the hall.

"Muchas gracias, Señor Argotta," I say as he gives me the voucher. I can't tell which of us looks prouder.

"You deserve it." He looks at me with an earnest expression. Then he holds his finger up and gestures with his head toward the room, as if he has more to say but can't speak openly until the rest of the students are gone. I start to fidget as I picture Bennett standing outside the door, waiting for me.

"Señorita, as you probably know, I run the summer exchange program," he says when we're finally alone. I nod. "Well, this year, we had more families participate than usual, but we didn't get as many applications as we typically do. I know it's rather late notice, but there's still a spot." When I don't reply, he fills the silence: "If you're interested."

I haven't even considered my summer plans. Come to think

of it, since Bennett arrived, I haven't considered much beyond the current day.

Argotta opens his desk drawer, pulls out a shiny yellow folder, and hands it to me. "It's a really fantastic opportunity. You'd get to spend ten weeks in Mexico with a wonderful host family. Here, take this and talk it over with your parents."

I take the folder. A few months ago, I would have considered this the opportunity of a lifetime, but now, with the ability to see any location in the world, a single one doesn't sound quite so appealing. "Thank you. I'm really honored that you'd consider me." I unzip my overstuffed backpack and push the folder down into it. "I'll think about it."

"Good. The family knows they might not be getting a student, but we need to give them some time to prepare either way, so just get the paperwork back to me as soon as you can—end of May at the very latest. I'm not expecting any more applications at this point, so if you think you'd like to take the spot, it's yours."

"Okay. Thanks again." I race toward the door, and when I round the corner, Bennett throws his arm over my shoulder.

"You did it!" He smiles and pulls me to him as we start down the hall. I lose my balance in a good way. "So, where are you going with that ticket?"

"Mexico, of course. It would be a shame to waste a perfect, well-paced trip that allows time for surprises." I mimic Argotta's accent and look up at him with a flirty smirk. "I happen to like surprises."

"Yeah," Bennett says, "I've heard that about you."

may

26

I put my bookmark in between the pages of *Rick Steves' Best of Italy 1995* and turn off the light, thinking about museums and cobblestoned streets and gelato. It's been almost a month since Bennett took me to Thailand, told me the first of his secrets, and handed me a postcard. He promised to take me to Italy next, but ever since the do-over with Emma, he's been reluctant to use his little talent, even for tourism. I haven't asked—I've been happy just having him here, and pretending that everything about him is normal—but I'm studying my phrase book just in case.

I close my eyes and think about him, and just as I'm starting to drift off to sleep, I realize that something doesn't feel right. Like a weight is pulling me toward the edge of the bed.

"Hey," a voice says into my ear. "It's me." My eyelids shoot open and the beginnings of a scream escape my mouth. *"Shhhh,"* the voice says, and a hand covers my mouth to muffle the sound. My heart is racing and my eyes are wide with terror, and I blink until I can finally make out his form in the dark.

"It's me. It's okay." He repeats the words while I try to talk my heart into slowing down. "It's okay, Anna, it's just me."

"Whan aer ew uing er?" I whisper-yell it into his palm, so it comes out garbled.

"What?" He laughs under his breath and removes his hand from my mouth.

"What are you doing here?" I repeat, clearly this time, as I sit up straight and punch him in the arm. "You scared the crap out of me."

He's still trying not to laugh. "I'm sorry. I would have knocked, but—" he says as he taps his watch. "Your mom loves me, but I don't think she'd appreciate a visit at eleven thirty on a school night."

I feel my heart slow down a little, and I pull the covers tighter around my waist. "Is everything okay?"

"Yeah, everything's fine. I'm sorry. I didn't mean to scare you. I was just lying in bed, and suddenly, I couldn't wait until tomorrow to see you. So I got up, put on my sweats, pictured your room, and *poof*, here I am."

"Poof?"

"Poof. You weren't asleep, were you?"

"Nearly." I rest my head on my pillows again and sigh.

I'm not sure how I feel about him—*poof*—appearing in my bedroom uninvited.

He lifts the covers up to my chin. My room is dark, barely lit by the full moon outside, but he must see the look on my face. "Hey . . . are you mad?"

I shake my head. "No, not really."

"But a little?"

I crinkle my nose. "Yeah, maybe."

"I'm sorry. I didn't mean to just show up. I'll go."

Now I feel bad. He looks so sweet, flustered like this, and just as he's about to stand up, I reach over and grab his arm. "Don't go," I say.

"Really, it's okay. I'll just see you tomorrow," he whispers as he plants a soft kiss on my forehead, and that's all it takes for my heart to start racing again, but this time it has nothing to do with fear. Five minutes earlier, I was missing him, and now he's here in my room, sitting on my bed and backlit by moonlight.

"Really. I'm not mad." Without even thinking about it, I grab his arm and pull him down on my bed, and he lands sprawled out next to me, looking a little surprised. I roll over onto his chest and smile down at him. He looks adorable on my pillow. "Don't go."

He looks at me for a moment, and then his hand finds the back of my neck, and he kisses me, harder than usual. And even though there's still a bit of the bulky comforter between us, I can feel the heat radiate from his body, feel the intensity of every one of his kisses, regardless of where it lands. On my lips. On my neck. On my chest. And for a good five minutes, I'm completely lost in him, kissing him, running my fingers under his shirt so I can feel how the muscles in his back tense up every time he pulls me tighter. But then I find myself again, realize where I am, and move away from him, so I can sneak a look at my bedroom door.

"It's okay." He's whispering in my ear, but I can feel his breath on my neck. "Don't worry about it."

I pull away just a little. "My parents . . ."

"Don't worry about it," he repeats. And for a few minutes, I follow Bennett's lead and let myself get lost in his kisses. But I can't seem to ignore the door for long. I steal another glance at it and he catches me.

He stops, breathing hard, and smiles up at me. My hair is everywhere, and he sweeps it to the side so he can see my face. He rests his hand on my cheek. "It's me, remember?" he says. "If they come in, I'll just . . . disappear and come back five minutes earlier." His smile grows more mischievous. "They'll never know. *You'll* never even know. Then you can pull me down on the bed like you just did, and we can do this," he grins, "all over again."

I look away from the door and lean in close to kiss him again. But suddenly, I have this thought. I have no idea where it comes from, why it would be here right now, or why I've never thought to ask it before, but here it is, coming at me full force. I pull away and look down at him. "You've never actually done that to me, have you?" I'm smiling, but my face is all crinkled up. "Done something over. And I never even knew?"

His smile disappears too quickly.

"Bennett?"

He doesn't say anything. His head falls back and sinks deep into my pillow. "Once." The word floats out with his heavy exhalation.

I feel the lump forming, growing in my stomach as I glare at him and wait for more. He doesn't say anything else. He just lies there, waiting for me to make the next move.

"When?" I sit up, tighten the covers against my body, and wait.

He faces me. "Remember that first night—the night you came to Maggie's and I was so rude to you?"

I nod.

"I went to the bookstore to apologize, and we went for coffee."

I nod again.

"And I walked you home."

I just keep nodding, because, yes, I remember all that. I want to know about the part I *don't* remember.

"I kissed you."

"You kissed me?" I would have remembered that.

Now it's his turn to nod. And I can only stare at him. Because that's impossible. All I wanted that night was for him to kiss me, and instead he spoke some nonsense about whatever happened last time not happening again. I didn't know what he meant at the time, but now I do. He'd kissed me. That's what happened.

"It was too much. I was afraid of what it meant for you and—" He grimaces. "I kissed you. And then I went home and realized what I'd done. So I went back and did it over again, the way I'd meant to do it. I walked you home. I said good-bye." While I stood on the sidewalk, shivering and confused, watching him walk away and thinking I'd done something wrong. While I spent the twenty-four days that followed wondering why I felt something for this person who didn't seem to care about me at all.

I can't look at him anymore, so I recline against the head-board, close my eyes, and rub my temples. When I open my eyes again, he's looking at me, sincere and apologetic. I shut my eyes tighter this time.

"When did you do it?" I ask. "I want to know the exact moment you went back." He couldn't risk running into himself and, that night, there were no moments when we were apart. And it all comes back to me. I'd made a dumb joke about him losing people, and he had gone to the bathroom. I remember how I thought he came out a completely different person. Turns out, he had. "The bathroom," I say.

He nods.

I huff in exasperation. "You weren't ever going to tell me, were you?"

"There was no reason to, but I'm telling you now," he says,

and I stare at him, fuming. "Look, I didn't want to hurt your feelings. It was before—"

"So you lied to me? To protect my *feelings*?"

He shushes me. "I didn't lie to you. I just didn't tell you. That's not the same."

"It is to me."

"Keep your voice down, Anna. You don't want your parents to come in."

"My parents? Why do you care about my parents? You'll just disappear and I'll be the one left here to come up with some way to explain why I'm yelling. Alone. In my bedroom." I lower my voice anyway and continue in a whisper. "Or, better yet, why don't you just do it over? That way you won't have to have *this* conversation again."

"I would not do that." The five words come out one at a time, like he means every one.

"Why not? It's perfect. Just go outside, come back ten minutes ago and do it all over again. I'll tackle you and make out with you like I did this time. Not that I'd *know* there was a 'this time.'"

I feel the tears start to well up and I fight, with everything I have, to keep them locked behind a wall where they can't do any permanent damage. If I cry now, he'll think I'm sad. But I'm not—I'm furious. These are hot, thick tears filled with the kind of anger that make some people punch holes in walls.

"Anna," he says in a calm voice, "I did it once. I didn't do it again. Not after I decided to tell you everything. Not after I decided to be with you."

I nod. "Oh. I see. After *you* decided." I think back to those weeks—nearly a month—when I walked into Spanish every day, wondering why he'd stopped looking at me after that night. Wondering why I felt such a strong connection with someone who seemed to hate me. "Well that night you *undid*, even before you *undid* it, that was the night *I* decided I wanted to be with *you*. But I guess that doesn't count for anything, does it?"

The room is silent. I stare at him. He looks down at the bedspread.

"I made a mistake," he finally says. "I did it once. I haven't done it again. I would *never* do it again." I feel my face soften, so I press my lips together to keep from caving in. And to keep these damned tears where they belong.

"I think I need you to leave."

"What?"

"Leave. Now. Please." I intentionally use the same words, the same tone of voice, that he used to kick me out of his house two months ago.

"Come on. . . . Anna."

"You're a hypocrite." I shut my eyes, and for a moment, there is no movement except my trembling. No words except the words that have already been said, still crowding the space in the room. I open my eyes, shoot him a stern look, and say, "Go. *Poof.*"

I feel the mattress rise back up as he lifts his weight off the bed. I open my eyes, expecting him to be gone, but instead I find him standing there. He looks sad as he closes his eyes, but I don't move or say a word. I just watch the map on my wall come more sharply into focus as his transparent shape disappears from in front of it.

27

The May mornings are still cold, but I can run in my lighter clothes now, without the gloves and the wool socks and the beanie. I hardly recognize the man with the gray ponytail, in shorts and a light T-shirt, and when he gives me a friendly wave, I return it with a dim smile. It's sunny and green and beautiful, but it's not enough to make up for my dark, angry mood. So my feet connect with the pavement harder than they should, and before I even reach the track I can feel the pain burn my shins from the steady drumbeat of abuse. Later today I'll pay the price for letting my feet do the screaming I can't seem to do.

When I arrive at Spanish, I find Bennett sitting at his desk, exactly where he's supposed to be, and his eyes bore into mine as I walk down the aisle in his direction. I take my seat wearing a frosty expression.

A few minutes later, I feel a tap on my shoulder. Argotta's

back is turned to the class as he writes a series of conjugations on the board, so I reach back, grab the folded slip of paper, and open it.

We need to talk.

I squeeze the note into a little ball and throw it on the floor in Bennett's direction.

Argotta turns to face the class, and we spend the next ten minutes talking as a group through each of the conjugations. When he turns around to write out another set of verb infinitives on the board, I feel another tap on my shoulder.

Bennett shoves the crumpled paper at me again.

I'm so sorry. It will NEVER happen again.

I stick the note in my pocket as I rise from my seat, walk to the front of the room, and lift the bathroom pass off the hook. I sprint through the safety of The Donut to the bathroom and splash cold water on my face. Now that I've seen him, I don't know how to be this angry with him. I'm too drawn to him, too completely caught up in everything I've come to know about him, to feel this way. I want to understand why he did what he did, and I want to tell him why it hurt me so much, and I want to believe that he's sorry, so that I don't need to be this angry with him anymore.

I stare into the mirror for a long time, watching my own reflection until it blurs and morphs and no longer looks like anyone I know, and I breathe and stare and gather my strength. As I walk back to class, I practice what I want to say.

But when class ends, there's no time to stop and tell him what's on my mind. As soon as we're out in the hallway,

Bennett leads me upstream, defying the laws of The Donut, moving against the current of hungry bodies making their way to the dining hall. He pushes open the double doors that lead to the quad and stops in his tracks. The bright day has pulled nearly everyone outside, and there's not a quiet spot to be seen.

Without talking, we both turn back toward the hall, looking for a quiet corner. "Follow me," he says, as if I have a choice, and he pulls me along, weaving through the remaining groups of people until we're at a bank of lockers clear on the other side of the school. He stops at locker number 422, which I realize, for the first time, belongs to him. He dials the combination and lifts the metal lock with a click. Unlike my locker, decorated with pictures and schedules and stuffed with books and packs of gum, his is empty and completely devoid of personality. Like his room at Maggie's—functional but temporary.

He piles our backpacks inside and slams the door. "Can we get out of here?" He grabs my hands and looks around the empty hallway to verify that we're alone. Before I can comprehend what's happening, I feel the not-yet-familiar sensation of having my intestines twisted and wrung. I keep my eyes closed, breathe in, and know a moment later from the smell around me, from the sound of the birds calling to each other, that we aren't in The Donut.

I open my eyes.

It's early morning, but the weather is already warm in the small harbor, and I spin around and take it in. Everything around me is yellow, blue, or red, a sea of primary colors, surrounded on three sides by hills and by the open sea on the fourth. I see a church topped with a bright green cross. A hillside covered with brightly painted houses, divided into sections by twisted staircases built into the steep mountainside. With the exception of a few fishermen on the dock, we're alone in this small, beautiful town, with its residents still sleeping before making their way down for coffee and breakfast.

I smile at the ground so he can't see me—he doesn't deserve the satisfaction. As incredible as this moment is, he's not playing fair. "Okay," I say, with venom seeping into my voice, "I give up. I have no idea where we are."

"Somewhere quiet."

He leads me past the harbor filled with colorful fishing boats toward the boulders jutting out like a pier into the sea. When we reach the shore, he steps up onto the smooth rocks, and I follow him as he hurdles them. He finally sits down in between two giant stones on a shorter one in the middle that creates a narrow bench just wide enough for the two of us to squeeze onto. He looks at me sideways, his face right next to mine, and gives me a hopeful smile. "Still mad?"

I can't decide if I want to hug him or shove him off the rock.

"Yes, Bennett, I am *still* mad. What, you're just going to bring me to an island every time you screw up? You didn't even ask my permission."

"I was just looking for a quiet place to talk. And it's not an island. It's a fishing village." He looks more miserable than I think he should. "It's Vernazza."

I close my eyes and listen to the sound of the surf hitting the rocks instead of the sound of my heart hitting my rib cage. Vernazza. Italy.

"I'm so sorry." I've lost count by now of how many times he's said it. He holds my chin and forces me to look at him, but I pull away. "I should have told you."

"It's not that you didn't tell me earlier." I look down at the rocks and collect my thoughts again. I can forgive him for not telling me. I can almost understand why he wouldn't have. What I can't get past is that he did it in the first place; he stole my free will.

"What is it, then?"

"You have the power to change people's lives, Bennett. And I don't mean that in a cheesy, romantic way. You can *literally* alter my life. That night, you changed it without giving me a choice, and you just can't do that."

"You didn't give Emma a choice. Or Justin a choice," he says. "We changed their lives, and if I recall, we didn't get their permission first."

"That's totally different."

"No, it's not," he explains. "We have no idea what happened from the time they each woke up that day to the time they got hit by a speeding car. Maybe one of them did or said something especially important, and we just wiped it out. We changed it. But we did that because we thought we were doing the right thing; we wanted to protect them from pain. My reasoning was no different."

"And I had to *beg* you to even consider that do-over. What

happened to you not changing things, huh? What? The rules only apply when they're convenient for you?"

"I was protecting you."

"You can't protect me. Not all the time."

"See, that's the thing. I can. I will. Even if I have to lie to you to do it."

I can't look at him. Instead, I look out at the small waves and watch them wash up against the rocks and roll back out again. "I don't want you to protect me, Bennett, not like *that*. Just because you're *special* doesn't mean you get to choose what I experience. You don't get to decide what I know and don't know. What I get to feel or don't feel. That isn't the way it works."

"Look, Anna, when I changed what happened that night, things were different. I was trying to stay as far away from everyone as possible. I didn't want this."

I glare at him.

"I do now," he says, clarifying things. For a long time after that, we're silent. "I haven't done it since," he finally says. "I'd never do it again."

He's looking directly at me, and I can tell he means every word—and I can tell how much he wants this to be over—but I still don't think he understands how hurt I am that he crossed a line I never thought I needed to define, especially for him.

"Remember when you asked me to make the choice to be with you or not?" I ask. "You told me all your secrets, and you let me decide if I wanted this."

He looks out toward the water and nods.

"That meant so much to me—the fact that you had *me* choose. And that's what makes it so hard to understand how you could have made a choice *for* me."

"I made a mistake."

"And—" I begin, but I feel the words catch deep in my throat. "We lost three weeks. We could have been together three weeks longer."

He lets out a sigh and his face falls as everything clicks; he took something away from me, but he also took something away from *us*. When he apologizes again, I finally hear the remorse I've been waiting for, and when he wraps his arms around me and pulls me tightly to him, I feel the anger begin to melt away. "It won't happen again."

"I know," I say with a sad nod, and I pull away so he can see my eyes as I say the next words. "Look, Bennett, I'm somehow okay with the fact that you can alter the events of my life— bizarre as that is." I give him a little smile, the first genuine one he's seen since I found out what he did. "But this is my life. I'm the only one who decides what comes next." I hold out my hand. "Deal?"

"Deal," he says, and he shakes it.

"So, are you going to show me around this place, or what?"

Vernazza is just like he'd described it. We walk away from the harbor toward what looks to be the main part of town, through narrow streets paved with large cobblestones and lined with small shops that haven't yet opened for the day. Bennett walks up to a door with an Italian flag hanging above a striped awning and pulls it open for me, and I walk in. The bells on the door jingle, and for a moment I think I'm walking into my dad's bookstore. That is, until I smell the bread, sugary and warm, filling every crevice of the bakery.

The woman behind the counter shuffles over, slides a mountain of twisted rolls onto a platter behind the glass, and looks up at us. *"Buon giorno."*

"Buon giorno," Bennett says. *"Cappuccini, per favore."* He holds up two fingers, and she takes her place behind the oversize espresso machine.

A rack of postcards near the window catches my eye and I walk over to it and give it a spin, watching the colorful photos of Vernazza and the surrounding towns pass by me. I feel Bennett watching me. I turn around just in time to see him point at a glass jar on the counter. The woman removes two chocolate-dipped biscotti and places them on bright blue plates. Bennett points to me, standing just under the sign that reads *6/£1,000* in a flowing script I assume to be hers. "Will you add six postcards to that too, *per favore*?"

"Six thousand lire, dear," she says.

"Can I borrow these?" I hear Bennett ask, but I can't see what he's talking about. He balances the biscotti on top of the coffee cups and pushes the door open with his hip, leaving me inside. "Pick six you like. I'll meet you out at a table." The bells jingle as the door closes behind him.

When I arrive at the table, Bennett is leaning back in his chair under one of the bright yellow umbrellas, sipping his coffee. I sit down in the chair next to him, and he motions to the stack of postcards. "What did you get?"

I spread them out across the glass-topped table.

"Pick one."

"Any one?"

"Any one," he says. "Pick one and give it to me."

I select the picture of the harbor and the small fishing boats, the first things I saw when we arrived here, and I hand it to Bennett. He pulls two pens out from under the rim of one of the little blue plates and passes one to me.

"Now, you pick another for yourself. I'll write you a postcard, and you can write one to me." He leans secretively over his card and begins to write. I look down at the little boats on my postcard, and it hits me for the first time in a while: *He doesn't stay.* Someone soon we may not be together the way we are now, and these postcards will be what we'll turn to when we're missing each other most. The pressure to live up to a high romantic standard starts to close in, and I compose my thoughts before taking pen to paper. Then I write:

Dear Bennett,
For as long as I can remember, I've dreamed of seeing
what lies outside the only world I've ever known—
outside my safe, normal life. And now, here I am, in a

*small fishing village as far away from home—as far
away from "normal"—as I can possibly be. And as
amazing as that is, I know one thing for certain—none
if it would matter if you weren't sitting here next to me.
You can take me anywhere. Or nowhere. But wherever
you are in this world, that's where I want to be.*

I stop and hesitate, looking over at Bennett before I write the next two words. Maybe the word *love* is too much, but I feel it pushing against my chest, wanting to make its way onto the paper. So I let myself write the words:

Love,
Anna

Before I can chicken out, I slide the postcard over to him. I watch as Bennett completes his thought, flips the card over, picture-side up, and slides it across the table to me. We each pick our notes up off the table and read them at the same time.

Anna,
*I'm so sorry I didn't tell you, but I promise it will never
happen again. From here on, you'll always have a say
in your own future.*

Love,
Bennett

At least he used the word *love* too. I place the card back on the table so his words are facedown in the glass, and I force a smile. "Thanks."

He looks at me, confused, knowing he's missed the mark but not sure how. I can feel him watching me as I pick up my biscotti and take a bite.

"What?" he asks.

"Nothing."

"No, you're disappointed."

I shrug and swallow my bite. "That's just . . . kind of a lame postcard." I look over at him in a forgiving way. "And besides, you don't need to keep apologizing." I thought by now he would have known me better: Once I make up my mind, I don't look back. "Is that what you really wanted to say?"

"No," he says. "I know exactly what I want to say. But I don't need a postcard to do it."

"Okay, I'm listening."

"Okay, here goes." He takes a deep breath, like he's preparing himself for something epic. "I . . . You're . . . You're amazing, Anna. And I love your passion to travel the world, but I have to admit, I don't completely get it. When I look around at this 'normal' life you're so eager to leave, I don't see *boring* or *predictable*—I see friends who love you and a family that would make any sacrifice for your happiness. I see the kind of security I've never had and always wanted. I may have given you access to the world I know best, but you and your family have given me a world that doesn't exist on a map.

"When I'm here, we both have the lives we want—you have

your daring adventure and I have my perfectly acceptable *nothing*. And more important, we have each other."

"Now, there's your postcard. I expect you to write this all down." I slide him a new one and smile, but I'm only half kidding.

He continues as if I never interrupted. "I don't think I can go back to a life without you."

My face goes blank and I just stare at him. "What are you saying?"

"I'm saying . . . I'm completely in love with you. And I guess I'm wondering . . . what if I didn't leave, after all?"

The word that was just pressing against my chest minutes ago is now coming from his mouth, and even though I wanted so much to see it on paper, I guess I wasn't prepared to hear it spoken out loud. He loves me. He wants to stay with me. I can't completely process either idea, but I feel light-headed from all of the hope that's surging through my veins. And I think I'm still staring at him.

"Is that okay with you?"

"Which one?"

He smiles. "Well . . . both, I guess."

"Yeah." I'm just sitting there, nodding, not sure how to say it back but knowing I want to. And instead of telling him how I feel, I take the easier route. "How long will you stay?"

"Through graduation?"

I think again about the words he said in the bookstore the night he first kissed me—*I never stay*—and now I'm pretty sure he can see the disbelief in my eyes. "I thought you couldn't."

He shrugs. "I didn't think I could, but, well . . . I've been here this long."

"What about Brooke?"

"When she finally gets home and I no longer have an excuse to be here, I'll just tell everyone that Maggie needs me and I want to stay here with her. I'll tell them all about you—"

"Come on, do you seriously think they're going to be okay with this? Won't they be furious?"

He shakes his head no but says, "Absolutely." Then he breaks into a huge grin.

I feel my face light up as his words run in a loop in my head: *I'm completely in love with you. What if I didn't leave, after all?* He wants to stay with me. "That's a lot of Tuesday-night dinners," I say. "Think you can take it?"

"That's a lot of traveling," he says. "Think *you* can take it?" and he leans across the rest of the postcards, pushes my cappuccino out of the way, and takes my face in his hands. Buried deep in his kiss is a new kind of promise for our future, but on the surface, all I can feel tickling and teasing every nerve ending is the intensity of what we have right here in the present.

We spend the rest of the day in the Cinque Terre.

And then we spend the night there.

28

I push a pin into the little town of Vernazza and stand back, enjoying the way the newest marker has bridged the gap between Southeast Asia and the state of Illinois.

Thanks to Bennett's talent, I've made it home without my parents even realizing that I was gone overnight, and while I don't know for certain what happened back here, I have a pretty good idea: I didn't return to school. Or show up at the bookstore for work. Or come home for dinner. At some point, my parents may have become exhausted from worrying. Police may have been called. Neighbors could have walked the streets with flashlights. Posters might even have been printed and stapled to telephone poles. But twenty-two hours later, when Bennett returned me to the spot in front of his locker—the place where we had taken a brief hiatus from our fight to hold hands, close our eyes, and leave the hallway the day before—it turned out that less than a minute had passed, and no one was ever worried, because no one ever missed me.

Despite knowing how awful the undone day might have been for the people I love, I can't bring myself to regret it. In those twenty-two hours, Bennett and I climbed the mountain steps to the trail that leads from Vernazza to Monterosso, the steepest of the trails connecting the five villages. It wound us through olive orchards and vineyards, challenged us with rough climbs and narrow pathways, and in the end, rewarded us with the most incredible views of both villages and of the Mediterranean.

We spent the afternoon in Monterosso, but when we tired of the tourists and longed for the more peaceful Vernazza, we chartered a small boat to take us back to where we had begun. As it sped through the blue water, jumping and bouncing over the waves, I reclined lazily against Bennett's chest and smiled up at the clouds. Just before we reached the dock, he enfolded me in his arms, leaned forward, and whispered in my ear, "Spend the night with me." Thinking back, I never even questioned my reply. And I certainly didn't think about panicked phone calls and posters and police and neighborhood searches, even though I should have. Instead I stayed, selfishly wrapped in Bennett's arms, and watched the Tuscan sun rise up over the bay from a tiny *pensione* tucked into the hillside.

29

A shrill series of wailing beeps fills the room, and before I can mentally process the action, my palm comes down hard on the top of the digital clock on my bedside table to buy myself another ten minutes. It isn't until the guilt climbs in under the soft covers and snuggles up next to me that I finally give in, throw both feet on the floor with an audible thud, and mind-over-matter myself through the darkness, arms extended for safety, to the closet.

Ten minutes later, my music is throbbing in my ears as I take the customary turns, pass the man with the gray pony-tail, and reach the spongy surface of the track. I run, lost in my thoughts and singing along with the chorus when a movement in the bleachers catches my eye. I look over and see Bennett sitting there on the metal bench—just like he was that first day, wearing the same black parka and the same little smile—and this time I don't hesitate. I turn and run across the center of the grassy green field, waving at him as I approach. I take the cement steps two at a time. "See? You are stalking me," I pant when I'm finally within earshot. "I knew it."

He stands up, looks around the track, and steps down to meet me.

"Hi. I'd kiss you, but I'm all sweaty." I stand next to him and lift the hem of my T-shirt up to wipe my forehead. "What are you doing here? And what's with the jacket—it's, like, sixty-five degrees out here already."

"Oh, my God. You know me. Anna, you know me?"

"Yeah. Ummm . . . why wouldn't I?"

He tightens his lips and presses his temples with his fingertips, and I start to realize that something's not right.

"I've been trying to get back." His voice is sharp, his eyes wide and panicked. "I haven't been able to get back. What's the date?"

"Tuesday. May . . ."—I think for a moment—"the sixteenth, I think." I add what would be obvious to most people but may not be to him: "It's 1995. Bennett, you're scaring me. What's wrong?"

"Oh, my God," he says again under his breath, "I'm still here." Then, to me, "I'm still here."

He is, in fact, standing in front of me, so I nod. I take a step back and watch his face as he processes the information. "Anna, I'm so sorry. I've been trying to get back to you, ever since—"

It's sinking in. *"What?* Ever since what?"

"Anna, listen to me. This is important. Brooke's home. Tell him . . . er, *me* . . . that Brooke's home. And tell me to show you—" But before he can say another word he's gone.

"What?" I beg. "Show me what?" But I'm talking to empty space as I stand there wondering where and when he'd come from and what he's supposed to show me. I search the bleachers, looking for him like he might still be there, but I know he's not. When Bennett disappears, he's gone.

I sprint down through the bleachers, through campus, and back into the street. *Brooke's home.* Trees are blurring by and I'm stopping only for traffic lights, and I'm trying to block the vision of his fading against his will. My heart's beating so fast it feels like it's going to explode by the time I reach Maggie's porch and knock hard on the door. I double over trying to catch my breath while I wait for Bennett to answer.

"Anna." Maggie's clearly surprised to see me sweaty and flushed, and the tone of her voice as she says, "Good morning," makes it clear she doesn't think I should be here this early.

"Good morning, Maggie." I pant. "I'm sorry. I know it's early. Is Bennett here?"

She opens the door wide and invites me in. "I don't think he's left for campus yet. Go on up."

"Thanks," I say as I race past her, up the stairs, and down the hall to Bennett's door. I knock and listen for movement, and when I don't hear anything, I start to panic. He said he was trying to get back here. *What if he's already gone?* But he opens the door wearing nothing but a pair of sweats, a headful of wet hair, and a smile. I take in a sharp breath. He's still here.

I throw my arms around his neck, relieved to smell his shampoo and feel the warmth of his still damp skin. "Hey, what's up?" he says brightly, but he seems to realize from the vise grip I still have on him that I'm here for a reason. "You okay?"

I back away. "Something's wrong."

He pulls me inside and closes the door behind him. I haven't been here since we sat on his bed and I begged him to do a day over again. That was only a month ago, but it seems like years have passed since then.

"I saw you at the track, just like that time in March."

"That again? I keep telling you, I was never—"

"Bennett. I just saw . . . another . . . *you*." I'd planned to break the news a little more gently, but at least I have his full attention now. "You were at the track again, but this time I could talk to you, and you knew me. And you were shocked that I knew you too."

"Are you sure?" he asks, and I nod, wide-eyed and absolutely certain. "What did I say? Exactly? What were the *exact* words I used?"

"You asked me the date, and when I told you, you were surprised. And you realized that you"—I reach out and rest my hand on his chest—"*you* were still here." He stares at me, eyebrows knit, forehead tight with confusion. "You told me to tell you that Brooke's home."

"What?"

I nod. "That's what you said."

He looks at his watch like the time of day is going to help him puzzle this out. "She's home?" he says, to no one in particular.

I nod. "There's more." I have his full attention again. "You said you'd been trying to get back here 'ever since.' And you told me to tell you to show me something, but you never told me what. You were in midsentence as you disappeared, like you couldn't stop it from happening." *Like you were out of control*, I want to say, but don't.

He looks around the room, out the window, anywhere but at me. "Bennett, what's going on?" I press my fists into my thighs hoping he'll say something, anything, that will make me feel better.

"I don't know."

30

Dad is driving us home from track-and-field sectionals, where I got the top time in the 3200-meter and guaranteed myself a spot in the state finals, when Bennett pipes up from the backseat, "Will you drop me off at home on the way, Mr. Greene?" His voice is robotic, just as it has been since the full impact of my conversation with the other Bennett hit.

I don't know what's going on. I do know that Brooke is back home and he's still here and there's something he's supposed to show me. I know that all week, he's replied to my questions in monosyllables, with forced smiles, before disappearing into his thoughts again. He's already blown me off twice this week to sit alone and think, and now I'm not even sure if we're still going to the movies with Emma and Justin tonight.

"I'll pick you up at seven," he says without looking at me. I watch him get out of the car and disappear through Maggie's front door.

At least now I know one thing.

—◦

The phone starts ringing the second I walk through the door, and I've barely even gotten the word *Hello* out when Emma's voice booms through the receiver. "We're going shopping. In the city. I'm picking you up in a half hour."

I look down at my shoes and at the number still pinned to my chest. "Not today, Em. I just walked in the door from my meet." And, besides, I want to add, I already have plans for today. I'll be spending the afternoon trying to figure out how to get things with Bennett and me back to the way they were.

And on top of that, just the words *the city* and *I'm picking you up* leave me with horrible visions of Emma lying in a sterile room with cuts all over her face, and tubes and needles sticking out of her body like alien appendages. I can practically hear her pout over the phone line, but the mental image only strengthens my resolve. "I am not shopping, Emma."

"Anna. Greene. The auction party is next weekend. What are you wearing?"

"I'm borrowing something from your closet. Like I do every year."

She clicks her tongue like she can't figure out how she got stuck with me for a best friend. "Well, then help me pick out *my* dress. I need something new and shiny and gorgeous."

"I really don't feel—"

"Come *on*," she whines into the phone. "I need your advice."

She doesn't, but I look at the clock and sigh.

"Thank you!" she blurts out. "I'll give you forty-five minutes to get ready!" She barely gets the last word out before clicking off.

"I take it you're going shopping with Emma," Dad says, and I flip around. I didn't realize he was standing there.

"Apparently so."

"Well," he says as he pulls out his wallet and offers me his credit card, "here. Now you don't need to borrow a dress."

⌒

We drive into the city—Emma chatting away, me silent and white-knuckled because of my grip on the door handle—and spend the sunny Saturday shopping on Michigan Avenue. Emma picks out a graceful dark orange gown for the auction party that looks beautiful against her olive skin. I pick out a black sheath that's much simpler, and much more *me* than anything Emma owns. As I turn around in the three-way mirror, I picture Bennett leading me past students with their dates, staff members and their spouses, moms and dads, as we round the skydeck on the ninety-ninth floor of the Sears Tower, and my chest constricts with the thought I don't want to have: What if he isn't here next Saturday?

I realize he'll need to go home eventually, but that he'll come back and stay through graduation. *Won't he?* I want to believe the words he said in Vernazza two weeks ago—*What if I didn't leave after all*—but they keep fighting with the words I heard at the track five days ago—*I've been trying to get back to you ever since.*

Two more shopping bags and four hours later, Emma decides we need to return home immediately, before she spends another penny. As we're walking to the car, she has an idea.

"Oh, Anna!" I jump as her squeal echoes through the parking structure. "Come home with me, and I'll get you ready for our dates tonight! I'll put together an outfit and do your hair and makeup! Come on! It'll be fun!"

Fun? I've been her project before, and I wouldn't use that word to describe the experience.

When we're settled in the Saab, bags in the trunk, music on the stereo, Emma turns to me and says, "I know the perfect outfit!"

⁓

Emma and I spend the rest of the afternoon getting ready. She dresses and undresses me, pokes and belts me, tugs and brushes me. And finally she throws her arms up in the air, declares her work complete, and turns me around by the shoulders so I can stare into her full-length bedroom mirror.

"Ta-da!" she yells as I stare. Okay, I have to admit that I look pretty good. She's piled my dark curls up with a clip and pulled some of them down at the sides so they are wispy around my face. The makeup feels thick on my skin, but she's done a great job with the colors, and I don't look like a clown.

I glance down at my feet—I'm practically on tiptoe, thanks to the chunky heels—and back up past the black tights to the clingy little skirt. The tight cotton shirt is a lot more low-cut than what I'm used to, and I cross my arms over my chest like I need to cover something.

"Stop that." She forces my arms to my sides and holds them there. "You look stunning."

I sigh, but relax my arms. "Are you sure?"

"Positive." She walks over to the window and looks outside. "Where are those guys? They're twenty minutes late."

As I stand there, staring at my reflection, my heart starts racing. What if he's not coming? What if he's already gone?

"Stunning!" Emma says again. "Oooohh. And guess who is about to tell you the same thing." I rush to join her at the window, pressing my face against the glass, and watch as Bennett and Justin get out of the car and walk up to the front door. I let out a breath I didn't realize I was holding. "Awww . . . just look at them. Our boys are awfully cute." Emma blows an air kiss down in Justin's general direction, grabs my hand, and pulls me toward the stairs. "Come on."

She races down to the front door like she's about to burst with excitement, and as she opens it to greet the guys, her accent is even thicker than usual. I can't help smiling at her. Or maybe I'm smiling because the guys really are cute. Or maybe it's that even though I'm dressed in high heels, a skirt far shorter than anything my mom would ever approve of, and more eyeliner than Marilyn Manson, there's something about this moment that feels more normal than anything I've felt all week.

Bennett must feel it too, because when he sees me, he launches right into compliments and pulls me into a big hug that signals that he's here—*really* here—and for the first time since we found out that Brooke was home, it feels like I'm all that matters to him and there isn't someplace more important he's supposed to be.

When we get to the theater, we walk in side by side, Bennett with his arm draped over my shoulder and Justin and Emma holding hands. While we're waiting in line for popcorn, Justin tells me, in a brotherly sort of way, that I look really nice tonight. Emma tells me to stop trying to steal her boyfriend, and Bennett jokingly threads his arm through hers, tells her he'll be her date, and leads her into the theater cradling the jumbo-size popcorn.

And that's how it goes for the rest of the night. The four of us are just the four of us, and Bennett and I are just the two of us, and everything feels so normal, not in a pretending-everything-is-normal kind of way but in a real, comfortable kind of way that makes me think that he's found a way to fix things. That this is still the life he really wants—safe and boring and utterly normal.

I snuggle into his shoulder, grab a big handful of popcorn, and watch the screen, happy to act like I didn't run into *another* him and learn about an *ever since* neither of us has any control over. Like double dates and popcorn with extra butter and Twizzlers are the most important things in the world to us, our daring adventure is still in full swing, and there are no clocks to be seen for miles.

⁓

Bennett drops Justin and Emma off at their respective houses, and when he points his car toward mine, my heart sinks at the thought of going home. I don't want my normal night to be over. I don't want to think about when Bennett may leave or when he'll be back, and I certainly don't want him to wake up tomorrow morning so absorbed in his thoughts that he forgets that tonight was fun.

"You okay?"

I reach over and touch his arm. "Not really. I want you to talk to me."

He drives for a couple more blocks, then pulls into the small parking lot of an office building and cuts the engine. The headlights go dark, and the two of us sit there in silence, staring out the windshield at nothing in particular.

He finally twists in his seat to look at me. "I meant what I said in Vernazza." His voice is low and steady, his eyes sad and faraway.

I wait for the word *but*. It doesn't come, so I fill in the blanks for him. "But you don't think you can stay?"

He sighs. "I don't know, Anna. This is completely uncharted territory. Nothing like this has ever happened before." He stares past me out the window into the dark.

"What are you supposed to show me, Bennett?"

He shakes his head. "I've been trying to figure it out, but the only thing I can think he—*I*—might have been talking about is something I can't show you."

"Why not?"

"Because . . . it's in my room. My *real* room, in San Francisco. In 2012. I don't think it's a good idea for me to bring it back here, and I *know* it's a bad idea to bring you into the future."

"But at the track, *you* told me about it. That I needed to *see* it, whatever it is. I think you're *supposed* to show it to me, Bennett."

He presses his lips together. "I'd rather just tell you about it."

"You need to *show* me. That's what you said." I reach down to the console and grab his hands. "And I want to see your room."

"No way." He takes his hands out of mine and grips the steering wheel. Then he looks me in the eye. "I told you, Anna, I'll take you anywhere in the world you want to go, but never before or after this exact date and time. You can't see your own future."

"I'm not—I'm seeing *your* present. I'm observing, just like you do."

"I'm not supposed to bring you forward."

"Says who?"

"Me."

"What if you're wrong?"

"What if I'm not?"

"You didn't think you should undo a car accident either, but that turned out pretty well in the end. Look," I say, "you're supposed to show me something, and besides, if you do go— if for some reason you really can't—" The words get stuck on the way out. I can't say them. "I just need to know where you'll be."

He stares at me for a long time. I have no idea what he's thinking.

"Please," I beg. "Just a few minutes. Just show me what I need to see, and bring me right back."

He closes his eyes, and the car is completely silent as I sit and watch him. Minutes pass, and finally he pulls the keys out of the ignition and stuffs them into the pocket of his jeans. I give him my hands.

I close my eyes as I hear him say, "Five minutes."

31

"We're here."

I open my eyes. It's dark in the room, but we're standing at the center of a curved wall of windows that look out upon the city below, and all I can see is lights twinkling across the horizon and stretching to the dark waterline. "Wow. This is your *room*?" I hate to leave the view, but I turn around and take in the rest of my surroundings.

It doesn't look any more lived in than his room at Maggie's; it's far too clean and devoid of personality, but at least I spot a framed piece of art on one of the walls. His bed is neatly made, and on the oversize glass and metal desk in the corner there's a silver and black screen and a digital clock that reads 11:06.

"What's the date?"

"May 27, 2012." I'm seventeen years away, in Bennett's real bedroom. I walk toward his desk and spot a single framed photo of Bennett with his arm draped over Maggie's shoulders. The two of them are smiling. The fact that he looks younger throws me for a moment, but it's the sight of this completely different Maggie that really jars me. She looks so old and frail, gaunt, and nothing like her 1995 self. Bennett takes the picture away from me and puts it facedown on the desk, and I can tell from the look on his face that she must have died shortly after it was taken.

I look around again. I picture my room—its walls plastered with paper race numbers and photos, its shelves lined with CDs and trophies—and realize there's a lot less of *him* in his room. But then I spot an oversize glass bowl on the nightstand next to his bed, and I know exactly what's inside. Something that's uniquely him.

I sit on the edge of his bed and start removing stubs. U2 in Kansas City, 1997. Red Hot Chili Peppers, Lollapalooza, 1996. The Pixies at UC–Davis, 2004. Lenny Kravitz at the Paramount in New York, 1998. The Smashing Pumpkins in Osaka, 1996. Van Halen in L.A., 1994. The Ramones at the Palace in Hollywood, 1996. Eric Clapton, Cleveland, 2000. I see a bunch of tickets stamped with band names I've never heard of and assume they started playing sometime after 1995. There are hundreds of tickets in here.

I look up and see Bennett at his desk, digging deep in the bottom of the largest drawer, and I watch him remove a wooden box and lift the cover. Then he walks over to me, holding a piece of paper.

"What's that?" I ask.

"A letter."

I drop the tickets back into the bowl. "You're supposed to show me a letter?"

"I think so." He looks at me and inhales like he needs a deep breath of courage. "Last year, I was hanging out in the park with my friends when a woman walked up to me." He hesitates but I keep looking at him, and suddenly his face relaxes into the smile I know so well by now. "She was beautiful. She had these big brown eyes and a headful of dark curls. She asked if she could talk to me in private, and she handed me this." He smooths it flat and pushes it toward me.

"What does it say?"

"You need to read it."

"I don't want to read it." I push it back and look away from the words. I begged him to bring me here, to show this to me, but now that I'm here, I know this isn't what I want. I want to go back to Evanston. I want to go back to pretending that everything is normal.

He pushes the letter toward me again. "I need you to know everything now."

I feel my face contort. "I thought I already knew everything. Bennett?"

"You don't. Please."

I look down and read:

October 4, 2011

Dear Bennett,

I'm worried about saying too much and breaking any of the rules you once taught me. I hope I've chosen my words carefully enough. Someday, my visit and this letter will make a lot more sense. For now, you'll just have to trust me.

The last seventeen years have given me a good, solid life. It hasn't been the daring adventure I'd hoped it would be, but I've been happy. Still, I've never forgotten that you once gave me a choice between two paths and somehow, against my will—and I think against yours, too—I got stuck on the wrong one. The one I didn't choose. Giving you this letter is the riskiest, scariest thing I've done in my whole life, but I just have to know where the path I chose would have led.

Someday soon, we will meet. And then you will leave for good. But I think I can fix it—I just need to make a different decision this time. Tell me to live my life for myself, and not for you. Tell me not to wait for you to come back. I think that will change everything.

Love,

Anna

I've always signed my name with a capital *A* that looks more like a large lowercase *a*—rounded instead of sharp. Apparently, in 2011 I still do.

"This is from . . . me?"

He nods.

"What, like, a future . . . me?" Those words would sound bizarre to anyone but Bennett Cooper, but he just nods like it makes perfect sense.

"How long have you had this?" I ask, as I remind myself to inhale.

He rests his finger on the date. "Since last October." At least his voice sounds guilty when he says it.

"So you read this . . . before you came to Evanston."

"Many times." I watch him nod and think back to that first day in the dining hall, when I told him my name and the color left his face. He knew me. He'd already met me. Five months earlier. Sixteen years later.

He grips my arms with both hands, which is a good thing, since I'm not feeling very steady. "You have to understand, Anna. I went to Evanston to find Brooke. Honestly. I figured I'd find her and be home in a matter of days. I only went to Westlake because I promised I would. Can you imagine how it felt for me that day in the lunchroom? To hear your name and see your hair and your eyes and *know* it was you? That you were *Anna.*" He gestures to the letter. "*This* Anna. That you were the person I'd met five months earlier on a random day in a random park in 2011. And there you were, in a high school lunchroom in 1995 in a town I had no desire to even *be* in." His voice cracks.

"I tried to avoid you at first. I probably should have just avoided you. These words were just rattling around in my head those first weeks, and I didn't know what I was supposed to do. I didn't want to create this life for you," he says, looking down at the letter. "I didn't want to hurt you."

And suddenly it hits me. I don't know why I didn't see it before, but now it's there and completely unavoidable. He doesn't come back. He doesn't stay. We lose each other for seventeen years, or longer; maybe forever.

Someday soon, we will meet. And then you will leave for good. And he's known all along.

"How could you not tell me?"

He just looks down at the floor, not speaking. "I don't know; I thought I could stop it," he finally says. "When I kept getting knocked back here, and returning to Evanston, it felt like I was building up strength or something. Like I was teaching myself how to stay somewhere for a long time. The letter never says how long I was there—it just says I *left for good.* I figured if I came back and stayed—if I didn't leave . . ." His voice trails off, and when he looks up at me his eyes are full of remorse. "It wasn't until you saw the *other* me at the track last week that I realized I hadn't fixed it after all."

"You should have told me." I can barely get the words out. He's still too confident in his own ability, still lying to me, thinking *that* will protect me from pain. But he can't protect me. Not when I'm the one who needs to make a different decision—when I'm the one who supposedly knows how to fix it. "What am I supposed to do differently?" I ask, and I wait through the silence for him to speak up and educate me on some finer point of time travel that I've missed somewhere along the way—something that makes all of this logical.

To tell me exactly what happens next and reassure me that everything is fine.

But he brings his gaze to the rug again and says, "I don't know."

The last time he let me down, it took everything I had not to cry in front of him, but this time I don't care. This time, I can't hold back, and I let those hot, angry tears fall without even trying to stop them.

I'm crying because he really has lost control and because he's actually admitting it, because he's been carrying this around with him all along, still keeping secrets he swore he wasn't keeping, all to protect me. But mostly I'm crying for her, the thirty-one-year-old me who spent nearly two decades missing a shaggy-haired boy with smoky blue eyes that changed her life one snowy day in Evanston, Illinois.

How could he not tell me about a letter that spelled out our fate and made it clear he could never stay? And that he'd known all along? "How could you—" I start to say, but I can't finish my sentence. But I need to, because if I don't, I know exactly what he'll think. That he's ruined my life. That he shouldn't have stayed with me in the first place. That he should have left when he first had the chance. That he should do these last months all over again. And I love him far too much let him think that.

I wipe my tears, and before either of us can say another word, my stomach muscles clench and I double over, reaching down to grab fistfuls of his comforter. It feels like my insides are on fire. I can't move or speak, but I can hear Bennett yelling my name and feel him reaching for me. Everything seems far away and muffled. His face is fuzzy and distorted, like I'm looking at him through a camera lens that's out of focus. My stomach twists and curls with a force that makes me double over again, and I hear myself scream. Loud.

Then it's dark and silent.

32

My face is wet and all I smell is leather, and when I uncurl my legs and reach down to steady myself in the seat, all I *feel* is leather. I open my eyes.

I'm in the dark parking lot, back in Evanston and completely alone in Bennett's Jeep. "No . . ." I have no other words, so I repeat the only one I can get out. "No. No. No!" I look around and feel panic traveling through my limbs. I keep looking over at the driver's seat, waiting for Bennett to magically appear like he does, but he never materializes, and neither do the keys, which should be in the ignition but aren't. I remember Bennett leaning back in this seat and stuffing them in his jeans pocket.

The digital clock on the dashboard reads 11:11. I have only been gone for five minutes after all.

Now I know what Bennett was feeling in the park that

night—getting knocked back against your will is nothing like traveling. I can't sit up straight or draw a real breath; all I can do is pant and try not to panic. My stomach churns again, even more violently this time, and I look around the too-clean car, but there's nothing I can throw up into—not even a stray coffee cup—so I cover my mouth and lean back against the seat.

Breathe.

Hold it in.

Breathe.

Hold it in.

I need to throw up.

And then I need a giant glass of water.

Breathe.

Hold it in.

I reach for the latch, but just as I start to pull it toward me, a small flashing light on the dash catches my eye. The alarm is set. As soon as I open the door, it will go off. But I feel a metallic taste in my mouth again as my stomach cramps into a tight ball, and when I throw the door open the alarm yells in the background, covering the sound of my retching over the cement.

When there's nothing left in me, I wipe my mouth on my sleeve and look around while the car alarm continues to remind me that I don't have the keys. I see a light go on in the house across the street and I know I need to get out of here before someone calls the police. I scour the car one last time for keys I keep hoping will magically appear.

I'm nowhere near home, but I take off running, heading for my neighborhood at the fastest pace I can manage in this outfit. If I could run at my usual speed, I would be home in fifteen minutes, but it's closer to a thirty-minute walk, thanks to Emma's tight skirt and chunky heels. And because I keep stopping to look for Bennett's Jeep. There's a small part of me that thinks he'll pull up to the curb at any moment now and we'll stand here in the dark, fighting about the letter, and eventually I'll forgive him, because I'm just so happy to have him back. But his Jeep never comes.

When I finally arrive at home, I trudge up the front steps and let myself in; I try to sneak past the kitchen, but Dad spots me.

"How was the movie?" He peeks out the window, looking for the car. "Where's Bennett? Why didn't he drive you home?"

I don't even want to imagine what I look like right now. Tearstained and puffy, sweaty and frazzled. "We were at the coffeehouse," I lie.

Dad looks down at my little skirt, up at my frizzy hair, and then he stares at me with a hardened expression I've never seen on his face before. He squints at me. "You look like hell. What happened, Anna? And you'd better tell me the truth."

The truth. I was at the movies. Then I was in San Francisco. I was looking at concert stubs, and I was happy for a second, and suddenly I was furious. I threw up in a parking lot, and now I'm home. I say the first thing that pops into my head. "We got into a fight. Bennett doesn't know where I am. I'm sorry." I feel the tears stream down my cheeks again. "It's been a really horrible evening."

"Are you okay?" Dad's face softens as he asks, and I try to say no, but nothing comes out. He pulls me toward him and holds me tight while I sob into his shoulder. Eventually, the tears stop. "Next time, go to the bookstore and call me to come get you, okay?"

"Okay. I'm sorry."

"It's all right. I bet everything will be better in the morning." He pats my back, and I head for the stairs. "Annie." I turn to look at him. "If it's *not* better, come find me. Okay?"

I smile and trudge up the stairs. My room looks just like it did when I left it. I was supposed to wash that pile of clothes this morning before I went shopping. My textbooks and notebooks are stacked haphazardly on the desk. My bed is still unmade.

This can't be it. I walk to the window and look down, hoping to see Bennett's car pull into the driveway. I picture him sitting on his bed, holding the letter, and the helpless look on his face when—for the first time ever—he watched someone disappear before *his* eyes.

The letter.

That day he heard my name in the dining hall, he knew exactly who I was. He knew we were together here. And he knew he would leave and not come back. He knew it all, and I knew nothing.

And suddenly, everything about his first month in Evanston makes sense. He didn't want to meet anyone because he didn't plan to stay, and he didn't want to know me because he knew eventually we'd be separated. But he gave me the choice. I remember exactly what he said that day, when we sat on the top of the rock we had just climbed. *You exist in 2012, just like I do, in a future that doesn't include me. Just knowing me . . . will change your whole life.* He wasn't only letting me choose to be with him while he was here. He was letting me choose whether or not I wanted to be *that* Anna. The girl he left heartbroken at sixteen, who grew up and hadn't forgotten about him.

I remember her words. My words.

I got stuck on the wrong path.

You will leave for good.

I just need to make a different decision this time.

I think that will change everything.

I have no idea what those words mean. What different decision am I supposed to make? What's supposed to change?

The street is quiet and dark, lit by a full moon and a cloudless sky full of stars. I cross the room until I'm standing in front of my map, and I touch my finger to Evanston, Illinois. I run it all the way to the left until it stops on the spot marked SAN FRANCISCO, CALIFORNIA. If only we were separated by this distance. But we're not. We're separated by this distance plus seventeen years.

I take a pin out of the box and stare at it. I spin it between my fingertips. Maybe if I just picture it, maybe if I want it enough, I can take myself somewhere else too. I bring the red plastic tip to my lips and close my eyes, as if *I* have Bennett's gift, and I will myself to disappear from this room and reappear in his. I picture the view from the window and the bowl full of ticket stubs and the desk and the bed, and I close my eyes tighter and let the vision of the space fill my head as I repeat the words "May 21, 2012. May 21, 2012" aloud, over and over again, in a whisper.

When I open my eyes, I'm still here, holding my pitiful little pin and standing in front of my map of the world with tears streaming down my face.

I look at the dot marked SAN FRANCISCO. The pin makes a sad little pop as it pierces the surface.

33

I sit up with a start and grab the clock from the nightstand. Ten twenty-two. In the *morning*? When did I get into bed? How could I have fallen asleep? That's when it all comes back to me: I got knocked back here, and Bennett's still gone.

I throw on my running clothes, race downstairs, and bolt out the door, ignoring my mom's chiding about sleeping the day away, her prodding me to eat before I exert myself, and her questions about why I'm training on a Sunday in the first place. But I'm not training; I'm running.

When I arrive at Maggie's, four blocks away, I notice immediately that Bennett's car isn't in the driveway, and my stomach plummets so far and with such speed that I fear I may throw up again. I leap onto the porch and ring the doorbell.

There's no answer.

I ring again and wait.

I peek through the sheer curtains into the living room for any sign of activity, but there's nothing. No movement. No sound. Where is he? Where is Maggie? I lean my back against the window and bury my face in my hands. What now?

My brain doesn't come up with any good ideas, so I obey my feet instead, which are telling me in no uncertain terms to go back to the parking lot—to the last place I saw Bennett where he was supposed to be. Or rather, *not* supposed to be— but where I wanted him to be. Here. In *my* town.

My gait feels stiff and awkward as my feet pound against the cement, but as the scenery goes by in a blur, it's what my eyes are taking in that's just plain wrong. The sun is casting a warm glow on each house I pass, igniting the patches of rose-bushes and new tulips that act as colorful dividers between red-brick walkways and lawns so green they nearly spar-kle. The air I'm breathing in is warm and humid, and unlike the cold that prickles against the lining of my lungs, this air makes me feel like I've inhaled a pillow and it's suffocating me from the inside out.

Two miles later, I finally arrive at the office building and come to a full stop. Bennett's car is gone, and for a moment, I let myself think maybe the whole thing was just a dream after all. But then I spot the amorphous blob of puke chang-ing color in the hot sun, and that's all I need to confirm that it was real.

I feel the tears start to well up behind my eyes, but I push them down and turn back the way I came instead. There's nowhere else to go, so I run back to Maggie, the only person who might know where he is. Or at least where his car went.

I wind back through the same neighborhood, past the same houses and cars I ran by just minutes before. When I see the street sign for Greenwood up ahead, I pick up my pace, and that's when I see Bennett's Jeep moving toward me. The right-turn signal starts flashing and the car turns and moves out of sight.

I fly around the corner just in time to see his car pull in to the driveway. He's home. I feel my feet kick into a totally new gear I didn't even realize I had. I knew he'd come home. "Bennett!" I yell as I slap my palm against the rear window and race around to the driver's-side door. "Bennett!"

The door opens slowly and I watch Maggie plant her feet on the cement and carefully lower herself onto the driveway. "I'm afraid not." Her voice is soft, controlled. I crowd Maggie's path as I lean past her, looking in at the passenger side, into the backseat. It's empty.

"Where is he? Maggie, where's Bennett?"

She closes the door behind her, shutting off my view of the interior. Her silver hair glimmers in the sunlight, her face is drawn, and her eyes—Bennett's eyes—seem to be searching mine for something she can't quite put her finger on. "You really don't know where he is, do you?" she asks.

I shake my head, even though it's not entirely true. I know where he is. I could tell her, but she'd never believe me.

She wraps her arm around my shoulder and guides me toward the porch. "Come on in. Let's talk." On shaky legs I let her lead me up the steps, and I follow her into the house and wait while she hangs her coat and purse in the closet. I trail after her into the kitchen and stand in uncomfortable silence while she takes two teacups out of the hutch and fills a kettle with water.

She looks back and sees me leaning against the doorframe for support, shuffling and fidgeting. "Relax. Have a seat." Maggie points to the kitchen table and turns her attention back to the tea bags. I sit.

I should be thinking about what I'm going to say to her, but instead I just look around the room, taking in the stark white cupboards, the dark granite countertop, the flower vase on the windowsill. My eyes settle on a stained-glass mountain scene that's affixed to the kitchen window by a suction cup and a hook, and I follow the stream of sunlight as it shoots through the colored glass and transforms itself into orange and blue and green streams of light that streak across the room and land on the white table.

"My daughter made that for me in high school," Maggie says from across the room. She doesn't give me time to respond, which is good, because I don't know what to say anyway. "I love the way the light comes through that window. Those colors just take my breath away." She puts the teacup in front of me, and a streak of blue light bounces off its side.

"I've just come from the police station," Maggie says as she takes her seat. "They found Bennett's car in an empty parking lot last night. The alarm was sounding, and a neighbor finally called to complain." She lifts her cup to her mouth and takes a sip.

"Oh, really?"

She gives me a suspicious look over the rim of her cup. "Weren't you together last night?"

I reach for the tea but my hands are shaking too much, so I just slide the saucer closer to me instead. "Yes, we were together. We went to the movies with some friends. We parked in that lot." I look at her. "And then we got in a fight, I walked home, and I haven't seen him since." To my own ears, I sound rehearsed, but I hope I'm telling her enough pieces of the truth to keep her suspicion at bay.

"And you don't know where he went?"

I shake my head no, even though this time it's a lie. I know where he went, but again, she'd never believe me.

"Well, I have no reason to spend my time trying to track down a Northwestern student who's simply renting a room from me. Why would I go through all that trouble for a complete stranger, right?" There's a certain bitterness and sense of bravado in her words that confirms what I already know: she's come to care about Bennett, too. I hide my hands under the table and clasp them together for stability. "What I find most interesting is that the police called *me* when they found the car." The lines on her face seem to deepen with concern, confusion. "Do you know why I was the one they called?"

I feel my face squish up, and I say, "No."

"First, because I'm on the registration as the *owner* of his car. And second, because, according to Westlake Academy—where he apparently attends high school—I'm his grand-mother." She slowly takes another sip of tea and rests her forearms on the table. "I assume you know I was under the impression that he was a student at Northwestern. I also assume you know, that I am, in fact, *not* his grandmother."

I try again to bring the cup of tea to my lips, but when I start to take a sip I discover it's still hot enough to scald. I return the cup to its saucer.

Maggie takes a big sip of tea, unaffected by the temperature. "Do you have any idea why he lied about me, Anna?" *Stay calm. Breathe. Take a sip of scalding tea.* "Why he listed me as his grandmother?"

All I want to say is "Because you are," and then run through all the events of the last three months, starting with the day Bennett moved to town. But I can't tell her that the boy in the photos on her mantel and the boy who's been living in one of her spare bedrooms are the same person. "I don't know, Maggie." Her expression doesn't change. "I don't know." I repeat the words like that will make them true.

She stares at me with those eyes, and my stomach turns over with guilt. She lets out a heavy sigh. "I really don't know what to do. The police want me to file a missing-persons report if he's not back in twenty-four hours. If you know anything, Anna, you have to tell me. Please."

I look down into my cup and take a sip.

"This boy has been living in my house and lying to me the entire time. I've liked him, but now it turns out I don't even know who he is. I never did." Maggie stares right into my eyes. "But something tells me you do."

She's right, of course. I know. And right now, all I want to do is tell her everything, because I want her to know who he is, and because I'm tired of being the only one who does and, mostly, because I want her to like him again. And she would, if only she knew who he really was and what he'd done for her.

I want to tell her that four years from now, she'll be diagnosed with Alzheimer's. The decline will be gradual, until 2000, when it will speed up and never slow down. By 2001, she'll start forgetting more than small details and minor events. She will forget to pay her bills, forget where her investments are located, forget to tell anyone enough to help before it's too late. By 2002, she'll no longer be able to function on her own. She will have forgotten her family. Her daughter, Bennett's mom, will be too far away in too many ways to make it better. And then, when Bennett is eight years old, Maggie will die.

But five years later, Bennett will start coming back to 1995. To 1996. To 2000. To 2003. Eventually, he'll start bringing Brooke. The two of them will knock on Maggie's door, pretending to be students soliciting donations, just to hear her voice. When she's really sick, they'll show up in the middle of the night to clean her kitchen and pay her bills. When she leaves for appointments during the day, Bennett will mow her lawn, and Brooke will plant new flowers. They'll stuff cash into strange hiding places around the house, because, even though they know it will cause her confusion, they also know she'll find it. And eventually, Bennett will let Maggie in on his secret. Even if she doesn't remember it for more than a moment, she'll die knowing that the last years of her life would have been very different if it hadn't been for Bennett's gift.

"Anna?" Maggie interrupts my thoughts.

"Don't let the police search for him." My voice catches in my throat, and even though I want to say so much more, I don't.

Her eyes grow wide with curiosity. "Why not? Please, you have to tell me. What do you know, Anna?"

I look at her, holding her gaze in mine. Finally, I return my eyes to the tableful of colored light. What do I *know*? Well, at least that's a question I can answer. Sort of. I run my fingertip along a streak of green. "I truly don't know how to find him. But I know he's safe," I begin, my voice a whisper. "I know he's back in San Francisco. I know he didn't want to leave, but he didn't have a choice. I know he didn't want to lie to you. Or to hurt you."

"Who is he?"

Over the past two months, I've never been tempted to divulge Bennett's secret—not to my family, not to my best friend—but sitting here, looking at Maggie's sad eyes, I just want her to know him like I do. But I remind myself that it's not my place. "I can't tell you, Maggie. It took him a long time to confide in me, and when he finally did, I promised I wouldn't share his secret with anyone. It's killing me not to tell you right now, but it's his story, not mine. But he's not a bad person." I want to add *He loves you,* but I stop short of saying too much. "He's just going to have to tell you himself when he gets back."

She leans forward. "And when will that be?"

Another question I can't answer, but this time it's not because I can't break my promise. It's because I truly don't know. "I have no idea. But he told me once that he'd come back, and I have to believe him."

I sit there watching her, waiting to hear what she'll say next. I feel sick.

"What should I tell the police?"

I think quickly. "There was an emergency back at home. An illness . . . in his family. A friend gave him a ride to the airport, and he left his car in the parking lot. But now he's called, and he's fine. He's . . ." I take a deep breath so I can finish my sentence without breaking down. "He's back in San Francisco with his family."

"I'm supposed to lie? To the police?"

"It's not a lie. That's where he is. You can tell them that, or you can say nothing, file a missing-persons report, and let them search for him. But they won't find him."

"If he comes back—"

"When," I clarify. "*When* he comes back, I'll be the first to know. I'll make sure you're the second. And I'll be sure he tells you everything. Okay?"

She nods a few times as she considers my solution. "What am I supposed to do about all his things? What about his car?"

The car. He told me the SUV was Maggie's, and now that I

think about it in context with everything else, it fits. "I think Bennett bought the car for you."

She furrows her brow and stares at me again. "Why on earth would he do that? He doesn't know me well enough to buy me a brand-new car."

I smile at her and let out a sigh. "He doesn't. But he does. And I know that doesn't make any sense. . . ." My voice trails off while those last words echo through my mind, and somehow, I find myself repeating the words I read last night in San Francisco. The words I will write in a letter to Bennett seventeen years from now. They worked on him. Maybe they'll work on his grandmother. "Someday," I say, "it will all make sense. For now, you'll just have to trust me."

34

For the last hour I've been leaning against the foot of my bed, dressed in the oversize sweatshirt Bennett wore after our first date in Ko Tao and staring up the black silk sheath I've bought to wear to tonight's auction party. When I first brought it home and hooked the hanger on my closet door frame, this dress looked almost magical, like something cartoon birds and mice had stitched together from scratch while I slept.

But tonight's the one-week anniversary of the night I got knocked back. Of *ever since.* And now the dress is just another museum piece, in good company with my map, a bag of sand, six postcards, and four new pins. All the things I can no longer look at without thinking of him.

I'm still staring up at the dress when I hear the knock at the door. I've been expecting it, but I'm not sure which one of my parents lost the coin toss.

"Come in," I mutter.

Emma?

I stare up at her from my spot on the floor. She's wearing the dress I helped her pick out, the strapless, floor-length gown in a deep, dark orange that looks as incredible on her now as it did in the dressing room. Her hair is pulled back in a tight twist at the nape of her neck, with a few strands of hair pulled out to frame her face. "Wow. You look gorgeous."

"Thanks." She takes a seat on the floor next to me, leans against the footboard, and reaches for me.

I look at her sideways. "You're gonna get all wrinkled."

"That's okay." She scans me from top to bottom, from my frizzy hair and bloodshot eyes down to my leggings and—to her horror, I'm sure—my unpedicured toes.

"What are you doing here, Em?"

She gives my hand a little squeeze. "Sorry. I know you want to be alone, but your mom put me up to this." I turn my head away from her and roll my eyes. Both Mom and Dad have been bugging me all week about this stupid party, and I've made it more than clear I'm not going. Under any circumstances. But to send Emma in as reinforcement? That's just cruel.

"And I wanted to be sure you were okay."

"I'm fine."

She looks at me in disbelief, then stares at the dress. "It would be a shame if I was the only one who ever saw you in it. You looked so beautiful."

I can't look at it without feeling sick. "Thanks."

We're silent for what feels like minutes, me looking down at the carpet, Emma looking back and forth between me and that dress. "I'm not going to change my mind," I finally say.

"I know. But we should stay here for at least, like, fifteen minutes so your mom thinks I really tried." She turns to me, smiles, and bumps me with her shoulder. "Okay?"

I give her a sad smile. "Thanks." Emma understands. She understood right away. Last Sunday I left Maggie's, ran straight to Emma's, and fell apart on her porch. We sat in her room while she passed me tissues, let me talk for hours, and believed every word of the story I made up. Someone in his family got sick. He had to take a red-eye back to San Francisco after we left the movie theater. He wasn't sure when or if he'd be back and was sorry he wouldn't have the chance to say good-bye. He'd miss us.

The next day, I told a few more people the same story and waited as it made the rounds of The Donut. And that was it. Within hours, everyone knew why Bennett had gone home, and I was the only one who knew it was all a lie.

Now I look at my best friend, all made up and happy and ready to go to the party she's been looking forward to for the last six months, and I know I should go tonight. I should be there to see what Emma and Danielle helped plan and to watch my parents dance and to see Justin in a tux. But I can't go out and pretend to be happy. Not without Bennett. Not yet.

"Are you mad at me? For not going tonight?"

She shakes her head. "No. I'm not mad. I just . . ." I stare at her, waiting for her to continue, but she doesn't. She looks down at the floor and twirls a loose thread in the rug with her finger.

"What?" I ask.

"Nothing."

"What?" I repeat.

She takes a deep breath and lets it out with a sigh. "I just miss you, that's all. I know you miss him—we all miss him too—but . . . I really miss *you*."

I force out a little laugh. "I'm right here."

"No, you're not."

I look at her and know she's right. Ever since the day I saw the other Bennett at the track and he told me he'd been trying to get back here, I've been doing exactly the opposite: I've been slowly disappearing.

She stops playing with the rug and stares at me. "Look, Anna, you're my best friend, and I love so many things about you. I love that you make me laugh, and that you love music and books, and you want to travel the world, and you're so committed to running . . . but you know what I love most about you? You know what I've loved about you since the moment we became friends?"

I look at her and wait.

"You're the strongest person I know. You're independent and you don't care what anyone thinks and you trust your instincts and . . . you've got *fight*. I've always envied that about you. If Justin left town, left me here, *I'd* be a blubbering basket case. But . . ." Her words hang in the air like she didn't mean to say them. *But what?* She expected more from me? She didn't think I'd be so weak?

"Where's your *fight?*" She stares at me for a minute and then reaches down and grabs my hand again. "Listen, I know it's only been a week, it's just—" She brings my hand to her face and kisses the back of it. "I want my friend back."

I look at her and wish I could tell her everything. I want to get back to her and the rest of my ordinary life too—to Mom and Dad and running and travel books—and I just don't know if I can find my fight with all these secrets weighing me down.

Emma doesn't let go of me, and we sit like that, waiting for our requisite fifteen minutes to tick by. "I'd better go. I have to greet the VIPs." Emma stands up and smooths out her gown. Then she checks her hair in my mirror and pats her eyes with her fingertip.

"I'm sorry, Emma."

She reaches for the doorknob, stops to blow me a kiss, and walks out, closing the door behind her.

I can't hear them, but I picture Emma at the bottom of the staircase, talking with Justin and my parents in hushed tones. I go to the window and peek out as Justin and Emma walk out to the car. Just as he's about to open the door, he looks up, sees me there, and gives a sad little wave. He gets in the car and they drive off.

Soon enough, Mom and Dad shout their good-byes and are-you-sure-you're-okays up the stairs and then they're off too. I look down at the sidewalk and stare at the spot where Bennett first kissed me—even though I don't remember him doing it. I look at the tree across the street, where his car rolled backward and settled because he didn't time our do-over exactly as planned. Even if he was a little off here and there, he'd always been in control. If he could get back, he would.

And that's when it hits me. He would have been here by now. Bennett was wrong and the letter was right. He's not coming back. He's stuck, against his will and most definitely against mine. Unless I make a different decision. And I have no idea what that means.

I leave the window open and walk back to the map. I stand there and study it for a minute, and then I reach forward and begin tracing invisible lines between the eight little red pins with my fingertip, running it back and forth, up and down, tracing patterns to connect them. Then I stop. I bring my finger to Evanston and make a tiny circle around the four I started with: Springfield. Minnesota. Michigan. Indiana. And then I rest my finger on San Francisco and make a much larger circle going all the way to Ko Tao, back to Vernazza, over to Wisconsin, and back to San Francisco.

I should have more. I'm supposed to have more.

I reach into the Lucite container and pull out a pin. Look at it. Stare at the map. Stick it into Paris. I pull out another one. Study the map. Stick it into Madrid. I stand back and consider the map again, enjoying the new look, and reach into the dusty container again. I push a red pin into Sydney. Then I grab the container and turn it upside down in my hand, feeling a few stray pins prick my palm.

I press pins into Tokyo.

Tibet.

Auckland.

Dublin.

Costa Rica.

São Paulo.

Prague.

Los Angeles.

And I just keep going and going, picking up pins and stabbing them into the paper until the map is covered with places I'll never see and the clear plastic box is as empty as I am.

june

35

Last week I was sad. This week, I'm just angry. I'm angry at him for not telling me about the letter and angry at my friends for acting like he was never here, but mostly, I'm angry at myself for letting my guard down so completely—for accepting this whole thing as perfectly normal.

My hands are balled up in two tight fists when Señor Argotta announces, *"¡Practiquemos la conversación!"* and walks down the aisle pointing out partners and passing out cards. He points to me. Then to Alex. I roll my eyes as I turn my desk toward him.

"¡Hola!" Alex says with a smile. "Hey, where were you on Saturday? We missed you." I'm not sure why it's taken him until Thursday to ask.

I shrug. "I'm training for state finals."

"On a Saturday night?"

"No, Alex. Every morning. I run *every* morning now. Even

on Sundays." Before I've said the last word I'm embarrassed by my tone, but I don't apologize. Instead I continue talking to him with this attitude, because it's actually making me feel better to see him uncomfortable for once. "So, do you have the conversation card, or what?"

He mutters something under his breath, picks the card up from his desk and reads to himself. "Oh, this one's pretty good." He reads it aloud. *"Partner number one, you are interviewing for a job as a waiter/waitress at one of Madrid's finest restaurants. Partner number two, you are the restaurant owner."*

I look around for something to punch.

"That's not such a bad one, right?" Alex decides without looking at me to notice that I'm gripping the sides of the wooden desk. "Do you want to be the waiter or the owner?"

"Neither." I push my chair away and run for the door, leaving my backpack on the floor and my textbook on my desk. Leaving Alex and that stupid conversation card. Leaving Señor Argotta calling after me in an accented voice that's full of concern, then frustration. But I don't stop. I don't even turn around. I run through The Donut, past the lockers. And I literally run into Danielle.

She crashes into a bank of lockers and her wooden bathroom pass goes sliding across the floor. "What the—!"

I'm wiping tears from my eyes as I help her back up to a standing position. "Danielle, I'm so sorry."

She starts to say something, but then she realizes I've been crying. "Anna? Are you okay?"

"I need to get out of here," I say.

324

"Anna!" She calls after me, but I'm already gone, through the double doors, racing toward the only thing I think may make me feel better.

⁓

He's here.

Not the way I want him to be, but in the only way I can have him now, in pictures of an infant, framed and displayed on a mantel, and in the eyes of his grandmother, who makes me tea and doesn't even question why I'm sitting in her kitchen at eleven twenty in the morning on a school day.

We sip from our respective teacups. We try to think of things to say, but come up with very little. She has plenty of questions and I have plenty of answers, but she can't voice hers because she knows I won't share mine. So we sit there, stuck in a thick silence that's interrupted every few minutes by the sound of porcelain cups connecting with their matching saucers.

Maggie finally breaks the silence. "I started cleaning out his room last week. I thought I'd put his things in the attic until . . ." Her voice trails off and I smile a little. I like the idea that she thinks he'll come back. "Do you—" she begins, looking at me like she'll let my expression determine whether she should continue her sentence or not. "Do you want to hold on to anything for him? Until he returns?"

I nod. And since there's nothing left to talk about, we carry our cups up the stairs and down the hall, past the photos of Bennett's mother as a child, of Maggie as a young woman, and into the mahogany-furnished room he once called his.

"I'll get you some more tea," Maggie says, and she grabs my nearly full cup and carries it out, closing the door behind her and leaving me alone in his room.

There are a few boxes stacked near the wall under the windows, but otherwise, it looks like it always did. I slide open the closet doors and peer inside. His uniform is there, along with a bunch of clothes I never got to see on him. His wool coat is hanging on a hook within easy reach, and even though it's ninety degrees outside, I put it on, lift the collar to my nose, and inhale his scent.

I shut the closet door and walk toward the desk. There is nothing on the surface—not even a pen or a photograph. I sit down in the wooden chair and open the top drawer. And that's where I find the rest of him. I take each of the items out one at a time and pile them on the desk. His Westlake student ID. One of my red pins. A blank postcard from Ko Tao. The postcard I wrote him in Vernazza. A stubby yellow pencil. A carabiner. A single key.

I push everything aside, take out the key, and walk over to the armoire. I work quickly, stacking the photo albums and old yearbooks in a pile, until I see the small gold keyhole in the back corner. I twist the key in the lock and pull up on the small door. Inside, I find stacks and stacks of rubber-banded dollar bills, hundreds, and twenties.

On top of one of the stacks, I see his notebook and remember how he used it to plot the do-over that probably saved

Emma's life. I pick it up and flip through it. Every page is covered with timelines and mathematical equations, charts documenting age conversions and historical events, and company names with dollar signs next to them. Finally I get the page he once showed me—the time conversions he did that landed us in my driveway and eventually kept Emma from driving to Chicago.

I flip back to the first few pages of the notebook and see something else familiar. My words, but in his handwriting:

Someday soon, we will meet. And then you will leave for good. But I think I can fix it—I just need to make a different decision this time. Tell me to live my life for myself, and not for you. Tell me not to wait for you to come back. I think that will change everything.

He's circled key words and terms like *for good* and *leave* and *fix* and *change everything*, adding his own comments and question marks and exclamation points like he was studying it, attempting to figure it all out. But he didn't. Not after months of trying. And now it's too late—he's gone for good. *Why didn't he tell me?* He was supposed to tell me *everything.*

I check the door for Maggie. Then I put the red notebook back on the top, lock the cabinet, and put the scrapbooks and photo albums back where they belong. Once everything looks just as he left it, I return to Bennett's desk.

I open the drawer and put the key inside, and then I look at the rest of the items. I pick each one up and turn it over in my hands, starting with the postcard from Ko Tao. I remember the day he presented me mine on the lawn at school. I couldn't believe he'd gone back, just for that. "I got one for myself, too . . . to remember the day," he'd said.

"Here," Maggie whispers, and I jump and turn my head. She's traded our teacups for a small shopping bag, and now she's holding it out to me.

"Thanks."

She looks down at the pile of things on Bennett's desk and rests her hand on my shoulder. "Are you okay, sweetie?" I give her a sad nod. "He's such a sweet boy. I hope he comes back."

I hold the bag under the edge of the desktop and brush everything inside. Then I stand up, pull Maggie into a hug, and thank her for letting me hold on to his things. She squeezes me tightly.

"You should go to California for a visit," I say as I pull away from her embrace. "Meet that grandson of yours. I bet it would mean a lot to your daughter."

"I don't know. . . . My daughter and I aren't very close these days."

I stare straight into her eyes, and even though they're exactly the same as her grandson's, I don't see him at all. I just see Maggie. "You should go anyway."

"Maybe I will."

I look at her and smile. There's no need to wait for Bennett to get old enough to start making little changes that will affect her future. Not if I can help her get it right the first time.

I kiss her on the cheek and close the desk drawer, leaving the key inside.

⟶⟝

I'm back on campus a half hour after last bell, and as I walk through The Donut I can hear my footsteps echoing in the empty halls. I hope the classroom is unlocked, my backpack is still there, and Argotta's already gone for the day. The probability of all three being true is extremely low.

When I reach the classroom door, the first thing I see is my backpack, propped up against Argotta's desk. When I look up from the floor, I spot him there, correcting papers.

"Señor Argotta?" When he hears the sound of my voice, he stops writing but keeps his eyes on his work.

"Señorita Greene. How nice of you to return."

"I'm . . . really sorry. It's just—" Now he looks at me, first curious, then horrified. My T-shirt is soaked with sweat, my face is all blotchy and red, and the humidity has caused my curls to tighten up and frizz. Argotta blinks fast a few times but doesn't ask.

"No need to explain. Your friend, Señor Camarian, filled me in on the . . . impact . . . that Señor Cooper's departure has had on you." I'm not sure if Alex has the necessary information to explain this "impact," but if The Donut is as all-knowing as Danielle says it is, he probably does. And now my chest feels heavy with guilt. How could I have been so mean to him today?

Argotta leans down and reaches for my backpack like he's

about to hand it to me, but when he feels its weight he sort of scoots it in my general direction instead. I step forward, pick it up, and hoist it over my shoulder. "Thanks." I turn to leave.

I'm almost at the door when I hear him clear his throat behind me. "Are you aware of the date, Señorita Greene?"

I stop. "It's June first, señor."

"*Exactamente.*" I roll my eyes. I'm not in the mood for this.

"Which made yesterday the last day of May." I turn around and look at him. "I was really hoping you'd consider taking that spot in Mexico, señorita. Perhaps now that your summer plans have changed . . ."

I flash back to the day he gave me the shiny yellow folder and realize I never even bothered to open it. I should probably know all the details, but I don't. "Oh. Right. Where is it again?"

"I think you had it as a destination on your travel plan, did you not? It's a beautiful town called La Paz. It's getting very popular. Now is really the time to see it."

"La Paz?"

"*Sí.*" He watches me while I try not to look confused. *La Paz?* "You have your travel voucher and you would have an excellent family to live with. The trip is practically free. I'm sure you already have your summer all planned out, but it really is a great opportunity, and if you're interested, I could still pull some strings."

Argotta watches me while he waits for his answer. And finally, when none comes, he leans back in his seat and folds his arms across his chest. I want to go, but I don't think I can.

330

What if Bennett comes back? I can't leave. I have to wait here. But my whole body starts to tremble as I remember the words I just read in Bennett's notebook—the words I will write in a letter to him seventeen years from now: *Tell me not to wait for you to come back.*

"Are you okay, señorita?"

I think that will change everything.

I feel far away as I nod, and when I speak, my voice doesn't sound like my own. "This is a good chance, isn't it? To leave?"

"*Exactamente!*" he yells as he throws his arms up in the air, and I startle. "Go! Go! There's nothing stopping you! Go see the world, señorita!"

He smiles at me, and I feel myself smiling back. Because this is it. *This* is the moment.

I don't know how it happened before. Maybe Argotta never mentioned it again. Maybe all the spots were full from the beginning. Maybe everything was exactly the same, but she decided to stay here all summer, sulking and waiting for Bennett to return. But right now, there's no question in my mind that *Anna* stood here in front of Argotta, politely thanked him, and turned down his offer. And that's not what I'm going to do.

"Do you still have the application?" he asks, and I nod. I'm not exactly certain where it is, but I know I'll find it; and now I can't wait to get home to dig through my desk.

"I'll give you until Monday. Let me know what you want to do."

My parents may need until Monday, but I don't. I rush

around to Señor Argotta and hug him. "Thank you so much, señor!" When I pull back, he looks a little shocked, but it hits him that the hug was my yes, and there's nothing but delight in his expression. "You're making a good choice, señorita."

I hope it's a good choice. I don't know for certain that it is, but I do know that it's a different one.

And suddenly it hits me. I'm smack in the middle of her do-over.

36

Depending on the season, Schiller Woods can be beautiful or eerie; the perfect place for either a wedding or a horror-film shoot. As Dad rounds the corner through the gate, I see that what was once a blanket of gray slush is now a bright green meadow. I step out of the car and take a deep breath; the whole park smells new.

"I've missed this," I say as I close the car door, feeling truly content for the first time in weeks. Dad looks surprised to see me so happy, but I can't help it; I love this event. The cross-country coaches in our division created the noncompetitive but mandatory race, just in case six months of running on a spongy track instead of sticky mud, and leaping metal hurdles rather than downed trees, had caused us to question our true passion. I've run this course enough to know how the path will dip and turn for the next three miles, where the tight spots will be, and where the obstacles are likely to be placed.

My teammates and I gather around a picnic table a few feet away from the starting line, stretching and looking across the open field for our biggest competitors while Dad goes in search of coffee. A few minutes later, he returns with a paper cup and a folded map.

"How are you feeling?" he asks me as he lays the paper flat on the table and huddles over it.

"Good." He looks up, waiting for me to elaborate, but I don't. Still, I do feel good. I've been feeling increasingly like myself since I made the decision to go to La Paz two days ago. Now I just need to find a way to tell my parents.

"Where is she?" Dad asks under his breath.

I lift up my arm and stretch in his direction while I point with my chin. "Over there. Number thirty-two. Blue shirt." I stretch deeper and give him time to find her. Size her up.

"Hmmm." He's watching her, but for what exactly I can't be sure. "Okay, remember to pace yourself. Don't hold back just to blast her at the end. Keep the pressure on all the way. Keep passing, keep in front. Then get that blue shirt in your sights and turn it up even more at the last marker." He's searching the crowd again. He shouldn't be so nervous, since I don't have a scholarship on the line this time.

"Got it."

"Where's your marker?" Dad asks, pointing back to the map.

I rest my finger on the drawing. "This water pump looks like it's about an eighth of a mile before the finish."

He studies the other options and finally nods. "Yeah. That's good. I think that's your best bet. Okay. I'm going to take my place with the other worried parents." He pats me on the back. "Don't break anything."

"I won't." I take a deep breath and drop forward. As I stretch, I stare at the upside-down paper number 54 pinned to my chest and listen as my teammates and competitors collect around me. I shake out my limbs and take my place.

We stand side by side at the starting line. It's only seven a.m., but we're already dripping with sweat from the heat and the humidity as we stretch and visualize the course. When the shot signals our start, we run at a controlled speed across the grass and into the woods. I already miss the mud and the slush. We push ourselves up a steep hill littered with fallen tree branches and debris, and then we drop down into the deeper woods where the footing is even more uneven.

We run as a pack for the first mile, sliding past one another when we reach narrowly spaced trees. At the end of the first mile, we cross a shallow creek and jump over a series of logs. I'm pushing and climbing and hurdling, and I know there are people around me, but as I cross the miles they seem to disappear as I move past them and fight my way to the front of the pack.

This is better. I'm not as light on my feet as I usually am, but at least while I'm running, surrounded by forest and sky, my head starts to feel clear again. I'm in control here, moving with the pack, but I can tell that I'm not pushing and fighting like I should be if I want to win this thing.

I run, feeling both the pounding of my shoes on the trail and my heart beating fast in my chest, and I look ahead at the girls in front of me. And just as we come around a bend and start to descend a narrow trail, I see the water pump far ahead in front of the leader. My marker. At first, I slowly increase my pace so I won't seem like a threat to the five girls in front of me. I slip quickly past one. Then another. I'm in third place when we hit the quarter-mile mark, and that's when I lock my eyes on that blue shirt and chase after it with everything I have left. For a moment, I feel something familiar returning. My feet move faster. *Where's your fight?* I hear Emma ask.

"Right here." I breathe out, without even caring if anyone's overheard me, and I kick it up a notch. Something has changed. Something feels different today. I picture the words in her letter—*I think I can fix it*—and they echo in my ears as I keep my eyes glued on the runners ahead.

The two girls in front of me hurdle the last obstacle, and then it's my turn. I run up on the fallen tree, leap forward, and my feet leave the ground. But I feel the tip of my shoe catch on a knot, and I fall forward in a stumble, taking wide steps to keep from falling. The girls I just passed shoot ahead of me again.

I rebalance myself, take a deep breath, and force myself forward again. I climb the hill at top speed, legs burning, until the two girls fall behind me again. Then I overtake the next. But the girl in the blue shirt is too far in front. I can see the finish line from here—see that she's closer to it than I am—and that makes me switch into a completely different gear. I steady my gaze on the blond ponytail swinging in front of me. I give myself one last push and speed up to catch her.

But she's faster. She's the one to break through the tape first, though I am right on her heels. I come to a stop and fall forward, pulling in breaths, wiping the sweat from my face, and smiling at the ground.

"Good race," I hear her say, and I twist to my side to see the girl I barely beat at state finals doubled over next to me and breathing just as heavily. She holds out her hand to shake mine.

I don't even care that I came in second, and my smile is geniune. "Thanks," I reply between breaths as I take her hand. "You made me fight for it." Her eyebrows pinch together in confusion but I don't feel the need to clarify. I may have lost that first-place trophy, but somewhere on the course I found what I was missing.

⌒◦

At home, I fly up the stairs, flop down on the floor, and start rifling through my backpack until I find the yellow folder I unearthed from the bottom of my desk last Thursday. I open it and read the letter from the host family again, for the hundredth time, and stare at the eight-by-ten picture of them. They're standing in front of their house with their arms locked around one another. Four kids. A girl my age. A boy that looks a little older. Two small girls in dresses, standing in front, who look like twins.

And now when I look up at the map, suddenly all I want to do is make it real again. I pull the pin out of Prague and listen to the *plink* it makes when the metal connects with the plastic container. I pull the pin out of Paris. Cairo. Amsterdam. Berlin. Quebec. A few minutes later, I've removed every false pin that pierced its surface, every destination I've never seen but marked as if I had, and placed them back in the home where they belong.

Only the eight pins remain:

Springfield, Illinois.

Ely, Minnesota.

Grand Rapids, Michigan.

South Bend, Indiana.

Ko Tao, Thailand.

Devil's Lake State Park, Wisconsin.

Vernazza, Italy.

San Francisco, California.

Eight pins aren't nearly enough, but at least they're real. The ninth one will be too.

37

Everyone's in a good mood at dinner, perhaps because I am finally smiling and not casting a depressing pall over the dining room table. But the mood, I sense, is about to change.

"I want to talk with you about this summer," I say.

Mom glances up at me as she chews, and Dad keeps his eyes on his plate while he takes a knife through his chicken. "Sure. What's up?" he asks.

I take a deep breath and go. "I've been talking with my Spanish teacher about an exchange program in Mexico. He organizes the trips and personally selects students to participate and he just told me that there's a great family that can host me this summer. In La Paz." I didn't expect to blurt it all out quite so fast. And now all those words are hovering above the table while my parents look at each other, confused.

"I know, it's sudden," I continue, "but I've thought a lot about this. I've always wanted to travel, and you know, I really need time away . . . from here." No one moves or says anything, so I just keep talking. "It won't cost you anything. I won the plane ticket in Señor Argotta's class, and I'd have a place to stay with this amazing family. It's basically free." I hear myself repeating Argotta's words and feel like he's here with me, cheering me on.

"La Paz?" Mom can't hide her concern.

"Yeah. It's on the Baja peninsula. On the Sea of Cortez. In Mexico," I clarify, just in case she missed that part.

"That's far away."

I smile at her and shrug. "That's sort of the point, Mom."

"No way." She sighs and shifts in her chair. "What do you even know about this family?"

I walk over to the counter where I laid the packet of information earlier and bring it back to the table. I lay the photos and the letter out for them to see, and describe what I've learned about them. He's a businessman. She's a nature photographer. They have a daughter my age. I take the completed form out of the folder and place it next to the photos.

"It just needs your signature."

Mom picks up the form, considers it, and sets in down on the table. "When would you leave?"

"In two weeks."

"Two weeks!"

"It's a bit last-minute."

Dad's too quiet. I can't tell on which side of the fence he is, so I look at him, pleading with him to stand firmly on mine.

"How long would you be gone?" he asks.

This part isn't going to go over well. "Ten weeks."

"Ten weeks? That's the entire summer!" Mom pushes her chair away from the table and walks to the kitchen. Dad looks at me and I look back with pleading eyes.

"Please, Dad," I whisper. I hear the water running in the kitchen.

"That's a long time," Dad says, loud enough for Mom to hear, and I picture her bent over the sink and nodding vehemently. "But even so," he continues, "it sounds like a really good opportunity." Mom returns to the table wearing a panicked look that morphs into an angry one, like she can't believe he's voiced this opinion without consulting her first. But Dad holds his ground. "She's been wanting to travel since she was little," he says to her. "This is a good way to see the world, to experience a different culture."

I mouth the words *Thank you* when she's not looking.

Mom sets her glass down with a little too much force. She sits down and looks across at Dad. "You're seriously considering letting our sixteen-year-old daughter live in a foreign country, for two months, with people we don't even *know*?"

"Argotta says it will really help my diction. It will help me develop an ear for the language. I probably won't be fluent in only two months, but I'll be closer."

"I don't know." Mom's looking from me to Dad, and Dad is looking from me to her, and we're at a stalemate.

"It's a huge honor to be selected," I offer. She doesn't need to know that no one else wanted this spot. It's funny to hear myself argue with such passion, given how dismissive I was when Argotta first made his offer, but that was when Bennett was here and permission slips weren't required for international travel. "Mom. This is something for *me*. I need to do this."

She won't look at either one of us, so we all sit in silence, pushing food around on our plates, and trying to ignore the photos of the happy family on the table in front of us.

***

"Drop me off here, would you?" I ask, even though we're still two blocks from the bookstore.

"Why here?" Emma pulls over to the side of the road and when she's stopped, follows my finger up to the bright blue awning of the Going Going Gone Travel Agency.

"Oh." She sounds so sad. "Wait. I'll park and come in with you."

I start to argue with her, but then I decide it might be therapeutic for her to witness me purchase the ticket, to see that this trip is actually happening, because she can't seem to fully process the fact that we'll be spending a summer apart for the first time in three years.

When we open the glass door, we're greeted by the same jingling bells we have at the bookstore. Emma and I sit down in the only chairs in the office just as a youngish woman with thick glasses and a mop of split-ended, outdated hair comes around the corner and takes a seat in the chair across from us. I can hardly see her behind the giant monitor.

"Hi. I need to purchase a round-trip ticket to La Paz, Mexico, please." I reach into my backpack and grab the now-tattered copy of *Let's Go Mexico*, flip to the dog-eared page on La Paz, and pull out the voucher I wedged into the binding.

"I'd like to use this." I slide it across the desk and picture the satisfied look I saw on Argotta's face this morning when I gave him my completed, parent-signed form.

She picks up the voucher, turns it over, and sets it on the desk in front of her.

"Sure! When do you want to leave?" She's a little too perky, and when she turns her attention to the computer screen, Emma rolls her eyes.

"June twentieth, please. It's a Tuesday." The travel agent's fingers begin flying across the keyboard. Every few minutes she stops typing to consult the screen, and then the fingers start flying again.

"Here, let me see this." Emma grabs *Let's Go Mexico* and starts thumbing through the pages, stopping every once in a while to show me some photo of a beach at sunset or to tell me about the great scuba diving or the delicious food.

"Look at this!" Emma twists in her seat and pushes the book at me. "Look at these markets—all this pottery and food. This isn't fair; you don't even like shopping."

The travel agent clears her throat and reads me my choices of departure times.

"I'm driving you to the airport," Emma chimes in. "Take that one at noon."

"Are you sure?" I ask.

"Yes. Absolutely," she replies, without looking up from the book.

"I'll take the twelve fifteen flight," I tell the agent, and she goes back to pounding on the keyboard.

Emma flips back to the photo of the open-air market. "Look at these hats. It's says they're woven so tightly they can hold water. Why would you want to hold water in your hat?" She looks up at me and shrugs. "I don't know why, but lately I've been thinking I need more hats. What do you think? Do I look good in hats?" she asks, and I suck in my breath. Even though she's sitting next to me, without even a single scar, for a moment all I can see is her lying on a stark white sheet, her frail body covered with cuts and punctured by tubes while I tell her about my Mexico travel plan. I jump when the printer comes to life and starts whirring and plinking just behind the desk.

"Hats?" I ask.

"Yeah. Hats. Those contraptions people put on their head to block out the sun and hide bad hair. Hats." She looks at me wide-eyed. "What do you think? Do I look good in hats? Some people can't pull them off, you know, but I think I might be able to."

I just stare at her, and finally I find my voice. "Yeah, you look good in hats." I feel pale. *You look really good in hats*, I remember saying that day I sat on her bed and held her hand and told her about the Yucatán Peninsula. Then I broke down. Then I told her to hold on and I'd fix it.

"Here you are." The agent smiles brightly and gives me a thin envelope decorated with colorful fish. "Have a fantastic time on your trip! And come back and see us again, Miss Greene!"

Emma locks arms with me and leads me out of the office. "Now that we did your thing, it's my turn. Let's go see Justin," she says, pulling me down the block to the record store.

School ends on a hot, muggy day, and while everyone heads to the lake carrying food, music, and picnic blankets, I spend my afternoon waiting in line with a bunch of sweaty people in the downtown Chicago passport office. Four hours later, passport in hand, I get off the El at the Evanston stop and trudge down the cement staircase toward home. At the intersection, I look down the street and see the sign on the record store.

It's been over a week since Emma and I went to buy my ticket and bounced happily into the record store to tell Justin all about Mexico. After she finished imitating the perky travel agent, he threw his arm around her and made a joke about being stuck all alone with her for the whole summer. He told me to come back next week and he'd load me up with CDs for my trip.

"There you are! I thought you forgot." Justin beams at me

as I push through the doors and walk inside the empty store. The music's loud, as usual.

I shrug. "How could I forget free music?"

He fakes a pout. "And here I thought you were coming in to see me."

"You?" I give him a confused stare. "No. Nothing to do with you. I'm just here for the tunes." I break into a smile.

"You're mean." He takes a step back and grabs both of my hands, just like Bennett used to do right before we closed our eyes and opened them elsewhere. "You excited?"

"Yeah. Very."

"We're gonna miss you."

"I'll miss you guys too." I look around the record store. "But it'll be nice to do something different, you know?"

"I know." Justin's been listening to me talk about traveling the world for the last decade, and the look on his face proves that he's genuinely excited to see me finally going somewhere. "Well, since you're only here to sponge music off me, let's stock you up." He takes my hand again and leads me through the store, down the skinny aisles carved out between roughly sanded wooden bins. He stops at a kiosk of new releases.

"Here, this is brand-new. Just came out this week." He passes me the CD, and I turn it over and read the track list. "She's good. Some pissed-off Canadian chick. Great breakup music."

"We did not break up."

"Of course you didn't, but you know . . ."

I fake a glare and the room goes silent as one song ends and another is about to begin. We start walking again, just as piano notes come in through the overhead sound system and a soft melody begins. Justin stops in the Rock section and reaches into the bin for a CD. "I've been meaning to tell you about this local Chicago band; they're playing at the coffee-house next week," he says, and I try to listen to him, but all of my attention is now focused on the melody being piped in from the ceiling. It sounds familiar, and when the lyrics begin, even though I'm supposed to be listening to Justin tell me about this band he's excited about, I find myself straining to hear the song over his voice.

> *Take me to another place, she said.*
> *Take me to another time . . .*

I feel that hole in the pit of my stomach start to grow again as I listen.

"Here it is," Justin says, and I almost *shush* him.

"The drummer is—"

> *Take me where the whispering breezes . . .*
> *can lift me up and spin me around.*

Now I can't look at him, because I'm afraid if I let go of the wooden bin I might not be able to stand. He's waving the CD around, his facial expressions all animated and enthusiastic, so I know he's still talking. And I think I'm saying, *"Uh-huh,"* or something like that, but I can't hear a word from either one of us. All I can do is listen to the lyrics.

If I could I would, but I don't know how.

"Anna? Are you okay?"

Just when I've stopped looking back at what I did wrong and stopped being angry at Bennett for what he did wrong—just when I've finally found my fight and made a decision that could change everything—the sadness and the anger flood over me again, and before I can talk myself into stopping them, the tears start falling, landing with little splashes on the plastic jewel cases.

"Stay here." Justin leaves and I watch him walk over to the front door and bolt it with one hand as he flips the BACK IN TEN MINUTES sign to the glass with the other. I release my grip on the bin and let my knees bend as I sink down to the floor, and I lean against the shelving, my knees pulled tight to my chest, and listen to the song. The adrenaline surge that makes my hands ball into fists has returned, and I open my eyes to find my short fingernails stabbing little smiles into my palms.

I'm melting into nothing. . . .

First I sense Justin standing over me, then I feel him on the floor, facing me and pulling me into a hug. As soon as I feel the warmth of his body I sort of fall into it. His proximity to me—the position itself—feels far too intimate, and I know I should pull away from him, but I can't. I need this connection. So I cry and breathe and enjoy the feeling of his hand, heavy on my back. We used to just be two best friends who'd known each other since we were little kids. Now he's my best friend's boyfriend, and that means we probably shouldn't be sitting here on the floor, listening to music, and holding each other quite so tightly.

I'm just about to say this to him when he pulls away from me and rests his chin on my knees. When we're eye to eye like this, he looks so different. The sun has tanned his skin, blending his freckles together, and his smile is so . . . Justin, so sweet and kind and ready to be there for me. Something in my expression must change, because he's suddenly leaning forward, closing his eyes, and moving much further into my space than he should. I know what's about to happen, and I know that I don't want it to, but I'm not quite sure how to stop it. I feel trapped between his mouth and the wooden CD bin.

I turn my head so fast that when our lips brush, it's an awkward, almost accidental movement. "Justin . . ." My accusatory tone makes his face fall. To break the tension, I collapse against his shoulder, let out a nervous laugh, and punch him in the arm. "What are you doing, you idiot?"

If it's possible, his laugh sounds even more nervous than mine. "Wow," he says, looking down at the floor. "I guess I misread that. I'm sorry." He can't even look at me.

And now I feel horrible for my other best friend. "Justin, I'd never do that to Emma. I didn't think you would either."

"I wouldn't. I didn't . . . I don't know, I just lost myself for a minute there."

He scoots away from me, and I feel like I need to say something to lessen his guilt. "Don't worry, nothing happened. Besides"—I let out a nervous laugh—"I guess it's kind of nice to know I wasn't crazy. Until you started seeing Emma, I always thought you had a thing for me."

Justin looks up into my eyes. "Of course I did."

"Shut up." I reach out and punch him in the arm again, mostly because I can't figure out what else to do with my hands.

He shakes his head. "How could you not know that?" he asks, and I just stare at him, because I have no idea what to say. "Do you remember that time in the sixth grade, when I came over to your house? Our parents were playing cards, and you and I spent the night hanging out in your room. You kept telling me you had a surprise for me." I smile at him, but so far, I don't remember any of this.

"When the room got dark, you told me to lie down on the rug, and then you clicked off the light and stretched out next to me. We spent the next hour looking at those little plastic glow-in-the-dark stars on your ceiling, making up our own constellations and laughing until we couldn't breathe. You told me how you looked at the stars at night and pretended to be somewhere else in the world until you fell asleep. Then you told me all about your travel plans, how you wanted to be a photographer or a journalist—someone who got to tour the world—and you were planning to live in Paris first. You were going to take a French class that summer and move there right after graduation."

"That sounds like something I would have said." I can't believe he even remembers this. We were eleven. Even now that he's reminded me, the details that are so vivid in his mind are murky and vague in mine. "How on earth do you remember all that?"

He laughs under his breath. "That was the night I stopped thinking about you as my best friend . . . well, as *only* my best friend." I feel my eyes narrow, and I inhale sharply, watching him, waiting for me to tell me he's kidding, but he just smiles and shrugs, like he can't help it.

"Why didn't you ever tell me?"

"I didn't want to ruin anything. I figured if it was going to happen it would eventually." He shrugs again and looks at me.

"So what are you saying? What about Emma?"

He gives me a genuine smile. "Emma's incredible. She's gorgeous and funny and totally amazing. But she's still not you. She's not my best friend."

"That's not fair to her. You've only known her a few months and you've known me my whole life. Give her a chance."

"I know. I am. It's just that, most of the time, I can't even believe we're together. When I first asked her out, I honestly didn't expect her to say yes. Maybe part of me asked her out just to see if it would make you jealous. But she completely surprised me when she agreed, and I don't know . . . she seemed like she was really into me."

"She was. She *is*." And until this moment, I thought he was too. I think back to the day we sat in the hospital cafeteria and he told me about his date with Emma, how they talked and talked—how she surprised him. I picture him huddled over Emma's broken body, stroking her hair and whispering jokes into her ear, with eyes for no one but her. How could I have been wrong?

Then I remember there was no hospital. Aside from Bennett, I'm the only one who knows there were two versions of that day: the first one ended with a horrible accident, but the second one ended with all four of us at the movies, eating popcorn, the two of them wearing smiles instead of hospital gowns. The first one ended with Justin comforting a very broken Emma, but the second one ended with him on a double date with me and Bennett.

Something important happened to them that day— somewhere between Emma's house and the poorly timed arrival at the intersection—that brought them together. Or maybe it was the accident itself that made all the difference. Either way, we wiped it out. We did it over. We changed it.

Maybe Bennett was right—testing fate, toying with it, may not have any obvious impact at first, but eventually something has to backfire.

39

It's six thirty a.m. and already it's eighty degrees outside. I dress in my lightweight shorts, pull my hair through the back of my pink running hat, and pop on a pair of black Oakleys I splurged on for my trip.

When I run past the man with the gray ponytail, I wave and give him the most enthusiastic "Hi!" he's ever heard from me. He's seen me every Monday, Wednesday, and Friday for the last three years. For a moment I want to stop and tell him that I'll miss him and that he shouldn't worry about my absence, because I'll be spending the next two months running on sand.

When I finish my three-mile loop, I stand on the porch, stretch into a runner's lunge against the banister, and look around. I wonder if this place will be different when I return. Maybe the trees will have noticeably grown or maybe there will be new cracks in the sidewalk or maybe Dad will have painted the house.

I open the door and stop cold. There, leaning against the banister, stands a black case with the word TRAVELPRO stamped on it in shiny silver letters and a giant red bow attached to the collapsible handle.

Dad and Mom emerge from the kitchen. She's still in her bathrobe, and he's pulling her along, holding her hand like she might turn and run if he didn't.

"A suitcase," I say. I've never owned luggage. "Thank you." Mom gives me a sad smile, moves to my side, and practically yanks me into a hug.

"Ew. Stop. I'm all sweaty."

"I don't care." She squeezes harder, and I feel her warm tears land on my bare shoulder. "I'm so proud of you," she whispers into my ear.

"Thanks, Mom." I squeeze her back and plant a kiss on her cheek. "Don't be sad. I'll be back before you know it."

"I know," she says. She wipes the tears away and locks her eyes on mine. "You're so much braver than I ever was."

I reach up and take her face in my hands. "That's not true. Look how brave you're being right now." I smile at her and hug her tight.

"Annie, your Brit's here!" Dad yells from downstairs.

I look around my room one last time and zip up the last compartment of my suitcase. I don't imagine that I'll need that much for a summer on the beach, so I've packed light. I have running clothes and shoes, my Discman, batteries, a collection of CDs, and a few light dresses. Flip-flops. Some makeup. Hair clips.

I zip my suitcase, roll it to the door, and stand in front of my map. I consider the little red dots sprinkled across its surface, remembering the soft feel of the sand in Ko Tao and the smell of the dusty rocks at Devil's Lake and the deep red of the Vernazza sunrise. And then I stare at the newest one, kiss my fingertip, and bring it to the pin in San Francisco. I close the door behind me and pull my new luggage toward the stairs.

When I get to the porch, Emma's standing there, telling Mom all about her and Justin's plans for the summer.

"Are you sure we can't take you to the airport?" Dad's in the driveway wearing a tight smile.

"Emma really wants to take me."

"So do we."

"Yes, but Emma doesn't have a bookstore to open or a hospital shift to make."

"Okay." He hugs me hard, but quickly, and then pulls the suitcase out of my grasp and rolls it toward the Saab's open trunk. The convertible soft top is down in celebration of this hot summer day.

I hug my parents one last time, say good-bye, and promise to write. Then I open the passenger door and see a small box wrapped in colorful paper waiting on the seat. "What's this?"

"Open it," Emma commands as she backs out of the

driveway, honking like a madwoman while I hold the small wrapped box with one hand and wave good-bye to my parents with the other. When we're out of sight, I rip the paper off and find a black leather case. I flip the top open.

"Em." I remove the delicate piece, turn it over, and twist the leather strap. "I don't need a watch. I have a watch."

"You have a running watch. This is a dressy watch. In case you meet some wonderful, handsome boy and he asks you out to dinner." I'm surprised to feel myself grin when she says it.

"And I need to know when to be home before I turn into a pumpkin?" I touch the glass face with my fingertip and look up at her. "It's beautiful. You didn't have to do this."

"I know. I just wanted you to always remember that I'm here counting the minutes until you return. Har-har-har."

I laugh. "Seriously, Em. Thank you. I love it." We both fall silent while I struggle to fasten the watch around my wrist.

"I can't believe you're missing Pearl Jam at Soldier Field. We've been waiting for this for more than a year."

"It's okay. You'll go with Justin." I feel a pang of sadness when I say his name. I wouldn't change what Bennett and I did for her, but I wish I didn't feel so responsible for the subtle shift in Justin's feelings. I look at her, wondering what's going to happen between them this summer, and hoping Justin gives her a chance like he promised me he would.

She sighs. "Justin thinks Eddie Vedder is 'pedestrian.' That was his word. 'Pedestrian.' The man's a genius." And with that, Emma turns the stereo on. "Case in point."

She twists the knob, and the opening guitar licks of "Corduroy" fill the car. As always, we sing. Loud. Off key. People in neighboring cars stare at us and shake their heads. But then I stop. Emma's still drumming hard on the wheel and singing, but I'm just listening to the lyrics of the chorus.

Everything has chains . . .
Absolutely nothing's changed.

Has anything changed? He blew into our lives and back out again, and on the surface, maybe it looks like he didn't leave any marks, but I know he did: they're all over me. And as painful as it is to be in this town without him, if I could do the last three months again, I'd make the same choice—to know Bennett Cooper. Even though it kills me when the song ends with the words *I'll end up alone like I began.*

Emma pulls into the international departures terminal and screeches to a halt in front of the curbside check-in, punches the gearshift into park, and turns to face me.

"Send postcards, love."

Postcards . . .

"I will. I promise." I hug her tight. "Have a fun summer. I'll see you in August."

I soften my grip on her but her arms remain firmly locked around me, and when she tries to say something, I hear her voice catch in her throat. "Em . . ." I tighten my hold on her again. "Stop. You're going to make me cry."

She lets me go and pulls away. "You're right. Happy moment. No crying." She rushes to wipe the tears from her face and we air-kiss on both cheeks. "Until August," she says.

"Until August." I give her another quick hug and bolt from the car before her tears become contagious. I pull my bag from the trunk and walk into the airport, then stop and look back to give Emma a final wave good-bye.

After the agent hands me my boarding pass, I walk on wobbly legs toward the line of people waiting at security. I've never felt more alone, but on the flip side, I don't think I've ever been braver.

I act like I know how to board a plane. People move quickly. And slowly. My heart races as I make my way through the seats, and it feels like it's about to burst out of my chest when I see 14A. My carry-on bag is filled with magazines and travel books and, of course, the eight things I couldn't leave behind.

After I take my seat and buckle in, I reach into my bag and remove the small stack of postcards and look at each one. Most of them are blank, but the one in his handwriting and the two in mine say the same thing—we meant something to each other. We didn't want it to end.

The plane taxis down the runway, and we lift into the sky. And that's when I feel it. Finally, something I can compare to the feeling of traveling with Bennett. A small twist. A lightness in my stomach. I feel this incredible rush of adrenaline, and I can't help smiling when I think of what's about to meet me. I adjust the pillow between the seat and the wall of the plane, grip my postcards, and lean my head against the small double-paned plastic window. I watch as Illinois slips and shrinks away below.

40

My neoprene belt is strapped tight around my waist, my music is thumping loud in my ears, and the soles of my shoes are leaving little impressions in the damp sand as I run. I look over my shoulder at the sun climbing fast on the horizon, and I let my head keep turning, following the line that divides the turquoise bay from the deep orange sky. I still can't believe I'm here.

I just wish he were too. The change of scenery helped, but it still aches to miss him so much, to look for his face among strangers on the street and to think of him every time I pass one of the hundreds of postcard racks scattered throughout this tourist town. And even though it's Bennett I miss most, I also hate knowing I'll never feel that twist in my stomach again, the one that made me feel queasy but completely alive.

Up ahead I can see the tall rocks and jagged cliffs that mark the end of the beach, and I feel my arms pump harder, pushing me toward them. I fix my gaze on the rock closest to the water and sprint with everything I have, stopping only when my fingertips touch it.

I shake out my arms and legs, walking back and forth along the beach as I cool down. When my breathing has returned to normal, I find a dry spot on the sand and recline on my elbows so I can take in the view. Then I lie back into the heat. I close my eyes, and for a long time I don't think about anything but the feeling of the sun on my face and the sound of the water lapping against the shore.

My head falls lazily to one side, and I exhale as I open my eyes, but instead of seeing the rocks that mark the end of the beach, I find myself staring at a picture of the San Francisco skyline. My heart starts racing again, maybe even faster than it did as I ran. I twist onto my side, reach forward to remove the image from the sand, and stare at it.

I flip it over.

You didn't get your postcard.

I want to look behind me. I have a feeling he's there, but I shut my eyes tight, because I don't think I can handle it if I look around and discover that the beach is still empty. But I remind myself that the postcard is real and tangible in my hands, and I force myself to sit up and look over my shoulder.

Bennett Cooper is sitting in the sand just a couple of feet away from me, and I take him in, from his mess of hair, down to his concert T-shirt, past his jeans, and finally to his flip-flops. I stare at him, my lips pressed together, slowly shaking my head back and forth. This can't be happening.

"Hey, you."

I feel tears slide down my cheeks, and I think I say, "Hi," but it doesn't matter, because within seconds he's right next to me, and all I can feel is his fingers on the back of my neck. His kisses land everywhere, on my wet cheeks and my forehead, on my eyelids and my neck, and finally on my mouth, and we pull each other close, neither one allowing even the smallest gap between us. "I missed you so much," he murmurs into my hair, and I want to say it back, but I just can't.

He brings his thumb to my face and wipes my cheeks dry, and I finally find my words. "You're really here," I say, and he nods and kisses me again.

"Yeah," he says. "I'm really here."

I can't help smiling at him. "I didn't think I'd ever see—" My words catch in my throat, but there's no reason to finish the sentence. He's here, and I just want to remember how it felt when I didn't wonder if he would be. I bury my face in his neck, warm from the sun and salty from the heat, and I stay there for a moment, just breathing him in. "I've missed you." This time I say it out loud, and when my hands find his hair again, I let my fingertips get lost in it, then pull back so I can see his face. He looks gorgeous and sun-kissed and so . . . here.

He stretches out next to me and we prop ourselves up on our elbows facing each other, and suddenly I feel like we're back on Ko Tao, lying on the beach, wishing we were kissing, and wondering what to do with our hands. But this time we both seem to know exactly what to do with them, and when he kisses me again, my hand goes straight for the bit of skin peeking out between his T-shirt and jeans, and I grip his waist, feeling the curve of his hip beneath my fingers. I'm relieved when he tightens his arms around me, because I still can't seem to get close enough to him to believe this is actually happening. We finally separate from each other, but just barely, and I rake my fingers through his dark tumble of bangs and let them linger there as I watch his face, lit by the morning sun but brightened by something else entirely.

"You look surprised to see me," he says.

I laugh under my breath. "How are you here right now?"

"I told you I'd keep coming back until you were sick of me." The corners of his mouth turn up in a half smile. "What?" he asks. "You didn't believe me?"

"No." I shake my head. "I wasn't sure what to believe." I'm still not sure. But right now, I just want to know that he isn't going to disappear at any second. I rest my forehead against his. "Are you back for good?"

"Yeah," he says as his eyes light up, "I'm back."

"How do you know you won't . . ."

Bennett looks at me and his expression turns serious. "I was here yesterday." His eyes move behind us to the grove of trees at the top of the beach and I follow his gaze. "I wanted to be sure I was really back in control again before . . ." His voice trails off and he lets out a heavy sigh. "It was all I could do to stay away, but . . . I was looking at you, and for a second

I thought that maybe it was better if I—I don't know. . . . You just looked so happy."

"I was. But I'm happier now."

He smiles. "Are you sure?"

"Yeah, definitely."

"La Paz, huh?"

"Where else?" I picture the circuitous routes of our travel plans, how the lines crossed in one only place. I rest my hand on his waist again, tracing tiny circles on his bare skin. "Tell me everything," I say. "Where have you been? What have I missed?"

He leans forward and kisses the tip of my nose. "You haven't missed much. I spent the last month and a half watching you."

"Watching me?" I lean back so I can see his face.

"You were right. That morning at the Northwestern track—I *was* there. I just hadn't done it yet." He reaches over my shoulder, grabs a little bundle of my curls, and twists them around his finger. "Ever since the night you got knocked back, I've been stuck in San Francisco. I tried to travel, but no matter what date or time I chose, I'd arrive at the same place: Monday, March 6, 1995, 6:44 a.m. At that damned track. God, it was like being stuck in *Groundhog Day*. I could only stay for a minute or so before I got knocked back, but it was the only place I could go, so that's where I went."

"I *knew* it was you." I knew I wasn't crazy.

He shoots me a small smile and keeps talking. "For some reason, at the beginning of this month, something changed.

Instead of landing at the track on March 6, I arrived on a sunny day in May and you *knew* me. And since then, everything's been slowly returning to normal. Every day I could travel a little bit further, stay a little bit longer, but I still couldn't get back to you—to Evanston or here—until yesterday."

"So what changed?"

"I don't know," he says, "but I bet *you* do. What did you do differently?"

I think back to the beginning of the month and it all comes back to me to me in a rush. *Are you aware of the date, Señorita Greene? June first, señor.* That was the day I decided not to stay in Evanston, moping around town and waiting for Bennett to return. The day I listened to *Anna's* advice and put myself on the other path—the one I wanted to be on. The day I made it possible for Bennett to come back.

"I decided to come here," I say. "You never came back. When Argotta told me about this trip, I just knew I needed to come here."

"Without me." He looks at me with a sad smile and I nod, and for a long time after that, we're quiet. "I should have told you about the letter."

"Yeah, you should have." I bring my fingers to his cheek, and when his eyes find mine I give him a smile that says he's forgiven. He smiles back, but I can tell he's thinking about something. I wonder if he's wishing he could do it over again, but I have a feeling his rules are back in place and we won't be changing our own history again any time soon. "So, do I know everything *now*?"

He lets out a laugh and looks at me again. "Yeah, you're all caught up. I have absolutely no idea what happens from here."

"Good." I watch him, thinking that my whole future suddenly looks different again. I'll get to feel that uncomfortable twist in my stomach and I'll poke the sharp end of little red pins into my wall-size map and I'll kiss him in romantic little villages and we'll drink lattes in hidden coffee shops.

"You know what you need to see next?" he asks, and I smile and shake my head. "Paris."

I remember how we walked along the path back at Devil's Lake, Bennett excited about teaching me how to climb a rock and me wishing we were in a Parisian café. He stops, and an impish grin forms on his face. "Are you hungry for breakfast?"

"Breakfast?" I laugh and look around the empty beach. "Now?" He wants to take me to breakfast. In Paris. Right now. I look down at the running clothes, dried on my skin.

"Why not?" He stands up and holds out his hand.

I consider my clothes again, but within a matter of seconds, I've decided I don't care, because after all, it's *breakfast in Paris.* I let him help me up.

We stand there on the beach, and I put my hands in his. He smiles, and I can see how excited he already is to show me something new. "You ready?"

I start to say yes. But then I stop. I look around at the water, at the rocks and the cliffs and the mountains that serve as a backdrop. And suddenly I don't want to be in Paris. I don't want to be anywhere else but here. I drop one of his hands, breaking our ability to travel in the way to which we've become accustomed, and I wrap myself up in his arms as I lean back into his chest.

"See that yellow umbrella way down there?" I point to the other side of the beach and look up at his face.

He squints as he stares into the distance. "Yeah." He looks down at me with a puzzled smile.

"That place has the *best* Mexican coffee in town."

His smile turns soft with understanding. "Does it, now?"

I nod as if I'm some kind of expert on La Paz. And I am. At least as far as present company is concerned. "It does." Bennett brings his hand to my face and kisses me like there's no better place in the world to be right now anyway.

I knit my fingers together with his. Then I reach down and pick up my San Francisco postcard from the sand and wave it in the air. "Come on," I say as we start off for the umbrella. "My turn to buy you one."

He bumps my hip. I bump his back. And we walk down the beach toward something he's never seen before.

time after time

Time will explain.

JANE AUSTEN

august 2012

1

san francisco, california

Nothing's changed. I was gone for three months, I've been home for three more, and still, everything here is exactly the same as it was before I left.

"You guys going to Megan's party next week?" Sam asks.

My gaze travels around the circle as everyone nods. Of course they're going. Summer is almost over and Megan's parents are loaded and never home, a combination that pretty much guarantees copious opportunities to drink and hook up.

"What about you?" Sam points at me with his chin. "You in, Coop?"

"Can't," I say, avoiding his eyes. "I'll be out of town." I tip my head back and down my Gatorade. The eight of us have been skating around Lafayette Park for the last hour and I'm parched.

"Again?" He reaches in for a handful of Doritos and then passes the bag around. "You missed her last party, and that was epic." Everyone nods again. Ryan parrots Sam with a "Seriously epic."

I look away as I shrug it off. "I hate to miss it, but I promised my mom I'd go see my grandmother before school starts." I feel a little guilty about these back-to-back lies: I probably wouldn't go to Megan's party, even if I was sticking around, and my mom has no idea that I'm going to see my grandmother.

Sam clears his throat and looks around the circle. "Who's got the chips?" Drew takes a big handful and everyone keeps the bag moving until it eventually makes its way back to Sam. "You sure there isn't another reason you're leaving town?" he asks. The crunching stops as all the guys turn and look at us, waiting for me to reply.

I lean back on my skateboard. "Like what?" My heart starts racing, but I force myself to stay still. To look cool and unfazed. I push Anna out of my mind, hoping that will make me look more convincing.

A smile tugs at the corners of Sam's mouth. I can feel the rest of the guys shifting in place around us. Sam suddenly reaches into the bag and chucks a chip at my head, and I duck out of the way as it flies past me. "I'm just giving you shit," he says, and everyone laughs as the crunching sounds return.

Ryan pulls his phone from his pocket and checks the screen. "Break's over." He stands up, pops his board into his hand, and takes off for the flat cement area surrounded by NO SKATE-BOARDING signs. He's right. We've probably got another ten minutes before one of the neighbors calls the cops.

Everyone else takes off, but Sam and I hang behind. I hold the chip bag out to him, and just as he's about to take it, I tip my head back and shake the rest of the crumbs into my mouth.

"Here." I hand it to him.

"You suck," he says, but he's smiling as he takes the empty bag from me and stuffs it into his backpack. I can see him staring at me out of the corner of my eye, but then he shakes his head hard and looks away. "So," he says, intentionally making his voice sound lighter. "Lindsey and I ran into her at the movies the other night."

"Her?" I wipe the grease and chip dust from my mouth with my shirtsleeve. "*Her* who?"

He looks at me like he can't believe I'd ask. "Megan." Then he adds, "*Hot* Megan."

"The one who throws all the parties?"

"Yes, that Megan. How many *hot* Megans do you know?"

I shrug. "I don't know. At least"—I count on my fingers— "four." He rolls his eyes.

"Well, I don't know about the other three, but this one asked about you. Again. She told me to make sure I bring you to her party this time." He looks at me expectantly, as if I should leap up off the ground and hurry home to rearrange my flight. Instead, I stand up slowly and reach for my board.

"Sorry, I would, but—"

"I know," he says. "Your grandma. In Illinois. Who's sick."

"Exactly."

Sam stands up too, and steps hard on the end of his board so it flips into his hand. "Look, you've managed to avoid her all summer, but when school starts next week, you won't have a choice. The way I see it, there is only one reason you wouldn't ask Megan out."

"Because she's kind of . . . vacuous?" She's a junior, a year younger than all of us, and I haven't spoken to her long enough to know if this is true or not. But I feel compelled to steer Sam away from his "one reason."

He looks back at me. "If you really don't like her, I get it. But she's Lindsey's friend, you know? The four of us could go out sometime. It might be fun." My mind flashes on an image of Anna, Emma, Justin, and me, walking into a movie theater, my arm draped over Anna's shoulder and Emma's arm threaded through Justin's. I already have a "four of us." Or at least, I did.

I run my hand through my hair. "I'll think about it, okay?" I won't, but hopefully I put enough sincerity in my voice to make him think I will.

"Don't think about it. Just ask her out. Because, seriously, she's nice and really cool and, in my humble opinion, not at all vacuous. And Lindsey likes her," he adds, knowing that could be a selling point.

The rest of the guys come back to grab their stuff and I'm relieved. They mutter good-byes and start down the path that leads to the bottom of the hill. Sam follows them, but then stops and looks back at me. "You coming?"

"I'm going to grab a coffee," I say, gesturing toward the Fillmore Street shops in the opposite direction. He gives me a quick "See ya" and takes off with everyone else as I head the other way.

When they're out of sight, I double back to the bench overlooking the bay and watch the sailboats skim across the water.

Nothing's changed, but everything's different now. Because Anna sat here once, right next to me, and handed me a letter that told me I'd meet her someday. I wish she'd warned me that once I had, I wouldn't quite know how to be here without her.

2

When I reach our house at the top of the hill, I open the front door and toss my skateboard and backpack on the floor in the foyer next to the giant houseplant. I'm heading upstairs to my room when I hear something strange coming from the kitchen. It sounds like chopping. And . . . singing.

Dad shouldn't be home from work yet and Mom had a planning meeting for one of her fund-raisers tonight. I turn around and head for the kitchen, and that's where I find my sister, Brooke. Her hair is pulled back in a ponytail and she's standing at the island, surrounded by vegetables.

She's now humming under her breath as she brings her knife down hard and slides it through a bundle of asparagus.

"What on earth are you doing?" I ask, and she looks up wearing a smile and gives me a little wave with the knife. She goes back to chopping as I walk around the kitchen, staring at the mountain of fresh produce, assessing the situation.

"I thought I'd make stir fry for dinner," she says proudly.

I stand next to her, leaning back against the counter. "Since when do you know how to make stir fry?"

She shrugs and continues chopping. "I don't. I'm practicing for my new dorm-food-free life. Caroline texted me earlier and right this minute, as we speak, she is lugging boxes from her Prius into our new apartment. Shona will be there tomorrow." She looks over at me. "One of us is going to need to know how to cook."

Brooke sets the knife on the cutting board, then gathers up the asparagus and drops it into a bowl. Then she brushes her hands together. "In a few more days I'll be back in Boulder, done with the dorms forever and settling into my new room." She looks right into my eyes. "And I'll be living with people I actually like again. Cool roommates. Like I had in Chicago."

Brooke and I have spent most of our summer talking about the three months I spent in 1995 Evanston while she was stuck in 1994 Chicago. She told me about the two roommates she found through the *Sun-Times* and the loft they shared in Wrigleyville. How she spent her days waiting tables at a local restaurant and her evenings watching live music at the local clubs. Her roommates liked everything, from jazz to punk, and they saw it all. Even folk night every Tuesday, where a heavyset woman sat on a wooden stool with her acoustic guitar, playing old songs like "American Pie" and "Leaving on a Jet Plane" to a packed house that sang along. As I suspected she would, Brooke settled in just fine. And like me, she would have been happy to stay where she was a lot longer.

But one Sunday afternoon, she and her roommates were hanging out on the rooftop deck, enjoying the sun and reading the paper, when one of them spotted a story about the city's plans to demolish the Chicago Stadium. Brooke's ears perked up. She hadn't been back in over two months—not since the night the two of us lost each other.

That afternoon she took an El train and two buses to the stadium. It was closed, but she walked around, peeking through the windows, trying to get a better view, and remembering how she watched me disappear before her eyes while Pearl Jam played on stage.

She made it all the way to the back entrance before she felt the stabbing pain in her stomach, and less than a minute later she was doubled over, screaming and squeezing her eyes shut. When she opened them again, she was crouched down in the same position, but the Chicago Stadium was gone, her Chicago roommates were gone, and she was alone in my room in San Francisco in the exact spot we originally left from.

"So . . ." Brooke reaches for the broccoli and goes back to chopping. "Are you still going to see Anna?"

There's no one else home, but I still take a paranoid glance around the kitchen before I answer. "Yeah. She gets back from her exchange on Saturday. I thought I'd go on Wednesday. Give her a few days to see her friends and get settled post-Mexico."

"And what are you going to tell Mom?"

I shrug. "I already told her: I'm going on a climbing trip with Sam."

Now it's Brooke's turn to scan the room and verify that we're still alone. "You know," she says quietly, "you'd make things a lot easier on yourself if you'd just go to Evanston and return back here as if you never left."

I stare at her but she doesn't look up. "And do three whole days over again? If *I* do those days over, I'm pretty sure that means *you* do, too. You really want to do over three entire days of your life?"

"That depends," she says. "If I got another speeding ticket, that'd be a plus. But if I met some amazing guy and you wiped him out, I'd never forgive you." Brooke glances up and shoots me a grin. "Not that I'd remember any of this."

"Well, I have no idea what I'd wipe out the second time around. So, if it's all the same to you, I'm going to stick with the climbing thing."

Brooke clears her throat. "Of course, you could also make it easier on yourself by just telling Mom and Dad where you're going."

"You know I can't do that."

Brooke knows everything, but I've said very little to my parents about my time in Evanston. Surprisingly, they barely asked any questions, not even about my grandmother, Maggie. They just sat me down in the living room and told me that the traveling needed to stop immediately. That it's far too dangerous, and I don't have control over it. And that it's time I started "living in the present," as Mom put it. "Like a normal person." I don't think Dad agreed completely, but he sat by her side and nodded anyway.

⌒⌒

That was three months ago. I don't even want to think about how furious Mom would be if she found out about all the concerts Brooke and I have traveled to this summer. Or that I went to 1995 La Paz last week. Or that, say, Anna Greene exists.

"I have an idea." Brooke elbows me and says, "Take me with you," like it's no big deal.

I laugh.

"No way, Brooke." She gives me a pleading look, as if that will have an impact on my decision.

"No," I repeat, this time with a little more weight in my voice. "Besides, you'd blow my cover. Climbing trips require *camping*." I raise my eyebrows and stare at her. "Mom and Dad would never believe you'd go camping."

"I can camp!" She crosses her arms, tapping her manicured fingernails against her skin. "I can camp," she repeats. I look at her sideways.

Then she brings her hands to her hips and looks me straight on. "Look, I'm your sister," she says, her tone serious, "and she's your girlfriend, and it's not like you can bring her here, you know . . . *ever*. And you're definitely not going to bring Mom and Dad there. So you might as well have the whole 'meet the parents' moment with me."

"No. Way."

"Please . . ." She presses her palms together in front of her. "You know she wants to meet *me*." She looks at me out of the corner of her eye and shoots me the look she reserves for moments when she knows she's right. And she is. When I brought Anna to present-day San Francisco, she got knocked back right away. She would love to know the people in my world the same way I know the ones in hers, but she never will.

I take off for the refrigerator but I can feel Brooke's eyes boring into my back. Eventually she gives up and heads for the stove, and the room fills with the sound of sizzling oil. "Brooke?" I say, and she takes a quick look over her shoulder at me. She doesn't say anything, but I know she's listening. "If anything comes up, will you cover for me?"

"Again?" she asks.

"Yes," I say. "Again."

I see her nod. "Of course." Things get quiet for a while, and then she adds, "What are you going to do with the Jeep?"

"What do you mean?"

"You can't leave it in the garage if they think you're going camping. They know Sam doesn't have a car."

"Hmm. Good point." If I park the Jeep on a random street or in a parking lot somewhere, it will definitely get towed. I can't leave it at Sam's house without coming up with some complicated excuse. I can't believe that the Jeep didn't even occur to me.

"You know my friend Kathryn?" Brooke asks.

"Yeah."

"She didn't need her car at school, and her parents didn't

want it taking up room in the driveway, so they rented a garage." There's a long pause. "They found it on Craigslist."

"Thanks," I say, making a mental note to hit the website after dinner.

"See? You kind of need me." Brooke doesn't turn around, but I think I hear smug satisfaction in her voice. Until she looks over her shoulder wearing a disheartened half smile, and there isn't a trace of smugness in her expression. She just looks sad.

"Hey, what were you humming earlier?"

She thinks about it for half a second. "Coldplay."

I pull my phone out of my pocket and do some speedy research. "Munich? In two thousand two? Looks like a small club."

Her head whips around and she lets out a squeal. "Really?" she asks. Her hands are clenched into fists by her sides, and when I nod, she dances back and forth in place. She turns the dial on the stove so the blue flame disappears underneath the burner and looks around the kitchen. "Mom and Dad are going to be so pissed when they come home to this mess."

"Yeah, but they'll never remember it." *This* we'll do over. Messing with multiple days feels dangerous. Going back a few hours in time so we don't have to tell Mom and Dad we were in Munich for a Coldplay concert feels like a perk I should capitalize on. "When we get back, you can pick right up where you left off. We'll have dinner and pretend we're a happy family."

"We are a happy family."

"Trust me," I say as I navigate over to the club's website, "That's only because they're so glad you're back home, they've temporarily forgotten that they're furious at me for losing you in the first place. As soon as you're back at school, the three of us will be our usual bickering selves again." I click around until I find an interior view, and I pan and zoom on the best photo I can find. I have no way of knowing if it looked like this back in 2002, but chances are, even if they've done a remodel or two, the bathrooms are still in the same spot.

"Okay, we're set." I steal a glance at the clock on the microwave and by the time I turn around again, Brooke's standing in front of me, arms extended.

She looks down, assessing her outfit. "Am I good?" she asks, referring to her jeans, a plain-looking shirt, and a pair of flip-flops. I'm not so sure about flip-flops in March, but I don't want to waste time waiting for her to pick something else.

"Yeah. You're good." As soon as I take her hands, she grips mine hard and gives her arms a nervous shake like she always does. Then she squeezes her eyes shut.

I close mine, and we're gone.

On Wednesday afternoon, I pack up the Jeep with all my camping and climbing equipment, and then do one last check of the stuff that actually matters. The white plastic container is sitting on the front seat, and inside I've stored everything I'll need when I return: a dozen plastic bottles of water, a Starbucks Doubleshot, and a Red Bull six-pack.

The music's on loud and I'm so lost in my thoughts, I jump when I feel a tap on my shoulder. I slam the cover closed and flip around to find Mom with her hand over her mouth, looking amused. "Sorry!" She yells so she can be heard over the music. "I didn't mean to scare you."

"It's okay. Hold on." I lean in through the open window to turn down the volume.

"How's the packing going?" She glances from the hood of the car to the back cargo area, now filled to the brim with camping gear and colorful ropes. The soft top is already off and secured in place.

"Fine. I think I have everything."

"Good . . . that's good." She stands there, nodding and smiling, like she's gathering the nerve to say something else. She distributes her weight onto both feet and roots herself in place.

"What?" The tone of my voice makes it pretty clear that I don't really want to know.

"Is there any chance I can get you to change your mind about this camping trip?" She folds her arms across her chest. "It's just that . . . Brooke is going back to Boulder this weekend and then you'll be starting your senior year, and these are the last few days we have together as a family."

I want to tell her that we've had a whole summer and we haven't done anything "together as a family" with a single second of it. I'm not sure what makes her think this is the week to start, other than the fact that I'm leaving town and she doesn't want me to.

"It'll be fine, Mom. I want to go climbing with my friends,"

I say, smashing my sleeping bag deep into the back of the Jeep so it won't blow away when I start driving. "It's only for a few days. I'll be back by Friday." That part's true, so I turn around when I say it.

"You won't have *any* cell phone coverage?"

"Probably not. You know how it is out there. You can try, but it's really spotty." Yeah. Mainly because my cell phone will be in the glove compartment of the Jeep, locked in a clown-car-sized garage I found on Craigslist yesterday.

"Bennett?"

"Yeah?"

"You're not traveling, are you?" she asks, her forehead creased.

I freeze, then force my expression to look relaxed. "You told me *not* to travel."

"Yes. I did."

I shrug and look straight into her eyes. "And that's why I'm packing up my car to go camping." Is that a lie? Technically it's not, but I'm pretty sure Mom wouldn't see it the same way. She stares at me and I wait. I don't know if I just said the right thing or the wrong thing, or something so in between the two that she can't quite figure out what to do with it.

She looks worried and, God, I wish she wouldn't be. If only she'd relax and trust that I have this whole thing under control, I could tell her *everything*—about Maggie and Anna and the Greenes. And then she'd know exactly where I'm going and when I'll be back and what's inside the box on the passenger seat that she keeps eyeing but hasn't asked about.

"Be careful, okay?"

"I always am." I kiss her on the cheek. "You worry too much, Mom." I want to say more, but I don't.

I can tell from the look on her face that she has a lot more to say too, but instead, she just gives me a somber-looking smile and says, "You make it pretty hard not to, sweetie," and leaves it at that.

august 1995

3

evanston, illinois

When I push the door open, the little cluster of bells bangs against the glass and a guy standing over at the New in Paperback table turns around and gives me a quick glance. I step inside and look around. I've never seen the bookstore so crowded.

I walk down the main aisle, looking for Anna between the bookshelves. I'm halfway through the store when I see her behind the counter. She's ringing up a customer, so I keep a bit of a distance and wait, and try to ignore my heart smacking against my rib cage.

Her hair is longer than I remember it, and it occurs to me that every time I saw her in La Paz over the summer she was wearing it up in a clip or a ponytail. It's even curlier now, and I feel the familiar urge to pull on one of those strands so I can watch it spring back into place. What's different about her?

She looks tanned and happy and . . . somehow even more beautiful than before.

She's making small talk with the customer, fingers flying as she punches numbers into the register, and then she takes his credit card and runs it through some loud contraption and hands his card back to him. And that's when she sees me.

I just smile. I watch as her expression changes, morphing into this perfect mix of surprise and relief.

Anna looks back at the customer and pushes the overstuffed bag in his direction. "Here you go," she says with giddiness that the moment doesn't call for. Her eyes keep darting in my direction.

"Thanks," he says.

"Any time. Have a good quarter."

Instead of reaching for the bag, he rests one hip against the counter and watches her, like he's expecting her to say something else. I wonder if he thinks that smile is for him. He is standing right in front of her, after all. But I can tell from this vantage point that she's not looking *at* him, she's looking *past* him. Anna has lots of different smiles, but the one she's wearing right now is one she reserves for me.

"Bye," she says, pushing the bag across the counter again, this time with more force, and he must get the message because he grabs it with both hands and heads for the front door.

She starts heading in my direction. "Shoot," the guy says, "I almost forgot." He turns around and struts back to the counter, and Anna returns to her spot behind the register, looking official again.

I watch her, picturing that surprised look she wore on her face just a moment ago. I think about how nice it would be to see it one more time.

No one's ever in the Travel section, so I take a chance. Ducking back behind the shelves, I hide from her view and close my eyes. I picture the row on the opposite side of the store, and when I open them, I'm standing in it. I take my backpack off and set it down by my feet.

I can still hear her voice at the counter but now I'm too far away to make out what she's saying. I stare down at the shelf marked with the word MEXICO, remembering the night I came in here last April.

I should have been studying, but couldn't stop thinking about her. All day, I'd been looking for a chance to get her alone so I could tell her the second part of my secret, but I never found one. So before I could change my mind, I fed my arms into the sleeves of my jacket and walked to the bookstore.

Her face completely lit up when she saw me walk in, and all I wanted to do was kiss her. Instead, I told her I was there to pick up a book on Mexico. She led me over here to the Travel section.

At first, we talked about our assignment, but then she stopped me in midsentence and said, "I want to hear the rest of the second thing." When I looked in her eyes, I knew she meant it. And so I told her everything. That I was born in 1995. That I'm seventeen in 2012. That I wasn't supposed to be here. That I could visit, but I couldn't stay.

And then, against my better judgment, I finally did what

I'd wanted to do since the day I met her. I came up on my knees and I kissed her, no longer caring about my rules or where and when I was supposed to be. Just as I was about to pull away like I knew I should, I felt her hands on my back, drawing me in until we were pressed against the bookcase and there was nowhere else for us to go but closer to each other. I kissed her harder.

The bells on the door jingle, snapping me back to reality.

"Bennett?" I hear Anna call from across the room.

I duck around the corner and press my chest into the end of the shelving unit, keeping my eyes fixed on the aisle and waiting for her to walk by. I don't see or hear her, so I stay silent as I listen for breathing and wait for her to come into view.

I'm just about to take a step forward when I feel her hands grip my sides. I jump.

"Gotcha," she whispers in my ear. Her forehead falls against the back of my neck and her arms wrap around me. I can feel her breathing.

"That's an understatement," I say, bringing her hands to my face, kissing her fingers.

"I didn't see where you went," she says.

"Yeah." I let out a small laugh. "Remember? I do that."

"Just to mess with me." I can hear the eye roll in her voice.

"Just to mess with you."

"Maybe you should start thinking about doing more with this little talent of yours than surprising your girlfriend."

"Say that last part again."

She laughs. Squeezes me harder. "Surprising your *girlfriend*."

I smile. "I like the way that sounds." I loosen her grip on my waist and turn around. Her whole face is lit up so bright, I swear we could turn off all the lights in the bookstore and still see each other perfectly.

"Hi." I twist a strand of her curls around my finger.

"Hi." She reaches up and musses my hair. "You're here," she says, but something in her voice makes her sound unsure.

"I'm here." I bring my hands to her cheeks. "I've missed you like crazy." She presses her lips together and gives me the slightest nod, and before she can say anything I tip her head back and kiss her, softly, slowly, savoring the feeling of being here in this room with her again. I kiss her harder. And just like that first night, she kisses me back, pulling me into her, like she still wants me here and still trusts me with her heart, even though she probably knows by now that she shouldn't.

4

When the clock reads 9:02, Anna walks the perimeter of the store, shutting off lights and adjusting books as she goes. I flip the sign on the door from OPEN to CLOSED, and we step outside. She presses some buttons on the keypad by the door to set the alarm, and clicks the deadbolt in place behind us.

I reach for her hand and we walk in silence toward the end of the block. The familiar sounds from the coffeehouse grow louder with each step, and I take a big whiff of the air, inhaling the scent. We're about to pass the entrance when Anna stops. "Do you want to go in and get something? We could hang out for a bit."

I peer through the window. It's not nearly as busy as it is when bands play on Sunday nights, but it's still pretty crowded. All of the couches are taken and the only option I see is a high table in the middle of the room. I've hardly been alone with her all summer, and I really don't feel like sharing her with anyone else tonight. "I was hoping for something a bit quieter."

She pivots so she's facing me and reaches for my other hand. "In that case, you have two choices: my room or yours. Who do you want to face first, my parents or Maggie?"

I make the sound of a game-show buzzer. "I don't like either of those. What's my third choice?"

She laughs and shakes her head slightly at me. "There's no third choice."

"Sure there is."

Anna raises her eyebrows and stares at me.

"We'll bypass the parents and just sneak up to your bedroom. No one needs to know I'm in town yet."

"Too late. I already told them you were coming tonight."

I snap my fingers and laugh under my breath. "Damn." Anna shakes her head at me again while I think about my options. "I'm not ready for Maggie yet," I say, and Anna gives me an understanding nod and drops my other hand. We continue walking toward her house.

"So, how did they take it?" I ask.

"My parents?" She shrugs. "Pretty well, I guess. Mom was cooler about you being back than Dad was, which kind of surprised me. Actually, he wasn't too upset until I mentioned that you came to visit me in La Paz. He wasn't at all pleased about that." Her head spins toward mine. "Oh, and I said you visited twice, not four times, so stick to that if he asks, okay?"

I silently hope he won't ask. I'm also silently disappointed that she's started lying to her parents. She didn't do that before I showed up.

"I can't tell what they really think," she says. "The other night, my mom came into my room to tell me that she likes you, and that she's glad we'll get to spend our senior year together. She actually looked giddy when she started talking about homecoming and prom and stuff." I feel the lump rise in my throat and I swallow it back down. "But then she and my dad must have talked about it again, because last night at dinner, they laid it on thick. I got this big lecture about making sure I continue to focus on my running and not let my grades slip because of you."

"Because of me?"

"I know, right?" She winks at me. "As if."

I raise one eyebrow. "As *if*?"

She shrugs again. "Come on, you're not *that* big a deal."

"Nah. Of course I'm not," I say, suppressing a grin.

She squeezes my hand. "You are, you know?"

I squeeze hers back. "You are too."

We pass the hedge that lines her neighbor's yard, and Anna's house comes into view. It looks exactly the same as it did when I left last May, with its wraparound porch and overgrown shrubs. There's a soft light glowing from the kitchen window like it always does at night.

Once we're inside, Anna leads me toward the sound coming from the living room. We turn the corner and I spot her parents. Mrs. Greene has her feet curled up underneath her and she's resting her head on Mr. Greene's shoulder. They're watching some old TV show. Which, I instantly remind myself, probably isn't old at all.

Anna stops at my side and grips my arm with both hands. The movement must catch her dad's attention, because he suddenly looks up and sees us. His eyes grow wide and he gives Mrs. Greene a little nudge that makes her sit up straight. "Hi. We didn't hear you come in." He aims the remote at the TV and mutes the sound.

Mr. Greene stands up, extending his hand, and even though it feels overly formal for him—for us—I reach out and shake it politely. Anna's mom gives me a halfhearted wave from her spot on the couch. "It's nice to have you back," she says, but her voice sounds hollow and insincere. Then she adds the word "Finally." It's not an afterthought; it's more like it was the one word she was trying *not* to say, but couldn't quite keep from slipping out.

"It's good to see you both too," I say. Then I stand there, nodding and waiting for one of them to say more and feeling my stomach sink. I should probably be happy they aren't outwardly furious with me. After all, not only did I disappear on their daughter in the middle of a date, I disappeared from all of their lives in the middle of, well, *everything*. I know it would be too much to expect a motherly hug or a fatherly back-pat, and I was hardly expecting tears of joy at the sight of my face in their living room. But I was sort of hoping we wouldn't be starting from scratch. Or, as it appears to be, less than scratch.

Anna gives my arm a squeeze and I look over at her. Unlike her mom's blank stare, her expression speaks volumes. She's beaming at me, her eyes full of joy and wonder, like she can't believe I'm actually standing here. Without even thinking about it, I let out a relieved sigh and kiss her on the forehead; and she tightens her grip on my arm again and lifts herself up on her toes. She bounces in place a few times.

When I look over at her parents again, their eyes are locked on Anna. But then Mrs. Greene's gaze slowly travels over to me and the corners of her mouth turn up in a half smile, almost as if she can't help herself. I give her a grateful nod.

"How's your sister doing?" Mr. Greene's voice takes me by surprise and my head snaps in his direction.

"Um . . . She's good." I quickly come up with a way to phrase the rest of my response to give him as little information as possible. "It was touch and go for a while there, but she's back home now." I leave it at that and hope that he doesn't press me for more information, because if he does, I'll have to lie to him and I'd really like to stop doing that.

"All great to hear." He waits for a moment, and then it looks like he's about to say something else. "Ah, never mind, you probably don't want to talk about it."

"Not really," I say.

The cagey thing probably isn't winning me any points, but now that I think about it, that could be a good thing. If I'm starting at the bottom, I won't have as far to fall once they learn the truth.

"We're going to go upstairs," Anna says, jumping in with

a rescue. Before her parents can say anything else, she leads me out of the room. We've only climbed the first two stairs when we hear her mom yell, "Leave your door open." Anna stops, gripping the banister with one hand and hiding her face behind the other.

She shakes it off. "Follow me. I'm dying to show you something."

Not much has changed since the last time I was in this room. Anna's impressive CD collection takes up every bit of shelf space, broken up only by the dozens of racing trophies that hold the alphabetized jewel cases in place. The walls are plastered with paper race numbers that were once pinned to her jersey and photos of her breaking through finish-line tape.

The bulletin board over her desk still holds the same lonely Pearl Jam concert stub from March 1994, but next to it I spot something new: a framed photo of Anna, Emma, and Justin. Emma's mouth is open wide, like she's squealing. She's standing behind Justin with her arms wrapped loosely around his neck, and Anna's on his right, her head resting on his shoulder. The picture must have been taken last June, after I left town but before Anna took off for La Paz. They look happy.

"How's Emma?"

"Eh, not so good. I went over to her house right after I got home and she told me that she and Justin broke up over the summer."

"Really? Why?"

Anna turns her back to me, runs her finger along the jewel cases, and selects one. "I don't know *why* exactly, because I haven't heard Justin's side of the story yet—I stopped by the record store the other day and he was too busy to talk—but according to Emma, he doesn't think they have enough in common . . . that they're better as friends."

She drops the disc in her CD player, and when the music begins, it sounds familiar, but I can't place the song. But then the lyrics begin and I instantly recognize Alanis Morissette's voice. I'm trying to recall which album this is when Anna says, "Have you heard this before?" She waves the case for *Jagged Little Pill* in the air, and I nod. "I love her. I've been running to this CD all summer." I wish I could tell Anna that she has a lot more Alanis to look forward to, but I keep it to myself. Instead I tell her that I'll look up the tour schedule and take her to a concert.

I spot the map that takes up the largest wall in her room. I walk over to it and stand there, counting the number of little red pins Anna uses to mark her travels. Nine, including the new one at the bottom of the Baja peninsula. Five more than the first time I stood here, admiring Anna's intense desire to see the world and enjoying the idea that I could give her a small piece of it.

I turn around and find her standing next to me. "Here." She hands me a small bag and I peek inside. My Westlake student ID. A blank postcard from Ko Tao. The postcard Anna wrote to me in Vernazza Square. A stubby yellow pencil. A carabiner.

One of her pins. "You left them in your desk at Maggie's. She thought I should hold on to them for you."

"Thanks." I remove the postcard from Vernazza, shooting her a glance as I run my finger across the edge. Anna's watching me as I read it, and I feel myself suck in a breath when I get to the last line, *wherever you are in this world, that's where I want to be*, and a wave of guilt washes over me. My chest feels heavy as I drop the card back in the bag and then toss the whole thing on the floor next to the door along with my backpack. "Is that what you wanted to show me?"

Anna's eyes light up. "Nope." She turns on her heel and crosses the room. She crouches down low, wrestling with something underneath her bed.

"Close your eyes," she calls over her shoulder.

Less than a minute later, I feel her behind me, her hands on my waist, pushing me forward. "Keep 'em closed. A few more steps. Okay, stop." I feel her next to me. "You can open them now."

It takes a moment for my eyes to adjust, and I'm not exactly sure where I'm supposed to be looking. But then I see something lying flat on top of her bedspread, and I take a few steps closer.

It's a photograph, printed on a huge sheet of thick-looking paper. I recognize the tall rocks and jagged cliffs immediately. "Is that our beach?" I ask, but I already know it is. That's the spot where I found her in La Paz. The same place I've arrived off and on all summer to surprise her during her morning runs. I lean in close to get a better look. "This is incredible. How did you find a print of the *exact* spot?"

"It's not a print," she says as she rests her hands on her hips. "I took it."

I know nothing about photography, but it looks pretty impressive to me. I can see every tiny crack in the rock face, and the tall cliff is perfectly mirrored in the water below. "You took this?"

"Señora Moreno helped me." I remember her telling me that her host mom in La Paz was also a local photographer. "I thought you could hang it on your bedroom wall." She doesn't clarify which bedroom and I decide not to ask.

"But wait . . . get this," she says, holding up a finger. Anna undoes the Velcro on a black canvas bag and removes a 35-millimeter camera. Her thumb glides along the back and over the buttons. "Look what she gave me. I guess it's pretty old, but I don't care." It looks ancient. I watch her twist the long lens, remove it from the body, and replace it with a fatter, stubbier one. She brings the camera to her face, and I can't see anything but her mouth. I hear the shutter snap and a weird, motorized sound.

Throwing the strap over her shoulder, she reaches under the bed again and returns holding a large envelope. She plops down on the floor and motions for me to join her. We sit close together, our hips touching, and she shakes a pile of images onto the shag rug and tells me the backstory on each one. There are lots of beaches and rocks and vista point views, but my eye goes straight to a close-up photo of a man with dark, wrinkled skin, holding a guitar and wearing the warmest smile.

"These are really good," I tell her. "*Really* good." I watch the flush creep into her cheeks.

"They have this darkroom in their basement. I spent hours in there with Señora Moreno and her daughter, learning how to develop film. It was incredible." She shrugs. "When I told Dad, he said he might be able to build one for me in that old shed in the backyard." She reaches for her camera and aims it at my face. "Until then, it's one-hour photo. Smile. I don't have a single picture of you."

I reach around her waist and pull her down onto the rug next to me. "There's no reason for a picture of me if you're not in it."

She laughs as she extends her arm as high in the air as she can and aims the lens at us. *Click.* She kisses me on the cheek. *Click.* She sticks out her tongue and I crack up. *Click.* And then, in one fluid series of motions, I take the camera out of her hands, set it on the floor, and roll over on top of her, kissing her like I've wanted to all night.

But the longer we kiss, the guiltier I feel. I promised I wouldn't keep secrets from her any longer. "Anna," I say. "There's something I need to tell you."

The knock is soft, but startling enough to send us scampering in opposite directions. The door was ajar as instructed and we didn't have much time, but we move so quickly that by the time Mrs. Greene's head pops in, Anna and I are already sitting up, a generous amount of shag rug between the two of us.

"Your dad and I are going to bed," she says.

"Okay. Good night," Anna says brightly.

Her mom clears her throat. "That means that Bennett needs to leave now."

"Mom—" Anna huffs.

"It's okay." I stand up quickly and cross the room toward my backpack. "I'll see you tomorrow," I say to Anna. I squeeze past Mrs. Greene and into the hallway, heading for the front door.

I'm just about to turn the knob when I hear Anna's voice behind me. "Wait a sec!" I turn around and find her halfway down the stairs. "Where are you going?" she whispers.

I shrug. "I don't know. I'll probably just go home and come back in the morning."

She looks around to be sure her dad's out of earshot. "What, like, home-home? San Francisco *home*?" She doesn't add *2012 home*, but I know that's what she means.

"Yeah, it's too late to go to Maggie's now. Don't worry. I'll be back tomorrow. I'll go over to her house and then we can go do something together."

She shakes her head hard. "No. I mean, you're here. You can't just . . . *leave*."

I don't want to leave, but I picture the look on Mrs. Greene's face a minute ago and think it's probably better not to push my luck tonight. I go could back to San Francisco, to the tiny garage, and crash in the Jeep. Or I could go back to my room and hope my parents don't walk in and find me. Come to think of it, maybe Anna's right. I might be better off staying put. I could always sleep on the couch in the back room of the bookstore.

Anna holds up a finger. "Don't move. I'll be right back." Before I can say another word, she's gone, flying back up the stairs.

I stand in the foyer and look around. On my left, I see the built-in bench, and on the wall above it, a row of empty coat hooks. It reminds me of the first time I came to this house. Anna had stayed home from school, and when I showed up, she took my jacket and hung it there. Then I told her my secret, showed her what I could do. Took her somewhere warm and far away. I consider doing it again tonight.

I hear her bare feet padding down the stairs. She's holding an armful of bedding. "You're sleeping on the couch."

My eyes dart to her parents' bedroom door at the top of the stairs. "No way." I rub my forehead hard with my fingertips and think about the idea. "Your parents actually said I could sleep on your couch?"

Anna nods. "Just for tonight. They agreed that it was too late for you to walk home in the dark. I told them you'd call Maggie and tell her not to expect you until tomorrow."

"I can't call Maggie," I whisper in her ear.

"I know. Just pretend to do it." She gestures toward the kitchen and I see the phone hanging on the wall next to the microwave. I cover my face with my hand. I wish I'd just said good night, gone outside, and *poof,* appeared back in her bedroom ten minutes later like I originally planned to.

"You can change in the downstairs bathroom." She points to a door I've never noticed before. "I'll go get you set up."

5

I fluff up the pillow and twist around in the blankets. For possibly the tenth time in the last hour, I sit up, resting my hands on my knees and staring out the sliding glass door and into the Greenes' backyard. According to the clock on the mantel, it's a quarter after midnight.

The last time I sat on this couch, Anna and I were wrapped up in this exact corner while Justin and Emma curled up on the opposite side. We watched a movie and took turns reaching into an enormous bowl of buttered popcorn that her mom made for us.

I throw my feet onto the floor and stand up. I walk through the kitchen and into the hallway, stopping at the bottom of the stairs. Her parents' door is open a crack. Anna's is completely shut. I'm about to close my eyes and bring myself to her bedroom, when I think of the look on her parents' faces tonight. Sure, if they caught me in their daughter's room, I could just go back five minutes, ten minutes, and do it all over. But going up there at all feels like a violation of their trust and I'm already on thin ice here.

There's no reason to rush things. I have plenty of time to see her tomorrow, the next day. I turn around, shuffle back to the couch, and collapse with my head in my hands. After a while, I settle into the pillow again and close my eyes, attempting to empty my mind. I finally feel like I'm about to drift off when I hear something that sounds like breathing.

I crack my eyes open, lift my head up, and see a silhouette in the doorway. "Oh, God. I'm sorry," Anna whispers. "I didn't mean to wake you."

"It's okay. . . . I wasn't sleeping." I sit up a little bit and gesture for her to come closer. She sits across from me on the coffee table. The sight of her, the sound of her voice in this room, fills me with relief. "What are you doing down here? What about your parents?"

"I checked. They're asleep. Trust me, once they're out, they're out."

She sweeps her hair away from her face and twists it around a finger, holding it against the back of her neck. "I couldn't sleep either. I've just been lying in bed, staring at my map, and thinking that, for the last few months, we've had all this distance between the two of us, you know?" She lets her hair fall, and then pushes it behind her ears. "And it suddenly dawned on me that tonight—finally—there was nothing between us but a door and a staircase, and it seemed"—she blinks fast—"silly."

I nod. "That's definitely silly." Even though the room is dark, lit only by the porch light on the back patio, I can see her blush. "I'm glad you remedied that." I say.

"Yeah, me too."

"But there's still more, you know?"

Her eyebrows lower and pinch together. "What do you mean 'more'?" she asks.

I stretch my arm out in her direction, angling it so my fingertip comes within a centimeter of her knee. "There's this distance here—a whole arm's length—which is really quite a lot if you think about it. This is, like, seventh-grade-dance kind of distance."

She laughs quietly. "That's not even silly. That's just . . . unacceptable."

"Right? And then there's this," I say, pinching a corner of the wool blanket she covered me with a little earlier. "What do you make of this?"

She reaches out, rubbing the fabric between her thumb and her forefinger. "Yeah, that's definitely a problem."

"Exactly what I was thinking."

I start to pull the blanket back, but before I can, Anna moves from the coffee table to the couch, sealing the opening shut with her weight. "What did you want to tell me earlier?" Her dark eyes fix on mine and I feel a sudden chill that hits my core. I wasn't expecting this turn in the conversation, and I'm trying to decide how to start, but she doesn't give me time.

"You aren't staying this year, are you?"

I shake my head no.

She rolls her shoulders back and looks up at the ceiling. "I knew it. Every time I've mentioned something about school, you've looked away and changed the subject." Her gaze ping-pongs around the room. Now she won't look at me. "Why not?"

"I can't."

"Can't or won't?"

"Can't." I sit up so I can face her straight on. "Look, I've been experimenting with this all summer. I even told everyone I was going on a two-week climbing trip and took off by myself. I pitched a tent where no one would find it and went to London. I wandered around, enjoyed the sights—missing you the whole time, by the way—but after three days, I was knocked back to the tent. The migraine was excruciating, but just like I did when I first got to Evanston, I immediately closed my eyes and brought myself back. It worked. I stayed another day, almost two. But then I got knocked back to the tent again. I kept bringing myself back, but each time . . ." I trail off, shaking my head, remembering migraines so debilitating I could barely open my eyes for nearly an hour. "The side effects got worse, not better. After a week, I closed my eyes and nothing happened."

"Why could you stay last time?"

I shake my head. "I don't know. I think it's because Brooke wasn't where she was supposed to be, you know? Like . . . things were off and once they were righted again . . ." Anna just stares at me, and I look at her, trying to figure out what she's thinking. "The two must be connected, because once she got back, I couldn't return here. And now it looks like my ability to stay here has changed too."

She still won't look at me and she clearly doesn't know what to say. She brings her hands to her forehead and rubs hard, like that will help the information sink in or something. "So, what? This is how it's going to be?" she asks.

"I don't know. This is the way it is right now."

I feel horrible. Back in the beginning, I prepared her for the fact that I couldn't stay here with her. I never should have let her believe that I could. I never should have let *myself* believe that I could.

"But I want to come back. A lot. I figure I can't visit too frequently or your parents will get suspicious, you know, but we can come up with, like, a schedule or something."

She doesn't say anything.

"If you think about it, this is how we always thought it was going to be, right up until Vernazza. Remember?" I stop one step short of saying what I'm really thinking: *You already agreed to be part of the most screwed-up long-distance relationship on the planet.*

She wrings her hands while she weighs the pros and cons of everything I've just said. We'll be together, but not every day, like we were before, and not on either of our terms. We won't go to the same school or hang out with the same people and, at least while we're both still living at home with our parents, we'll spend most of our days seventeen years away from each other. So many people take proximity for granted. We just want to be in the same place at the same time.

Her eyes are fixed on the carpet. "I can handle a lot, you know? I can handle everything about you and what you can do, but what happened last time . . . I can't let that happen to me again." She lifts her head and looks right at me. "I know you didn't *want* it to happen, and I realize you didn't do it on purpose, but you were here and then you were just *gone*, and when you didn't come back, I . . ."

She grabs a strand of hair and twists it around her finger. I'm just about to speak when she opens her mouth and looks me straight in the eye again. "Here's the thing. When you left, I sort of . . . fell apart." Her shoulders hunch forward and she starts breathing faster. "I mean, I *completely* fell apart," she repeats. "I don't fall apart, Bennett, and I don't want to *be* someone who falls apart and . . ." She inhales deeply and wraps her arms around her waist. "I can't let that happen again."

I look at her, bracing myself for what she's about to say. What she *should* say. She wants me to leave. She doesn't want me to come back here again.

"I need to think about it," she says.

The words aren't as bad as the ones I was expecting, but they still take me by surprise. "Yeah." It takes effort to keep my voice steady. "Of course you do."

She presses her lips together, hard, like she's holding something in, and I realize she's trying not to cry. But I wish she would. I wish she would just sit here and fall apart, like she apparently did when I left, because unlike last time, I could actually be there for her now. I could tell her everything I would have said then: That we'll be okay. That this whole thing is weird and twisted and unfair to both of us, but especially unfair to her, because it's always harder to be the one who's left behind than the one who leaves. And I'd tell her that I love her, and that I'll do anything to be with her, any way I can be.

"When are you leaving?"

I swallow hard. "Friday. I promised my mom I'd be home for the weekend. Brooke's heading back to college on Sunday." I start to tell her about our plans to take the boat out on the bay but I decide against it. "Then I start school on Monday."

She gives me a sad smile. "Me too."

We're both silent for a long time. She scoots back to her spot on the coffee table, and I think she's about to say good night and head back upstairs, but she doesn't move. I can tell she's contemplating what to do next, and I should probably stay silent and not say anything that might sway her decision to stay, but I can't help myself.

"I'm here now," I say quietly.

She looks up from under her lashes. Then her expression softens and a smile spreads across her face. "I'm glad." She reaches over, grabs the edge of the wool blanket, and rubs it between her thumb and her forefinger again. "There's still the matter of this, you know?"

My heart starts racing and I laugh, happy to follow her lead. "Is that *still* there?" I lift up the edge of the blanket and Anna climbs underneath, stretching out next to me. Her arms wrap around my waist and she wedges one of her legs between mine.

"Much better," she says, sliding her hands under my T-shirt, up my back, kissing me. In a matter of minutes, we both seem to forget about the complications around this whole crazy thing we're doing. For the rest of the night, it doesn't seem complicated at all.

6

I wake to the faint sound of water running. I try to lift my head off the pillow to take a better look, but my movement is restricted by the weight of Anna's head, buried in the crook of my neck.

I kiss her cheek. "Anna," I whisper. "Wake up." She tightens her grip on my shoulder and, without opening her eyes, settles into my chest and lets out a happy sigh.

The water sound stops and it's almost instantly replaced by a light plinking noise. I'm trying to place it when I hear the unmistakable—and extremely loud—whir of a coffee grinder.

Anna jumps and her lids pop open. The second she sees me, she lets out a gasp. She lifts her head and scans the living room.

"It's okay. We just fell asleep."

"My *dad's* in there," she whispers, her eyes darting back and forth between the kitchen and me.

"I know. It's okay," I repeat, thinking she didn't hear me the first time.

Her eyes grow even wider. "It's not *okay*! He can't find us like this. He'll never—" She comes closer, within an inch of my face. "I'm dead."

"Come on . . . just tell him we were talking and we fell asleep." I try to look at the scene from her father's point of view. Anna's shirt is back where it belongs but I have no idea where mine is.

"He'll never believe that."

I start to speak but she covers my mouth with her hand. *"Shhh."* The coffee grinder comes to a stop. She looks at me, wide-eyed. *Do something*, she mouths. *Please.*

It takes a second or two for understanding to kick in, possibly because I'm still a little groggy and she's whisper-shouting at me in the near dark. "You sure?" I mouth back, and she answers my question with a quick, panicky nod.

I find the clock immediately—God knows I stared at it enough last night—and check the time. A little after six thirty. I slide my hands under the blankets, feeling for hers, and when I find them I grip them tight.

Her eyes are already shut.

I kick the blanket onto the floor and squeeze my eyes closed as I picture her room. When I open them, we're on her bed, wrapped up in the exact same position we were on the couch— Anna curled up into my chest, our hands clenched together, our legs intertwined. I really don't want to move, but I have to twist away from her so I can read the clock on her nightstand. Six o'clock on the dot.

Minutes pass as we lie side by side, silent and unmoving. Then Anna bends her knees to her chest and starts quietly cracking up.

"See why you need to keep me around," I whisper, still looking up at the ceiling.

She stretches out and throws her arm over her forehead. Her head falls to one side and she looks at me. "There are lots of other reasons to keep you around."

I roll over on top of her, my legs straddling her hips, my face only inches away from hers. "So will you?" I kiss her. "Keep me around?"

She inhales sharply. "I'm still thinking about it."

"Good." I kiss her again. "How are you feeling?"

She crinkles her nose. "A little . . . twisty. But I don't feel sick or anything." She pushes my hair off my face but it just flops back down again. "How about you? How's your head?"

"It's good. But you know, I only feel the side effects on the return trip and only if I change time zones. I'm just popping back downstairs." I look over at the clock and kiss her again. "Unless you keep me here too long."

Anna glances at the time. "You should probably go. It's already ten after."

I plant a kiss on her cheek and then hop off the bed. I give her a little wave. She waves back. "See you downstairs," I say, closing my eyes and picturing her living room.

My eyelids pop open and I'm standing next to the couch, staring at the jumble of blankets we left behind. I see my shirt on the floor and pull it over my head. Then I crawl back under the covers, where I belong.

Twenty minutes later, Anna's dad peeks around the corner. He sees that I'm already awake and gives me a wave. I wave back and wonder if he checked in here last time and saw something quite different.

I hear the water running. The coffee beans tumble into the grinder. The whirring sound starts and stops. I wait for a few more minutes and then head toward the kitchen, where I'm greeted by the sounds of dripping and percolating and an unmistakable aroma that makes my mouth water. Anna's dad is wrapping the cord around the grinder and returning it to its home in the cupboard when he sees me out of the corner of his eye.

"Good morning."

I lift my chin in his direction. "Good morning, Mr. Greene."

He leans back against the counter. "How'd you sleep?" He crosses his arms and stares at me, and I feel the adrenaline start racing through my veins.

I rest my hip against the counter opposite him, hoping I appear calm and not at all guilty. I look at him straight on. "Great," I say. "Thanks for letting me stay last night."

He stares at me for what feels like a full minute. I hold my breath and try not to move.

Finally he uncrosses his arms and says, "No problem. Glad

we could help." His tone is friendly, and when he turns his back to me, I silently exhale.

He reaches into a high cabinet and pulls out two mugs. "Do you drink coffee, Bennett?"

"Yes, sir," I say, and he reaches into the cabinet again and grabs a third.

7

Two cups of coffee, three tall glasses of water, a bowl of cereal, and a couple of hours later, I leave the Greenes' and walk the four familiar blocks to Maggie's house. My heart is beating hard in my chest by the time I reach the porch, and speeds into a whole new gear when I pick up the lion's-head door knocker.

Sweat drips down the back of my neck and my shirt sticks to my skin. Today the weather may be different, but I'm just as nervous as I was when I stood in this same spot last March, bending the corners of an index card back and forth while I waited for her to answer the door.

I'd just come from the Northwestern student housing office. I had no way of recognizing the penmanship, but as I stood in front of the giant bulletin board, one card stood out, its letters carefully drawn and perfectly slanted, as if someone who cared how it looked had written it. I pulled out the thumbtack and turned it over to verify what I already knew. Then I went straight to the address.

When my grandmother opened the door, I introduced myself as a Northwestern student and asked her if her room was still available to rent. She wore a guarded expression, but nodded, and when I handed her enough cash for the remainder of the quarter—even though I had no intention of staying that long—she invited me in for tea and showed me my new room. But two months later I disappeared without saying a word, leaving behind a closet full of clothes, a brand-new SUV, and a bunch of questions Anna had to do her best to answer for me.

I hear the floorboards creak on the other side of the door. Maggie peeks through the curtains, takes one look at me, and disappears again. Everything's quiet. No floorboards creaking as she walks away, but no deadbolt snapping either.

Finally, the door opens. She's wearing a loose-fitting dress that hangs almost to the ground and, as usual, there's a brightly colored scarf draped around her neck. I look up at her face and when I see her eyes, I lock on to them. They're blue-gray and striking, but that's not the reason I can't stop staring at them. It's because I know them well. Her eyes are exactly the same color as my mother's. Exactly the same color as mine. I can't help wondering if she's thinking the same thing.

"Hi, Maggie," I say. For something to do, I shift my backpack from one shoulder to the other.

"Hi." She stares at me for an uncomfortably long time. But then her forehead wrinkles and her eyes light up and she actually looks happy to see me. "Anna told me you'd come by this week, but she didn't know when, exactly." She stands a bit straighter, bracing herself against the side of the door. "Do you want to come in?"

I step into the foyer and follow her to the living room. Sunlight streams in through the floor-to-ceiling windows that look out onto the street. I set my backpack on the floor and sit on the couch.

It's impossible to ignore the images around me. On every wall and every surface in Maggie's living room, I see framed photos of my family. Me as an infant in my mother's arms. Brooke as a little girl, with her long dark hair and her bangs cut straight across her forehead. My mom and dad on their wedding day. We're everywhere, decorating my grandmother's home, even though she doesn't appear in a single photo. I can practically hear the words my mother said every time Brooke or I asked about her: "She only met you once." Then Mom would show Brooke and me a photograph of the three of us at the zoo. When we'd press her for more information, she'd say that she and her mother had a falling out and that she didn't want to talk about it.

Maggie catches me staring at the pictures and crosses the room to pick up a silver frame. "Here. You'll like this one. It's new," she says as she hands it to me.

Maggie has a tiny infant me folded up in one arm, and

Brooke is by her side, holding Maggie's other hand. I stare at her. She looks happy. And then I notice the giraffes in the background.

"We went to the zoo," she says.

I squint at the photo, realizing that it's the same picture we have back home.

She taps her fingernail against the glass. "I hadn't met the baby before. You remember that you two have the same name, right?" She shakes her head in disbelief like she always does when she thinks about it.

Maggie settles in to her usual chair and leans forward, like she wants to get a closer look at me, and I feel myself move away from her, my back sinking further into the couch cushions. Something's not right about this. "You went to San Francisco?"

She adjusts her scarf around her shoulders. "Anna was actually the one who encouraged me to go," she says, and my stomach drops. "But it might not have been a good idea. My daughter and I got into a fight while I was there and . . ." Her eyes lock on mine and she looks at me wearing a sad smile. "Let's just say I'm not so sure when I'll be going back again."

I take a deep breath and try not to look panicked about what she just said. The only reason Brooke and I have a picture of the two of us at the zoo with our grandmother—the only reason we ever *met* Maggie—is that Anna told her to visit?

"So." She leans back into her chair. "I hear you left town so quickly because of a family emergency. Is everything okay?"

I nod vacantly.

"Good. So are you back here for school, then?" Her word choice is deliberate, and the generic reference to "school" isn't lost on me. Anna told me over the summer that Maggie found out I was really going to Westlake the whole time.

I avoid the school thing entirely. "I need to go back to San Francisco," I say, intentionally avoiding this perfect opportunity to come clean. "But I'm planning to come back. To visit." That is, if Anna wants me to.

Maggie doesn't say another word, but she doesn't take her eyes off me, either. She's waiting me out, and I know I'm supposed to tell her everything because Anna promised her I would when I returned. I check out the photographs again and feel sick to my stomach. Does she have any idea who I am?

I take a deep breath and open my mouth to speak. "There's—" I start to say, at the same time that she says, "Well—" We both stop in midsentence.

"Were you going to say something?" she asks.

"It's okay. You go first."

I wait for her to talk. To tell me she found my red notebook in its hiding place upstairs and pieced everything together. To call me out with such direct questions, I won't have a choice but to tell her everything. It will come out sloppy and rushed, possibly as a single run-on sentence with very few breaths in between, but the words will be out there and I won't be able to take them back. And my grandmother will become the fifth person in the world to know who I am and what I can do.

"I was just going to ask if you needed a place to stay when you visit. Your room is still available. If you want it."

I suck in some air, feeling disappointment that I didn't expect. "Yeah. Sure," I say. "That'd be great."

"Good. I haven't rented it out yet. I'd certainly prefer it to go to . . ." She pauses. *Say the words. Say, "my grandson." Tell me you know who I am.* Instead she finishes her sentence with "someone I already know."

She stands up and I do the same. I comb my hair off my forehead and cast my eyes down at the ground. *Tell her.*

"Maggie . . ." I say.

Her head springs up. "Yes?"

"I'm . . ." I can't do it. I can't say it. If she already knew about me, that would be one thing. But she doesn't. At least, I don't think she does. "I'm not supposed to be here."

And there it is, that warm smile I remember so well. "And yet, you came back," she says as she reaches over and grips my arm high up by my shoulder and gives it a reassuring squeeze. Maybe that's her way of giving me permission to *not* tell her. Or maybe I'm just looking to be let off the hook.

"I'm going to go get some sheets for your bed," she says. "All of your clothes are boxed up in the attic. You can put everything back where it belongs."

She starts to leave the room, and for some reason I start talking about logistics. "I'll pay you the same amount, of course. Even though I won't be here as often."

She's walking away, but I can hear her clearly. "It's your room, Bennett. Come as often as you like and stay as long as you want to." Then she stops and turns around. "You should decorate it a bit too. Hang up some posters or something. Make it your own."

Three hours later, I've reassembled my bedroom at Maggie's so it looks exactly the way I left it, a process which has left me soaked in sweat from hauling boxes from a 120-degree attic into a 105-degree bedroom. How can she not have air-conditioning?

As I suspected, my clothing options here are limited to long-sleeved flannels, concert tees, and an assortment of thick sweaters. I dig around in my backpack for a clean shirt and a pair of underwear, and then shuffle across the hallway.

While I was unpacking, Maggie must have been stocking the bathroom with me in mind. Fresh towels hang from the racks, there's a new bar of soap on the counter, and on the shelf next to the tub I spot a bottle of all-in-one shampoo and conditioner. I turn on the water and toss my sweat-drenched clothes on the floor.

After I'm showered and dressed again, I return to my room and crouch down in front of the giant mahogany armoire that dominates this room. I feel around on the bottom for the lock, and inside I find everything I left behind last time: big stacks of cash, all minted pre-1995, and the red notebook I've used to calculate my travels for the last year or so. I pick it up, give the rubber band that holds it together a little snap, and return it to the cabinet.

The twenties in my wallet are from home, so I take them out and stuff them into the opposite corner of the compartment where they won't get mixed up. Then I count out five hundred dollars in safe bills, fold them into my wallet, and shove all of it into the back pocket of my jeans. I put everything back the way it was.

Downstairs, I find Maggie standing in front of the narrow desk in the foyer with her purse wide open. She fishes out her car keys and then stuffs a bunch of envelopes inside. She looks up and sees me. "Are you all settled up there?"

"Yeah. And thanks for the shampoo and stuff." She gives me a dismissive flick of her wrist as if it were no big deal.

"I have a doctor's appointment, but I'll be back in a few hours." She gives her keys a little jingle but then stops cold. "Oh . . . Did you need your car today?" She gives me a confused stare. "I've been using it while you were gone."

When I walked into the dealership last March, I paid cash for the '95 Jeep Grand Cherokee and figured I'd leave it for Maggie when it was time for me to go home. Which is why I put the title in her name. It's also why I chose the color blue. "That's okay. I hoped you would."

She gives me a funny look, and I'm pretty sure she's about to start asking questions I don't want to answer.

"I've got to run. I'm meeting Anna in town. Drive the car as much as you want. I'll just tell you if I need it, okay?" I step onto the porch and pull the door closed behind me.

Anna and I spend the rest of the afternoon wandering around downtown Evanston shopping for clothes. Anna's dad gave her money to buy some new running shoes, so we start there. Then we start looking for clothes for me. Plaid Bermuda shorts appear to be in style, but I can't seem to bring myself to even try them on. Instead, I grab another pair of jeans.

Anna picks out a button-down shirt and holds it up to me for size.

"What do you think?"

I don't even look at it. I just grab her by the shoulders and pull her into me, and she looks down and laughs when she sees the shirt she picked out smashed in between our chests. "It's perfect," I say, and I kiss her, right in the middle of the Gap.

An hour and four stores later, I have a new pair of Chuck

Taylors and enough mid-90s fashion to get me through the next few months.

We head over to the deli and order huge subs to eat in the park. We hang out for a long time, talking about everything *but* the upcoming school year. I ask her about concerts she wants to see, and quiz her about the places she wants me to take her next. She asks me questions about San Francisco, and I tell her how I've spent most of my summer skateboarding around the city, climbing on an indoor rock wall, and missing her. I realize how pathetic I sound, but Anna must not hear it that way, because she scoots in closer and hooks her arms around the back of my neck.

She kisses me. When she pulls away, I look straight into her eyes. "What was that for?"

She shrugs. "I just love you."

"Good. I just love you too."

She kisses me again. Then she stands up, brushes the dirt off her shorts, and offers her hand to help me up. "Time to get you some music."

Justin is busy ringing up a customer, but he waves when he sees us come in. Anna waves back, and then leads me down one of the narrow aisles. I twist my head as we walk by the wooden bins, trying to get a better glimpse of the CDs.

We're near the back of the store looking through the Hot Summer Sounds kiosk when Justin comes up behind us. "You're back. How was the world?"

Anna flips around. "I don't know about the world, but

Mexico was really, really good," she says, throwing her arms around him. When Justin hugs her, he closes his eyes. But it must click that I'm standing here watching, because they suddenly spring open and lock on mine. I smile at him as his arms fall to his sides. He takes a big step back.

"Well, I'm glad you're home," he says to her.

"Me too."

He lifts his chin in my direction. "What's up?" He raises his hand in the air and I start to give him a fist bump, but then I realize that his palm is open. I correct quickly, giving him a high five instead. "So, you're back." The inflection in his voice makes it more of a question than a statement.

"Yeah. For now."

Anna shoots me a sideways glance and changes the subject. "What's this?" she asks, pointing up to the ceiling.

"Latest from Blind Melon." He gives a disappointed shake of his head. "Nowhere near as good as the last one. I think they're done." When Justin turns his back, Anna gives me a questioning look and I return it with a shrug. I've never heard of them, so I can only assume he's right.

"You two catch up, I'm going to go look around." I'm happy to leave them alone. This place is far too fascinating to spend another second talking when I could be thumbing through the bins.

Hand drawn signs hang from the ceiling and identify each section—R&B, Jazz, Rock. I wander around the record store, picking up CDs and turning them over to read the track lists, adding to my mental list of concerts I want to check out. I'm heading to the Ska section when I spot the poster rack in the far corner.

This proves to be even more entertaining. I stand there for a long time, flipping through the posters, wondering who half of these musicians are, and laughing out loud at the impressive collection of 90s boy bands.

I flip a few more frames and stop. "That one," I hear Anna say from behind me. I didn't even know she was standing there. She slides in front of me and taps on Billy Corgan's chest. "Please tell me you know these guys."

"Yeah." I nod, staring at the Smashing Pumpkins, marveling at the ridiculous amount of eyeliner they're each wearing.

"Have you seen them?" she asks.

I glance around to be sure Justin's nowhere near us. "Three times," I say. I rest my chin on Anna's shoulder and whisper in her ear, "Miami in '97, Dublin in 2000, Sydney in 2010."

She tilts her head toward me. I can tell from the look on her face that she's surprised to hear me share even the slightest hint of future information. "Good," she says with a satisfied grin. "They're from Chicago."

"I know."

Then I tell her what Maggie said about decorating my room and making it my own. "I could hang this one next to the window. Or maybe on the wall by the closet." I shrug. "Of course, it's kind of pointless to put posters on the walls if I won't be coming back here to visit."

She bites her lip and stares at me. Then she reaches down into the bin, grabs a rolled-up poster, and hands it to me.

When I take it, she turns on her heel and walks away. I'm smiling as I pick out a second one.

By late Friday afternoon, my room at Maggie's is starting to come together. Anna's photograph of our beach in La Paz is in a new frame and hanging above my bed. The closet is filled with enough new clothes to take me through the rest of the summer and well into fall, and I already had plenty of stuff to keep me warm this winter. I thumbtacked the postcards that used to be hidden in my top drawer onto the wall above my desk, and I hung a 1995 wall calendar there too, so I wouldn't forget *when* I am.

We hung the Weezer poster on the left side of the window and we're almost done hanging the Smashing Pumpkins on the right. "Down just a bit," Anna says. "There. Stop."

"It's good?" I raise an eyebrow and look over my shoulder at her. When she nods, I tape the corner in place and then take a few steps back to check out the result. "Better?" I ask.

She flops down on the edge of my bed and folds her legs underneath her. Reclining back on her hands, she slowly scans the room. "It's starting to look like you," she says. I take my own glance around. She's right: it does look more like me, but that wasn't my only intention. I wanted it to look more per-manent, partially for me, but also for her.

"What are you going to do if I tell you I don't want you to keep coming back?" she asks.

I walk toward her, shaking my head. "I don't know. . . . Show up in a few weeks, I guess. Say good-bye to you and Maggie. Haul all this stuff up to the attic as slowly as possible, hoping the entire time that you'll change your mind."

"You seriously want to keep coming back here?"

I plant both palms on the bed, right next to her hips, and lean over her. "I told you before. I'll keep coming back until you're sick of me." Her lower lip quivers, like she's trying not to smile. "I don't know. Something tells me you're not sick of me yet."

She stares at me but doesn't speak for the longest time. "No," she finally says. "I'm not sick of you yet."

I brush my lips lightly against hers. "Good," I whisper.

"So," she begins, never breaking eye contact, "how would this work, exactly, you . . . visiting but not . . . staying?"

"I'll be here for anything that's important to you—races, dances, parties, whatever. We'll plan it all out, down to the minute. You'll never be surprised." She fakes a pout. "Well, not in a bad way, that is." That gets the slightest hint of a smile before her expression turns serious again.

"I'll know when you're leaving?"

"Every time."

"And when you're coming back again?"

"Every. Time," I repeat, this time with more emphasis on each word. "I promise."

"How can you be so certain you won't get knocked back?" I think about what she said the other night. How she fell apart after I left.

"I'll never stay longer than a few days. I'll be in control the whole time. If I ever feel like I'm losing control, I'll tell you right away."

She licks her lips and considers me for a moment. I think she's about to say something, but instead she slides one hand up my arm and around the back of my neck.

"Okay," she says.

"Okay?"

She nods and I feel a smile spread across my face. "Yes," she says as she hooks her finger into my belt loop and scoots back, giving me a little tug. I climb up and settle in next to her. "But I have a condition."

I kiss her. "Let's hear it."

"You need to tell Maggie who you are." I pull away from her. My first instinct is to shake my head no, but when I see the look on her face, I decide against it. I bite my tongue and let her finish her thought. "You could come and go without having to hide anything. Besides, don't you think she deserves to know?

"Also—and this is totally selfish, I realize—but when you left last time, Maggie was the only person I could really talk to. And now you're going to leave again. And again. And when you do, it would be nice to have one person in my life that I can talk to about you—one person I don't have to keep your secret from."

I rake my hands through my hair while I consider her request. I was all ready to tell Maggie the other night, but only because I thought she already knew who I was. I didn't think I had a choice. But she seems content with the way things are. I certainly am.

I decide to stall. "Do I have to tell her before I leave tonight?" I ask.

She shakes her head no and I blow out a breath. "Just . . . whenever . . ."

Whenever. My mind starts racing with all the ways I could tell Maggie who I am, and each time, my stomach knots up. But then Anna wipes the whole thing from my mind when she scoots in closer and kisses me hard, her hands on my skin and her hair everywhere, reminding me of all the reasons I'm here and all the reasons I have to keep coming back and the fact that I'll do anything to make her happy. When she pulls away, she smiles and says, "Emma's eighteenth birthday is in three weeks and her parents are throwing her a party. It'll be embarrassingly over the top."

"Then I'll be here."

"I have a few cross-country races you could come to. And homecoming's in October. Wait, we need to write this down." She hops up off the bed and comes back holding a pen and the wall calendar, and over the next fifteen minutes, the rest of our schedule falls into place. Homecoming. Cross Country State Finals. Thanksgiving. Christmas. We have plans to see each other every two or three weeks, but I can already tell that won't be enough. I'm not sure how to do it yet, but I'm already concocting ways to squeeze in more time with her without making her parents suspicious or running the risk of getting knocked back.

Anna closes the calendar and tosses it on the floor. "When are you leaving?" she asks.

"Soon," I say as I play with her curls. "Maggie will be home in a few hours. I should take off before she gets back; otherwise I'll have to stage some elaborate cab ride to the airport or something."

She reaches up and brushes my hair off my forehead. "I want to be here when you go."

I can't imagine how that's going to make this whole thing easier, but she looks pretty determined. "Are you sure?" I ask.

She nods and says, "Positive. In fact, do you mind if I stick around for a little while . . . afterward?" Her nose crinkles up. "Or is that just weird?"

I smile as I picture Anna and Maggie, hanging out in the kitchen drinking tea. "Stay as long as you want to. I bet Maggie would like the company. You can even come over when I'm gone."

She rolls her eyes before she covers her face with her hand. "I did that last time you left. I moped around in here for hours." She looks at me and says, "I even put on your coat," and then hides her face again. She lets out a sigh and shakes her head, like she can't believe she's admitting this to me. But I like the idea of her wearing my coat. I like the idea that this room might help us feel some kind of connection to each other, even when we're apart. I pull her hand away from her face and knit her fingers together with mine.

Before I can say anything, she changes the subject. "You should probably leave Maggie a note before you go."

"Good idea," I say. I come up on my knees and pin her hands

above her head. I kiss her neck and she squirms underneath me. "I'll be right back. Don't move."

Downstairs on the narrow desk in the hallway, I spot the Post-its right away. I write a note telling Maggie I'll be here in three weeks, and stick it on the shelf next to the basket where she always drops her keys.

Then I stare at it. I picture Anna, sitting in my room after I've left, alone and wishing she weren't. I picture myself doing the same thing in a different room two thousand miles and seventeen years away. I don't want to leave. But at least I'm here now.

I race back up the stairs and open the door.

And she's right where I left her.

august 2012

9

san francisco, california

I shut my eyes tight and lift my forehead off the steering wheel. My neck goes slack and I fall back into the seat, gripping the sides of my head and trying to piece together where I am. There's a faint bit of light streaming in through the cracks on each side of the garage door, and I strain to read the clock on the dashboard: 6:03 P.M.

I rip into the box of supplies on the passenger seat, blindly groping for one of the water bottles. I down the first one without stopping and reach for another. My eyelids are still half closed when I pop the top on the Starbucks Doubleshot, and I let them fall shut completely as I tip my head back, letting the coffee slide down my throat. My whole body is shaking, and there's sweat dripping down my face even though I'm freezing.

It takes a good twenty minutes for the pounding to turn into more of a dull throbbing, and when it does, I reach into the glove compartment for the car keys and my phone. The screen shows two missed calls from Mom back on Wednesday night, and four texts from Brooke over the last two days. I open the texts first and read them in order:

> Ugh. Too quiet without you here. Having fun?

> Seeing a show @ the Bottom of the Hill tonight. In real time. Like normal person I am. Borrring . . .

> Worried about you. Reply when you're back, okay?

> No "mom" jokes in reply to last text, pls. Miss ya.

I squint at the screen, hit reply, and type out my message:

> No jokes. Back home now. C U soon.

My mouth is still dry and my limbs feel weak, so I reach for another bottle of water and recline back in the seat, looking around the garage. In his e-mail, the owner had mentioned that it was "on the small side," but that turned out to be a major understatement. When I first opened the door, I stood in the alley for the longest time trying to figure out if the Jeep would even fit.

It proved to be as challenging as it looked, but I folded the side mirrors flat against the frame, backed in slowly, and pressed the button on the electronic garage door opener, hoping for the best. I was a little surprised when it actually closed. I press that button again and the garage door jolts to life, squeaking and rattling and eventually settling into place over my head.

In the alley, I leave the Jeep running and hop out. There's not much back here other than trash cans and rusting garden equipment. I grab a water bottle and throw my backpack over my shoulder, heading toward an abandoned pile of old flowerpots, and then I take a handful of dirt, dump some water over the top, and work the mud into the grooves of the shiny carabiners that hang from the external straps of my backpack.

But my cover-up efforts turn out to be unnecessary. When I get home, there's a note from Mom on the counter saying that Brooke's out on a date, Dad's at a dinner meeting, and she's going to the movies with friends. So much for family night.

I make myself something to eat and flop down on the couch. For the rest of the evening, I flip through channels, stare at the empty space next to me, and wonder how Anna and I are going to pull this off. She should be here right now. Or I should be there. But we shouldn't be *this*.

I must eventually drift off because when I open my eyes again, the room is pitch-black, the television is off, and I'm covered with a blanket. I haul myself up to my room and fall into bed, still wearing the same clothes I had on when I left Evanston.

<hr/>

The voices coming from the TV in the kitchen are low but audible, and when I turn the corner, I find Dad with his hip against the counter, spooning yogurt into his mouth and watching the news. He looks up when I walk in.

"Hey. Welcome home. How was your trip?"

I'm grateful that he asked the question the way he did so that I don't need to lie when I answer. "The trip was great. A lot of fun."

Dad takes his glasses off and cleans them with the edge of his shirt. He puts them back in place and looks at me over the top of the frames. "The nights must have been cold."

It takes me a second or two to think about how to phrase this one. None of the nights in Maggie's house were even remotely chilly. "No, the nights were actually really warm," I say. Too warm, in fact.

Dad finishes his yogurt and pours himself a glass of orange juice. Once I start in on my cereal there's a lot of crunching, but the only voices in the room are coming from the television. He glances up at me a few times, as if he's trying to think of something to fill the uncomfortable silence. But then something on the screen gets his attention, and he's off the hook.

He reaches for the remote, turning up the volume, and pivoting to face the screen. "Breaking news this morning," the anchorwoman says. A red and blue graphic that reads TRAGEDY IN THE TENDERLOIN flies in from the side of the screen and stops in the center—large and ominous, for effect—before it shrinks and settles at the bottom where it can't interfere with the video footage of a building ablaze against the backdrop of the early-morning sky.

An apartment fire in the Tenderloin district claimed the lives of two young children in the early hours this morning. Five-year-old Rebecca Walker and her three-year-old brother, Robert, were asleep when a fire broke out in the bedroom they share on the third floor of an apartment complex on Ellis Street. The parents were rushed to the hospital for smoke inhalation. Firefighters were unable to rescue the two children.

I take a big bite of cereal and walk over to the counter to pour myself a cup of coffee, listening as the anchorwoman passes the story to the on-the-scene reporter. I'm only half paying attention, but I catch the gist. The parents were unable to get to the children, there was no smoke detector, and an investigation is underway to determine the cause. I peek at the screen when the downstairs neighbor describes hearing screams through the ceiling and calling 911. After one more shot of the high-drama burning-building footage, they move back to the studio and the anchorwoman wraps up the story and moves along to a new one about a fender bender that's currently being cleared from the Bay Bridge.

"That's horrible," Dad says, staring at the screen. I'm pretty sure he's referring to the previous news item about the fire and not the minor car accident. "Those poor parents. They must feel so guilty." He's tips his head back, downing his juice, and brings his glass to the sink. He won't look at me, but he doesn't have to. I can feel it. The space around us is already filling up with all the things he wants so badly to say right now.

Until recently, I bolted from any room that contained both Dad and news. I'd learned my lesson. If some horrible tragedy took place and I stayed silent, he'd shoot me this contemptuous look and say something like, "Doesn't this even *bother* you?" On the flip side, if I made a comment that expressed even the slightest bit of remorse for the situation, he'd whip out a pen and paper and start plotting out all the ways I could go back and stop the plane crash/bus crash/shooting/stabbing/ explosion/carjacking/terrorist attack/etc. Either way, my response to him would be the same. I don't change things. It's not my place to change things, just because I can. And yes, of course it bothers me. All the time. I'm not heartless.

Losing my sister in a previous decade came with its share of complications, but as it turns out, there were also a few silver linings. Meeting Anna was one. No longer having these excruciating conversations with my dad was another.

Brooke nearly spills my coffee when she throws her arms around my neck. "You're home!" After a quick hug, she bounces over to Dad and gives him a peck on the cheek. She stops suddenly, and her gaze darts back and forth between the two of us. "Uh-oh," she says, wiggling her fingers in the air. "There's tension . . ." Brooke slips into her usual role, using humor to restore peace to our somewhat dysfunctional family. She slaps Dad's arm with the back of her hand. "So, what'd he do this time?" She looks over at me and gives me a wink.

"Nothing," Dad says. "Nothing at all."

The double meaning isn't lost on me.

He cleans his glasses again, this time with a dishcloth, looking out the window the entire time. "It's going to be a gorgeous day." His voice is higher that usual and that enthusiastic tone sounds forced. "Let's get that boat on the bay, shall we?" He checks his watch. "I want to leave in a half hour. Can you two be ready?"

Brooke and I nod.

"Good. I'd better go see if your mom needs help."

As soon as he's out of earshot, I turn to Brooke. "Family day," I say flatly. "Super."

She raises an eyebrow at me. "Come on. They're not that bad, you know?"

"Easy for you to say. *You're* not a huge source of disappointment to one and a constant worry to the other."

"And neither are you, but whatever . . ." She lifts herself onto the kitchen counter and points to the half-empty coffee mug I'm holding. "Hurry up, we only have a few minutes. Top off your coffee, pour me a cup, and tell me *everything.*"

So I do. In hushed tones I speed through the details, telling her all about Maggie and the reason there's a photo of the three of us at the zoo. Brooke's eyes grow wide, and she asks for more details about the stuff I try to breeze past, like Emma and Justin's breakup and how the Greenes let me crash on their couch the first night. She sips her coffee, hanging on every word, and after I've given her a play-by-play of practically the entire trip, I shake my head and tell her how Anna decided—once again, and for reasons I honestly can't fathom—that she'd rather put up with the oddities of this bizarre relationship than tell me to stay where I belong. I tell Brooke how hard it was to leave, and with every word, I'm more relieved to have one person here who understands. The thought makes me remember Anna's request for a confidante of her own. I wish I hadn't left town without giving her one.

Mom and Dad walk back into the kitchen carrying bags over their shoulders and jackets in their arms. Dad heads straight for the garage, but Mom takes a detour to give me a peck on the cheek and tell me she's happy I'm home. Then she asks me to carry the cooler out to the car.

As I'm picking it up, Brooke leans in close and nudges me with her elbow. "I'm glad you're home too," she says.

It feels so strange to lie to Brooke, but I do it anyway. "So am I," I say.

10

People keep walking by, but so far no one seems to have noticed that I'm sitting here alone in the Jeep, staring at the door that leads to my locker. The warning bell sounded thirty seconds ago, but I can't bring myself to leave this spot.

It would be so easy to close my eyes right now, disappear from this car, and open them in a secluded corner of Westlake Academy. I'd go straight to the office and tell Ms. Dawson at the front desk that my family's plans have changed, I am back in town for my senior year after all, and, if possible, I'd like a class schedule. Then I'd walk the hallway until I found Anna. We'd eat lunch with Emma and Danielle like we always did. That night, while we were sprawled out on her bedroom floor studying together, I'd surprise her by grabbing her hands and transporting her to a quiet spot far away, like a beach in Bora-Bora.

The final bell rings. I reach down for my backpack, throw it over my shoulder, and slam the Jeep door. As I cross the student parking lot, I look down at my jeans and T-shirt. I never thought I'd actually miss the Westlake uniform.

I don't pass a single person as I climb the staircase that leads to my locker on the third floor, and when I pull up on the latch, the click echoes in the empty hall. Inside, there's nothing but empty water bottles, a few granola-bar wrappers, and a bunch of loose papers that someone fed through the slats while I was gone. Collectively, they represent everything I missed last spring. There's a prom court voting ballot, a sign-up sheet for the annual senior class Olympics, and a flyer for the spring musical. I push them back in my locker and shut the door.

I printed out my class schedule this morning, but I barely even glanced at it before I shoved it into the front pocket of my jeans. I haven't the slightest clue where I'm supposed to be right now, so I dig it out and open it. First period: AP World Civilizations with Mrs. McGibney. Building C, the one farthest from my locker, clear on the other side of the quad. I check the time on my phone. I'm already five minutes late.

It takes me another five minutes to reach the classroom door, and when I open it, a roomful of faces I haven't thought about in months turns to look at me. I take a few tentative steps inside, and the next time I look around I see Cameron in the back row. He lifts his hand and gives me a nod.

"You must be my missing student." McGibney doesn't look up or stop writing on the whiteboard as she addresses me. "Are you Mr. Cooper?" she asks, but she keeps talking and doesn't wait for me to answer. "I was just going over the rules of this class. The first one is that I expect my students to be sitting in their seats when the bell rings."

"Sorry," I mumble under my breath.

"I give one freebie, and you just used it." She still hasn't looked away from the board. I have no idea how she can talk to me and write at the same time, but I'm a little bit impressed. She's already written the words "First Civilizations" and started a bulleted list below: "agriculture," "significant cities," "writing systems." "Are you going to sit down and join us, Mr. Cooper, or would you prefer to stand by the door for the rest of my class?" She adds a bullet and the words "formal states" as she speaks.

The only empty seat is in the first row, directly in front of her desk, and I can feel every eye watching me as I shuffle across the room and settle in. Trying not to move too quickly, too slowly, or too loudly, I unzip my backpack and remove my notebook and a pencil.

A pencil. I run it back and forth between my fingers as I picture Anna piling her curls on top of her head and using my pencil to hold them in place.

"Hi." The voice jolts me from my thoughts, and I look to my left. Megan Jenks is leaning over her desk, writing in her notebook, and looking at me from behind a veil of blond hair.

"Hi," I say under my breath.

She smiles before she turns back to her notes. I return to mine, madly copying the words on the whiteboard into my composition book, as if the exercise alone will give them some kind of meaning. McGibney asks a question but I only half hear it. Not that it matters since I have no idea how to answer.

Megan's hand shoots up next to me. "Miss Jenks," McGibney says, pointing at her.

"The Neolithic Revolution."

"Yes. Good." McGibney returns to the whiteboard and writes something under the word "agriculture" as Megan looks over and sends another quick smile my way. I give her a nod, turn to my notebook, and write "Neolithic Revolution." It's the first day of school, and I'm already wondering if I missed some required reading or something, because I have absolutely no idea what they're talking about.

⁓

The day moves at a painfully slow pace, and I muddle through Statistics, Spanish, and Physics until it's finally time for lunch. I make small talk with the people in line. When they ask me how I am, I tell them I'm fine. When they ask me where I've been, I give them one of several answers: Traveling around. Seeing the world. And, I'd prefer not to talk about it.

Everything happened so quickly last spring. When I lost Brooke in 1994, Mom insisted I get as close to her as I could, and it was my idea to stay with my grandmother in 1995 Evanston. It wasn't 1994 Chicago, but it was close enough. Against my better judgment, I left it to Mom to come up with an excuse to explain why I was missing school here.

She panicked. At first she told them I was "Away, sorting

out a few things." But when a week turned into two, she had no other choice but to expand upon her story, and suddenly I was "sorting things out" at a treatment center for troubled teens on the east coast. They had no idea when I'd be home. That was up to the doctors.

At least word didn't get out to my friends, who seem to believe my version of events: I tapped into some latent rebellious streak and took off to backpack around Europe.

I grab a sandwich and a huge bottle of water, head into the cafeteria, and immediately spot the guys on the other side of the double glass doors. They're sitting outside on the deck at the long table that overlooks the quad.

When I arrive, Adam scoots over and I slide my tray next to his. He has a mouthful of food, but after he finishes chewing and washes it down with his water, he looks at me like I'm the new kid or something. "Hey. I almost forgot you were back here."

I glare at him like I'm offended. "Thanks . . . missed you too."

Cameron has been talking nonstop all summer about his new girlfriend, but since I've barely seen him outside the park, I haven't met her yet. Now she's watching me with a curious expression, but he's too fixated on his pasta to notice.

I reach across the table. "Hi," I say. "I don't think we've met. I'm Bennett."

She brings her hand to her chest and says, "Sophie," before she extends it in my direction. Cameron looks up and attempts a smile even though his mouth is full of noodles and sauce. He gestures back and forth between the two of us and then sticks his thumb up.

Another tray slides across the table, and Sam slaps me on the shoulder as he sits down. "Hey. How's the first day going?"

He looks different. It's only been a few days since I saw him last, but his hair is cropped closer to his head than I've ever seen it, and it doesn't look like he has shaved in the last day or two. He looks older or something.

I shrug and say, "Good, I guess," as I look around campus. "Just . . . different." I've always found the glass walls and metal railings interesting, but today they serve as a reminder that everything about this place and its modern architecture is in such stark contrast with the refined look of Westlake Academy. I can't imagine what Anna would think of these buildings. I'm pretty sure she'd have no idea what to make of the solar panels next to the living roof above the art studio.

"What do you have after lunch?" Sam asks as he bites into his burger.

I lean back, digging into the front pocket of my jeans for my schedule. I unfold it and look for the fifth-period box. "English. With Wilson."

Sam wipes his mouth with the back of his hand and says, "Hey, me too. Good." Just as he says the last word, someone lets out a gasp from behind us and we both turn our heads. "Hey, Linds," Sam says, sliding down the bench to make room for her between us.

"*What* did you do to your hair?" Lindsey puts her food on

the table and stares at his nearly bald head in wonder. She reaches out like she's going to touch it, but then pulls her hand back again.

"I cut it."

"With what?"

Sam laughs as he rubs his hand back and forth over the top of his head. "I love it. It feels cool. Here," he says, leaning over in her direction. "Touch it."

"No." She smacks his shoulder with the back of her hand but laughs along with him. Then she plants her palms on the sides of his face and kisses him on the forehead. "I just saw you yesterday. You couldn't have warned me?" Lindsey's shaking her head as she sits down.

He shrugs. "It was spontaneous."

She stares at me pointedly. I resist the urge to laugh. And to touch my own hair. "See, Coop, this is the kind of stuff that happened last year when you weren't around to keep him in line. Where were you during yesterday's head-shaving debacle?"

I hold my hands up in front of me, palms out. "Not my night to watch him." Lindsey rolls her eyes and takes a long draw of soda from her straw. She's still shaking her head as she digs into her pasta.

Sam runs his hand over his head wearing a wide grin. "I like it."

Lindsey and Sam have been together since the beginning of our junior year. She's a full inch taller than any of us, including Sam, and dominates on the volleyball court. We'd always been friends with her, but at some point during our sopho-more year, she started eating lunch at our table. I don't even remember it being weird. She just sat down.

I think she had a falling out with her friends. I once asked her about it, and she admitted that, aside from her teammates, she didn't have a lot of close girlfriends. *I like to know where I stand with people*, I remember her saying. *None of this today we're friends, tomorrow . . . poof.* She had pinched her fingers together and made them explode apart. *Guys are so much easier.* A long pause. *That's a compliment, by the way.*

Maybe we're more complicated than you think, I'd said, keeping a straight face. *What if we don't like you at all and we just don't know how to tell you?*

She'd looked at me right in the eyes. *Do you guys like me, Coop?*

I couldn't help but smile. *Yeah. We do.*

She had shrugged. *See.*

Months later, a bunch of us were hanging out at the beach. Sam was on one side of the bonfire telling one of his *remember that time* stories, complete with animated facial expressions and exaggerated gestures, when Lindsey wrapped her hand around my arm and rested her chin on my shoulder. "I think I like him," she admitted, and I stared at her in disbelief. "Sam?" I asked, and she shrugged and said, "Look at him. He's kind of adorable."

I looked at him. I didn't find him adorable. But then I looked back at her and saw that she meant every word. Sam caught her looking his way and shot her a smile that made her turn red and bury her face in my shoulder, and just so he wouldn't get the wrong idea, I subtly motioned back and forth between the two of them. Two weeks later, they were Sam and Lindsey. I gave her endless amounts of grief for blushing so hard that night.

She twists her pasta around her fork and looks at me out of the corner of her eye. "So tell me everything. I barely got to see you this summer. How was it? What did you do?"

"It was fine." I can't think of anything interesting to tell her outside of the concerts I went to with Brooke or my trips to visit Anna in La Paz, so I leave it at that and ask her what she did. She tells me she spent most of the summer driving back and forth to beach volleyball tournaments in Southern California.

It reminds me that it's been a long time since I saw her play. "When's your first game?" I ask.

"A week from Saturday," she says. "You should come. Sam will be there." She elbows him and gives him a half smile. "He'll be the one wearing a hat."

Sam ignores her comment and leans forward on the table, resting his chin in his hand. "What are you doing after school today?" he asks me.

"Homework." I think about the mountain of assignments that have been doled out over the last four classes, and the sad fact that I still have three more to go.

"That's it?" Lindsey asks.

"I don't know. I guess I was thinking about heading over to the climbing gym." I look at Sam. "Want to come?"

"Sure. But it'll have to be on the late side. I'm tutoring tonight."

Since when does Sam tutor? "You're tutoring?"

He shrugs. "I must've told you. I started at the end of last year, but this year I'm running the sixth grade math program, so it's a lot more intense." He takes a big sip of his drink. "It's fun. You should do it. It'll look good on your college apps."

I haven't even thought about college applications. "Are the kids cool?"

Sam shakes his head. "Hell, no. They're a bunch of spoiled brats with some serious entitlement issues."

I laugh. "Way to sell it."

"I'm kidding. There are, like, two cool ones. But seriously, you'd be good at it," he says to me. "You're good with kids and stuff."

"Yeah," I say sarcastically, "I'm super patient. Especially with the spoiled ones with entitlement issues." I give him a wide smile and two overly enthusiastic thumbs-up.

I reach for my water, suddenly realizing what Lindsey meant by her *That's it?* question. Everyone's afternoons are filled with sports, clubs, and community service projects that look good to a college admissions staff. I haven't even thought about what I'm doing next year, let alone boosting my application.

The bell rings and everyone dumps their trash in the bins before taking off in their separate directions. Lindsey gives Sam one more eye roll before she pushes his head in my direction. "Watch him," she says with a wink. I laugh, thinking how much Lindsey and Anna would like each other. The four of *us* would have fun together.

I'm glad Sam and I are going the same way, because I didn't even look at the room number before I stuffed my schedule back into my pocket. As we walk through the halls toward our lockers, my mind drifts back to Anna again, and I start piecing together her schedule, wondering what she'd be doing back in 1995 Evanston. Would she still be in class, or out on the track? Would it be her day to work at the bookstore? Did she, Emma, and Danielle talk about me over lunch? Did Anna tell them that I'm coming back? Did Emma lose it when she found out?

Sam comes to a stop.

"What?"

He points at a row of lockers. "Don't you need your stuff?"

"Huh? Oh, yeah. . . ." It suddenly dawns on me that we're standing in front of *my* locker.

Sam shakes his head and gives me a pitying look. "I swear, man, it's like you're back but you're not."

I avoid his eyes as I spin the combination dial.

I couldn't have said it better myself.

After an hour at the climbing gym with Sam and a rushed dinner with my parents, I head upstairs to start on my homework. I navigate to the school website and check this week's assignments. I have a couple of hours of reading for Chemistry, a paper due in two weeks on the rise of the Tigris-Euphrates civilization, and an essay I'm supposed to begin writing for English.

I lean back with my arms folded behind my head, staring up at the ceiling. Until recently, I'd never really thought much about my bedroom. Mom had it professionally decorated when we moved in four years ago, and I don't recall picking out a single thing.

Unlike Anna's room, there are no posters on my walls, no maps of the world, no bookshelves filled with trophies and CD cases. It's just really white. White walls. White ceiling. White rug. White comforter. The desk is glass and metal, but that does very little to break up the monotony. The only color in the room comes from the huge canvas painting my mom bought at an art auction a couple of years ago, and the red glass bowl—overflowing with ticket stubs from every live concert I've ever seen—that's perched on the nightstand next to my bed. Aside from that bowl, this room could belong to anyone.

Anna was only in my bedroom for a matter of minutes, but in that short amount of time, she must have seen it for what it is: a room that looks like it's staged for an upcoming sale.

I should start on homework, but instead I reach for my phone. It's a little after nine o'clock here and an hour later in Boulder. I type out a message to Brooke:

> U there?

I wait for her to reply, and finally the phone chirps.

> Yup. Studying.

> How was your first day back?

I type in one word:

> Sucked.

Brooke's reply appears quickly.

> Sorry. :(

I stare at the screen, thinking about what to say. Finally I type:

> I miss her.

I look at the words before I hit send. A few minutes pass before Brooke replies.

> I know. Go do something to take your mind off it.

That's what the climbing was for, but it just made me wish I were outside on real rocks and reminded me of my first date with Anna.

> Like what?

I picture Brooke letting out an exasperated huff when she reads my message. She comes back with three rapid-fire responses:

> IDK.

> Something fun.

> Something good.

I go back to my computer, where I find myself drifting off into thoughts about college admissions and catching up with everyone else on extracurricular activities. I search for volunteer opportunities and find hundreds in San Francisco alone, ranging from part-time jobs that support senior citizens to working with kids in the city's poorer neighborhoods.

This one site catches my eye, and the reason isn't entirely lost on me. I click on it, check out the programs, and watch the video. Then I navigate back to the map. The building is in the heart of the Tenderloin, only a block away from where last Saturday's fire took place.

It's not as if I've forgotten about it. It's been hanging out in the back of my mind for the last three days. But now that this map is filling the screen, I can't block it out of my mind anymore. Without even thinking about what I'm about to do, I move the cursor to the search field and type the words "Tenderloin fire."

There's a long list of links and I click on the most recent one. It basically says the same thing the TV news story reported last Saturday morning: an apartment fire on the third floor killed two children, a five-year-old girl and a three-year-old boy. Neighbors called 911. Source of fire remains unknown. Investigation underway.

I scroll down to the bottom of the screen and find an update to the story: investigators are still trying to determine the cause. The parents aren't speaking to the media.

When I click the corner of the window, the browser closes and the story disappears. I push my chair away from my desk and reach for the enormous English book I was given today during class. I flop down on my bed and start reading. I'm only a couple of paragraphs into the homework assignment when my mind starts wandering again.

I stand up and return to my desk. I open the bottom drawer and dig deep, shuffling through a collection of postcards I've bought to give to Anna, little scraps of paper I've saved for no particular reason, and climbing maps folded haphazardly and stuffed inside. At the bottom, I feel the red notebook I hid when I got back from Evanston last weekend. I open it to a dog-eared page near the back.

The calculations are especially messy, stretching across the binding and continuing down the sides. Even the pencil marks themselves have a bit of a manic look to them, but with complete clarity, I remember writing them and know precisely what they mean.

I barely knew Emma at the time, but I stayed up all night calculating and weighing the risks of altering an entire day to prevent an accident and possibly save her life. Sure, I'd gone back before—five minutes here, ten minutes there, each time changing totally minor, completely insignificant events. But I'd never gone back that far or deliberately changed *that* many minor things. I didn't even know if it would be possible. And even though it was, I decided I would never do it again.

But looking at the dates and calculations reminds me how I felt when it was all over and I saw the look of pure relief on Anna's face. She practically skipped down the driveway after seeing Emma that Saturday morning—all of her various internal organs intact and the skin on her face scratch-free and perfect—and as I stared at her through the windshield, this feeling of intense pride washed over me. *I* had done that. *I* made that happen. It was the first time I'd ever felt that maybe I had been wrong about this gift of mine. It was the first time I'd wondered if maybe Dad was right.

Now I run my finger along the pages, thinking about the look on his face as we stood in the kitchen last week, watching the news on the screen. He wanted to say something, but he knew I wasn't supposed to travel anymore. Besides, I'd told him so many times that he probably knew it was senseless to bring it up again: I don't change things.

I wonder what he'd say if he knew that I once did.

For Emma, I'd gone back fifty-two hours. Could I go back even further?

I turn to a clean page and start scribbling some new calculations. I know I'll never be able to answer the big ethical questions with any certainty, but a few minutes later, I've figured out the math. I'll need to go back about sixty-four hours. Two and a half . . . almost *three* days. I'd have to stay back there, just like I did with Emma, and repeat those three days again to be sure that the do-over stuck, that nothing unintentional got altered along the way. I slam the notebook shut, bury it deep in my drawer again, and go back to my homework.

⁓

This is officially insane.

I'm standing in my room, zipping up my backpack. It's

heavy, filled to bursting with water bottles, Doubleshots, Red Bulls, a wad of cash, a flashlight, a smoke detector, and a fire extinguisher. I look around the room and shake my head. What am I doing?

Before I can give it another thought, I close my eyes and visualize my destination. When I open them, I'm in the alley I found on Google Maps, just one block south of the apartment complex. I've never been here before and already I hope I won't have to come back again.

To describe this neighborhood as sketchy would be a massive understatement. It's only a little after five A.M., but there are pockets of activity everywhere. A group of guys are hanging in front of a liquor store on the corner, and the doorways are filled with homeless people curled up in sleeping bags. There's an eerie buzz around me, and I feel my guard go up as I walk down the street toward the address. I keep my eyes up, my feet moving.

I'm relieved to find the apartment and somehow feel a little bit safer as I slip into the entryway. I scan the directory on the wall, reading the last names next to each of the little black buttons until I find Walker. I check to be sure no one's watching me.

I close my eyes and when I open them again, I'm on the other side of the main entrance. There are no lights on the lower floor and the staircase is barely visible. I reach into my backpack for my flashlight, and I shine it on the stairs as I climb the three flights that lead to 3c. Closing my eyes, I visualize the other side of the door.

In the apartment, I sneak down the hallway with my flashlight. School pictures line the walls, and for the first time tonight, I don't question whether or not this will work, I just hope it does.

I creep around the corner, past the living room and toward the bedrooms. After I pass the bathroom, I stand frozen, facing two closed doors. I have no idea which one belongs to the kids, so I think back to the video footage of the building on fire and make the educated guess that it's the door on the right; the one closest to the street. I twist the handle and the door creaks open.

On the far side of the room, two twin beds bookend a large window that looks out over the street below. A thin stream of light is coming in from between the curtains, casting a soft glow on the dingy carpet.

The kids are breathing, low and soft, and neither one of them moves as I remove my backpack and cross the room. I crouch down, remove the brand-new smoke detector I found buried in a box out in our garage marked HOME IMPROVEMENT, and position it as high on the wall as I can reach. Back in the hall, I grab the small fire extinguisher I snagged from under our kitchen sink and prop it against the short wall between the two bedrooms.

I close my eyes and visualize the exact same spot I was in before the fire broke out last Saturday in the early-morning hours. My bedroom.

By the time I open my eyes, the other me has already disappeared, sent back to who knows where and when, and I'm free to take his place.

The last time I was here, I had just hauled myself up from the couch downstairs. My head was still aching and my mouth was uncomfortably dry. But right now my heart is racing in a good way, and I'm so full of adrenaline I'm about to burst out of my own skin. I don't know if I was successful or not, and I won't know until the news comes on in a few hours, but somehow, I have a feeling it worked. This wasn't what Brooke meant when she said I should do "something good," but I'm pretty sure I just did.

12

The first time around, I had climbed into bed with my clothes on and fallen back into a deep sleep. But there's no way I could have fallen asleep tonight. I've been sitting here for the last hour waiting to see the first signs of daylight, and thinking about what I just did.

Suddenly it dawns on me. In fact, it's odd that I didn't think of it until now, or factor it into my decision process as I sat in my bedroom on the Monday night I just wiped away. I'd been three days closer to returning to Anna. Now I have to do those days all over again, like I just rolled the dice and landed on the square that reads, *Go back three spaces*. I don't know if this do-over will work, but one thing's certain: it may actually be the most unselfish thing I've ever done in my life.

The TV is the first thing I hear, and when I turn the corner I find Dad in the exact same place he was the first time:

leaning against the counter, spooning yogurt into his mouth, watching the news.

The expression on my face must look different this time, because he takes one look at me and breaks into a grin. "Well, someone's in a good mood," he says. "Nice trip?" My heart starts beating fast and I force myself to keep a straight face.

It's a completely unfounded superstition, but I still feel the intense need to keep things exactly the same—at least until I know if the do-over was a success. So even though I'm not at all hungry, I head for the pantry and emerge with the same box of cereal. "The trip was great."

"The nights must have been cold."

It takes me a second to remember what I said last time. "No, the nights were actually really warm."

Dad finishes his yogurt and pours his juice while I force down a spoonful of cereal. There's the same uncomfortable silence. The only voices in the room are coming from the television. Three. Two. One.

"Breaking news," the anchorwoman says. I set my bowl on the counter and my head flips around. There's no fancy TRAG-EDY IN THE TENDERLOIN graphic today. Instead, the first thing I see is similar-looking video footage of the apartment building ablaze against the backdrop of a dark night sky.

An apartment fire broke out in the Tenderloin district in the early hours this morning. Neighbors say they were awoken by a smoke alarm and helped all four

residents of the apartment escape before the flames
engulfed the building. Two children, their parents, and
a neighbor are currently being treated at San Francisco
General for smoke inhalation. All five are expected to
be released later today.

I look over at Dad. He's glanced up at the newscast here and there, but this time, he doesn't set his yogurt container down or reach for the remote to turn up the volume. On screen, the anchorwoman never breaks to an on-the-scene reporter, because there is no on-the-scene reporter. Instead, the camera goes to a wide shot of the studio, and she turns to her coanchor, who flashes her most concerned expression. "A good reminder to check those batteries in your smoke detectors."

The newscast moves to the fender bender that's currently being cleared from the Bay Bridge. Dad doesn't notice me staring at him, unable to speak or move or take in a good deep breath.

I did that.

"Do you remember that apartment we lived in when you were born?" Dad asks. "It was way out on the edge of the city. We moved to a different building when you were four, but when you were really little, your mom and I lived on the third floor of an apartment complex."

I actually did that.

Now that I know the do-over was a success, I no longer feel the urge to keep every element of our conversation exactly the same as it was the first time around. Which is good, since I'm frozen in place, staring at him while I try to force my jaw back where it belongs.

"Your mom hated living on such a high floor. We had this rickety old fire escape, and I thought it was kind of cool, but she was always afraid of a fire breaking out and all of us having to use it. She's still terribly paranoid about fires. Have you seen all the smoke detectors we have in this house?" He laughs. "She even makes me keep spare ones in the garage. Are you okay, Bennett?"

I have to speak. Now.

"I did that." My voice shakes.

"Did what?"

"That," I say, pointing lamely at the TV.

He turns and looks at it. "Oh? Really? I didn't know that. I always thought that looked a bit dangerous."

The newscast has moved on to a story about this Friday's Critical Mass bike ride through downtown. "No. Not that," I say, and Dad looks back at me quizzically.

I'd better talk quickly. If everything goes roughly the same way it did last time, I have about three more minutes before Brooke arrives. I want Dad to be the first to know what happened. I want to tell him while we're alone.

I keep my voice low and strong. "Dad, listen to me. I did that over. The fire in the Tenderloin." I gesture to the TV again, but he doesn't look away from me this time. His eyes are locked on mine, hanging on every word. "We've been here before, and that story was different then. Those kids didn't make it out of the fire. They died."

My heart was already racing, but now that I've said the word "died," it kicks into a whole new gear. My legs are shaking, so I rest a hand on the counter to steady myself. Dad looks at the TV, then back at me, then back at the TV. "What?" he asks.

"Those kids died. But I went back and changed what happened."

Dad's staring at me like I told a joke and he doesn't get the punch line.

I give the kitchen a paranoid glance to be sure we're still alone before I blurt it all out. "I came downstairs—just like I did ten minutes ago—and when I walked into the kitchen there was a news story about a fire in the Tenderloin that killed two kids. You didn't say anything, but I knew you wanted to. And you probably thought I didn't care, but I did."

Dad pulls his glasses low on his nose and watches me over the top of them. "Later, we went sailing, and the next day we drove Brooke to the airport, and then I started school on Monday and, frankly, it was kind of a shitty day and I couldn't stop thinking about those kids anyway so I thought . . . why not try it? I wanted to see if I could fix it. I wanted to know if I could stop it from happening the way it did."

Dad opens his mouth to speak, but he stops. He looks at me for a full minute, his face contorting into new expressions the whole time. I'm waiting, watching him, holding my breath and trying to figure out what he's thinking. Finally, his whole face relaxes. His eyes shine. I can tell he's proud of me.

"Hey! You're home!" I startle as Brooke wraps her arms around my neck and whispers, "God, it sucks here without you." She takes two steps back and looks from me to Dad. "What's up? You okay?" She rises to her tiptoes and pecks him on the cheek.

"Yeah, I'm okay." Dad gives her a small smile, but he doesn't look at me at all.

Brooke bounces over to the refrigerator and opens the door. She stands in the chill while she tries to decide what to eat.

Dad looks a little unstable. "We should get going soon. I'm just . . ." He trails off as he looks around the kitchen. "I'll go see if your mom needs help."

Brooke pours herself a bowl of cereal and lifts herself up to sit on the kitchen counter. "Okay, we only have a few minutes. Tell me *everything*."

Exactly like last time, I speak in hushed tones, telling her all about Maggie and the reason there's a photo of the three of us at the zoo, Emma and Justin's breakup, and how the Greenes let me crash on their couch the first night. She sips her coffee, hanging on every word, and after I've given her a play-by-play of practically the entire trip, I lower my head and say, "There's more."

I tell her about two kids who were killed in a fire in the Tenderloin.

And then I tell her how they weren't.

13

My second first day of school starts off differently. I don't sit in the car, listening as the bell rings in the distance and wishing I could close my eyes and open them at Westlake. Instead, my car is one of the first ones in the student lot, and I'm one the first people in the building.

I head straight to my locker, drag the recycling can over and park it underneath the door, and scoop all the papers and granola bar wrappers into the bin. I give my locker one more sweep with my hand and I look inside. With the exception of the VANS sticker I put on the inside of the door freshman year, it's as empty at my locker at Westlake was.

When the first bell rings, I'm already more than halfway across the quad. I open the door to my World Civilizations classroom and discover that it's still empty, so I take a seat in the row closest to the window about halfway down the aisle, nowhere near McGibney's desk.

I grab my notebook and a pencil from my backpack, and as I'm doodling, she walks through the door. She crosses the room and sets her briefcase down next to her chair. "Punctual," McGibney says, and I look up at her.

"Excuse me?"

"You're punctual," she says plainly. "What's your name?"

"Bennett Cooper." I hold my hand up and she nods.

"Ah," she says, and I can practically see the wheels turning, my mom's ridiculous story clicking into place in her mind. "Welcome back, Mr. Cooper. I hear you have some catching up to do." She says the words plainly and without a trace of the sympathetic stare I know I'll be getting from the rest of the teachers today.

"Yeah," I say. "I do."

"Well let me know how I can help, okay?"

People come into the room, look around for a desk, and settle in. Cameron spots me, and as he walks down the aisle, we give each other a fist bump. He takes the seat behind me, just as Megan steps in and looks around. I turn to talk with Cameron and I can't say I'm surprised when I see her take the seat on my left.

"Hey, Bennett," she says.

"Hi," I say. I'm feeling good. Chatty. Full of adrenaline, like I could run a marathon and still have energy left to burn. "How was your summer?"

"It was good. Thanks. How was yours?"

"Good," I say, and Megan nods, like she's encouraging me to continue. And I would, but the bell rings and McGibney immediately launches into detail about the year's syllabus.

She goes over the rules of class, putting extensive emphasis on the importance of being on time and in one's seat at least a full minute before the bell rings. After she looks around the room and declares that everyone's present, she gestures toward the whiteboard in one big, dramatic movement.

"Now. Let's get right into it. We'll be talking about early civilizations for the next two weeks." She writes the words "First civilizations" and draws a line underneath, then begins adding bullet points. I remember this part, and now I start to predict what she's going to write next. "Significant cities," I guess accurately. Next, "writing systems"... She ends with the words "formal states."

She turns around and addresses the class. "Does anyone know the term we use to describe the transition from hunting and gathering to more formal agricultural systems?"

My hand shoots up and so does Megan's. McGibney calls on her, but I'm a little puffed up because this time, I knew the answer. Even though I cheated.

⁓

It takes more effort than I anticipated, but for the next three weeks, I "live in the present" as the bumper sticker wisdom says. I try *not* to think about my past with Anna, or even speculate about what my next visit with her will bring. I go to school during the day, make small talk with my parents at night, and do my best to fill my time on the weekends. I stay fixed in place on the timeline, avoiding concerts and news, and extinguishing any thoughts that creep in about do-overs.

I try to live like I'm normal. I force myself not to think about Anna every time I meet my friends for coffee, or skate at the park overlooking the bay, or pass a gift shop that sells San Francisco souvenirs and postcards. As hard as it is, I try not to think about the fact that she can't come here and meet my family and friends. I ignore the reality that I can take her anywhere in the world, but I can't show her the city I love more than any place I've ever been. And for the most part, I'm successful. But every few days, I find myself autopiloting over to the garage, where I pull the Jeep inside its rank-smelling walls and listen to music for a while.

september 1995

14

evanston, illinois

Before I even open my eyes, a cold breeze slaps me in the face. I'm expecting clouds and fog, but when I look up at the sky, I find it bright blue and cloudless. I peek out from behind the side of Maggie's house and see the sun is shining bright on her tomato garden.

I've been stumped about how and *where* to return. It was one thing when I was living here, coming and going every day, but now it feels weird to show up and just let myself in the front door as if this were my home, even though Maggie gave me a key and told me to use it. I'm not looking forward to telling her who I am and what I can do, but it would sure be nice to come back here without having to worry about my arrival giving my grandmother a heart attack.

There's no answer when I knock on the door. After a full minute, I let myself in.

"Maggie?" I call out from the foyer. I walk through the

house, checking the kitchen and the living room for signs of her, but there's nothing. She might be in her bedroom, but I'm not about to check there, so I head straight for mine.

My new posters are up on one wall and Anna's photograph of our beach in La Paz hangs above the bed. I drop my backpack on the chair by the door and head for the closet.

My new T-shirts are folded and stacked on a shelf and the new dress shirt Anna helped me pick out hangs in front. Smashed in the back of the closet are all of the winter clothes I bought during my first visit here. It's hard to imagine that next month I'll need those wool button-ups and long-sleeved T-shirts again.

My backpack is full of stuff I need but can't buy here: more cash, even though the hidden compartment is still sufficiently stocked. The fake State of Illinois driver's license I paid some guy to make for me, perfectly mimicking the photocopy I gave him of Maggie's, but with my photo and my birthday stated as March 6, 1978, rather than March 6, 1995. I open the top drawer to stick everything inside and spot a note:

Go look inside the cabinet.
Love,
Anna

I cover my mouth with my hand, hiding the smile that spreads across my face when I see the boom box. Resting against the handle is a postcard with a shot of downtown Evanston. I pick it up and flip it over:

Welcome back. I thought you might want to <u>play</u> those
CDs you bought last time you were here. ☺
   I have to help Emma set up. I'll see you at her house
at 7:00.

The boom box is heavier than I expected it to be. I set
it on top of the desk and sit down so I can study the vintage buttons and knobs, check out the dual tape deck and the
radio dial, and press the button marked with the words "Mega
Bass." When I press one of the buttons on top, a door slowly
opens. Inside, I find one of the CDs we bought last time I was
here.

I barely stifled a laugh when Justin pushed this CD into
my hands. I already considered *The Bends* a classic, but
around here they refer to it as the second album from a new
band called Radiohead. I press play and the room fills with
music—a steady guitar lick and soft drums, then voices and
melodies—and I close my eyes, taking it in, feeling a smile
spread across my face. I look around the room at the posters,
realizing why they helped but felt a little insufficient. Music.
That's what this room needed.

When I'm dressed and ready to go, I head to the kitchen to
find something to eat. As I walk down the stairs I can't shake
the feeling that I'm being watched by photos of my mother,
now in reverse-chronological order starting with her wedding at the top and ending with her kindergarten photo near
the foyer at the bottom.

Maggie still doesn't seem to be home. On the desk in the

hallway, there's a stack of bills underneath a Post-it cube, and I sit down and write three notes telling Maggie I'm here. I leave one on the kitchen table, another on the end table where she always sets her tea, and I stick the last one on the end of the banister, just in case she makes it to the stairs without spotting the other two.

I'm still a good six or seven houses away from the Atkinses' when I hear the music drifting through the neighborhood, but it's not until I'm standing in front of the house that I begin to understand what Anna meant when she described Emma's birthday party as "over the top."

A long line of alternating dark-pink and white balloons line the driveway, creating a colorful path from the sidewalk to the side entrance of the enormous brick Tudor-style mansion. I look around. I think I'm supposed to walk through it.

At the end, I see a woman with short blond hair wearing a bright pink dress. She's standing next to a small table under a comically large balloon arch.

"Welcome!" she says, beaming. I'm not sure who she is until she asks, "Can I start you off with something to drink?" in a British accent so thick that she must be Emma's mom. She hands me a glass of pink lemonade and I take it and thank her politely. "Everyone's in the backyard," she says.

She turns her attention to the big group coming in behind me. "Welcome!" I hear her say as I turn the corner and walk into the "backyard." Which is really more like a small park.

Bright pink and purple flowers are bursting out from behind short hedges, and the grass is so green I feel the impulse to reach down and touch it to be sure it's real. The walkway takes me past smaller patios and hidden sitting areas until it ends at a huge lawn. There's a DJ parked on the far end.

I look around for Anna. Right in front of the DJ, I spot Alex and Courtney dancing. He's grabbing her by the hips and pulling her toward him while she shoots him fake smiles and pushes him away. I keep scanning the yard, and finally Danielle pops her head up from the crowd, gives me a wave, and starts walking toward me.

"She's going to be so happy to see you," she says, pulling me into a hug. "You're all she's talked about for the last few weeks."

I'm not sure what I'm supposed to say to that, but I'm glad to hear that she's been thinking about me as much as I've been thinking about her. "Where is she?" I take a quick sip of lemonade and I feel my whole face pucker up. I set my glass down on a small table next to a rosebush.

Danielle rises up on her toes but it doesn't give her much of an advantage. "I saw her earlier, but—oh, wait . . . there she is." She points off toward the edge of the garden and I follow her finger but still don't see Anna. "She's over by that big tree, talking with Justin."

I finally spot her. Justin's leaning against the tree and Anna's standing in front of him. She's wearing a short skirt that looks a lot more like something Emma would wear, and I'm pretty sure that means that Anna let Emma dress her for the occasion. Her hair is up on the sides, held in the back by a clip, but the rest of it is long. She's twirling her curls around her finger.

Justin sees me before she does and I hear him say, "He's here."

Anna turns around, and before I can take another step she throws both arms around my neck. Justin glances around the yard like he's looking for an excuse to leave.

"I'm going to grab a drink," he says, and then tells me where to find the beer they stashed in the bushes.

"Thanks." I don't tell him that I don't drink. I tried once, at a party my sophomore year, and it was a disaster. After two beers, all I had to do was *think* about needing to take a leak and I'd wind up back home in my bathroom.

Anna gives me another squeeze. "Did you get my present?"

I nod. "Thank you. It's perfect. Exactly what the room needed." I step back and take a closer look at her. "You look amazing."

Anna looks down at her outfit and shakes her head. "Emma's doing, of course." The shirt is lower cut than anything I've ever seen on her, but I don't want to make her self-conscious, so I don't say anything.

"How was your trip?" she asks, raising her eyebrows jokingly.

"Very short."

"No little bags of peanuts on board?"

I run my thumb along her cheek. "Nope. No peanuts."

She fake-pouts. "Bummer. I liked the peanuts."

"Can you stop talking now so I can kiss you?" I start to move in closer to her but she pulls away, glancing over my shoulder at the party in full swing behind me, and reaches for my hand.

"Not here." She gives me a peck on the cheek instead. "I have an idea. Follow me."

She leads me to the other side of the lawn, past the DJ and to the edge of the garden. We're not exactly out of sight, but this is a little more private.

I think I'm finally going to kiss her, but then she ducks down low and pulls me into a small grove of fruit trees. We push branches and leaves out of our way and when we're able to stand up straight again, we're standing at the edge of a hill. A tall, wrought-iron gate hugs the slope, and Anna feels around in the dark for the opening. She finds the latch and the gate swings toward us with a squeak.

It's dark back here, but the narrow path is illuminated by a series of lights hidden in the surrounding ferns and grasses. Tiny rocks crunch under our feet as we follow the path to a wooden bridge, and once we're across, I see a cement bench next to a giant Buddha statue. I can still hear the music, but it's muffled.

Anna stops in front of the bench and steps in close to me, resting her hands on my waist. "So . . . you were saying something about peanuts," she says with a smile.

"No, I was saying something about kissing you." And before

she can say another word, my hands settle on the small of her back and I close what's left of the distance between us. I feel her hands on the back of my neck, her fingers traveling into my hair, pulling me into her, kissing me.

When we stop, she doesn't open her eyes or move away. I can feel her breath as she speaks. "I missed you." She runs her thumb along my jawbone and my pulse races. "Tell me about the last few weeks. I want to know everything."

Everything. I take a deep breath, preparing to launch in. I've been waiting for three weeks to tell Anna *everything.* How many times did I stare at my cell phone, wishing I could call and tell her about the fire, and two kids that are alive today but shouldn't be, and the look on my dad's face when I told him what I'd done? Finally, here she is, staring at me with this sweet, expectant look on her face, and my mind is totally blank.

I'm not ready to go there yet, so I decide to warm up with a few basics. I sit down, straddling the bench, and Anna sits right in front of me. When I talk, she leans in close, as if my class schedule is especially interesting, and when I tell her about my friends and how weird it is to be back with all of them, she scoots forward and takes my hand, lightly tracing the lines in my palm with her fingertip as she listens.

When I'm finished, I ask her about life at Westlake. She tells me about Argotta's class and how she has a new conversation partner, and that every time she turns around and looks at my old desk, it makes her happy to think that I sat there once but also makes her sad that I no longer do. Last weekend, she got the top time in her cross-country meet.

We're both quiet for a few minutes and I see my opening. I take a deep breath, preparing to tell her about the fire, but before I can, she squeezes my hand and says, "I have something to tell you."

I smile at her. "I have something to tell you, too."

"You first," she says.

"Yeah? You sure?" I ask, but I'm secretly glad I don't have to wait any longer. I was nervous at first, but now that we're all warmed up, I can't wait to see the look on her face when I tell her what I did.

Anna nods.

I shake my head, looking for the right words to kick off my bizarre story. It's still kind of hard to believe, let alone say out loud. "I did something really crazy. Or stupid. Or awesome. . . . I don't know. It's sort of hard to categorize."

She looks at me quizzically.

"My dad and I were watching the news one morning, and there was this story about two kids who were killed in an apartment fire. For the next few days, I—I—" I start stammering, and rake my fingers through my hair as I search for the right words. "I just couldn't get the image out of my mind."

I'm careful about what I say next, purposely withholding the future-specific things I can't tell her about, like the online news article and Google Maps. "It started as pure curiosity. I sat there, scratching equations and time conversions into my notebook, trying to figure out if it would even be possible, but before I knew it, I was combing the house for a fire extinguisher and a smoke detector."

"No way. . . ." Her eyes light up and a smile spreads across her face. "You stopped it?"

I shake my head. "I didn't stop it. I just . . . readjusted a few things."

"You . . . readjusted a few things?"

I tell her how I crept through the dark apartment. I describe the wall of school photos, and I explain how I worked quickly to mount the smoke detector without waking the kids.

"I went back and did nearly *three days* over again. Until Emma, I'd never gone back more than five or ten minutes, you know? I didn't even know it was possible. But it worked. When I went into the kitchen that morning, the news story on TV was about a fire that took out an apartment complex, not a fire that killed two kids. And when I told my dad what I did . . ." My words hang in the air. I look down at a cluster of plants and Anna rests her hands on my hips.

"You changed it."

I nod slowly. And then I can't help it. I break into a huge smile. "I don't know if it was right or not. It doesn't matter now, it was a one-time thing. Or, I guess, counting Emma, a two-time thing. I just wanted to see if I could do it again."

"And you did."

"Yeah."

Anna brings her hands to my face and kisses me. She pulls away and stares at me for what feels like a really long time, and I assume that she's trying to think of something to say. Finally I remember that she had something to tell me too.

"Hey, you said you had news too? What did you want to tell me?"

She checks her watch.

"Nothing. It can wait." She stands up and holds out her hand. "We've been gone a long time. Emma is probably starting to look for me."

I realize that tonight's supposed to be about Emma, but I'm not ready to go back out there and share Anna with the rest of her friends yet. I wish I knew when we'd get to be alone again.

Before I can say anything, she shrugs and says, "Really. It's no big deal. I'll tell you later."

We wind back up the path and reemerge from the trees. I spot Emma right away, but that's not saying much. She's pretty hard to miss, dancing with a big group of girls in her short skirt, tight half-shirt, and a huge fabric hat in the shape of a birthday cake.

When Emma sees us, she bounces over and gives me a big hug. I wish her a happy birthday and she grabs each of us by the arm and leads us back out to the patch of grass that's become a dance floor. I try not to think about the fact that I'm the only guy out here.

We've been dancing for about five minutes, and I'm thinking that's more than sufficient. I'm just about to leave when Emma throws her arm over my shoulder and pulls me in close to her. "I've missed you, *Shaggy*." She musses my hair and I can't help smiling. No one's called me that in months.

"I've missed you too, Em."

Then she stands up on her tiptoes and gets right in my face. "I hear you've turned my sweet little Anna into a big fat liar," she says, shaking her head.

That's the last thing I'd want to do. I look at her, genuinely confused. "How so?"

She stares at me like I should know what she's talking about. "Tonight?" she says, raising her eyebrows, waiting for it to sink in.

I'm starting to feel a little dense because I'm still not sure where she's going with this. "I have no idea what you're talking about."

She pulls away and studies my expression, and I guess she comes to the conclusion that I'm telling the truth. "She didn't tell you?" she asks, and I shake my head no. Resting a hand on my shoulder, she whispers in my ear, "Her parents don't know you're in town."

When she pulls away, I just look at her. I'm still not getting it.

"She told them she's spending the night here, at my house. She brought an overnight bag and everything." She winks.

I turn and look over my shoulder at Anna. She's dancing with a big group, but she keeps looking over at Emma and me.

"Really?" I say without taking my eyes off Anna.

"Yes, really." Emma musses my hair again. "I believe somebody owes me one," she sings.

We have a whole night together. We've never had a whole *planned* night together, and I know exactly what I'm going to do with it. But right now, I just need to get off this dance floor. I spot Justin over by the tree, talking with a couple of guys I don't know. "What if I go chat with your ex and see what I can do about getting you two back together again?"

She huffs. "What makes you think I want to get back together with him?"

"The way you've been looking over there the entire time I've been talking to you." The corners of her mouth twitch, like she's fighting back a smile.

She pokes me in the chest four times as she spits out each word: "We. Are. Just. Friends."

But you're not supposed to be, I want to say. *You're supposed to be together. You might still be if I hadn't wiped out the first four hours of your first date.* I flash back to the Saturday that Anna and I went back and changed. How we basically created two versions of the same day, one that ended with a horrible accident that left Emma in the ICU and another that ended with Anna, Emma, Justin, and me at the movies together. The first one ended with Justin telling Anna how he and Emma had this incredible morning hanging out at her house, bonding over a conversation that left him surprised and unquestionably interested in her. The second one ended with them breaking up a few months later.

It would be nice not to feel so responsible for the second version, but I *am.* "So, you don't want me to talk to him?" I ask.

She looks over at Justin and back at me. I wait her out. "Okay," she finally says with a heavy sigh. "If you want to."

I give Anna a small wave, thrilled to be honorably

discharged from the dance floor, and squeeze through the crowd toward Justin. On my way, I grab a Coke from a bucket of ice and pop the top.

He introduces me to his friends, two guys he works with at the radio station, and we spend the next ten minutes talking about music. Eventually they take off to find the hidden beer, and I'm standing alone with Justin.

"So," I say. I take a sip of my drink. "Can I ask you a question?"

Justin nods.

"What happened with you and Emma over the summer?"

He looks in her direction. Emma and Anna are buried somewhere in the crowd of people jumping up and down because the song is telling them to.

"I don't know," he says without looking away from the dance floor. He stares into his red Solo cup, like he might find the answer he's looking for somewhere at the bottom. "At first, I thought we were a good match, you know? But after a while, it seemed like we were both trying too hard or something. Or . . . maybe I just was."

We both look back at the dance floor again. The song ends and we see Emma emerge, one arm hooked through Danielle's and the other around Anna's shoulders. She's leading both of them away from the dance floor toward the big bucket of drinks in the corner. She grabs three sodas, passes them around, and pops the top of her own.

"Don't get me wrong," Justin says. "She's funny and gorgeous and I'm sure everyone here thinks I'm crazy for breaking up with her. But honestly, I don't think I ever really got used to the idea of the two of us together."

"Maybe you didn't give her enough of a chance."

He laughs. "Now you sound like Anna." He looks away when he says her name, and there's something in his expression I can't read.

I think about how many times I sat in San Francisco, remembering the months I spent in this town, and not only missing Anna, but Justin and Emma too. "I know you broke up, but would it be too much to ask for the four of us to go out while I'm in town this weekend?"

"Sure. We still hang out. We're good friends."

"But that's it?" I ask. When I look over at Anna, I see the three of them heading our way.

Justin sees them too, and when he does, he looks down at the grass, suddenly bashful. "Yeah, that's it. But I like her. A lot," he says. "I always have."

I watch as his gaze travels toward them, and for a second I wonder if he's still talking about Emma.

⌒

Emma's mom sidles up next to Anna and asks her if she'll come inside and help with the cake, and I finally see my chance to get away from the party. Tracing the route Anna showed me earlier, I sneak past the food table and out toward the edge of the garden, under the fruit trees, through the wrought-iron gate, and deep into the backyard.

I follow the winding path that leads to the cement bench at the bottom and make my way over to the tiny gardening shed I noticed earlier. It's angled into the corner and, while the squeeze is tighter than I expected, it works well enough. I close my eyes. When I open them, I'm back in my room at Maggie's.

I work quickly. My red backpack is leaning up against my desk, and I fill it with a couple of shirts, a sweater, and a huge stack of cash from the cabinet. I check to be sure that my Illinois ID is in my wallet, and I add a few more bills in there for backup. I find the cardboard box I stuffed deep into the closet and remove the rest of the things Anna and I need: four plastic bottles of water, two bottles of Starbucks Frappuccino, and an unopened sleeve of saltines.

In the bathroom, I find that Maggie has now filled the drawers with me in mind. There's a new tube of toothpaste, still in its box. Three toothbrushes in sealed plastic packages. A six-pack of disposable razors.

I head downstairs and call out to Maggie a few times, but there's no reply, so I go to the desk, quickly scratch out new notes, and replace the ones I left earlier. I'm standing in the hallway, about to return to the party, when I have an idea. It's a huge risk but I'm assuming that by now, everyone's busy singing "Happy Birthday," so I close my eyes and open them in a quiet corner of Emma's bedroom. Right away, I spot Anna's overnight bag on the floor by the bed. There's plenty of room in my backpack, so I stuff the whole thing inside.

I close my eyes again picturing the tiny spot behind the

shed in Emma's backyard, and when I open them, I'm standing there. I drop my backpack, peek around the corner, and sneak back to the party.

"Cake?" Anna asks when I return to her side. My face still feels hot and my hands are shaking with nervous energy as I take the plate from her hand, but she doesn't seem to notice. She sees a group of her cross-country friends and pulls me in their direction, saying that she wants me to get to know them better.

When the temperature begins to drop and the balloon arch has started sagging, the DJ announces his last song. I watch Emma leave the lawn, find Justin, and pull him out to the makeshift dance floor with her. He says something and she throws her head back as she laughs. She stands on her tiptoes, kisses his cheek, and puts her birthday cake hat on his head. He tries to give it back, but she keeps pulling it down over his eyes.

I nudge Anna with my elbow and subtly gesture toward the two of them. "That's interesting."

Anna follows my gaze and then looks back at me wearing a huge smile. "Yes it is."

Now Justin is dancing. Like, actually dancing. He's jumping up and down and grabbing Emma around the waist, and she's smiling like this is the best birthday she's ever had.

When I look over at Anna, she's still watching her two best friends, and I wonder if she's thinking about what we did that day. I wonder if she looks at them the same way I do, knowing that they should be together and feeling responsible for the fact that they aren't. But suddenly, Emma and Justin disappear from my thoughts, and now I'm looking at her and all I can think about is the backpack stuffed behind the gardening shed at the bottom of the hill. Without meaning to, I let a small laugh slip out under my breath.

That gets her attention. "What?" she asks. There's this lilt in her voice, like she wants to know but at the same time she's a little bit afraid to.

"You had something to tell me," I say, fighting a grin.

She presses her lips together and takes a sharp inhale. "I did, yeah, I—" She starts to finish her sentence but I cut her off.

I push her hair back from her face and plant a kiss on her forehead. "Go say good-bye to Emma and meet me in the garden in ten minutes . . . where we were earlier. Don't let anyone see you."

Anna looks puzzled at first, but as she watches me, her mouth turns up at the corners and she nods without asking any questions. I turn and walk away from her, and for the third time tonight I follow the path until I reach the bottom of the garden. I wrestle my backpack out from behind the shed.

I pace the ground. I sit on the bench and stand up again. I examine the Buddha statue. Finally I see Anna's face peek out from behind the trees. The latch on the wrought-iron gate clicks and I hear it squeak open and closed.

Her feet crunch on the gravel as she winds down the path, and she stops when she finds me in the shadows, leaning up against the shed.

"Why are we down here?" she asks, and without saying a word, I step forward, wrap my fingers around the back of her neck, and kiss her. I can feel her smiling as she lets go of all her questions, parts her lips, and kisses me back. She tastes like cake.

Her hands settle on my hips and as she kisses me harder; her fingers creep under my shirt and up my back. I'm starting to wonder if we'll ever be able to get out of here, when she whispers, "Why are you wearing your backpack?"

I kiss her again. "Give me your hands."

She's breathing hard. "Why?" she asks, but doesn't hesitate for even a second. I can already feel her fingers sliding back down to my waist, feeling for my arms, following the bend in my elbow until they find their home in my hands.

Hers are shaking with anticipation or nerves or a combination of the two, and I take them, the whole time never letting her lips leave mine. All I can think about right now is that I'm so grateful for this crazy gift I possess; that I can take her away with me, just for a little while, disappearing completely into a faraway place where there's no people or voices in the background, and no one looks even vaguely familiar to either one of us.

Her eyes are already closed. I pull her hands behind my back, our fingers still locked, still connecting us, and I keep her body pressed into mine as I picture our destination.

I close my eyes.

And we disappear.

15

I open my eyes in a secluded area I found a few years ago
when Brooke and I came here for a U2 concert in '97. Anna's
hands are still locked behind my back and she's smiling, lids
tightly shut, waiting for me to speak.

"We're here," I say. "Open your eyes." As soon as I say the
words, my heart starts pumping hard.

I take a look around, but there's not much to see yet. Until
we get out from behind this shrub, we could be anywhere. I
follow Anna's gaze as she takes in the chain-link fences and
the back windows along a line of similar-looking houses. She
runs her toe across the gravel underneath our feet, like she's
trying hard to piece it all together. There's hardly any light
back here, but I can still make out the baffled expression she's
wearing as she turns slowly in place. And then she looks up,
beyond the shrubs, and sees the tower, its iron beams lit up

with so many lights it looks like it's made of gold. She covers her mouth with her hand and laughs.

"No way . . ."

"I told you. You needed to see Paris next."

She takes a few steps backward, stops when she hits my chest, and without turning around, feels for my hands and wraps them around her waist. She twists her neck so she can see me, and even though we're nowhere near Emma's backyard anymore, we pick up right where we left off two minutes ago.

⁓

We hop over the short fence that leads to the park. Once we're out in the open we can see the entire Eiffel Tower, base to top, gleaming in front of us. It's only nine o'clock and, surprisingly, there aren't many people back here. Anna and I walk toward the base with our fingers knit together. She keeps looking over at me, smiling and shaking her head.

She suddenly drops my hand. "Race you," she says, and she takes off. Her speed keeps her well in front of me at first, but she has to keep adjusting her skirt, and that slows her down. I pass her just before we turn the corner that leads under the structure, and that's where we find everyone. The crowd is thick and the lines are long.

"Come on," I say as I start walking toward the end of the shortest one, but Anna grabs me by the arm. She tips her head back and looks straight up. Then she looks back at me. "We're waiting in line?"

"Yep."

"Oh." She looks up to the top of the tower again, then back at me. "Why?"

I rest my hands on her shoulders and give her a quick kiss. "No cheating." In the time it's taken us to have this discussion, at least ten people have stepped into the line. I jump in at the end.

"Why is, you know . . . *that*"—she makes this weird gesture with her hand—"cheating?"

"Because it is. It's like rock climbing. You can't just magically find yourself on top of a mountain, staring out at an insane view. You've got to earn it. *Without* cheating." She presses her lips together, like she's trying not to smile. "Besides, there aren't a lot of discreet places up there." She shoots me a confused look and I step closer so I can't be overheard. "There's nowhere to arrive without being seen by a bunch of people."

"Oh."

"Which, you know, some might find shocking."

"Yeah, I suppose some might." She nods and tries to hold a serious expression, but I can see that smile still trying to peek through. "So we're taking the elevator?" It's a question, but she says it more like a statement.

"Nope. That's cheating too." She starts to say something, but I hold my finger up, and say, "Wait a sec."

I haven't exchanged my American dollars for French francs yet, so I've been subtly scanning the people in line for the perfect target and I just found him: older guy, jeans and tennis shoes, fanny pack with an American flag pinned to the belt.

When the line snakes around, I hold up three twenty-dollar bills and ask him if he'll buy us two tickets to the second deck via the stairs in exchange for them. He checks the prices on the board, calculates the profit, and happily takes the money from my hand.

"The stairs?" Anna asks.

I just grin.

"How many stairs?"

"I don't know. A lot. We can count them if you want to." She smacks me with the back of her hand. "Trust me, you'll love this. We can stop and look at the view on the way up." Fanny-pack Guy hands me our two tickets and we head to the entrance.

As it turns out, there are six hundred and seventy steps, and we don't even have to count them, because every tenth one is conveniently painted with a number. The higher we go, the more frequently Anna stops, saying she has to catch her breath. But I notice she's refusing to look around, and whenever I point out the sites, she just nods and keeps climbing. She looks relieved when we finally reach the second platform.

Down on the ground, it was already much colder here in Paris than it was in Evanston, but up on the tower, it feels like the middle of winter. Anna's trying to play it off like she isn't cold, but I can see her shivering as we stand here, leaning against the railing, staring out over the city. I suddenly remember that I brought my sweater, so I take it out of my backpack and hand it to her. She pulls it over her head. It

507

hangs almost to the edge of her skirt and the sleeves go past her fingers and she looks completely adorable.

Someone taps me on the shoulder and I turn around to find a woman grinning wide and holding a camera out in my direction. She says something in a language that's not English or French as she gestures between herself and the man standing to her right. I take the camera from her and hand it to Anna.

"You're the photographer," I say, and Anna looks grateful as she brings the camera to her face. She snaps a few pictures and hands it back to them.

"I hope one of those pictures turns out," Anna says when they're out of earshot. "They probably won't have another night on the Eiffel Tower again." I'm about to tell her that they're probably checking the pictures right now when I remember that cameras don't work that way yet. Then I realize that Anna's staring out at the view and not talking. I wish I'd thought to go to her house and get her camera for her.

"Stay here," I say, and without giving her any time to reply, I double back toward the elevator bank, past the people in line, and into the crowded gift shop. Right behind the counter, I find what I'm looking for. I convince the cashier to accept an American twenty in exchange for a ten-franc item, and less than ten minutes later I'm heading back to Anna with a plastic bag swinging by my side.

But when I return to the spot where I left her, she's gone. I walk all the way around the deck, but she's nowhere to be found. I head back toward the center of the platform and see her there, pacing back and forth in front of the elevators.

"Hey." I come up behind her and grab her by the waist. She jumps. "You okay?"

She flips around, arms crossed, eyes narrowed. "You left me on the Eiffel Tower?"

"Just for a minute," I say, and her eyes grow wide. I'm clearly not supposed to find this amusing, but I can't help it. She's just standing there, looking small and pissed off and adorable in my sweater.

"You're laughing at me?" Her eyes grow even wider and I think she's going to start yelling at me or something, but instead she steps forward and takes my face in her hands. "What if something happened to you? What if you got knocked back?" She shakes her head. "I don't even know what date it is," she practically whispers.

I'm still finding this amusing, even though I'm clearly not supposed to. "I'm sorry. I didn't mean to scare you." I kiss her and I'm relieved when she lets me. "I'm not going to get knocked back. And besides, you know I never take you out of your time. Never. You're always a really awkward phone call and an outrageously expensive plane ride away from your parents, but that's it. Okay?"

She presses her lips together and nods.

"I just wanted to get you this." I hand her the plastic gift-shop bag, and she peeks inside. Her whole expression relaxes as the grin spreads across her face.

"You bought a disposable camera?"

I shrug. "You looked a little sad about taking that couple's picture." I guide her over to the railing. "Smile," I say, holding the camera out in front of us. I press the button and the shutter snaps, but when I press it again, nothing happens. I'm turning it around in my hands, looking at it from all angles and trying to figure out what to do next, when Anna takes it from me, chuckling as she runs her thumb along a little wheel that must advance the film. She holds her arm out and presses the button.

After she's taken four or five shots, she stops and looks at the camera. I can tell by the way she's staring at it, running her finger along its edges, that this small cardboard box contains so much more than a few images of the two of us on an undeveloped strip of film. It's not a memory or a postcard, it's more than she's ever had—tangible proof that we exist together, outside both her world and mine.

"Bennett?" she says, still looking down at the camera.

"Yeah."

"Are we going back home tonight?" When her eyes find mine, I shake my head no.

Her gaze travels up to the brightly lit iron beams above us, and a grin spreads across her face. "I never thought I'd be standing on the Eiffel Tower and saying this but . . . can we get out of here?"

16

Clouds are filtering the morning sun but it's still bright enough to stir me from sleep. I rub my eyes as I take in the unfamiliar room, remembering little by little where I am right now. In Paris. With Anna.

She's sitting in the window ledge, her bare legs bent and visible below the hem of one of my T-shirts. Her chin is resting on her knees and she's staring out the window at the city below.

I kick off the covers and cross the room. "What are you doing way over here?" I pull her hair to one side and kiss the back of her neck.

"I couldn't sleep." She's quiet for a few seconds, and then she says, "I keep having to remind myself that this is all happening. That I'm actually here."

"Then we should get going. We have a whole day in Paris and we still won't come close to seeing everything."

Anna turns her head and gives me the biggest smile. And then she sits up straighter and spins in place, wrapping her legs around my waist and her arms around my neck. "I didn't mean Paris. I meant here, with you."

⌒⌒⌒

We grab coffees at the café downstairs and make a game plan. We decide to skip the obvious sights, the museums and cathedrals and monuments, but agree that we can't miss the Seine, so we order our *pain au chocolat* to go and head toward the river. We find a place to sit on the bank, and Anna pops a chunk of bread into her mouth. She closes her eyes, letting the dough and chocolate melt on her tongue.

"God, that's incredible. Why can't we make bread that tastes like this?"

"You and me?" I joke and she stares at me.

"Americans."

"Oh. Because we aren't French," I say matter-of-factly.

She tears off another chunk of bread and pops it into my mouth, presumably to shut me up.

We spend the rest of the morning wandering around aimlessly, meandering down the smallest alleys we can find, popping into bakeries when they smell too good to simply walk past. Anna stops at a corner store that appears to sell everything from drinks to cheesy Parisian trinkets, and heads for the cooler. She grabs two bottles of water and tosses one to me.

The clerk is ringing us up when Anna sees a display on the counter. "Ah, here you go." She hands me a laminated map.

"This is what we need," she says, tapping the surface.

I take it from her hand and slip it back into the rack where it was. "We don't need a map."

"Why not?" She looks confused at first, but then her face falls. "How many times have you been to Paris?"

"Twice. Both times for concerts, and I barely even walked around the city." Anna waits patiently for a better explanation. "I just prefer to get lost."

She raises her eyebrows and stares at me. "You want to get lost? In Paris?"

"It'll be fun."

She looks unconvinced. She might also look a bit terrified. So I grab the map from the rack and set it down on the counter. "Fine. We'll get a map. But it's purely for backup."

The cashier gives us the total but I hold my hand up in the air and tell her to wait. "Stay here. I'll be right back." Anna cocks her head to the side, and gives me a *Haven't we already covered this?* expression, but I laugh under my breath and take off anyway.

I have to snake around a few aisles, but I finally find a small section of bike accessories, and that's where I find the padlocks. I return to the counter, using a little sleight of hand to keep it hidden from her view.

"Here," I say as I take my backpack off and hand it to Anna, along with the map. "Find an extremely inconvenient pocket for that, would you?" While she's busy with the zipper, I remove the padlock and its key from their packaging, and slip them into the front pocket of my jeans.

513

I look at her and say, "Now we have a destination."

"We do?"

"Yeah. I want to show you something."

"Do you need the map?" She smiles.

I look at her and shake my head. "No, I do not need the map."

<hr />

I may need the map. We've been walking along the banks of the river for a good forty minutes, and we keep passing bridges, but so far, I haven't seen the sign that marks the one I need. I give myself one more bridge before I fold. Then I spot it: a dark green sign with white type that reads PONT DES ARTS.

The pedestrian-only footbridge is more crowded than I expected it to be. Couples are sitting on the benches in the center and people are clustered in groups along the railings. Everyone seems to be speaking French.

I find a spot against the railing and sit down. I lean back against a post and Anna sits between my legs. Just as she's reclining against my chest, a police siren blares by and fades away. "I love how even the most common sounds remind you that you're somewhere else," she says.

We're quiet for a long time, looking out over the water, until Anna twists her neck and looks up at me. "I've been dying to ask you something," she says. I must be wearing an affirmative expression because she suddenly spins around to face me and looks me right in the eye. "When you stopped the fire, did you feel the same way you did after we changed things with Emma?"

Her question catches me off guard and I react by dodging it. "I didn't stop the fire. I changed a few things leading up to the fire. Big difference." But Anna stares at me, not letting me off the hook.

I look at her, remembering how I sat in my room that night, picturing the look on Anna's face when she first saw Emma, unbroken. "Before, during, or after?" I ask.

"All of the above." She reaches out for the hem of my shirt and plays with it, running her finger back and forth along the edge.

I start to fall back on the things I say when I don't want to let people in: simple words like "fine" and "good" that slip so easily off my tongue. But instead, I feel myself lean in a little closer, like I'm ready to tell her everything.

"Before? Scared," I say flatly. "When you asked me to go back and help Emma, I honestly didn't think I could do over that many days, and even if I could, I had no idea if it would work. Anything could have happened. We could have been knocked back right away. Or we could have changed the sequence of events, but the car accident might have happened a few hours later regardless. The number of things that could have gone wrong were just . . ." I trail off, shaking my head.

"I thought Emma would be the first and last time I'd ever do anything like that. But when I heard what happened to those kids, I guess I just wanted to try it again. I mean, if could go back two days, why not three? And if it *did* work, if I could *change* it . . . Still, I'd be lying if I said I wasn't terrified the entire time."

Anna doesn't say anything, but she's tracing tiny circles in my palms again, just like she did in Emma's backyard last night. I think that means I'm supposed to keep talking.

"During, I didn't think about anything else. I just hoped it would work." I'm hit with a vision of the school pictures that lined the hallway of apartment 3C.

"And after . . ." I stop. I don't know what to say about the after. After I installed the smoke detector and came home, I waited to see the news, and discovered that the do-over had worked. My dad looked proud and shocked at the same time, like I'd hit that inexplicable home run in a tied game, bottom of the ninth.

"After," I repeat. "It was like being in one of those Choose Your Own Adventure books and I chose a different ending. Those two kids were alive and safe, and I knew they shouldn't have been. And that was . . . strange . . . to know that they died."

Anna brings my hand to her lips and kisses it. "And what about the side effects?"

"Nothing," I whisper. "No migraine. No dehydration. No side effects at all. I felt like I could have run around the block." Another tour boat goes by and we stop to listen to the guide rattle off the interesting facts about this bridge that we've heard twice now.

"Do you think—" Anna begins. She stops, waiting for a group of kids in matching soccer uniforms to walk past us.

"Do you think it's possible that do-overs aren't such a bad thing?"

I shake my head. "What do you mean? That I'm *supposed* to change things? No way. I did it once for you. I guess I did it this second time for my dad. But those were isolated incidents that I *chose* to do. It's not like I'm now on a mission to stop the world's tragedies. Besides, I still don't know if there are ramifications or not." I can't even say it aloud, but part of me is still wondering if the people whose lives I've altered are affected by their changed pasts. Does Emma know at some unconscious level that she was in a massive car accident? Will those two kids . . . I can't think about it. "Look, nothing's changed. I'm purely an observer. I'm not supposed to alter the future."

"I'm not saying you're *supposed* to, just that it felt good when you did. I mean, Emma and Justin are fine, right? Nothing horrible happened to them, they just . . . got a second chance. And because of you, so did those kids."

I look past her, staring out over the water. A second chance. I sort of like the idea of that. Not that it matters, since I'm not doing it again.

"Hey," I say, as I lean back and reach into my front pocket. "I almost forgot why I brought you here in the first place."

She looks at me with a curious grin. I open her hand and rest the brass padlock in her palm. She takes her eyes off me to look down at it. "Why am I holding a padlock?" The sunlight bounces off the surface as she twists it around, examining it from all sides as if that will enlighten her.

"I probably shouldn't tell you this—it involves a few future details—but I heard this story and thought it was cool." I shift in place and take a deep breath. "No one really knows when it started exactly, but by the end of two thousand nine, all of the railings on this bridge will be covered with padlocks. Couples who came to Paris from all over the world started writing their names on them, clipping them to this railing, and tossing the key into the river as a symbol . . ." Anna's wearing an expression I can't read, and I suddenly realize how lame I sound. ". . . of, like, their . . . Oh, never mind." I reach for the padlock, but she snaps her hand closed.

"Stop it. You're not taking our lock."

"Yes, I am." I reach for it again but she laughs and pulls her hand behind her back.

She looks me in the eyes. "Go on."

"No. I heard that story and thought it was kind of romantic, but now that I say it out loud it sounds so cheesy."

"No, it doesn't." I lean back against the post. Once she can tell I'm not going to try to take it away again, she brings her hand back to her lap and opens her palm. "I love it."

"Yeah?"

"Yeah." She turns the padlock over in her palm again, this time as if she's admiring it. "We don't have anything to write with."

I lean back and pull a black Sharpie from my jeans pocket. When I hand it to her, she laughs. "Typical. Here," she says, handing me the lock. "You should write it. It was your idea."

I shake my head. We're in 1995, in her world, and it seems

like something she's supposed to do. When I tell her this, she uncaps the pen and brings the felt tip to the metal.

"What should I say?"

"Whatever you want to say."

She thinks about it for a moment and writes ANNA ♥ BENNETT across the surface. "That's not very inspired, is it?" She stops and looks out over the water like she's trying to decide how to finish what she started. She brings the pen back to the lock and writes '95/'12. She stares at it.

"I like it," I say. "Now it's both cheesy *and* mysterious."

"Aww. Just like us."

"Nah, nothing like us," I say. "We're not at all mysterious."

I hand her the key and she slips it inside. The latch opens with a tiny click, and she threads the lock through the chain-link fence and snaps it closed. She runs her fingertip across the surface and lets out a little laugh. "Wouldn't it be funny if we're the ones that start the whole lock thing?"

"Maybe we do."

"I like that," she says.

I don't have the heart to tell her that in 2010, all the locks will be removed. Or that, in 2011, they'll start reappearing, and by 2012, there will be very few spaces left on the railing again. They can cut our lock off. We'll just come back here together—in 1998 and 2008 and 2018—and replace it every time it gets removed. I stare at the key in Anna's hand, wondering if it's realistic to think that we will still be together years from now, living this way.

I never even wished for her, but right now, all I want is for this person who gets me so completely to be part of my present and my future. As long as I don't think about the logistics, it seems possible.

Anna kisses me. Then we both kiss the key and she tosses it into the river.

Anna and I spend the rest of the afternoon wandering around. We don't have a destination in mind, so we turn when we feel like turning and stop when we feel like stopping and poke our heads into shops that look interesting. We pop into record stores so we can buy CD imports that would cost a fortune back in the States. We pick out postcards.

We stop at a bakery for a baguette, and then, without even discussing it, we head through a set of wrought iron gates and into a park. It's alive with activity, and as we meander down the path, people jog past us and in-line skaters roll by. Anna surprises me when she pulls me off the walkway and behind a dense cluster of trees to kiss me.

We spot a soccer game and sit on the grass to watch. The whole thing is nonstop action, but we both find it difficult to take our eyes off this one guy in a bright green shirt. He's the shortest one out there, and he's *so* quick, but it's more than that—he's just fun to watch. His face is completely serious until he takes a shot, but then he throws his hands up in the air in victory and lets out a yell, even when he misses.

A half hour later, we're still glued to the game, and it's now tied, two-two. Green-shirt Guy kicks the ball and takes off running toward the goal. Then he's open, waving his arms in the air, and the ball comes sailing back in his direction. But just as he's about to kick it, another player comes running at him from the opposite direction. The two of them collide hard, and Green-shirt Guy falls to the ground, clutching his leg. Everyone gathers around him, so it's impossible to see what's going on.

A few minutes later, he emerges from the crowd with his arms draped over two of his teammates' shoulders. His face is full of agony as he hops on one leg to the closest bench. He sits down and buries his face into his hands while they remove his shoe.

"I wonder if it's broken," Anna says.

All I can think to say is, "They hit hard."

"Bennett," she says quietly.

I look over at her. "Yeah?"

Her eyes are still glued to the guy in the green shirt and she's wearing the strangest expression. "What if you gave him a second chance?"

I shake my head. Hard.

She looks at me. "You could test yourself. See if the side effects kick in or not. And if they do, I can help you."

It's a ridiculous idea. I don't even know what time it is or how long we've been here, but I do know that we've been completely out in the open, in full view of everyone. We'd need a safe point we could return to without being seen, and we don't have one. But then I remember how Anna pulled me behind the bushes to kiss me.

"There was a clock in the bakery," she says. "It was 2:10. We got to the park and walked around and it was, what do you think, 2:30 when we sat down here?" She's talking fast, thinking too much, and getting way too excited about this. But before I can say anything, she stands up, heads back to the path, and returns less than a minute later. "It's 3:05 right now."

I look back over at the guy in the green shirt. His face is pinched and his leg is stretched out in front of him, and I still can't tell if it's broken or not, but he's definitely in a lot of pain. I think through the times Anna just rattled off to me and before I know it, I'm grabbing her hand and steering her back to that spot behind the bushes.

"This is crazy," I say.

When we arrive, she pivots to face me. When were we here last? 2:20? 2:23? I can't be sure, and I have to be sure, or the Anna and Bennett back on that part of the timeline will disappear into thin air in the middle of the street, or at the entrance to the park, or from the front of the bakery line.

I think through every step we made, and then I grab her hands and shut my eyes. When I open them, we're standing a few feet from where we started, back on the path, and in plain sight. We both speed back behind the bushes and hide there for a minute or two, until I'm certain that no one saw us.

We rush back to the soccer game in progress and sit in the

same spot, watching the same game. The guy in the bright green shirt is perfectly fine, speeding toward the ball, making solid kicks, and throwing his arms up in delight with every attempt. Anna's sitting closer to me this time, her legs folded in front of her and one leg resting on mine. She tightens her grip on my hand and we come up with a plan.

The score reaches two-two, and they're all lined up, about to make that last play. Before the ball gets thrown out, Anna looks at me, stands up, and races down the edge of the field near the goal. The play goes the same way. He kicks it and takes off running, but this time, just as he's about to throw his arms up, Anna yells, "Stop!" at the top of her lungs.

Most of the guys ignore her, but Green-shirt Guy turns around, just for a second, and looks at her. By the time he returns his attention to the game, it's too late. The other guy has the ball and he's taking it to the goal at the opposite end. He kicks it hard, scores, and the game is over. Green-shirt Guy throws his hands up in Anna's direction, and yells at her in French.

She takes off toward me, running and laughing, grabbing my hand as she speeds by. We spot a bench out of sight and collapse on it. My hands are shaking and my heart is pounding so hard I feel like it's about to burst out of my chest.

"I have no idea why I let you talk me into these things," I say, breathing fast. "You and Brooke." I shake my head. "You have far too much in common." I look over at her and she's sitting there, catching her breath, beaming and obviously quite proud of herself. "You look adorable when stopping tragedies, by the way."

She brings her hands to my face and kisses me, even though there are people everywhere.

I've spent all these years trying not to alter the slightest event, and now, in the seven months since I met Anna, I've purposely changed things four times. And none of them seems to have thrown the universe off-kilter or anything.

"How do you feel?" she asks as she pulls away.

"Good." I look at her and smile. "Really good."

⌐⌐

By the time the sun starts to set, our legs are rubbery from climbing so many stairs and hills, and now we're standing in a secluded corner of a dead-end street, holding hands, smiling at each other and stalling.

"You ready?" I ask.

"No," she says. "Not even close."

But we can't stay away any longer. I tell her to close her eyes and she does, but before I do the same, I take a glance around this Parisian street one more time. Then I let my eyes fall shut.

When I open them, we're in the exact same position, back in my room at Maggie's, and it's Saturday morning. I check the clock. Ten A.M.

Almost instantly, Anna lets out a quiet groan and her hands find her stomach. She slumps down on the floor and pulls her knees to her chest. I slide down next to her, and even though my head is throbbing and my vision is blurry, I remove my backpack and grope around inside, searching for the sleeve of saltines. When I find them, I tear into the package and hand it to her. Anna mumbles a thank-you as she starts in on a corner of the cracker, and I search for the water bottles.

We sit like that for a good twenty minutes, me downing waters and Frappuccinos, Anna nibbling crackers and trying not to hurl. "Now *this* is romantic," she says, resting her head on my shoulder.

I let out a weak laugh and let my head fall against hers.

Anna finally declares herself strong enough to stand. But when I try to say, "I'll walk you home," my words slur, and when I stand up, my legs wobble. I lean on the bed, resting my hand on the surface for stability. I'm utterly exhausted. I can't remember the last time I felt this tired.

"Lie down," Anna insists as she pushes me gently toward the bed and lifts my feet off the floor. I hear her tell me to scoot up a little. I feel her adjust my pillow under my head. I think she takes off my shoes. "Close your eyes," I hear her say, quiet and soothing, as she sits on the edge of the bed and runs her thumbs back and forth along my forehead.

I don't remember anything after that.

18

The faint sound of knocking wakes me up from a deep sleep. I sit up in bed and rub my head with both hands. The next knock is louder.

"Come in." I feel like my eyes have been glued shut, but I force them open when the door creaks and Maggie pokes her head inside. She looks surprised to see me twisted and disheveled on top of my comforter.

"I'm sorry," she says. "I didn't realize you were sleeping. I just wanted to know if you were going to be here for dinner."

I press my fingertips into my temples and glance over at the clock radio on the nightstand. Is it really 6:12? Have I been out all afternoon? The last thing I remember was Anna helping me lie down. Was that really almost eight hours ago?

"I'm making a pot roast." Maggie smiles as she says it, like I might need convincing. But I don't. I take a big whiff of something that smells delicious. I'm just about to tell her that

I'll be down in a minute when she crosses her arms and her expression turns serious. "Are you okay, Bennett?"

I force myself to sit up and throw my feet to the floor. "I'm okay. Just really tired."

"Jet lag," she says plainly, and closes the door behind her. If only she knew that I've never been on a jet.

I pull on a clean pair of jeans and reach into the chest of drawers for a shirt. I still feel shaky and a bit cold, so I throw on a flannel.

Downstairs, I find Maggie setting the table for two. She glances up at me and returns to folding the cloth napkins into triangles. I slip right into my old role here, reaching into the cabinet for two glasses and filling them with milk.

Maggie and I politely take our seats like I'm a guest in her home. I try to come up with topics for small talk, but all I can think about is Anna and our day in Paris. I block it from my mind as I dig into the pot roast, I tell her all about Emma's party, right down to the details of the balloon arch and the DJ in the backyard. Maggie gives me encouraging laughs and asks a lot of questions about the people I know here. Then there's a pause in the discussion and she looks at me pointedly.

"It sounds like you made a lot of friends at Westlake," she says without looking at me. I start to respond, but I freeze instead. It's the first time she's acknowledged knowing that I lied to her about being a student at Northwestern last year, but she throws it out there and goes back to eating like it's no big deal. "My daughter loved it there too."

This would be a great time to apologize for lying to her. It would also be a great time to tell her that her daughter and my mom are the same person. While both are true, I feel a little bit sick the moment I have these two thoughts, so I ignore them and try to go back to my dinner as if Maggie's statement doesn't require a response. But then I hear Anna's words in my head: *It would be nice to have one person in my life that I can talk to about you—one person I don't have to keep your secret from.* That, I can't ignore.

My stomach is turning and what I really want to do right now is bolt out the back door, run past the tomato garden, and find an empty spot to disappear from. I could be back in San Francisco in less than a minute.

Before I let my feet dictate my next steps, I force out the words, "Maggie, I need to tell you something." And there it is. Now I don't have a choice. There's nothing else I need to tell her.

"Sure." I think she's trying not to look at me now. And I'm definitely trying not to look at her.

I'm pushing mashed potatoes around with my fork like the words I need to find are buried somewhere underneath. "I'm not quite sure how to explain this. Thre's something about me that's . . . unusual." I cringe as I hear the words come out of my mouth. She's looking at me, waiting for me to continue, and I suddenly wonder if it wouldn't be better to just show her. After all, it worked with Anna. I push my chair away from the table and stand over by the counter.

I blow out a breath. Here we go.

Maggie sets her fork down and wipes her face with her napkin.

"Watch," I say. And I close my eyes, but before I let myself disappear, I add the words "Please don't freak out."

Seconds after I picture my room upstairs, I'm standing in the center of it. Downstairs, I hear Maggie scream. I count to ten and close my eyes again, returning to the exact same spot in the kitchen. She's standing right in front of me and when she goes to move away, she smacks me hard on the shoulder. She mutters something that might be an apology and reaches for the counter to steady herself. Perhaps this wasn't the best way to break the news.

I reach forward and grip her arms. "It's okay. There's nothing to be afraid of."

She stares at me, her mouth hanging open and her eyes wide. I lead her over to the chair, and she sits down, forearms pressed into the Formica, staring at her half-eaten plate of food.

I sit down next to her. "I want you to know who I am, Maggie."

She doesn't look up at me but I see her head nod.

"There's a lot you already know about me. My name is Bennett. I live in San Francisco. I think you know I'm seventeen and that I never went to Northwestern, and I'm sorry I lied and told you that I did."

This whole thing sounded so much better in my head. It isn't coming out at all the way I wanted it to. Maggie gives me a slight nod, but I don't know if she's following me or if she just wants me to continue in hopes that I'll eventually get to the point. "There's also a lot you don't know about me. Like . . . that . . . my mom is your daughter. Her pictures are all over your house." My hands feel clammy so I rub them on my jeans and keep talking. I can't stop now. "There aren't many of your grandson because he's only seven months old right now. And . . ." I pause to take a deep breath, but it seems pointless. I should just spit it out. "This is going to sound really weird, but . . . that's the reason your grandson and I have the same name."

This time, her head doesn't move at all.

"I'm . . ." I stop. Breathe. Go again. "I'm your grandson and I'm seventeen"—I stammer—"in two thousand twelve. Not in nineteen ninety-five."

Still no response. I have no idea what to do, so I keep going even though I'm stumbling over every word.

"When I was ten, I sort of . . . accidentally . . . discovered that I could . . . travel. I can go back in time—five seconds, ten minutes, four months, several years . . . all the way back to the day I was born. March 6, 1995. That's as far back as I can go."

Maggie's shoulders rise and fall.

"I'd never tried to stay anywhere in the past before, not until the last time I was here. Do you remember when I arrived last March . . . how I was so sick?"

Slight nod.

"I wasn't really sick. I kept . . . disappearing. I was trying to stay here but I kept getting knocked back to my bedroom in two thousand twelve. See, that's how it works. When I try to push the limits of what I can do, I get sent back where I belong. It's like time's way of saying that I'm not where I'm supposed to be. It's the only time I don't have control. And then it hurts. Sometimes a lot. I finally . . . trained myself, I guess, to stay here."

Maggie brings her hand to her mouth but still keeps her back to me.

"I was only here because I lost my sister, Brooke. She wanted to go to this concert in Chicago in nineteen ninety-four. Neither one of us thought I'd be able to do it or anything, but it worked. We made it. But a couple of minutes later, *I* was knocked back to my present and Brooke wasn't. She was stuck back in nineteen ninety-four. So I came here, to your house, here in nineteen ninety-five, trying to get as close to her as I could."

It's silent for a minute or so. "Did you find her?" I'm relieved to hear the sound of Maggie's voice, low and calm. She's taking in facts and I figure that's a good sign.

"Yeah. She got knocked back home after a few months. And I think that's why I couldn't come back here. Once she was home I couldn't really go anywhere for a while." I picture myself returning to the same day, over and over again, to watch Anna at the track. I start to tell Maggie, but decide that might be more information than she needs to know.

I pour myself a glass of water, not because I'm dehydrated, but because I'm eager to have something to do with my hands.

I fill another glass and slide it across the table to Maggie. She picks it up right away.

"Do your parents know?" she asks.

"I was twelve when they, sort of, found out by accident."

Now Maggie's hands are trembling. She looks at me. "Do they know you're here right now?"

I shake my head. "They knew I was here last spring, but they don't know I came back. Brooke does, but my parents . . ." I trail off, but Maggie looks at me like she's waiting for me to continue. I shake my head again. "They wouldn't understand this."

Maggie leans forward. The color seems to have returned to her cheeks. "Where do they think you are right now?"

"Rock climbing and camping with my friend Sam."

"Sam?"

"Yeah, Sam."

"So you're not . . . *in* . . . two thousand twelve San Francisco right now?"

"No, when I leave I'm gone. I disappear from there and come here. This time, I've been gone since Friday night." I rest my arms on the table, and tell her how it works. She listens intently but doesn't ask any more questions. "If I wanted to, I could return to San Francisco right now and arrive back on Friday, just five minutes after I left. And even though I'd been gone for two days, my parents would never even know it. But then they'd be doing those two days all over again and that seems like a pretty horrible thing to do to them. So I just, you know . . . say I'm camping."

Maggie looks confused. "Yeah, I guess that's probably best then." She takes another sip of her water. "Or you could . . . tell them you're coming here?"

I laugh. "I don't think that would go over so well." I push my plate to the middle of the table. "Mom wants a normal seventeen-year-old kid who skateboards and takes tests and applies to college, and *doesn't* rock climb in Thailand or travel to see his grandmother back in nineteen ninety-five whenever he wants to."

That finally gets a smile. "And your dad?"

"Dad wants me to do more with my 'gift,' as he calls it. He thinks I'm special and that I should be righting wrongs, fixing things, being heroic or something." I pick up my glass and swirl the water inside, thinking about the fire back in San Francisco and what Anna and I did in Paris and how, over the last few days, I've been starting to think he could be right. "I don't know. Until recently, I've pretty much used this thing I can do for my own benefit." I don't tell her that it's also been for hers. She doesn't need to know what Brooke and I will do for her years from now, when the Alzheimer's sets in and starts taking control of her mind and her life.

Maggie looks more relaxed now. She shifts in her chair and reaches for the glass of water. "That sounds like your dad."

"Really?"

She nods. "He's always been a bit intense. Far more so than your mom is." Maggie looks past me, over my shoulder, and when I turn my head to follow her gaze, I see that she's staring at the stained glass image that hangs in her kitchen window above the sink—the one my mom made when she was a kid. "But he's a good man, I think. She definitely loves him." She looks back at me again, and leans in closer. "And you . . . my goodness. I was only there for a short time, but from what I could tell, their whole world revolves around you and your sister."

"That might be true now, but everything will change once she discovers that she doesn't have a *normal* kid who keeps her busy with Little League games or school plays." I stop short of telling Maggie what I'm really thinking. Her daughter's stuck with me, a freak show who sneaks around behind her back and lies to her, all to keep doing the one thing she so desperately wants him to stop.

Maggie lets out a sigh and shakes her head. "I bet she thinks you're pretty remarkable." I have no idea how to respond to that, and it's quiet for a long time. Finally, she looks at me wearing a huge smile as she reaches across the table. She covers my hand with hers. "I'll go back after all. I'll see what I can do. Now that I know who you are, maybe I can use my trips to San Francisco to help your mom understand you a little bit better."

My stomach sinks as I think about the photo of the three of us at the zoo, and how Maggie would never have come that weekend if Anna hadn't told her to. I don't know what happened before that visit, but I know what happened afterward—Maggie never came back.

"I'm afraid you can't do that," I say. She doesn't seem to grasp Anna's involvement in the whole thing and I don't want to ruin the one memory she has by telling her that it never should have happened. "You came to visit us once, and that was it."

"Once?" She pulls her hand away from mine, and I watch her face fall as the information sinks in. She doesn't say anything, but she doesn't need to. Her expression says everything. *That can't be possible.*

I feel compelled to tell her everything, but I can't. And now I have to choose my words wisely and use them sparingly, because the more she knows about the future, the greater the risk of her inadvertently changing it. Who knows what could happen if she does.

"The two of you didn't speak for a long time. I don't know why, my mom never talks about it, but Brooke and I never knew you." I trip on the last two words and immediately wish I could pull them back in, but it's too late. Maggie heard me. *Knew.* Past tense.

She stares at me like she wants to ask the question but doesn't know how to voice it or if she should. I answer it silently. *You died without knowing us.*

I remember those weeks far too vividly. I'd never seen Mom cry before, but the day she found out that her mother had passed away—all alone in this great big house—she became hysterical. Brooke and I didn't know what to do, so we hid in her room, wrapped in each other's arms and crying together without really understanding why. The next day, Mom and Dad got on a plane, but they couldn't afford to bring Brooke and me along. Besides, they'd said, we were too young for funerals. I was eight. I didn't know what I could do back then; if I had, things might have been different.

Maggie looks away from me and her gaze wanders around the room before it settles on the table. "Are we both that hard-headed?" she asks herself, and I hear the disbelief in her voice. She slowly raises her head and looks at me. "But now that I know, I can change it. I can be the one who makes the effort, makes it better. Right?"

I press my lips tightly together and shake my head. "You can't change it, Maggie. You weren't part of our lives the first time, so you can't be part of them now. Who knows what might happen if you were?"

She gives me a stubborn stare, like she's considering doing it anyway.

"You have to promise me you won't go back there again."

She takes a deep breath and her eyes lock on mine. "I don't know if I can make that promise, Bennett."

I don't have a choice but to give her an ultimatum. "Then I'll go back in time, right after you came into my room tonight. That Bennett—the one who's thirty minutes *younger* than me—will disapper the instant I come back, and I'll take his place. I'll come downstairs, and you and I will have a nice chat and eat this delicious dinner. And then I'll get up from the table, help you with the dishes, and this whole conversation we're having right now," I gesture back and forth between the two of us, "will never happen."

She rests her elbows on the table and buries her face in her hands. The two of us sit like that for a long time, Maggie thinking about the future and me feeling horrible and helpless because we're all stuck with it.

"Fine," she says, her voice cracking. "I won't go back." Suddenly she sits back in her chair and crosses her arms. "You said earlier that it hurt when you traveled. What did you mean by that?" I'm surprised by the question but grateful for the subject change.

"It doesn't hurt when I travel *to* another destination—like when I come here from home—but when I return, I get hit with these terrible migraines and I'm completely dehydrated. I drink coffee because the caffeine helps the headache and I down a bunch of water for the dehydration, and after a half hour or so, it goes away."

"So did you have a headache when you returned earlier . . . from wherever you went?"

I shake my head no. "I really only get the major side effects when I . . . leave the timeline, if you will. Earlier, I just went upstairs, counted to ten, and came back. I used to get a little headache when I returned after doing those short hops, too, but that doesn't happen so much anymore."

Maggie nods and it looks like she's following me. But then she leans in closer and her forehead wrinkles up with confusion and concern. "I don't understand. If it hurts, why do you do it?"

At first, I think about all the places I've been—all the things I never would have seen and experiences I never would have had if I'd let twenty or thirty minutes of pain stop me from traveling. But then I look at her, and I don't think that's what she means. I think she wants to know why I come back here.

My eyes scan Maggie's kitchen until they stop on that same stained glass oranament my mom made. I think of the photos of my family that line the walls of the living room and the hallways, and how happy we all look. I remember how I opened the front door last Friday, stepped inside, and felt this invisible weight lift from my shoulders.

"I feel at home here," I say. I watch Maggie's eyes well up.

The phone rings and she stands, leaving me alone at the table, and I'm relieved to have a few seconds to catch my breath. After she answers it, she glances over at me. "Yes, he's right here."

She returns to the table and hands me the cordless phone.

"Hello?" I say.

"It's me." The second I hear Anna's voice my whole body seems to relax.

"Hey, you." I can hear her smiling on the other end of the line.

"It's nice to talk to you on the phone," she whispers. "I don't think I ever have."

"How do I sound?"

It's quiet for a second or two, and then she says, "Close."

I smile but don't say anything.

"So," she says. "Emma and I are going to a movie. We thought you and Justin might want to come along?"

I look over at Maggie and find her buzzing around,

gathering up pots, filling the sink with hot water. "Hold on," I say before I cover the receiver with my hand. "Do you mind if I go to the movies?"

"Of course not." Even though we were in the middle of a pretty big discussion here, Maggie looks like she means it.

I return to Anna. "Sure. What's the movie?" I ask. Not that it matters.

"Emma wants to go to some sneak preview of *Empire Records*," she says. "I haven't even heard of it. Have you?"

The words "cult classic" start to leave my mouth but I stop them. "Yeah," I say instead. "I hear it's good."

"Great. We'll pick you up in twenty."

I press the end call button and return the phone to its home on the wall. When I reach for my plate to clear it from the table, Maggie swats my hand away. "Stop it. I've got the dishes. You go have fun."

"You sure?" I ask. Her hands still look a little shaky.

"Positive." She turns her back on me and continues collecting the rest of the dishes in the sink. She turns the water on, and I'm about to leave the room, when I hear it stop. "Bennett?"

I look back as she wipes her hand on a dish towel.

Then she crosses the room and surprises me when she pulls me into a hug. "Thank you. I'm glad you told me," she says. I close my eyes as I wrap my arms around her. She feels small in my arms, and when she rubs my back, I squeeze her even tighter. I've spent all these years sneaking around, helping her secretly and always from a distance, and I'm filled with relief that I don't have to do that anymore. She knows who I am. And it suddenly hits me that I'm hugging my grandmother for the first time. I squeeze her even tighter and she does the same.

"I'm glad I get to know you now," she says.

I choke out the words "Me too."

She takes a deep breath and gives me a hard pat on the back. "Okay, scoot. You have a date." Then she takes two steps away from me and stops. "Bennett?" The tone of her voice is careful and questioning, the wrinkles on her forehead more pronounced as she asks, "How long has Anna known?"

I close my eyes, thinking back to the day I stood in Anna's kitchen and showed her what I could do. Then I let my memory take me back even further, to the day she handed me that letter in the park.

I open my eyes, feeling this overwhelming sense of relief as a smile slowly spreads across my face. "Anna's known from the beginning."

19

Anna and I spend most of Sunday hanging out in my room, listening to music and talking about the next time I'll be back: three weeks from now. Homecoming. Anna tells me that I'll finally get to see her in the dress she bought for the auction party last May and reminds me to get here in time to pick up a tux.

The room is getting darker, and when I glance over at the clock and tell her I should be getting back, I feel a pit form deep in my gut. It's followed by a rush of guilt for feeling that way about my own home.

"I have something for you." Anna says as she crosses the room and flips on the light. She pulls something out of her bag and hides it behind her back. "Pick a hand."

I point to her right side and she opens her hand, shows me it's empty, and pulls it behind her back again. She must switch hands, because when I point to her left side and she opens her other hand, it's empty too. She looks up at me with a mischievous grin, so, on impulse, I grab her wrists and kiss her while she twists in my arms, laughing and trying to keep whatever she has behind her back out of my grasp.

"Fine!" she says, cracking up as she squirms away and holds me at arm's length. "Here." She hands me a three-by-five-inch album with geometric designs and the word PHOTOS in block letters across the front.

I turn it over in my hands and Anna gives me a proud grin as she opens the cover for me. The first picture is the two of us, standing at the top of the Eiffel Tower. Her arms are wrapped tight around my waist, the inky black Parisian sky in the background, and we're beaming at the camera like there's no place in the world either one of us would rather be.

I flip page after page, looking at the photos we took as we walked around Paris that night and the following day. Me standing in front of the Fontaine du Cirque. Anna in front of the wrought iron gates that led to the park, holding a baguette like a baseball bat. Me at the base of *The Thinker*, mimicking the pose. Her on the bridge, standing next to our lock. God, was that only yesterday? I look through the pictures, feeling grateful for a talent that allows me to take her to Paris at the drop of a hat. I feel equally grateful that it allows me to buy a whole extra day with her.

"This is incredible," I say as I flip through the plastic pages.

And then I get to the last one. It's not from our Paris trip yesterday, but I remember the night we took it in vivid detail. She'd just come back from La Paz. We were sprawled out on her rug in her bedroom and she held her arm high in the air, balancing her brand-new camera in one hand. She'd planted a kiss on my cheek as the shutter snapped. I study the expression on my face. I look happy.

"I love it." I stare at the picture, and then look over at her again. I think I'm supposed to tell her how nice it will be to have something to look at when I'm home and missing her, because I'm pretty sure that's what she wants to hear right now, but the truth is, when I'm seventeen years away from her and wishing I weren't, subjecting myself to these photos will be the last thing I'll want to do. Still, I'll probably do it anyway.

"See." She taps on the cover of the book. "And now you have something to show your family." Her smile looks sweet and hopeful, but it's her words that snap me back to reality. "I figured since I'll never be able to go home with you and meet them, at least you could show them these pictures." She lets out a laugh. "You know, so they don't think I'm a figment of your imagination or anything." My stomach knots up into a tight fist.

She waits for my reply, and when nothing comes she continues talking.

"I made a photo album for myself, too, but of course I have to keep mine hidden from *my* parents. I've convinced them that the pins in my map are just wishful thinking, but I'm not sure how I'd explain photos of you and me on the top of the Eiffel Tower."

I look down at the pictures in my hands, thinking back on our weekend. Talking with her under a canopy of trees during Emma's birthday party. The look of anticipation on her face when I took her hands in mine and told her to close her eyes, and the sheer awe I saw when she opened them. Falling asleep with her in Paris. Waking up to her in Paris.

I shove the photo album into my backpack, avoiding her eyes. "Good idea." I wonder if she hears the guilt in my voice. I wish she hadn't brought this up now, when I'm minutes away from leaving and I won't see her again for three more weeks. "Speaking of my parents, I'd better get going." I zip my pack closed and feed my arms through the straps, and Anna looks down at the carpet.

I step closer to her and rub her arms. "Are you going to be okay?"

She nods without looking at me. I take her chin and tip her head up. "Go downstairs and talk to Maggie." Anna closes her eyes, presses her lips tightly together, and nods.

I muster a valiant smile, but inside, I'm thinking how I'd give anything to stay here another day, another week . . . another three months. This whole being strong for someone else thing is a lot harder than I expected it to be. I can tell she's trying to keep it together for my sake as well. "I'll be back before you know it," I say, and clench my jaw the minute the words leave my mouth.

"I know." She takes a gulp of air and lets it out in a sigh. "That was the most incredible weekend." She buries her face in my chest and wraps her arms around me. We stand like that for a long time, listening to the music in the background, trying to ignore the inevitable.

Out of nowhere, it hits me: this is how it's going to be for the next year. Every few weeks, *this* is how it will feel to say good-bye to her. What's worse, every few weeks for as long as we're together, this is how it's going to feel. Will we ever get used to this?

I block out the thoughts as I plant kisses in her hair and on her cheeks, which are now wet and salty. I kiss her forehead and then her lips. It takes everything I have to let go of her and step backward, but I do.

I close my eyes and fade away.

september 2012

20

san francisco, california

My forehead slams against something hard, and I struggle to open my eyes. When I do, I can make out the Jeep logo on the steering wheel. Everything's blurry, the interior of the car is spinning, and my arms feel heavy, like I've got weights attached to my wrists. It takes all of my energy to bring my hands to the wheel, but when I feel the leather, I grip it hard and push, throwing myself back against the headrest.

I let out a groan.

My eyes fall shut on their own, and I sit there in the dark, smelly garage, breathing in, breathing out, and trying not to think about the fact that this hurts more than usual. That's when I feel the tickle, something warm sliding down onto my upper lip. I lick it, and my mouth fills with the unmistakable taste of blood, metallic and sticky-feeling. I wipe my nose with the back of my hand and it comes back with a streak of red.

I tilt the rearview mirror toward my face. What the hell?

The box of supplies proves to be worthless for this situation, but it's not like I could have anticipated a need for Kleenex. I've never had a bloody nose in my life. I use the bottom of my shirt to pinch my nose together, and a few minutes later the bleeding has stopped.

There's a tiny patch of evening sun peeking in through the sides of the garage door. I down my Doubleshot without stopping and chase it with a warm Red Bull and two bottles of water. I sit there for a long time, eyes closed, willing the pain to stop. I look in the rearview mirror. My face is red and patchy, my eyes bloodshot. Then I look at the clock on the dashboard. I've been back for almost an hour.

Finally, when my head is no longer throbbing, I push the button on the remote control and the door lifts slowly and rattles into place above me. I twist the key in the ignition and pull out of the garage.

Before I close the door, I twist in my seat. Looking back inside, I can't help but laugh. If I'd ever allowed myself to think that my ability made me some kind of superhero, this would certainly put things into perspective. My secret hide-out isn't a subterranean cave or a cool arctic ice structure. It's a garage. A dark, smelly garage that an average-size car and average-size me can barely occupy at the same time. And exactly like I hoped it would be, it's perfect.

⌐⌐

Luckily, the house is quiet and I sneak inside, through the kitchen and into my bedroom, hoping to get there before

Mom notices the bloodstains on the bottom of my T-shirt. I undress, hiding my dirty clothes deep in the bottom of the hamper in my closet, and throw on a clean pair of sweats. In the bathroom, I wash my face hard with a washcloth.

Back in my room, I unzip my backpack and remove the photo album Anna made for me. I hold it in my hands, examining the colorful patterns on the cover. I start to open it, but I just can't bring myself to do it. Not yet.

I open my desk drawer, and down near the bottom I see my red notebook. I stuff the photo album inside with everything else and shut the drawer.

I'm halfway down the stairs when I look over the banister and see Mom and Dad by the front door. He pulls his suit jacket over his shoulders, looks into the hallway mirror, and adjusts his glasses. He grabs my mom's purse off the table and hands it to her. She thanks him as she throws it over her shoulder.

"Hey," I say. They both look up at the same time. Mom's face breaks into a wide grin.

"Oh, good. You're back. I didn't even hear you come in." She meets me at the bottom of the staircase. "How was your climbing trip?" she asks as she kisses me on the cheek. "Did you and your friends have fun?"

I ignore her question and change the subject by stating the obvious. "I take it you guys are going out?"

"We realized that we haven't been to a nice dinner together in weeks," Dad says. He stands behind my mom, rubbing her arms lightly.

"Do you want to join us?" Mom asks. "With all your homework, we've barely seen you since school started." Her expression is sincere, but Dad's standing there, looking at her like he can't imagine why she'd invite me to join them on their "nice dinner." From behind her shoulder, he stares at me wide-eyed and gives me a small shake of his head, just in case I didn't know how to answer.

I look at the two of them, maybe for the first time, through a different lens. I think about Maggie's comments last night, and how Dad was always more intense than Mom but she loved him. How their worlds revolved around Brooke and me. More than anything, I wish I could talk to Mom about Maggie. Every time I've tried to tell her about those three months I spent living there, Mom stopped me short and said she didn't want to hear it. I'm guessing that it's not because she doesn't want to know; it's because she can't handle the guilt.

"Want to come?" Mom repeats.

"No, thanks," I say, and Dad gives me a grateful nod. "You two have a nice date."

As Dad grabs my mom's hand and leads her outside onto the front porch, he says something under his breath. She's laughing as the door closes behind them.

After they're gone, I stand at the bottom of the stairs for a long time, looking across the room at the huge picture window that overlooks the bay and wondering what to do with myself. I drum my fingers against the banister and think about the week ahead of me. There's a physics test tomorrow and I have an interview with the tutoring organization Sam works for on Tuesday. I should start studying.

I make it back to my room, but just as I'm about to turn on the music and hit the books, I have a different idea. I open the largest drawer of my desk and dig down to the bottom. When I find the photo album, I return it to my backpack and head downstairs for my board.

The sun is just starting to set when I arrive at the park, and I'm relieved to find it relatively empty. It's still warm outside, and I look over the horizon at the San Francisco Bay, bright blue and full of sailboats. I sit down on the bench, remove the photo album from my backpack, and flip through the pages. This time, Anna's here with me.

october 2012

21

san francisco, california

I scroll through the calendar on my phone, looking at all the days that have passed since my last trip. I picture Anna doing something similar, adding one more x in today's square on her wall calendar before she heads off to school. We're getting closer and closer to the one marked with the word "homecoming." Three more open squares. Three more days to go.

I'm supposed to be writing an essay on the Zhou Dynasty for AP World Civ, but instead I'm staring at the tabs at the top of the browser: ZHOU DYNASTY—WIKIPEDIA, WORLD CIVILIZATION/ONLINE STUDENT RESOURCES, PANDORA.

I click on Pandora and change the station a few times before I settle on "90s Alternative." Without even thinking about it, I open a new browser window and a news page pops open. I scan the stories about the upcoming presidential election and watch today's most popular YouTube video.

I click on the Local News button and scroll through, reading the headlines: VICTIMS OF A SMALL PLANE CRASH IDENTIFIED. MAN ARRESTED FOR ARSON. WOMAN SHOT OUTSIDE MARKET. SIXTEEN-YEAR-OLD RUNAWAY FOUND DEAD ON LOCAL BEACH. The list of tragedies and near-tragedies that occurred in the greater Bay Area over the past twenty-four hours goes on and on.

I'm just about to close the window and return to my essay when a story farther down the page catches my attention: FATHER AND DAUGHTER KILLED BY TEEN DRIVER.

I click on the link and it opens to a picture of a light-blue bike, twisted and lying in the gutter. I read the story:

> *7:34 P.M.—A seventeen-year-old male driver struck a family riding bicycles shortly after 3:30 P.M. today. The teen's truck lost control and collided with a fire hydrant before hitting a man and his two daughters, killing the man and one girl and injuring the other. The driver was released from the hospital with minor injuries and was immediately arrested on suspicion of involuntary manslaughter.*

I tell myself to close the window, but instead, I scroll down and continue reading.

Identities have not yet been released, but according to police, the cyclists were a man, his nine-year-old daughter, and her twelve-year-old sister. Both the man and nine-year-old girl were pronounced dead at the scene. The twelve-year-old was taken to the hospital with minor injuries. The father met his two daughters at school every day to ride home with them, to make sure they got home safely.

The words make me sick, but it's the pictures that do me in. In addition to the one of the light-blue bike, there's a photo of the building that eventually stopped the car. Its stucco is scattered and stacked in piles on the ground, its framing exposed.

I stare at the screen, thinking about the driver, and how such a small mistake—something that happened in a fraction of a second—just changed his entire life. He's only seventeen, but his whole future came to a screeching halt today. Even if the jail time is minimal, how could he ever be the same knowing that a girl and her mother are now without a sister and daughter, and a father and husband. I picture him, sitting in an orange jumpsuit down at county, wishing he could do it all over again, wishing for a second chance. And two keystrokes later, the printer whirs to life. I grab the paper while it's still warm and head downstairs.

Dad's office door is ajar, but I knock before I push it open anyway. He's behind his desk, working at his computer, and he looks up and watches me with a curious expression as I cross the room. I don't say a word as I set the news story on the desk in front of him.

"What is this?"

"Read it."

He scans it quickly and looks up at me.

"Tell me it's a really bad idea," I say.

He's quiet for a long time, reading the article, then he grins. "It's a really bad idea."

"I know, right?"

He stares at me.

"Want to come along?"

⁓

I find Dad's old backpack on the shelf in the garage reserved for our family's neglected camping gear, and I shake off the thin layer of dust that's collected over the years. When I was little, I saw this pack nearly every weekend. I remember how big it used to look as I trailed behind Dad on Cub Scout hikes through the wilderness.

Now I work quickly to ready it for a completely different kind of adventure, filling it with two room-temperature bottles of water from a flat lying on the floor next to the refrigerator. I'm about to head back inside when I spot my skateboard leaning up against the far wall, and it gives me an idea. I jam it into my pack, one end sticking out through the gap in the zipper.

Back in my room, I add the rest of the essentials—large wads of cash stuffed into the front pockets of both packs and a clean T-shirt balled up in the main pocket of mine, just in case. As I pass the bathroom, I grab a big handful of Kleenex from the box on the counter.

Dad's pacing his office and cleaning his glasses with the hem of his shirt. I hand him his backpack and shut the door behind me.

"What's that?" he asks, pointing to my pack.

I turn around to look at it. "That's a skateboard, Dad."

"Thanks, Bennett." He shakes his head at me. "Why are you bringing a skateboard?"

"I'm sticking to my rules. I still don't believe I should change things deliberately, but I've been sort of . . . experimenting with altering little things: you know, small, insignificant details that could have a huge effect on the outcome." I give him a mischievous grin and gesture toward the board. "This is a diversion."

Dad seems relatively comfortable with the small amount of information I'm giving him, so I hold out my hands. He looks wary as he glances down at them. "It's been a while. Do you still remember how this works?"

He nods once. When he takes them, his grip is strong and his hands feel rough and large in mine, nothing like Anna's or Brooke's. For a moment, I feel like I'm ten again; small, fragile, and not at all like the person with the power.

"You ready?" I ask.

Dad doesn't say anything as he closes his eyes.

I close mine and lock in the time. I visualize the nondescript alley I found online, a half a block away from the intersection where everything just changed for four people. I muster a silent plea that I'll be able to fix it for all of them.

⌒

"Open your eyes."

Dad opens them and looks around. I can tell he's trying not to panic. "Where are we?"

I gesture toward the far end of the alley. Cars are zooming

past, and I start off walking in that direction and tell Dad to follow me. When we arrive, I peer around the corner and take in the surroundings. Halfway between the alley and the busy intersection, I see a wide cement stairway that leads to an office building. I didn't see that on the map, but it makes this spot even more perfect.

I point into the distance, across the intersection, and Dad stands next to me, following my gaze. "See that red fire hydrant on the next block?"

He squints. "Yes."

I tell him everything I know from the news story online. "The car went out of control and slammed into that hydrant, and a few seconds later, hit the bikers. But all of them passed through this intersection first, at different times, before any of that happened. We have about ten minutes before the bikes arrive at this spot, so here's our plan." Dad stares at me with wide eyes as I describe what I have in mind, and when I get to the part where I tell him his role in the whole thing, he lets out a series of "okays" and "got its." He might be a bit shell-shocked, but as far as I can tell, he's taking it all in.

"That's the plan?" he asks.

"Yeah." I brace myself for criticism or, at the very least, additions. Dad smiles and says, "That's really good."

I smile back. "Thanks. I kind of thought so too." He has a funny look on his face, like he's about to say something important, but instead, he looks over his shoulder and down the street. A bike courier zooms past us.

"You'd better get going," he says, pointing toward the

intersection. He heads off in the opposite direction.

In one swift string of moves, I pull my skateboard out of the backpack, start into a run as I throw it on the ground, and swing the pack over my shoulders as I skate away. I push with my back foot and glide, weaving back and forth to find my balance. A minute later, I'm at the bottom of the steps. I pop my board into my hand and race up to the top. It's perfect— the ground is smooth and there's no one here.

I'm floating around the empty courtyard, feeling the board under my feet and gathering my nerve, when I spot a short cement divider at the far end. I build up speed, heading straight for it. I'm feeling confident as I pop an ollie at the base. I clear it easily and land clean on the other side.

I turn around and skate back toward the steps. I leave my board at the top and race halfway down so I can check the scene. There are other bikers on the road, but I think I spot the three of them on the next block. They're riding slowly in a single-file line, and when the light turns, they stop. So far, so good.

At the top of the steps I grab my board, jump onto the ledge, do a 50-50 grind to the bottom, and land perfectly. Now I see Dad clearly as he rounds the corner, just in front of the bikers, all of them moving quickly. I run back up to the top of the stairs and skate deep into the courtyard so I can generate enough momentum.

Then I'm off, skating fast toward the steps, the wind pushing my hair off my face. I speed toward them, focused on nothing but the cement ledge that separates the steps from a cluster of trees. I ollie onto it, balance the trucks on the edge, and slide down—fast, but completely in control. And I land, bending my knees to absorb the shock and forcing the board into a quick turn to keep from going into the street. And that's when I fake my crash.

I let my board slip out from under my feet, sending me tumbling hard toward the ground. I fall onto my shoulder and roll it out like I've done hundreds of times, but I imagine the whole thing looks far more dramatic to a nonskater. In case it doesn't, I add a little flourish, taking the whole display up a notch or two.

Gripping my leg to my chest I lie on the ground, yelling loudly and writhing in pain. And that's when Dad arrives at my side, wearing his suit and looking like a concerned pedestrian. "Are you okay?" he keeps asking, while I respond with more yelling. And writhing.

He reaches for his cell phone and I have to turn away to conceal the grin on my face. I never thought I'd turn a do-over into a heroic act, and I sure as hell never thought I'd make Dad my sidekick.

Now the man has stopped and is straddling his bike and balancing his weight on the curb. His two daughters are stopped too, waiting curiously behind him and staring at me. I let out a high-pitched groan and return to thrashing on the ground.

Dad has to yell to be heard above the hum of the passing traffic. "My cell phone is dead and this boy needs some help. Can you call nine-one-one?"

I can't hear what the man says in reply, but he appears to be digging around in the pocket of his jeans.

This brilliant street performance should probably be my sole focus, but I can't stand not knowing what's going on. I look past the girls and into the street, and see the truck. Dad's watching it too, and I'm sure neither one of us is breathing as it shifts into the lane closest to us.

I sit up to get a better view, no longer caring if I've broken my cover. In a fraction of a second, no one will be looking at me anyway.

The truck speeds up to make the light and travels through the intersection, and a few seconds later, it veers off the road and up onto the curb. It sideswipes the fire hydrant, sending water shooting into the air. It doesn't stop moving until it slams into the side of the building. Stucco goes flying in every direction and smoke starts shooting up from the open hood.

I know how this scene will look a few hours from now—I clearly remember the "after" photo of the building: windows shattered, framing exposed, stucco piled on the sidewalk—but when I look at the little girl in front of me, I remember the other picture that ran with the news story. She's still standing astride her light blue, *un*twisted bike, and craning her neck to see what happened on the next block. Suddenly, she catches me staring at her. She hops off and hits the kickstand with her foot, and walks over to me.

She crouches down low. "Is your leg okay?" she asks.

"Yeah. I think it's okay." I'm sure I look ridiculous, sitting in the middle of the sidewalk, wearing this goofy smile.

Then my dad is by my side, his voice loud and direct. "Stay here. We're going to go check on the driver." The little girl and I watch as our fathers take off running toward the scene of the accident.

"I hope he's okay," she says.

"Don't worry," I say in a tone of voice that's probably far too enthusiastic for this situation. "I have a feeling he's fine."

22

Dad opens his eyes and looks around at his office, like he's seeing the bookshelves and paintings for the first time. "Did we do it?" He drops my hands and starts pacing back and forth in front of me. "How do we know if we changed it or not?"

I look at the clock above the door. It's only a quarter to four.

He crosses the room in three long strides and stands behind his desk, shuffling papers. "Where is it? Where's the story you brought in here?"

I keep my voice calm to offset the anxiety I hear in his. "It's okay, Dad. That hasn't happened yet." I point up at the analog clock above his desk. "I came down here and showed you that story around seven thirty. That's four hours from now."

His eyes follow my finger but he only gives it a quick glance before he returns to digging through the stacks on his desk. "Dad. Stop." I rest my hand on one of his. "We'll check the news tonight, but now there probably won't *be* a story. Or, I guess, there *will* be a story but it will be a completely different one. Are you okay? You look pale."

He gropes around for his chair, sits down hard, and rolls it toward the desk so he can rest his head in his hands. I can see his shoulders rise and fall with each slow, deliberate breath, but aside from the panic attack, he doesn't seem to be showing any post-travel reactions.

Which makes me realize I feel pretty good too. My heart is racing and my stomach feels light and I just want to . . . move. I want to go outside, hop on my skateboard again, and power down the hill, feeling the wind prickle my skin and lift my hair off my forehead. I feel incredible—no nosebleed, no migraine—just buzzy, like my whole body is vibrating, surging with adrenaline.

Dad's head springs up and he starts typing on his keyboard. I come around to his side of the desk and watch as he types in every possible combination of words that could lead us to today's events: "bicycle" and "accident" and "intersection" and "manslaughter."

He's not getting it.

"Dad, you're not going to find anything yet. The accident just happened. It won't show up for a while. Dad . . ." I lead his hands away from the keyboard. "We'll check later tonight, okay, but trust me, it won't be there. It worked. Everyone's fine, except the kid driving the truck, who's a bit banged up but probably being arrested right now for reckless driving and not vehicular manslaughter."

Before I can comprehend what's happening, Dad stands up

and pulls me to him and hugs me so hard I can't breathe. Eventually, he releases me, but he still keeps my arm in his grip. He stares at me like he's trying to decide what to say, and finally settles on "They were really nice people, weren't they?"

I let out a nervous laugh. "Yeah, Dad, they were really nice." I picture that little girl, worried about the condition of the driver who—in a version of a timeline that no longer exists— left her family fatherless and cut her life short at age nine.

"I'd better get back to my homework," I say, gesturing toward my bedroom. "I have an essay I need to start all over again."

Dad pats my arms hard and chuckles. "Sorry. That sucks," he says.

"That's okay. So did the essay."

<hr>

My backpack is a lot lighter without the skateboard. As I throw it over my shoulders and readjust the straps, I steal one last glance at the clock on my nightstand. I'm not supposed to be in Evanston until homecoming this weekend, but I can't help it. I have to see Anna right now. I have to tell her what I just did.

I grab my car keys off my desk and speed out to the Jeep, and a half hour later, I'm backing it into the garage on the other side of town. I switch off the ignition, lower the door, and close my eyes.

I open them on the cross-country course that sits adjacent

to the Westlake track. I've arrived exactly where I intended, in a quiet spot off the trail behind a cluster of trees and a fat shrub that conceals me from sight. Resting my backpack on the ground, I feel around inside until I find what I'm looking for. Then I sneak out toward the trail, listening for their foot-falls. I can't hear a thing.

It doesn't take me any time to find the perfect spot. Smack in the middle of the trail I spot a log, large and intentionally placed to be hurdled, and I jiggle the postcard into a crevice so it's standing up straight. Then I duck back out of sight.

The adrenaline is still surging through me, and even though I know I should stay silent and still, I can't stop pacing across the dirt. I'm waiting and listening and ready to burst out of my skin. Finally, a few minutes later, I hear the rhyth-mic sound of feet padding against the dirt, followed by heavy breathing and the occasional grunt. I force myself to relax, pressing my back firmly against the tree bark.

Then the footsteps stop.

"This was just sticking out of the log," someone says.

"What is it?" asks another.

"A postcard. From *Paris*." I still don't recognize the speaker, but I laugh under my breath when I hear the fascination in her voice as she says the word "Paris."

"That's weird."

More footsteps.

"What's up?" Ah, there's Anna's voice. I stand still, listening.

"It's nothing. Come on, we're losing time," another voice says, and I hear footsteps on the trail again.

"Here, check it out. This was wedged into the log."

"Huh . . ." I picture Anna taking it from her teammate, flipping the postcard around in her hands. "Weird. Come on, Stacy's right, we should go."

They run off and everything's quiet until I hear footsteps on the trail again, this time coming from the opposite direction. Leaves crunch and twigs snap, and Anna's face comes into view as she clears the short incline and peeks around a bush.

"What are you doing here?" she asks, clearly surprised to see me. "I'm in the middle of practice." She's taking long strides, beaming as she walks toward me. I wrap my arms around her waist and lift her off the ground. "*Ew*, what are you doing? Put me down!" She laughs and smacks me with her hand. "I'm all sweaty."

"I don't care." I tighten my hold on her and plant a kiss in her hair. I'd been hyperaware of the adrenaline surge, but now I don't notice it as much. I feel a headache coming on but I ignore it.

"Is everything okay? You're shaking."

"Yeah. Everything's fine. I have to tell you something." I comb my hands through my hair. "You're not going to believe what I just did—"

Suddenly, I don't know where to start. Anna stares at me, looking confused and curious and waiting for me to continue. Every detail of *everything* that happened over the last forty-five minutes is swirling around in my head, flying around too quickly for me to grasp on to just one. Did all of it actually happen? The bikes. The crash. The girl.

"You're not supposed to be here until Friday."

"I know, but—" A faint ringing in my ear makes me stop in midsentence, and before I can say another word it completely changes pitch—high and piercing and constant—and I grab the sides of my head and crouch down on the ground in front of her.

I hear Anna say my name, but her voice sounds far away. I try to take my hands off my head so I can steady myself on the ground, but I can't move. I feel my whole body grow weak, like my muscles are atrophying as I sit here. I feel my knees buckle and my cheek hit the dirt.

My eyes are open so wide they're stinging and watering, and I feel pebbles and mud collecting under my fingernails as I claw my way back to sitting. I fall into the ground again and my head hits something that feels like a rock. Without my ability to control them, my eyes shut tightly. And suddenly, the piercing sound is gone and everything falls silent.

23

The pain hits me all at once, so hard and so unexpected I don't even have time to grab on to anything for support. My head falls forward and my face slams against the ground, and when I open my eyes, I see the blood, pooling under my head. I stare down at the pattern that unmistakably places me in Dad's office.

No bushes, no trees, no Anna. And no garage, no Jeep.

I crawl over to the end table next to Dad's leather chair. Using it for support, I try to push myself to standing, but my knees can't hold me and I fall sideways, collapsing into the side of the ottoman. I feel it slide out from underneath me, and I try to keep my grip, but it's useless. I'm back on the floor in a crumpled heap within seconds.

The front of my shirt is drenched with blood, and it's only getting worse. I can feel it trickling down my upper lip, warm and thick, sneaking into my mouth so I taste it too, metallic, disgusting. Using a clean corner of my shirt, I bring my hand to my nose, pinching hard. I sit up again and I let my head fall backward, feeling the edge of the end table dig uncomfortably into the back of my neck.

Every time I blink, my eyes feel like they're on fire, and I can feel the sweat beading up on my forehead. My head is pounding and my mouth feels like it's full of cotton balls.

Everything goes dark.

⁓

"Bennett!" The voice is far away and muffled, unrecognizable. I try to open my eyes but nothing happens. "Bennett. Wake up. Drink this."

"Anna?" I can't see anything, and when I speak the words "Where am I?" I hear them come out slurred and unrecognizable. I try again to open my eyes and finally see a sliver of light. I feel the ground beneath me for clues. It's soft. Like a rug. "Anna?" I ask again.

"Bennett." There's a hand on my shoulder. My head wobbles and I send all my energy to my neck in a desperate attempt to keep it in one place.

"Where am I?" I try again. This time my voice sounds clearer, but still, there's no reply.

The hand squeezes my shoulder hard. "Drink this, son."

I feel something cold and smooth at my lips, and before I can even process what's happening, I feel the liquid, ice-cold on my tongue but searing my throat as it slides down. I cringe and push the glass away.

"Keep going," he says, and the glass is back at my lips. I take small sips at first, but the water feels so good, so wet, that I lean into it, suddenly desperate for more. The glass tips up and I take huge gulps until it's empty.

"Good. That's better." I open my eyes. Dad's face is full of worry as his hand settles on my shoulder again. I hear him set the glass on the table next to me. "Do you think you can sit up?" I give him a weak nod and use all my energy to push myself up from the floor.

This bloody nose is nothing like the last one. This time my T-shirt is soaked in blood. I remember the feeling, the taste, and it makes me slump down again, feeling nauseous. Dad grabs me by both shoulders this time and props me up again.

"I'm going to get you some more water. I'll be right back." I want to ask him to make it room temperature, but the door clicks shut behind him before I can get the words out. I stare at the ceiling and fix my gaze on a small crack in the plaster. I won't close my eyes, even though they're watering and burning and begging me to shut them.

A few minutes later, Dad's back at my side, pressing a glass of water into my hand and a cold washcloth against my forehead. He opens my other hand, palm up, and sets three pills in it. I give him a weak shake of my head. "They're just Advil," he says. "Take them. They'll help."

I start to tell him that the headache is normal. That it always passes on its own, and all I need is water, coffee, and twenty minutes to rest. But it occurs to me that this particular headache is different from others, and that what I know about what "always" happens most likely doesn't apply in this situation. I throw the pills into my mouth and chase them down while Dad watches me. I drain the water in a few gulps.

My hands are still shaking so I clench them into tight fists by my sides. "I'll go get you a clean shirt," he says as he heads toward the door.

"Dad." I stare at the crack in the ceiling again, but in my peripheral vision I can see him stop.

"Would you stay here? Please?" I ask, and before I know it, he's back by my side, sitting on the ottoman, watching me. We sit like that for a long time, neither one of us speaking.

"Are you ready to tell me where you've been?" he asks.

I rub my temples hard with my knuckles, and look across the room at the clock on the wall behind his desk. My eyes narrow as I strain to read it, but the hands keep coming in and out of focus. "Where I've been?" I ask, forcing myself to walk through everything that just happened. We were waiting to see the news story about the accident, to see if it was different from the first one I printed out for him. Then I went to see Anna, everything went dark, and when I opened my eyes, I was a bloody mess on the floor and Dad was here with water. "What time is it?" My voice still sounds weak, scratchy. I rub my throat.

Even though the clock is in plain sight, Dad looks down at his watch. "It's a few minutes after two. Bennett, I need to know where you've been."

"After two?" I repeat, ignoring his question entirely. I rub my temples even harder. That doesn't match at all. It had to be four o'clock when I left to see Anna.

Suddenly, everything falls into place and I start to realize what's happening. I was knocked back. Hard.

My heart speeds up as I piece it together in my head. The news story I printed and brought downstairs to show Dad said the accident occurred around three thirty. We haven't done it over.

Now I'm fully conscious, eyes wide as my head spins in Dad's direction. My sudden movement startles him and he recoils, but I don't even try to keep the fear from my voice. "Please tell me we stopped it. We stopped it, right?"

He looks confused. "Stopped what?" Dad asks, and my hands immediately start shaking. "Bennett, I want to know where you've been."

"The *bikes*?" It comes out like a question. My hands clench by my sides again.

"The bikes?" I can hear the confusion in his voice. He doesn't know what I'm talking about. We didn't stop it. I got knocked back and we didn't stop it after all. I cover my face with my hands.

"Dad," I say without looking up. "There was an accident with these bicyclists and we went back . . . I brought my skateboard and caused a distraction and you helped. This little girl—" I choke on the last word.

"I know," he says, as if he's now concerned about my mental state in addition to my physical one. "She's okay. They're all okay. Just like you said they would be."

I pull my hands away from my face and stare at him. "What? Are you sure?"

"Absolutely. I was waiting for you to get home so I could show you the article." He sounds pretty certain but I keep staring at him anyway, as if I'm waiting for him to change his mind. "The news story read exactly the way you thought it would. A kid crashed his truck into a building. There wasn't a single word about a family of bicyclists."

He remembers. If he remembers, it happened. I didn't wipe it out. None of it makes sense, but a huge smile spreads across my face anyway, and as it does, my face feels tight, like it's cracking. I scratch at my skin and pull my fingernail away. It's caked with dried blood, but I don't care. I let out a laugh.

"Bennett, that was yesterday."

I stop in midlaugh and the smile disappears. "What?"

Dad nods. He's still looking at me like I've lost my mind.

"Yesterday? No . . . that can't be right." I was just in my room. I was just with Anna.

"Bennett, it's Thursday afternoon." He scoots the ottoman a little closer to me, and he seems to be choosing his words carefully. "Your mother and I have been worried sick. You left my office, said you were going upstairs to work on an essay, and when your mom tried to find you for dinner, you were gone. You didn't come home all night. An hour ago, I found you here on the floor."

I think about the day. I can't even bring myself to say it out loud. *Thursday?*

"Son." Dad draws out the word, nice and slow, like I need more time than usual to process what he's about to say. "The accident happened yesterday. Do you remember what happened when we got home?"

I try to. I remember returning from the do-over and leaving his office. I walked upstairs, grabbed a postcard from my desk drawer, and stuffed it into my backpack. I closed my eyes and went to the cross country track at Westlake. I hid off the trail, listening to Anna and her teammates speculate about the mysterious postcard. She found me right after that, and we talked. I felt great until the piercing sound brought me facedown into the dirt. And then I was back here in Dad's office. It all happened fifteen minutes ago, twenty tops.

But it wasn't twenty minutes ago. It was yesterday.

"I need to know where you've been, Bennett. You need to tell me the truth. Why didn't you come home all night?"

The truth. I look away from him and shake my head. I can't tell him where I've been because I have no idea.

I look right into his eyes. "Dad, I honestly don't know."

He looks at me like he isn't buying it, and lets out a long sigh to make it even clearer. "Don't lie to me, Bennett. How could you not know where you've been for the last twenty-two hours?"

Twenty-two hours? My mouth drops open and I stare at him wide-eyed, shaking my head. I don't know. I really, truly, in all honesty have no clue where I've been.

Dad must be able to tell by the look on my face that I'm

telling the truth this time. "You seriously don't know, do you?"

I shake my head even harder, bring my legs to my chest, and bury my face in my knees. This can't be happening.

"What happened while I was gone?" I ask without looking up.

He hesitates before speaking, as if he's weighing his words carefully. "I told your mom everything," he says quietly, and my head snaps up. "When you hadn't come back by midnight . . ." He trails off. I let my head fall into my knees again.

"What's the last thing you remember?"

I lie. "Sitting in my room, working on my report."

"And then?"

I think about it for a minute, and decide to keep lying. "And then I was trying to peel myself off your carpet."

I need to get back to Anna and tell her that everything's okay. I left her standing in the woods, watching me fade away. I promised her I wouldn't leave like that again. And then it occurs to me. What if I haven't left at all? What if I've been there for the last twenty-two hours and just don't remember it?

"Look, you did a great thing the other day. You should be proud of yourself."

"But?" I ask.

"But this is dangerous." He points down at the bloodstains soaking into the rug. "Bennett, you're a smart kid and you already know this, but I feel like I have to say it anyway. This is it." He scoots the ottoman even closer to me. "Whatever is happening to you right now is because of the traveling. You know that, right?"

I stare at him blankly.

"Your mom was right all along. This is too dangerous."

I inhale slowly, processing his words. Mom's not the one who was right . . . I was. I knew all along that I shouldn't change things. There's no such thing as second chances, even when they're deserved.

It felt good after Emma. Even after the fire. There was the nosebleed after I returned from Evanston last time, but I didn't even think it was connected. Now I can't account for twenty-two hours of my life and I'm covered in blood; it's pretty obvious that it is, in fact, *all* connected. I can use this gift of mine for good, but not without a cost.

"Where's Mom?" I ask.

"Sleeping. She was up all night. I finally convinced her to get some rest. She'll be happy to see you home safe." Dad stands up and brushes some imaginary dust from his pants. "She's pretty angry at me right now. She thinks I made you do it."

"Why does she think that?"

He shrugs. "Because I told her I did. Besides, it *is* my fault. This might have been your idea but I'm the one who pushed you to do it."

"No you didn't," I say, but it doesn't help. He stares off across the room looking completely deflated.

"Dad?" He looks at me again. I think about my 50-50 grind

down the side of the staircase and how I faked my fall at the bottom. I picture the look on that little girl's face. I remember how hard Dad hugged me when it was all over. "It was really fun."

"It was pretty incredible wasn't it?" And there it is: the look I saw on his face when we first returned. He looks triumphant and proud, and I feel emptiness deep in my gut when I wonder if it's the last time I'll see this expression. "Actually, I was kind of excited to do it again, but . . . oh, well." He shakes his head and rests his hand on my knee. "Thanks for taking me along." He gives my leg a comforting little shake, and then, for something to do with himself, he reaches past me and grabs the glass off the table. "I'll go get you some more water. I'll be right back."

As soon as he's out of the room, I stand up. My legs still feel wobbly and weak, and I grab on to the side of the chair to steady myself. Just as I'm heading for the door, the glow of the monitor gets my attention, and I feel the urge to see that news story for myself.

I hobble over to the desk, sit down in the leather chair, and reach for the mouse. I start to open a new browser window, but I don't need to because there's already one on the screen. It's a news story from this morning, about a local boy who was last seen at his bus stop but never arrived at school.

Dad wasn't exaggerating when he said he was looking forward to our next do-over.

He'd already found it.

24

I'm halfway up the stairs when Mom sees me from the top landing. She starts racing down the stairs and I grab the railing. "You're home. . . . What happened to you?" She blinks fast, like she's trying hard to focus.

"I'm fine."

"You're *not* fine, Bennett!" Her eyes travel from my face to my jeans and back up again.

"It was just a bloody nose." I stare blankly at my shirt.

"*That's* a bloody nose?" She presses her lips together and her chin trembles. "Where have you been all night? Please, just tell me what happened to you."

She looks at me with this glassy stare, and I can see how hurt she is. There are so many things I'd love to tell her, but I'm in so deep now I don't even know where to start. When my eyes meet hers, I feel like a five-year-old who just fell off the play structure and needs comfort and reassurance. If I told her everything, I bet she'd give me that.

"Where have you been?" she repeats softly.

"I don't know, Mom." My voice cracks when I say it, and I suck in a breath. I can tell from the look on her face that she believes me. But I can also tell that it's not enough. If I ever want to make it to the top of these stairs, I need to come up with something better.

Mom rests her hand on mine, encouraging me to say more. "I woke up in Dad's office like this." I pull my T-shirt away from my body and shake my head. Then I look down at the banister, hesitant to go on, choosing my next words carefully. I've never really talked with my mom about what I can do. We always just, sort of, dance around it. But now there's no other approach than a direct one. "Dad told you what we did, right?" Mom nods. "I must have blacked out afterward."

She crosses her arms. From the neck down, she looks angry, but her face gives her away. "This whole time?" she asks, and she shakes her head as if she can't believe she's asking such a ridiculous question.

I shrug, trying to look cool, like it's no big deal. But I feel my face contort, blowing my cover. I look straight into her eyes. "I honestly don't know where I've been."

Mom's expression turns into this odd mix of sympathy and alarm.

The fight-or-flight instinct kicks in, making me tighten my grip on the handrail and pull my shirt away from my body again. "Can we please talk about this later? I'd like to clean up." Without waiting for her to respond, I plant a kiss on her cheek and squeeze past her.

"Do you need anything?" she calls from behind me.

Yes. I need to be able to be in two places at once. I need to not miss anyone and I need for no one to miss me. "No, thanks," I say as I turn the corner.

In the bathroom, I work quickly to wash the blood from my face with soap and hot water. I run a comb through my hair, but even when I'm done, it still looks greasy and stringy. I pull my shirt off over my head and toss it into the garbage can. It's one of my favorites but now I hope I never see it again.

I close my bedroom door and lock it behind me. My eyelids are heavy, and even though I feel the gravitational pull coming from my bed, I ignore it. After all that's happened, I realize it's the stupidest thing I could do and that the number of things that could go wrong are practically infinite. But I have to go back and see Anna. Just for a few minutes. Just long enough to tell her that I'm okay and to find out if my version of what happened on the cross-country course matches hers. Then I can sleep.

My jeans feel like they're glued to my skin. I peel them off and toss them into the hamper and dig through my drawers until I find my favorite sweats and a Cal Bears hoodie. I change my socks and slip my feet into my shoes. My eyes burn and start to water, but I wipe them with the back of my hand.

My backpack's loaded and I'm almost ready to go. I head to the mini fridge in the closet and grab a Red Bull and reach under the bed for a couple of room-temperature bottles of water, then set everything on the nightstand so they'll be in easy reach when I return.

I'm standing in the center of my room, about to close my eyes, when there's a knock at the door. I swear under my breath and chuck my backpack into the corner. "Come in," I say, once I'm lying on my bed as if I'm about to doze off. The knob turns and clicks a few times.

"It's locked," Mom calls out from the other side, and my legs feel heavy as I make my way across the room to open the door. "Can I come in?"

No. I'm about to leave. I *need* to leave. But I take a few steps backward and open the door for her. She walks in and heads for the turret window over in the corner that overlooks the bay. She runs her fingers along the molding, then crosses her arms, keeping her back to me.

"I remember the day we moved into this house."

"Mom," I say. "I'm really tired." I cover my eyes with my hand. Do we have to do this now?

She continues as if I hadn't spoken. "You and your dad were on your way over in the moving truck and I walked around, room to room, trying to figure out which ones you and Brooke were going to choose. I was standing right here, admiring this view, when Brooke walked in and said this was the one she wanted. But I talked her into taking the other one."

"Why?" I ask.

"This one was the nicer of the two. It had this view and I thought it should be yours. You're the one who got us this house, after all." She turns around and looks at me. "I gave your father a lot of grief about what the two of you did . . ."

"We just bought some stocks." It was more than that, but I don't feel like getting into it with her right now. I've been down this path before, arguing over the nuances of manipulating the market and buying stock based on information neither one of us should have had or been able to use. But last time I checked, insider-trading laws didn't mention anything about time travel.

"I'm not going to ask you to justify what you did, Bennett. Even though I thought it was wrong, I understand why you did it."

I don't say anything.

"You did it to make us happy. To give our family a better life."

"Yeah."

"And probably to get your dad off your back." She smiles.

I smile back. "Yeah, maybe that too."

She gives me this meaningful look and steels herself, like she's preparing to say something important. "I'll always appreciate what you did for our family, Bennett, but I want you to know something." She takes a few steps closer to me but stays just out of my reach. "You didn't have to do this." She holds her arms out to her sides and glances around the room.

I shoot her a skeptical look and she shakes her head. "Don't get me wrong. I appreciate all of this . . . I admit, I'm a bit of a sucker for the finer things in life, and life has been a lot easier with, well, everything we have. But I don't need it."

She looks resolute, but I can't help raising an eyebrow.

"I mean it. Your dad didn't like his job, and I didn't like living in that tiny apartment in an unsafe neighborhood. And yes, money was tight and we fought about it a lot. But you know what?"

I shake my head.

"Your dad and I love each other, and we love you and Brooke more than you two will ever know. This family would have been fine without all of this." She must see a trace of disbelief in my eyes because she adds the word "Really," and gives me a stern look to demonstrate her conviction.

I still must seem doubtful. I've seen the way she cherishes her car and her designer clothes. "You'd give this all away?" I ask, pointing to her pearls.

"Absolutely. In fact, it would be nice to be rid of the guilt."

I look in my mom's eyes and see that she means it.

"Dad told me what the two of you did for that family yesterday. And he told me about the fire . . ." She trails off. Then she takes three steps forward and wraps her arms around me. "I hope he didn't talk you into—"

I cut her off in midsentence. "He didn't talk me into anything, Mom. I swear. It was completely my idea." I feel my face getting hotter. "If you would just stop worrying and see that I have this under control."

"Do you?" Mom shoots me a sideways glare. She's right and she knows it. Two days ago I could say those words and mean them, but today . . . yeah . . . not so much.

"Look . . . I love what you did for those kids, Bennett, I

really do. But you're *my* kid, and I know it's selfish, but I don't want to trade your safety for *anyone* else's."

I shake my head at her. "Come on . . . This isn't about my safety."

"Yes, it is. I've spent far too many nights wondering where my kids are, Bennett. It is about you being here, in this place, living like a normal person."

I knew the word "normal" would pop out of her mouth eventually. Without even thinking about it, I hear myself say, "Mom. I'm still going back to visit Maggie."

Her jaw drops. I reach over to the desk and pick up the photo of my grandmother and me. "I told you this picture was taken when I was living with her a few months ago, in nineteen ninety-five, but that wasn't true. She didn't look like this in nineteen ninety-five. This was taken in two thousand and three, just before she died."

Her hands are trembling as she takes the frame from me.

"I've been going back there for years. I take care of her."

Mom looks for something to hold on to but there's nothing in sight, so she takes two steps back and sits on the edge of the bed. "You go back?" Her lip quivers when she asks, and when I nod, she covers her mouth with her hand.

"All the time," I say.

Mom sits on my bed staring at the photo, and as I watch her, I realize that now would be the perfect time to tell her about Anna too. All I have to do is grab the album from the bottom of the drawer, say something simple like *I also go back to see her. This is Anna,* and start turning pages. Then she'd get it. She'd have to.

But before I can move, Mom looks at me, her eyes welling up, and pats the mattress next to her. "Tell me about her." she says, referring to my grandmother, not my girlfriend.

And instead of going over to my desk, I sit down next to my mom and tell her everything, from the flowers Brooke planted in Maggie's garden and the bills we paid right down to the details of the room I've been staying in when I visit. The tears spill down her cheeks, but she hasn't even heard everything yet.

I ask her to tell me what happened between the two of them.

"Our fights were about such unimportant things, and I honestly don't know why I let it go on so long," she says, her whole body trembling as the tears fall even faster. "I let a few stupid disagreements keep me away from my mother and keep her from knowing my kids . . ." She takes a deep breath. "And she was all alone when—" She can't finish her sentence, but she doesn't have to.

I scoot in closer and fill the gap between us. "She wasn't alone," I say quietly and mom looks up at me. I tell her how Brooke and I went back to the day Maggie died, and how we held her hand as we watched her slip away. Brooke called 911 and we disappeared as soon as help arrived.

She hugs me hard and I relax in her arms, relieved to finally have everything out. I try to think of a way to tell her about Anna too, because it would be nice to come clean completely, but this doesn't feel like the right time. "Thank you," she says as she rubs my back.

Then Mom leans back and stands up. She brushes her hands on her pants and adjusts her shirt, looking around the room like the walls are closing in and she needs to escape. She gives me a peck on the cheek, tells me she loves me, and looks me right in the eye. "Please do me a favor," she says, her voice a bit steadier. "Don't travel for a while. I need to think about all of this, okay? For now, I just need to know you're here and safe. Will you do that, please?"

Without waiting for an answer, she says, "I should let you rest." She's about to leave when she stops and turns around. "Oh, and call Brooke, please." She glances over at my desk, like she's expecting to find my cell phone where it usually is. "She's worried." The latch clicks shut behind her.

I look at the door, thinking about my mother's request and wishing I could respect it. I look at my bed, wishing I could lie down and sleep for the next ten hours or so. I look out the window, hoping the Jeep is still in the garage and that my phone is still in the glove compartment, and wishing I could call Brooke and tell her everything. The risks are huge. But the pull to see Anna—to tell her I'm okay and let her help me piece together what happened yesterday—is stronger than all the others.

Once my backpack is out from under the bed and in place again, I stand in the center of my room and let my eyes fall shut. I'm tempted to picture the cross-country track and arrive there again, just a minute or two after I estimate I was knocked back, but I'm still worried about wiping out the bike accident. So instead, I lock my mind on yesterday, a little before midnight. I picture Anna's room. I visualize the clock on her nightstand. I let myself go. A few seconds later, I open them.

I'm expecting to take in her familiar shelves lined with trophies and CDs, but instead, my eyes open to a view of my boring white room. I close my eyes and try again. When I open them, I'm right where I started.

This can't be happening.

It's just like last time, when Anna got knocked back from my bedroom and I was stuck, unable to leave this room. Maybe my brain is simply too exhausted. Maybe it just needs some extra help. I stand in place, spinning a three-sixty, looking for anything that will help me visualize where I want to go.

The photo album is still buried deep in the bottom of the drawer, but I dig it out and flip to the very last photo—the one of Anna and me, lying on her rug in her bedroom. Her arm is extended in the air and we're both smiling. I bring my fingertip to the plastic and close my eyes. This is where I need to be.

I close my eyes. I open them. Again and again.

After six more attempts, I slump down on the floor next to my bed, feeling sick and utterly spent. The next thing I know, I'm waking up and the morning sun is streaming in above me.

25

I have no idea what's happening back where Anna is. All I know is what's happening here. The days keep beginning and ending and I've spent four of them trying desperately to get back to the day I left Anna in the woods. I'm closing my eyes, opening them, repeating the same actions over and over again, and hoping for a different result. I think Einstein was the one who called that the definition of insanity.

It's been three weeks and four days since Emma's birthday party, which means that homecoming weekend has come and gone. Even worse, I've left Anna exactly the way I did last time: alone, without any warning. Just like I swore I wouldn't do again.

Mom lets me skip school on Friday and again on Monday, but by Tuesday, she insists that I look just fine and completely capable of a day full of learning. So I drag myself from the parking lot and head straight for AP World Civ. I'm not the first one in the room but at least I'm not the last.

I pull my notebook and a pen from my backpack and start doodling while I wait for the bell to ring.

"Hey, stranger." I look to my left and find Megan taking her seat. "Welcome back."

"Thanks." I smile at her and go back to my drawing.

A minute or so later, she leans over across the aisle. "You missed the midterm yesterday. It covered all the material so far." I stop drawing and look over at her. "It was pretty hard, but . . ." She shrugs. "I think I did okay. Anyway, if you want to borrow my notes . . ."

Mrs. McGibney walks in, her briefcase swinging by her side, and looks right at me. "Mr. Cooper," she says flatly. She drops the case next to her desk and it lands with a thud. She starts writing the day's agenda on the whiteboard, but I can tell she's still talking to me when she says, "You missed an exam yesterday. You can come in at lunch and take it."

I sneak a peek at Megan as she grimaces.

"Today?" I ask.

"Yes, sir. Today would be perfect." She takes her eyes off the board to look over her shoulder at me. "Don't worry, you can bring your lunch." She returns to writing.

"I was kind of hoping for a couple of days to brush up."

"I announced this test last Wednesday, Mr. Cooper. According to my records, you were here last Wednesday. Judging from the scores, everyone in this class spent the last few days 'brushing up.' If you didn't, that is not my problem."

"But I was sick."

More writing. "I'm offering the test today at lunch. Otherwise, it won't be fair to the rest of the class." She finishes the agenda and brings the dry-erase marker to the board, punctuating the last line with a loud period. "Sound good?" She turns around and stares at me.

It doesn't matter. Today, next week, the grade I get on this test will likely be the same either way. I nod.

"Great. I'll see you then."

I spend the next forty-five minutes cramming. Every time McGibney turns her back, I thumb through my notebook, desperately trying to recall all the things I've learned about world civilizations since school started. The notes are fairly detailed in some places, but I honestly don't remember writing many of them. In other places, I find page after page with nothing but doodles. Apparently, a few weeks ago, I spent an entire class trying to figure out what to name my garage.

The bell rings and everyone rises from their seats and heads for the door. As I turn into the hall toward my next class, I spot Megan leaning up against the locker bank, smiling and clearly waiting for me. "Man, that was harsh," she says when I'm within earshot.

"Remind me not to get sick again."

She smiles. "Here." She reaches into her messenger bag and hands me a black-and-white composition notebook. The cover is bent and the pages are frayed, and as I turn it over in my hands I notice that it looks a lot more battered than mine does, as if she's actually been using it to take notes in class and then refer to them later on.

"Really?"

"Sure." She closes her bag and readjusts the strap on her shoulder. "Maybe you could skip your next three classes and go study in the library."

Under normal circumstances, that's exactly what I would do. And after I was finished cramming, I'd go back to the beginning of the day to do it over. The second time around, I'd be ready for both the test and for McGibney's question. When Megan wasn't looking, I'd slip her notebook back into her pack before she even realized it was missing. This conversation would never happen, and Megan would never know that there was a version of events that I wiped out, where she stood in the hallway and offered to let me borrow her notes.

But these aren't normal circumstances. I don't know if I could go back four hours even if I wanted to. If I had the ability to travel again, I certainly wouldn't be here at school, worrying about a test. I'd be with Anna.

"Thanks," I say. I shove the notebook into my pack and start thinking of excuses for missing my next three classes. "That's really cool of you."

"No problem." She stands there, looking at me like she has more to say. "Well, I'd better get to class. Good luck." Before I can respond, she turns on her heel and walks away. I turn on mine and head for the library.

I've been sitting in the same carrel, staring at the same page and trying *not* to stare out the same window, for more than an hour now. Megan's notes are clear and detailed, but the words seem to leave my brain faster than I can bring them in.

I twist my pencil back and forth between my fingers, thinking about Anna and the last words I heard her say: *You're not supposed to be here until Friday.*

But I can't get to Friday. And I can't get to Wednesday and I can't get to Thursday either. Every time I try, I open my eyes in the exact place I closed them. And suddenly it dawns on me. I've been trying to get back before homecoming so I don't let Anna down. But what if I'm trying too hard to go back to a precise moment, when I should just be trying to get *back?*

I grab my phone but leave the rest of my stuff at the carrel, and head for a computer kiosk. I look up a 1995 calendar and find the month of October. I open up the calendar on my phone to today's date and hold it up next to the screen. The calendars are nearly identical, only a day off. In 2012, it's Tuesday. In 1995, it's a Monday.

I head straight for the men's room and lock myself in a stall. I leave my phone on the back of the toilet and close my eyes. I think back to the layout of Westlake Academy, trying to remember the quiet spots I found to hide in every time I felt like I was about to be knocked back to San Francisco.

Right outside our Spanish building, there was a rarely used path obscured by overgrown plants and shrubs. I brought Anna there once, the day we cut class and I told her the last part of my secret.

I have no idea if this will work, but I close my eyes, mutter the word "please," and picture the location.

My skin prickles from the extreme drop in temperature and I breathe in fresh air that couldn't possibly exist in a men's room. As soon as I open my eyes, they dart around the empty field and I let out a gasp. I'm actually here.

I bring my hands to the sides of my face and peek through the glass doors. It's quiet, and even though I landed *where* I intended to, I'm still not sure if I landed *when* I intended to. I pull the door handle and it opens. At least it's a school day.

The hallway is empty. I look around for a clock and find one just above the next locker bank. I've timed it perfectly. I'm only a few feet away from where I need to be and I make it there with a minute to spare. I'm leaning against the lockers, trying to look like I belong here, when the bell rings. That's when I realize that I'm the only one who's not wearing a uniform.

Up and down the corridor, classroom doors begin opening and people start spilling out into the hall wearing the traditional Westlake black-and-white plaid. The girls are in skirts and white blouses. The guys are in slacks and dress shirts. I spot the occasional tie or V-neck sweater.

The rules are clear in this circular hallway dubbed The Donut, and because everyone's required to walk clockwise between classes, they all head in my direction at once. A few people notice me standing here, looking out of place in my street clothes, and shoot me a questioning look as they pass.

I'm combing the crowd for Anna, but I don't see her anywhere, and as the activity level dies down, I'm starting to question myself. Maybe I was wrong about her class schedule?

But then I see her come around the bend, talking with Alex, and my heart starts pounding hard.

When she's within a few feet of the classroom door, she finally spots me. She stops cold and covers her mouth with her hand. Her expression is impossible to read, and as she takes long strides in my direction, I can't tell if she's relieved to see me or furious that I didn't show up when I was supposed to. I brace myself for the worst, but as soon as she's close enough, she throws her arms over my shoulders and squeezes me tight. I've never been so happy to see her. "I'm so sorry," I whisper in her ear.

Alex walks past us into the classroom, and mutters the word "asshole" under his breath.

"Ignore him," she says as she buries her face in my neck.

I try to release her so I can see her face, but she tightens her grip. "I'm so sorry I missed homecoming."

"I don't care. You're here now."

The Donut empties out and I can tell the bell's about to ring. I take a step back and rest my hands on her shoulders. "I need to talk to you." I point with my chin toward the double doors that lead outside, and I can tell by the look on her face that she knows exactly what I mean. "I can't bring you back this time though. You're going to have to miss Spanish, for real. Is that okay?"

"Yeah." She says it with a little laugh, as if it's the only possible answer.

We follow the path up the slope until it ends at the big tree at the top of the ridge. We sit down next to each other, exactly the way we did last year when I told her the third and final part of my secret, and she became the fourth person in the world to know everything there was to know about me. But now, there's nothing but pain and worry on her face, and I can't help but wonder if I made the right decision that day.

"I didn't know what to do." Her voice is shaking and so are her hands, and I reach for them and scoot in even closer to her. "You were just standing there in the woods that day, all excited about something, and then out of nowhere you just collapsed. What happened? Why couldn't you come back?"

I shake my head. "I don't know. There's some stuff . . . missing. Was that the last time you saw me?" She nods but she's clearly confused as to why I'm asking when this is information I should already know.

She's breathing faster now and I can hear the panic in her voice. "Yeah. You got knocked back home."

Not home. Not right away at least. If I wasn't here and I wasn't there, where was I, passed out in the garage for twenty-two hours?

Over the next fifteen minutes, I talk nonstop, telling Anna about everything that happened last week—the news story and me on my skateboard, the two little girls and my dad on sidekick duty—and that I have no idea where I was for nearly a full day, and how I've spent the last five days trying to get back to her. Her face contorts when I tell her how painful the returns have become, and how they got progressively worse and a hell of a lot bloodier.

"It'll be fine now." I put on my best smile and hope I sound reassuring. "I'll just go back to doing what I've always done. Apparently, as long as I use this ridiculous thing I can do for my own selfish purposes, I'm free to come and go as I please," I say.

Anna takes my face in her hands and makes me look her in the eye. "You have to promise me. No more do-overs, okay? Never."

I nod. "Yeah, I'm pretty sure that's the message I'm supposed to be getting here." I let out a laugh, but Anna doesn't join in.

"Promise," she says.

"Yeah. I promise." As I say the words, I wonder why it's so easy to make this promise to her when I can't make it to my own parents.

I sigh. "Well, at least my mom and dad can now agree on one thing. They've both made it crystal clear that I'm not to travel ever again."

"Not even to see me?" she asks, and I stop laughing.

"No . . . well. Yes. Not exactly."

Anna drops her hands and leans away from me. "What does that mean, 'not exactly'? Did they tell you that you couldn't come back here anymore?"

I look down at the dirt. "Actually, they did. But that was five months ago."

She waits for me to explain, but I have no idea what to say next. This conversation was inevitable, and there have been plenty of times I walked through it in my head, but having it today was the farthest thing from my mind.

"My parents don't . . . exactly . . . know about you." I suck in a deep breath and wait while she stares at me for a painfully long time.

"They don't know about me?" I can't tell if she wants to cry or punch me. I shake my head no and Anna's eyes narrow in disbelief. "What about your sister?"

"Brooke knows," I whisper.

"Brooke?" Anna's voice cracks as she says her name, and there's a questioning tone at the end, like she can't believe that there's only one person in my world who knows she exists.

"Listen, please. My parents wouldn't understand. And I can't tell my friends . . . I mean, what am I supposed to tell them?"

"Tell them that I live in Illinois. Just like my friends think you're a normal guy from San Francisco." She scoots away from me, looking both confused and disgusted at the same time. "You don't have to tell them I live in nineteen ninety-five." She says that last part so quietly that I have to strain to hear her. But then she finds her voice again. "Look, I know you have a thing for secrets, but I thought we were done with that."

"We are. I don't have any secrets from you."

"No, just that I *am* one." She lets out a sarcastic-sounding breath.

She looks down at the dining hall windows, and this time, I'm sure she's wondering why she ever entertained the idea of letting complicated me into her rather uncomplicated life.

"Look," I say, "last June, when I was stuck in San Francisco and couldn't get back here, I thought I'd never see you again. I didn't know what to say to my parents or my friends."

Anna gives me a hard look and shakes her head. "Everyone in *my* life knows about you, even though they don't know your big secret." She says the last part sarcastically, wiggling her fingers in front of her face for emphasis. "Nobody here gets it. None of them understand why I'm in a relationship with a guy who lives two thousand miles away—and they don't even know the half of it." She huffs. "But they know about *you*.

"I could never keep you to myself." She says the last part quietly, but loud enough for me to hear.

I rub my forehead with my fingertips as I try to find the right words. "I didn't want to hurt you. And, I swear, I was going to tell them eventually, but it was just . . . easier not to."

Her head snaps up and there's that look again. "Easier?" she asks. Now I'm pretty sure she's about to punch me.

"Not more *convenient. Easier.*" I bring my hand to my chest. "On *me*. Look, you seem to enjoy torturing yourself with photo albums and things that remind you of the two of us, but I don't. That only makes it worse. It's *easier* for me to pretend you're not real when we're not together."

A tear slides down her cheek and she quickly brushes it away.

I reach for her hands, and I'm a little surprised when she lets me take them. "Do you have any idea how much I hate being there without you? When I'm supposed to be doing homework, I go for drives instead. I take the top down on the Jeep and turn up the music and cruise around the city I've always loved, and all I want to do is show it to you. I want to bring you to my favorite café in North Beach, where they serve lattes in bowls instead of mugs. I want to show you this wave organ that's built into a bunch of rocks and has an insane view of Alcatraz. I want to bring you to my school and introduce you to Sam and the rest of my friends, so you'll know them the same way I know Emma and Danielle and Justin. But I can't *ever* do that." She squeezes my hand. "We've already tried and it was a disaster. I guess I figured, the less I had to be reminded that you couldn't be there, the easier it would be."

Anna releases my hands so she can wipe the tears from her cheeks.

"Look," I say. "All I want is a normal relationship with you, and when I'm here, it feels like I have it. But when I'm there . . . I just miss you. All the time."

She grabs one of my hands in both of hers and squeezes it tight.

"I'll tell them about you, okay? I'll show my mom and dad your photo album, and I'll tell them everything. And I'll explain that I'm done with do-overs—that they're the only reason I've lost control—but that I need to keep coming back here to see you. Okay? I promise."

The bell rings but neither one of us move. Eventually the dining hall below starts filling with people, and I spot everyone taking their usual places and their usual tables and starting in on their usual conversations.

"Great," Anna mutters, watching the scene below.

"What?"

"Ten bucks says Alex has already told everyone about seeing you here." She stands up and brushes the dirt off her jeans. "This should make for a delightful lunch."

"Do you want me to stick around?" I ask.

Anna offers her hand to help me up and I take it. Then she looks at me and lets out a heavy sigh. "It's okay. I've got it." We start walking down the hill and she threads her arm through mine. "But I'll tell you, next time you're in town you better bring me a giant bouquet of flowers or something. If you show up empty-handed my parents might come up with something more painful than being knocked back to San Francisco."

"That bad?"

"Yup."

"I didn't get to see you in the dress."

She lifts two fingers into the air. "Twice now."

I wince. "Were you actually wearing it this time?"

She raises her eyebrows and nods slowly.

"God, I *am* an asshole."

"Yeah." She gives me a sad smile and bumps my hip with hers. "But not on purpose."

⁓

Exactly fifty-five minutes after I left, I open my eyes in the men's room stall. I push through the door just as the migraine hits. My eyes are burning as I stumble over to the sink, feeling my way with the help of the walls.

I find the spigot, turn it on, and stick my mouth under the stream. I drink as fast and as much as I can before cupping my hands and splashing cold water on my face. The fluorescent lights make it impossible to open my eyes, and my head is pounding, but at least it all feels familiar.

I push my hands into the countertop and keep my head down, breathing and concentrating, willing the pain to disappear. Twenty minutes later, the pounding subsides to a dull ache in my temples.

And it feels like everything is back to normal. Well, *my* normal, at least.

november 2012

26

san francisco, california

The sound of my phone chirping wakes me from a deep sleep, and I roll over, pulling the comforter over my head to block out the sunlight. I'm starting to slip back into sleep again when there's another chirp. I feel around on the nightstand for my phone and open my eyes to back-to-back texts from Brooke:

> Good morning!

> Hey, what r u doing tonight?

My eyes are still adjusting when another message appears.

> Party at our apartment. Come!

I stare at the screen as I consider it. Aside from a some-what loose plan to meet up with the guys and loiter around

Lafayette Park later, I really don't have anything else to do this weekend. But social conflicts aren't the real reason I think I should stay away. I only have one more week before I can go see Anna again and I'm not about to do anything to jeopardize it. Another message:

> I want my roommates to meet you!

A groan escapes my mouth as I fall back into the pillow. I lift the phone above my head and text her back.

> I think I'd better stay put.

I toss the phone onto the comforter and close my eyes. It hasn't even been five minutes when my phone chirps again. I'm expecting to see another overly enthusiastic message from Brooke, but this one's from Sam.

> Sup?

I type back:

> Sleeping.

Then I clarify:

> Was.

Sleep might be impossible at this point, but I let my hand fall to my side and the phone lands on the bed again. I'm lost in a restful daze when another text arrives, followed by another. I sigh and reach for the phone.

> Wake up.
> We're climbing.
> Outside.
> On real rocks.

> Pick me up in 20.

The sun's peeking in between the curtains. I haven't been climbing outdoors since last summer. Pretty soon the rain will start falling and Sam and I won't have any other option but the climbing gym. And it sounds so . . . normal. I could use a day of normal.

I throw off the covers and force myself into the shower, and ten minutes later, I'm feeling like this was the right call. I pour coffee into a travel mug, load my stuff into the Jeep, and pull into Sam's driveway right on time.

I have no idea where we're going, but he has our destination all figured out, and before I can even back out of the driveway, he's programming it into the GPS. The route starts with a short drive to the Golden Gate Bridge and ends at the base of a mountain three hours away.

"We're climbing Donner?" I ask as I pull up to a stop sign and consider the map.

Sam gives me an exaggerated shrug and gestures out the front window. "Have you seen this day?" He gives me a hard stare like he can't believe I'd suggest anything else.

I crane my neck to get a better view. It's one of those near-winter days: deep blue sky, bright sun, crisp wind. I hit the gas pedal with my foot and roll down the window, and as we cruise down the hill toward the bay, the car floods with cold air.

At the next stop sign, I turn left onto a residential street and pull over to the side. Sam looks at me sideways as I climb out, but it doesn't take him long to figure out what I'm doing, and when he does, he hops out and starts helping me unbuckle the Jeep's soft top. We pull it back and secure it in place. And then we're off again.

"Now it's a road trip." Sam crosses his arms behind his head and reclines the passenger seat. As he searches on my iPhone for music, we make small talk about the tutoring job I'm starting on Monday. He tells me about the kids, and how he'll point out the troublemakers, as well as the ones who seem to really care about being there.

I was great in the interview. The head of the organization offered me the job on the spot. Now I've pushed my start date back twice, like I'm avoiding it, and the more Sam says, the more I start to realize that I don't want to hear about it. There's something offputting about the whole thing.

The Jeep creeps forward until we finally arrive at the entrance to the Golden Gate Bridge. Out of nowhere, I remember the organization I stumbled upon when I was first researching community service projects. The one in the Tenderloin, down the street from the apartment that burned down but didn't take the lives of two kids.

I've don't even give it another thought, and I hear the words just slip out. "I'm going to pass on the job, Sam."

"What? You can't pass on it. You already took it."

I keep my eyes on the traffic in front of me. "I know. I'm going to un-take it."

I can feel him looking at me. "You need to do something for your transcripts," he says, and I assure him that I plan to. As we drive onto the bridge, I tell him everything I learned from the online video that day, and with every word, I'm more and more excited about getting home tonight and filling out the application.

"Whatever you want." Sam falls back into the headrest and stares through the open roof. "Check it out," he says as we pass under the dark orange gates that span the bridge. "Ah, best part . . ."

Without looking away, he tosses my phone into the console. "It's not too early for Jack White, is it?"

"It's never too early for Jack White." I hear the first song on the playlist I made a few months ago. It's a solid mix of the White Stripes, the Raconteurs, the Dead Weather, and White's solo stuff. The four electric guitar notes kick off "Sixteen Saltines."

Saltines. I smile as I picture Anna nibbling on the corner of one and I turn up the music as loud as it will go.

Over the next three hours we make our way to Donner,

listening to a lot of music, talking very little, and stopping only once along the way for lunch at In-N-Out. We down our shakes and stuff french fries into our mouths, but leave our burgers wrapped so we can eat them at the summit.

After we arrive at the parking area off the freeway, we grab our gear and walk thirty minutes to the base of the first route. Neither one of us has been here before and Sam's giddy, rattling off everything he learned during his Internet research last night. Clean granite. Lots of routes. Incredible views from the summits.

At the base of the first rock, I ready myself. I tie my shoes, clip my chalk bag to the loop on my pants, and stuff my sweatshirt into my backpack. I open one of the granola bars I grabbed out of the pantry this morning before I left and eat it in three bites. At the bottom of my pack, I feel for the six-pack of lukewarm Gatorades and I open one and drink it without stopping.

I look around. Sam and I are the only people out here. I point my head at the sky and let out a loud yell, and Sam jumps and scolds me for scaring the crap out of him. He returns to tightening the Velcro on his shoes. The air is clean and this place is amazing and I can't wait to see the view from the top. I had no idea how much I needed this.

"You want me to lead?" I ask as I start clipping the cams onto my harness.

Sam looks up at the rock. "Actually, this is a popular one to free solo. What do you think? You up for it?"

I consider it. It's not that vertical, and the holds look relatively easy to spot, even from here. "Sure," I say as I drop the gear back into my pack.

"You have the burgers?" Sam coils the rope and throws it over his shoulder, then clips his chalk bag to his belt loop.

"Yep." I pat the smaller backpack I brought along and feed my arms through the straps. I'm not hungry at all. Just euphoric and full of energy.

Sam checks his watch. "We made good time. It's only twelve thirty."

The climb is easy at first, and I have no trouble finding hand- and footholds. I pull myself up, slide to the left, and pull up again. The granite is cold and dry beneath my fingertips. I'm moving quickly through the route.

About a quarter of the way up, I see a good spot to take a break, and I wedge my hand into a large crack and find an equally large space for my toe. I let my arms slacken a bit.

I look for Sam. He's ahead of me, and he seems to be maneuvering the rock well. I see his fingers grip the edge and watch him pull himself onto a ledge to rest. He's only about ten feet higher, and I can see the sweat glistening on his forehead and dripping down his cheeks. He wedges himself into a position where he can free one hand, and he lifts the edge of his T-shirt and wipes his face dry.

It's time to move, so I chalk up my hands again and reach up for a hold. It's barely enough to grip on to, and within a few seconds, my knuckles are turning white and my forearms are burning. I see a better grip only inches away and swing my body around so I can grab on to it, rising to a ledge that's wide enough to stand on. I stop and catch my breath.

The summit is farther away than I expected it to be, and it'll be slow going from here. I don't know what I was thinking. It's been months since I climbed outside, and even though this was supposed to be an easy route, I'm starting to think the free solo climb was a bad idea. When I chalk my hands, my arms are shaking with fatigue.

I start back up the rock, and a little while later I see Sam reach the summit. I stop and consider my last few moves while he stands there, doubled over and beaming down at me.

"Dude, my mom climbs faster than you do."

I tighten my fingers around the hold with one hand, freeing the other one to flip him off. Sam lets out a loud laugh, and returns to sweating and panting. I'm waiting to feel the euphoria I usually experience at this point of the climb, but each move feels harder than it should be. I'm going to be insanely sore tomorrow.

I'm almost there. In just one or two more strategic, well-thought moves, I'll be at the top. I take one more deep breath and lock my eyes on my next hold. I make my move, then the next, and suddenly I'm gripping the shelf.

I breathe. My fingertips dig into the granite.

"Jesus, it's about time." Sam takes a swig of Gatorade and checks the time on his phone. "It's already one o'clock. Get up here, would you? I'm starving."

As I pull myself up, I feel the edge break in my hands. Dust and bits of rock tumble down into my eyes, and I grope blindly, reaching up for anything to hold on to. My right hand falls away and I grab the rock harder with my left, but it just slips off.

Sam reacts immediately, dropping his Gatorade and falling to his stomach. His hand juts out over the edge, but by then I'm nowhere near it.

My cheek skids against the surface and my hip hits something sharp. My shoulder slams against a boulder and that slows my momentum, but only temporarily. My already-raw fingers burn and sting as they claw at the granite.

I hear Sam yell from the summit.

I'm waiting for my body to shut down so I don't have to endure the pain of the crash. Suddenly, I feel my hip connect with something hard and I stop fast. I'm lying in a crumpled heap on the ledge I'd been standing on earlier, and it's wide enough to keep me secure, but I scramble to find something to hold on to anyway.

"Stay there," Sam says, and I laugh. He disappears from the edge and I keep laughing, but I'm not sure why. Maybe because it keeps me from thinking about how fast my heart is racing and that my legs feel rubbery.

A couple of minutes later he returns to the shelf, flattens his chest against the rock, and slaps a coil of blue rope by his side. He feeds it over the edge and I watch it fall, dancing and squirming its way toward me. When I look up, I see Sam.

His face is drawn, his eyes are full of panic, and his hands are shaking violently as he guides the rope down.

I tie the rope to my harness. Sam yells, "Hold on," and then he's gone for a full minute. I picture him tying the rope to the anchors at the top and feel the slack disappear. He returns and looks over the edge. "Okay. You're on belay. I've got you!" He gives me a thumbs-up and drops to the ground again. He's trying to sound stoic, but I can hear the worry in his voice.

I start climbing again, taking my moves a lot more slowly, thinking through each one more than I usually do. I try not to think about falling again. I don't look up, but I can feel Sam working to keep the rope taut.

I'm only a few feet from the top when Sam drops to the ground again, and when I'm close enough, he lowers his hand. This time, I grab it and let him pull me to the surface.

Neither one of us says a word as we collapse back on the sun-warmed rock and stare straight up at the sky. I don't even remove the rope from my waist. I just lie there. Eventually, I bring my hand to my face. My cheek is throbbing and my arms are covered in deep scratches. My right hip hurts when I try to sit up, there's a small gash on my shoulder, and my fingers are caked with blood.

"You okay?" Sam asks and I nod. I don't look at him, but his voice still sounds a little shaky. "Give me your pack." He holds out his hand and I slide it off, but the strap grazes the cut on my arm. I cringe. He rifles through my stuff, and when I look up a minute later he's dumping Gatorade onto an In-N-Out napkin. "All the water's at the bottom," he says as he hands it to me. "This will have to do."

I wash the dirt off my face and clean up my arm. Without saying a word, I hold my hand out to Sam and he tosses me the rest of the Gatorade. I dump a little more on a clean corner of the napkin, take a big gulp, swish it around in my mouth, and spit out a mouthful of dirt.

"Well at least you crushed your face and not the burgers," Sam says with a laugh. He reaches into the bag and pulls out his Double-Double, then tosses the bag to me.

I down another Gatorade, Sam takes a big bite of his burger, and neither one of us speaks as we stare out at the view. I take a few bites, but when I start thinking about what might have happened, I feel my stomach tighten up and my appetite disappears.

What if I had fallen to the bottom? I didn't think about doing it over—it all happened too quickly—but I could have. What if I'd locked in on a time before we started up that rock, closed my eyes, and brought myself back? What would have happened if I'd saved my own life? Could I even *do* that? If I had, Sam would have seen everything.

Out of nowhere, I think about something I once said to Anna. As I was envying her deep roots in Evanston and a normal life she couldn't wait to leave, I told her that, aside from my parents and my sister, everyone I knew back home was somehow temporary. Now I feel guilty for saying that. I watch Sam mowing his burger and wiping sauce from his face, and I can't stop picturing how he dropped to the ground and reached over the edge for me.

Sam's not temporary. He never was. And it occurs to me that, while I can't tell him my biggest secret, perhaps I shouldn't keep so many of them from my best friend.

We finish our burgers and I toss my backpack—now much lighter, since it's filled with nothing but trash—over the edge. I use the top rope to rappel down to the bottom, and Sam follows me.

We pack up and head down the path to the next rock. It turns out to be a lot more technical, and when Sam offers to lead, I accept immediately. We climb two different routes. At dusk, we start the half-hour hike back to the Jeep.

We're walking single file and almost at the end of the trail. "Sam," I say to his back.

He lets out a "huh" that's barely audible.

"There's something I've been wanting to tell you."

He keeps walking and doesn't turn around.

I take a deep breath. "I wasn't backpacking in Europe last spring."

He flips his head around and gives me a quick nod. Then he turns back to the path.

"I was in Illinois."

"Oh . . ."

"Living with my grandmother."

The fact that I can't see his face makes this easier.

"And while I was there, I sort of . . . met this girl."

He stops cold and I almost run into his backpack. He turns

around, his eyes wide with surprise. "Why were you staying with your grandmother?"

I stare at him. I wasn't expecting him to go there and don't have a great answer for this. "I was just . . . dealing with some family stuff. It was complicated. I just needed to get away." It's not the whole story, but so far, I'm not lying.

His eyebrows knit together. "Coop," he says. "We all know you were in rehab." Then he stops cold and stares at me. "Wait, did you meet a girl in *rehab*?"

"In rehab? Why would I be in rehab?" My mom swore she didn't tell that ridiculous story to anyone outside the school administration. And Sam has never seen me drink or smoke or pop a pill. Even if he'd heard that, how could he actually believe it? How can he just be telling me this now?

"Come on, why else would you take off suddenly in the middle of the school year, not come back for three months, and when you do, tell everyone you were traveling in Europe." He rolls his eyes. He's got a point. "Besides, your mom told Cameron's mom that you were away 'dealing with some issues.' What else would we think?"

Great.

I step in front of him and start walking down the trail toward the car. I didn't want to start some kind of major confrontation about where I was last spring; I just wanted to tell him about Anna. I'm tired. I could have died on that rock today. And now my brain isn't working fast enough to feed me new lies and help me keep up my cover. All this lying is exhausting, so I decide to give up, play it straight.

"Look," I say without turning around, "You don't have to believe me, but I wasn't in rehab. I was living with my grandmother in Illinois for three months and then I came back. Now I go visit her. And Anna." It feels good to say her name aloud.

I can hear Sam's footsteps behind me, but he doesn't say anything and neither do I. Once we reach the car, we silently load up our packs and get inside. I turn the key in the ignition and crank up the heat, and then I reach for my iPhone, looking for music.

Sam buckles his seat belt. "Is that why you stayed there for the rest of the semester?" he asks.

I don't look up but I nod.

"Because of Anna."

I inhale sharply when I hear Sam say her name, and I turn to look at him. "Yeah, because of Anna."

"Who lives in Illinois."

"Unfortunately, yeah."

He gives me this *let's hear it* gesture with his hand, and as I back out of the lot and turn onto the two-lane road that heads to the bottom of the mountain, the words just start pouring out.

Omitting details about the decade I visit, I tell him everything there is to know about Evanston, Illinois, and what I do when I'm there. I even give him the history, going all the way back to last March, when I first arrived at my grandmother's house and enrolled at Westlake. A half hour later, he not only knows all about Anna, he knows about Emma and Justin, Maggie, and the Greenes, too. Anna was right. My shoulders are lighter right now than they've been in months.

When we reach the bottom of the mountain, Sam points out a diner that serves twenty-four-hour breakfast, and I pull in and park. I'm just about to get out when my phone chirps. I pick it up and read:

> Miss you here.
> Come next weekend? There's someone
> I want you to meet. :)

"You want to get us a table?" I ask Sam. "I've got to reply to this message."

"From Anna?" he says, like he's enjoying being in the know. If he only knew how impossible that is.

"It's from Brooke. Give me a sec. I'll be right in."

Sam shuts the car door and heads inside. It occurs to me that, as much as I miss Brooke, and as much as I'd love to tell her what happened today, I'm glad I'm not in Boulder right now. I can't remember the last time I wanted to be exactly where I was.

I type the words:

> Miss you too,
> but can't do next weekend (Anna).

A minute later, her reply arrives:

> Bummer.

I'm just about to shove my phone in my pocket and join Sam when I have an idea. Anna told me I'd better bring flowers next time, but I can do a hell of a lot better than that. I start typing.

> There's someone I want you to meet too.

> Wanna come along?

november 1995

27

evanston, illinois

"God, it's freezing out there!" Brooke pulls her leg inside and slams the car door shut again. She tightens her jacket around her body and shivers.

"Actually, I was going to ask you to wait in the car. Do you mind?"

"Are you kidding? We just drove three hours, the last of it in an electrical storm, and now it's, like, twenty degrees out there." It's actually closer to ten but I decide not to tell her that. "I am *more* than happy to wait in the car." Brooke holds out her hand, palm flat. "Keys?"

"What?"

"Keys. Heat. Music." She points at the ignition. "Keys?"

I hand her the car keys and reach behind me to grab the huge bouquet of flowers I bought on the way here. "I'll be over there." I point at the crowd of people gathered in the field surrounded by white pop-up tents. "See the guy in the blue parka? That's her dad. As soon as you see Anna join us, give me ten minutes and then come over. Got it?"

"Got it." She turns the key backward in the ignition, cranks the heat up to ninety, and starts spinning the radio dial, looking for a station. She stops in midspin and shoos me away. "Go. I'm fine."

As I close the door, I hear the gunshot off in the distance and I follow the signs to the starting line. Anna's dad is still huddled up with the other parents, each of them clutching a matching Styrofoam coffee cup in one hand and checking a stopwatch in the other.

I stand in the empty space next to him. "Hi, Mr. Greene," I say quietly, and he turns to face me. I keep the flowers low at my side, but visible.

He studies my face and says, "You're here." Then he looks back at the course and takes a big sip of his coffee.

I shift in place. "Yes, sir. I'm here."

"Anna told me you would be, but I didn't believe her." He looks down at the flowers and brings his cup to his mouth again, tips his head back, and drains it.

"I wanted to tell you personally how sorry I was about homecoming. I would have been there if there was any way, but . . . I . . ." I trail off because I can't find any words that wouldn't be lies.

He stares at me. "Why didn't you call?"

I shift nervously. I'm searching for a way to explain this and still tell the truth, but I'm coming up blank.

"Did you know that she stood there for an hour, in that

dress, waiting for you? And you didn't even *call*. How could you do that to her?" He's not yelling, but I almost wish he would. That would be easier to take than his calm demeanor and the way his voice is dripping with disgust and disappointment. It's almost too much to take. It's almost enough for me to tell him everything, all my secrets, right now, so he can understand why I keep disappearing on his daughter when that's the last thing in the world I want to do.

"I can't possibly explain how sorry I am. I know I . . . let her down." He must hear the genuine remorse in my voice, because his eyes soften, but only for a second or two. He walks away without saying anything else, and I think that's the end of it. But then he drops his empty cup in a trash can and heads back toward me.

The hard stare has returned. "My problem, Bennett," he finally says, "is that you *keep* letting her down. And for some reason her mother and I can't comprehend, she keeps letting you do it." I feel my face contort. I didn't think I could feel more horrible than I did after I told Anna she was a secret.

The crowd starts moving into formation, standing on opposite sides of the bright yellow tape and making a path between the edge of the forest and the finish line. Mr. Greene checks his watch and says, "She should be here in a few minutes."

I think he's going to follow the other parents, but instead he takes a deep breath and turns to look at me. "Look, I'm not going to pretend to understand this thing between you two. She doesn't seem to care that you live two thousand miles away from each other, or that she only gets to see you every few weeks, but I do. It was fine when you lived in the same town, but this is ridiculous. Do you really think you can keep this up?"

I grip the flowers a little tighter.

He gestures toward the finish line. "Here they come," he says, and he walks away from me and squeezes in among the other parents. He's clapping and yelling in a deep, booming voice, even though there are no runners in sight yet. When Anna comes into view, he takes it to a completely different level. I step in to get a better view but keep a safe distance from him.

Three runners emerge at the same time, Anna in third, but tight on the heels of the girl in second. She passes her easily and then kicks it up a notch. Her feet are spinning so fast they're a blur, her arms are pumping hard by her sides, and she has this look of determination on her face that I've never seen before.

"Go, Annie!" Mr. Greene shouts. "Come on! Punch it! Let's go!"

I can see her eyes now, fixed on that yellow tape. She's gaining on the leader, but she's running out of time to close the gap. She's right on her heels, and the other runner speeds up again. Anna barely overtakes her at the very end. She breaks through the tape first and throws her arms in the air.

Mr. Greene is still hollering, but he suddenly stops and presses a few buttons on his watch. "Yes!" he yells. Anna's across the field, doubled over, hands on her knees, until she stands up and starts walking in circles, working hard to catch her breath. She stops next to the girl who almost beat her and reaches out to shake her hand.

Her teammates gather around her, bouncing up and down, blocking her from view. But a few minutes later, she emerges from the pack and I see her looking around, presumably for her dad. He spots her right away, and gives her an enthusiastic wave.

She starts running toward us and I watch him, pacing back and forth, as if it's all he can do to keep from running over to her and picking her up like she was six and not sixteen.

"Did you see that?" she asks. Her dad holds up his hand and she gives him a high five. "Man, I had to turn it on at the end there!" Her shoes are completely covered in mud, and as she gets closer, I can see that everything from her calves on up is speckled with it too.

"That's my girl!" I hear her dad say as he pulls her into a tight hug. She pecks him on the cheek and he squeezes her again, even tighter, and that's when she opens her eyes and sees me standing there. She pulls away from him.

"Hi," she says.

"Hi." I hold out the flowers and her eyes light up. Then she covers her face with her hands and says, "I was totally kidding about the flowers."

Mr. Greene clears his throat and Anna looks over at him and nods once, like she's dismissing him, but he doesn't budge. "Dad."

"Fine. I'll go verify your time," he says, and he leaves the two of us alone.

"Man, your dad's pissed at me," I say as I watch him walk away. My pulse is racing and my hands are still shaking as I hand her the flowers. "I'm afraid these didn't help much."

"Thank you anyway. I love them." She takes the bouquet with one hand and rests the other on my right cheek. "What happened to your face?"

"I scraped it rock climbing." I cover her hand with mine and kiss her palm. "I brought you something else, too."

"Oh, yeah?" She looks over my shoulder, like she's trying to get a glimpse of what's behind my back. "Where is it?"

"In the car. I was hoping I could drive you back home." Anna looks confused, so I keep talking. "I've been thinking about what you said last time I was here, and you were right. You should know my family. And I want them to know you." Her forehead crinkles up and she stares at me. "I'm starting with Brooke."

"Brooke?"

"Yeah. She's in the car." I gesture behind me, toward the parking lot. My face breaks into a huge smile, and I expect hers to do the same, but instead she looks horrified.

"In the *car*? I can't meet Brooke *now*. I'm not . . . I mean . . ." Her shirt is drenched in sweat and her cheeks are dotted with mud. She pulls her hair out of the ponytail, brushes it back off her face again, and puts it back exactly the way it was, but then her eyes grow wide as she stares over my shoulder.

"What's the matter?"

"Hi!" I hear Brooke's voice behind me. I'd forgotten that I told her to wait ten minutes before she got out of the car. I should have told her to wait there until I got her. I should have given Anna more time to get used to this idea. Surprising her with this suddenly feels selfish.

"Hi." Anna looks down at her clothes and shakes her head. "Wow . . . I was kind of hoping to meet you when I was . . . cleaner."

Brooke flicks her wrist in the air, like she's swatting Anna's comment away. "No worries," she says. But then she stands there awkwardly, crossing and uncrossing her arms, while she tries to think of something else to say. "I'm so excited about this road trip. I lived in Chicago for a few months, but I never saw the rest of Illinois."

"There's a good reason for that," Anna says. She lets out a nervous laugh and goes back to staring at Brooke like she's still trying to wrap her head around the fact that she's standing in front of her.

Then Anna's dad returns and I introduce the two of them.

Brooke is bouncing in place as she holds out her hand. "It's so nice to finally meet you, Mr. Greene. Bennett's told me so much about your family," she says. She's still shaking his hand, and Anna's dad looks down, as if he's wondering if she's planning to let it go anytime soon.

"It's nice to meet you," he says, stealing a quick glance at me. "We've heard a lot about you, too. I'm glad to see you in such good health." Brooke's whole face contorts and she starts to say something, but then she looks over at me and I stare back at her with this *Just go with it* look.

She nods and says, "Thanks," and drops his hand. When he looks away, Brooke shoots me a glare.

"There's a local reporter interviewing the team," Anna's dad says to her. He points off in the distance to a white tent with a sign that bears the Illinois High School Association logo. I recognize her coach and a few of her teammates. "You should probably join them." His eyes dart in my direction and then back at Anna. Everything, from the expression on his face to the way his arms are crossed, makes it clear that he doesn't want me here.

"I'll be right back," she says to us, and then to her dad, "I'm going to ride back with them, okay? I'll just go back to the hotel with you so I can shower first."

"What about the store?" He's talking to Anna, but he's staring at me, red-faced and expressionless. I can practically see his blood boiling. He finally looks away and I take a deep breath. "I only need you for an hour," he says to her. "I can't close in the middle of the day."

Then she and her dad exchange a meaningful look, and I have a feeling I've been a subject of a number of tense discussions in the Greene house over the last few weeks. After a few more uncomfortable seconds, he looks back at me, his arms still crossed, his forehead still tight. "She needs to be at the bookstore by three o'clock."

"She will be," I say.

He returns his attention to Anna, pointing at the flowers in her hand. "Do you want me to bring those back with me and get them in water?" His face relaxes and she gives him a grateful smile as she hands them to him.

When they head off to the tent for her interview, Brooke punches me hard in the arm.

"Ow." I grimace. "What was that for?"

"Nothing. Just proving that I'm in good health."

I laugh and rub my arm where she hit me. "Yeah, I'd probably better fill you in on that."

Brooke and I wait out in the car in front of the hotel, and we finally see Anna walk through the double doors. She climbs into the open passenger seat. Her hair is still damp and she smells likes soap.

"All the places we could go in the world, and you want to drive three hours from Peoria to Evanston."

"It'll be fun."

"Fun?"

"Yes, fun. In fact, Brooke and I have designed a trip that will have all three of us in completely new territory for the next three hours. We're taking the scenic route."

"There's nothing scenic between here and Lake Michigan. Trust me."

"Now, that's not true. We're going to pass eighteen lakes in the next hour."

"Really?"

I nod proudly. "I bet you've never even been to Oglesby." Anna raises her eyebrows at me. "No, right? How about Starved Rock State Park?" She's trying not to smile. "Did you even know that rocks could be starved?" I shake my head like it's an impossible idea.

"How do you even know about these places?"

I can't tell her that I've spent the last week researching this trip online, so I joke instead. "*Lonely Planet: Illinois.* What, you haven't heard of that either?"

She just stares at me. "Maybe you should start driving," she says, and I take off for Route 29.

Anna folds her leg underneath her and twists around to face Brooke in the backseat. "So . . . tell me everything about you," she says. For the next hour, they talk nonstop, and I don't even try to get a word in edgewise.

⁓

I spot a diner that overlooks Fox Lake, and the three of us get out and stretch our legs. Inside, the hostess seats us in a booth with a view of the water, and Anna and I take one side while Brooke settles in across from us.

"Coffee?" our waitress asks as she hands each of us our menus. After a round of "Yes, pleases" she returns with three steaming coffee mugs. Brooke and Anna reach for the milk at the same time and I laugh to myself.

We consult our menus and the waitress returns to take our orders.

"I'll have the special, please," Anna says. I quickly find it on the menu: eggs, hash browns, bacon, toast. "Eggs scrambled, please."

"I'll have the same," I say.

Brooke lets out a heavy sigh when the waitress asks her what she'd like. "I'll have the veggie omelet, but can you make it with egg whites only, please. And no bacon or sausage on the side. Just whole wheat toast. No butter, please."

The waitress stares at her. "Egg whites only?" she asks tentatively, and Brooke nods. "No yolks?" She squints and cocks her head to one side.

"That's right."

The waitress shakes her head and writes it down. "I'll see what the cook can do." As she walks away, Brooke looks at me and throws her hands up. "It's like she's never heard of an egg white omelet."

"You're in nineteen ninety-five," I remind her.

"You're in the middle of Illinois," Anna adds.

I put my arm around Anna's shoulders and she kisses me on the cheek. Our eyes lock on each other's for a moment, and I try to read her expression. "You okay?" I ask.

She thinks about it for a second. Then she nods. "Definitely."

"Good." I give her a small kiss.

"You guys are going to stop that when the food gets here, right?" Brooke says. I reach across the table for a packet of sugar and chuck it at her.

Brooke grabs it in midair and returns it to the container.

"So juvenile," she says, shaking her head. But then she lets out a laugh and presses her palms into the tabletop. "Okay, I can't stand it anymore. I have news."

Anna and I look at each other, and then at her.

"I met someone. His name is Logan and he's from Australia. He has the most adorable accent." She looks especially proud of that last part.

Anna looks at me sideways and leans forward on the table. "Where did you meet him?" she asks, and Brooke's whole face brightens again. She bounces in her seat and leans forward, mirroring Anna's pose. "We met at the Train concert."

I clear my throat. "Watch yourself . . ." I say, and Brooke throws her hands in the air and says, "What? They've been around forever!"

My eyebrows shoot up. "Not as long as you might think."

She sighs. "Got it." She starts again, choosing her words more carefully. "We met at this concert at Red Rocks." Brooke looks at me for confirmation and I give her an affirmative nod. "He's there with a bunch of guys and I'm with my roommates, Shona and Caroline. Shona recognizes one of his friends from a class, and so the two of them start talking, and pretty soon we're all hanging out together, waiting for the show to start. Then one of them asks if we want to sit with them." She stops to take a breath and a sip of coffee.

"Logan sits next to me and we start chatting." She beams. "He loves music too." She leans over toward me. "I was dying to tell him that I'd been to Sydney to see a Maroon 5 concert in two thousand eight."

"Again," I remind her.

"Oh, right." She leans closer to Anna and winks. "The lead singer is *hot.*"

I kick her under the table and she laughs.

"So we talk off and on throughout the show, and in the middle of the second set, he leans into me and asks—in this totally cute, kind of shy way—if I have a boyfriend. To which I, of course, say that I do not. And I can tell he wants to kiss me, right? But he doesn't. We keep dancing and brushing up against each other and stuff, but he doesn't make a move."

The waitress arrives and slides our plates across the table. Brooke looks down at her omelet, which looks like a totally normal three-egg omelet, and then looks up at the waitress. "Thank you," she says. She grabs her fork and starts picking all the vegetables out.

"At the end of the night we exchange numbers and say good-bye, and everyone starts walking their separate ways across the parking lot, but then I hear him call my name behind me." She beams. "So I turn around and he's standing there, and he asks if he can kiss me good night. Isn't that sweet?"

She leans on the table and Anna does the same. "He's an unbelievable kisser." I steal a glimpse at Anna. She's wearing a shy smile and the flush is already creeping up her chest again. She reaches for a strip of bacon and takes a bite.

"We went out the next night and get this . . . he lives a block away from me. Can you believe that? We've been inseparable ever since. We ride our bikes to campus together and meet for lunch and we're ridiculously cute." Brooke stops for a breath and takes a bite of her toast. Then she lets out a sigh. "I miss him already."

I look at Brooke and I feel a wave of jealousy. Anna and I will never know what it's like to live a block away from each other. We'll never plan our class schedules so we can ride to school together, and we'll never run into each other on campus and feel giddy when we unexpectedly spot the other one heading our way. It hasn't even been a full day since Brooke last saw this guy; she has no idea what it's like to miss someone.

But if Anna's thinking the same thing, she never lets on. "He sounds great." Then she picks up her fork and says, "I'm starving," as she starts in on her breakfast.

The three of us spend the next few hours on the road. We stop at Starved Rock State Park and wander around the trails, looking at the rock formations and waterfalls. Anna doesn't say anything, but she looks exhausted, and it hits me that this probably isn't the ideal time for a hike. After forty-five minutes of sightseeing, I suggest we head back to Evanston and she looks relieved.

When we arrive at the bookstore, it's only two-thirty, and the downtown area is busy. I don't find a parking spot until I reach the next block.

"This is perfect," Anna says as I pull the SUV into a tight space across from the park. "We can stop in the coffeehouse and grab a latte."

We pile out of the car and I feed some quarters into the meter. Inside, we head over to our couch in the corner and Anna and Brooke plop down facing each other. Anna starts telling Brooke about the bands that play here on Sunday nights while I order drinks from the barista.

The three of us sit together for a little while, and I can tell that Anna's stalling. She keeps checking her watch, and finally, when she can't hold off any longer, she says good-bye to Brooke. The two of them hug and exchange a few more words, and Brooke makes me promise to bring her back here again soon.

After Anna's gone, Brooke and I sit a little longer, sipping our coffees and talking about the day. "Mom and Dad would like her," Brooke says.

"Yeah." I let out a huff. "As soon as they get past the part where she lives down the street from our grandmother." I roll my eyes. "And that she goes to the high school our mother graduated from. And that she and Maggie have become close friends. But yeah, as soon as they get past all of that, I bet they'd love her." I set my coffee on the table, lean back against the couch, and fix my eyes on the ceiling. "I have to tell them when I get home tomorrow." My head falls to the side and I look at Brooke. "They're going to kill me."

"No, they won't. They might not get it completely, but what are they going to do? Besides, think about how nice it will be not to have to sneak around." I try, but I've been doing it so long I can't even imagine it.

Brooke tips her head back and takes another gulp, and then sets her cup on the table next to mine. Neither one of us say anything, but we both know it's time for her to go.

She follows me past the barista and down the long hallway

that leads to the bathrooms, and I check the men's room while she stands outside waiting. Once I've confirmed that it's empty, I open the door a crack and wave her inside.

I lock the door and without even saying a word, she reaches for my hands. She shakes her arms out hard like she always does and then kisses me on the cheek. "Thank you so much."

"Any time," I tell her, which isn't entirely true but sounds like the right thing to say.

She shuts her eyes and I do the same. When I open them, we're standing in Brooke's bedroom, right where I picked her up this morning. "I still want you to meet everyone," she says, and I tell her I'll try. Then I close my eyes. When I open them again, I'm standing in the bathroom alone.

I'm not sure what to do with myself for the next hour while Anna's at work. I head outside and start walking in the general direction of the record store when an ambulance turns the corner and flies past me, siren blaring, lights spinning. I'm just about to cross the street when I see it pull to a stop directly in front of the bookstore.

I take off running.

When I reach the entrance, the EMTs are wheeling a stretcher through the door, parting the crowd that's already started gathering outside. I follow behind them.

"Anna!" I call out once I'm inside, but I don't see her anywhere.

I keep following the stretcher as it turns down the Cooking aisle.

And that's where I find her. She's sitting on the ground,

her hands wrapped around her father, who's slumped down against the bookcases, his legs bent at an awkward angle. One of the EMTs reaches out to pull Anna away, but she looks at him with terror in her eyes and refuses to budge. "What's wrong with him?" she cries.

"I don't know," I hear him say. "I need you to move away so we can figure it out, okay? Please."

I can't get to her side fast enough.

When she sees me, she grips her dad's arm even tighter, but I kneel down next to her and pull her toward me. "Come here," I say. My hands are shaking as I reach for hers. "Let them help your dad."

I look over at Mr. Greene. His eyes are wide open, staring straight ahead. But then his head falls slowly to one side and he looks right at me and blinks in slow motion.

Anna's head spins toward me, then back to her dad, and back to me again. Finally she releases his arm and lets me leads her a few feet away. The paramedics lower Mr. Greene to the floor and start working to bring him back from wherever he is right now.

"What happened?" I ask her.

"I don't know. When I got to the store, I didn't think he was here." Her voice is trembling, and she's breathing so hard the words are coming out all choppy. "I walked around for a few minutes and finally found him." She gestures toward her dad. "I don't know how long he's been like this, Bennett. I don't know what's wrong."

Justin must have heard the sirens from the record store

because he bursts through the door, looking rattled as he scans the room. He's clearly relieved to see Anna, but his expression changes again when he spots the paramedic team that's gathered around her dad.

"What happened?" he asks us, but neither one of us knows what to say. "I just found him like this," Anna says. She's crying now, and I keep telling her it's going to be okay, even though I have no idea if that's true.

One of the EMTs stands up and walks over to us. He looks directly at Anna. "We're taking him to Northwestern Memorial."

"My mom works there," Anna says quietly. "She's a nurse." Then she looks at me. "We need to find her," she whispers, and before I can say a word, Justin says, "I'm on it," and takes off toward the phone in the back room.

The EMT pulls out a clipboard and dislodges a pen from the plastic holder. "Were you with him earlier today?" Behind him, the other two paramedics are strapping machines to Mr. Greene's chest and moving him onto a stretcher.

"This morning," Anna says, her voice quiet and weak. "He was fine."

He writes it down. "What time did you see him last?"

Anna speaks louder this time. "About ten o'clock." She looks away, and I don't know if she's thinking the same thing, but I have to ask.

"What would have happened if we'd found him earlier?"

The EMT shakes his head. "We don't know anything yet. I really can't say."

"What would have happened?" I repeat.

"I don't know. You may have seen signs that something was wrong." He looks straight at me. "Look, let us get him to the hospital first and find out what happened, okay?"

The other two paramedics give him a sign, and he snaps the notebook shut and starts moving toward the door. "You can ride to the hospital with us," he says to Anna. To me, he says, "Sorry, family only."

He looks at Anna again and says, "Follow me."

Anna starts to move but I tighten my hold on her. "Ride with me. We'll be right behind him."

The EMT's eyes narrow as he addresses Anna. "You're going to let your father ride alone?"

"We'll be right behind you," I say. The other paramedics pass us wheeling the stretcher to the ambulance, and he gives me a disgusted shake of his head before he follows them.

I push a few gawkers out the door, and the little bundle of bells rings hard as I slam it closed. I snap the deadbolt into place.

As the sirens blare away and the spinning red lights disappear from view, I grab Anna's hand and lead her to the other side of the bookstore. We walk by the front desk, and I spot the flowers I bought her this morning. They're in a vase. In water. Exactly as promised. I take a deep breath.

"We're going back to this morning." Justin's in the back room but I keep my voice low anyway. "Listen to me, okay? We have to go all the way back to this morning—back to the hotel. That's the only time we weren't moving or in plain sight today. I can't time it right otherwise."

Anna doesn't move or say a word.

"We're going back to ten fifteen, right before you left your dad at the hotel. You're going to ride home with him instead and that'll give you three hours to watch him for . . . whatever . . . some kind of sign that something's wrong."

She blinks a few times. "What if we get all the way back and nothing's happened?"

"I don't know, then tell him something's wrong with *you*. Tell him you're having trouble breathing, or come up with an excuse to stop by the hospital and see your mom. Do whatever you have to do to be sure he goes straight to a hospital."

Anna nods.

"Do you remember where he parked the car?" She thinks about it for a minute. "Yeah," she whispers.

She's ghost-white and trembling. "You have to pull yourself together now, okay? Don't worry. We'll fix it." A vision of my battered self, lying in a puddle of blood, stuck who knows where or when, flashes in my mind. I push it away. The side effects don't matter. All that matters is getting Anna back to this morning.

I rest my forehead against hers. I don't even have to tell her to close her eyes. Before I close mine, I think back to this morning and try to lock in a mental image of the hotel and a precise moment I can let the other "me" disappear without disruption. I picture the circular driveway leading up to the hotel where Brooke and I picked Anna up this morning and—

"Brooke." I didn't mean to say it aloud, but I must have, because I open my eyes to find Anna staring at me. I drop her hands and rub my temples with my fingertips. "What will happen to Brooke?" I hear myself say.

She was with me the entire time. If Anna and I go back without her, what happens? Does Brooke disappear too? If she's in the car when I get back, what do I do with her? If she's not in the car, where has she gone?

I have to go back even earlier. I have to go back to this morning, before I picked Brooke up. I take Anna's hands again, but this time, it's not because we have a destination. Without thinking, I start voicing everything that's going through my head aloud. "I'm not sure how to do this. It's not clean, like the others were. It just . . . messes with so many things." I barely have time to get the words out when Justin peeks around the corner and flies down the aisle toward us.

"There you are. I found your mom," he says to Anna. "She's still at the hospital. I'm supposed to take you." Anna untangles her fingers from mine and follows Justin out the door. As he puts his arm over her shoulders, she stops and turns around. I'm still standing exactly where she left me.

"Aren't you coming with us?" she asks.

"Yeah." I stuff my hands in my pockets and follow them, still thinking through the morning in my mind, desperately looking for a loophole.

Justin's car is parked across the street, around the corner from the record store. He opens the door for Anna and she climbs in while I slump down in back. I've never felt so powerless.

When we pull up to a stoplight, Anna points out the window as she looks at Justin. "Would you pull over, please?" Justin drives through the intersection and stops on the next block, and Anna gets out of the car, pulls the bucket seat forward, and climbs in back next to me. She rests her head on my shoulder and whispers in my ear, "I can't let you go back."

I look up at the rearview mirror and my eyes meet Justin's. He stares at me for a moment, and then hits the gas.

29

Mrs. Greene spots us the second we round the corner and step into the ICU waiting room, and all three of us freeze in place as she bolts from her chair and speeds across the room toward us. She's still wearing her uniform.

She hugs Anna hard and then leads her away from us, returning to the chairs in the corner, where she fires questions at her. Anna sounds calm as she fills her mom in on everything that happened, from the moment she and her dad left the house the night before to the series of events that led to her finding him on the bookstore floor.

Justin gives me a look and I give him one back, silently confirming that neither one of us knows what to do with ourselves. He glances awkwardly around the room and I point at a couple of chairs a polite distance away. We spend the next twenty minutes in silence.

Then Justin's parents burst through the door, and that sends the energy level soaring again. "Where is she?" Mrs. Reilly asks as she heads straight for us. Justin hugs her and then points over toward the corner. I wish I didn't have to overhear Anna's mom repeat the same horrible details, but I'm close enough to pick up every word she says and every gasp that leaves Mrs. Reilly's mouth.

I lean over, resting my elbows on my knees so I can cover my ears and at least muffle the sound. I'm just about to go outside and get some fresh air when I hear Anna's voice.

"Do you have a quarter?" she asks as she collapses into the chair next to me. She kicks her legs out straight and lets her head fall back against the wall while Justin and I dig around in our pockets.

"Here," Justin says.

Anna reaches across me to take it and stands up. "I'm going to find a pay phone and call Emma. I'll be right back."

Anna's gone for a full ten minutes, and Justin and I return to our silent state. But then the doctor enters the waiting room and calls out, looking for Mrs. Greene. She stands up and crosses the room. The two of them speak in hushed tones for a moment.

Her mom's head spins in my direction. "Bennett, would you go find Anna?"

I move quickly, out of the waiting room and into the sterile halls, but I don't have the slightest idea where she is. I turn down corridors and double back when they look like dead ends, and I finally spot her at the far end of a hallway, leaning against the wall and playing with the steel phone cord as she fills her best friend in on what happened.

She sees me coming.

Doctor, I mouth, and Anna says something I can't hear before she slams the phone down hard. The two of us speed back to the waiting room.

As soon as she's within arm's reach, Anna's mom takes her by the shoulders and pulls her closer, then waves the rest of us over to her. "Go ahead."

The six of us stand in a semicircle while the doctor explains far too matter-of-factly that Mr. Greene has had a stroke. She goes into detail about the battery of tests they're running to determine exactly what time it occurred and the extent of the damage.

She looks right at Anna's mom, addressing her more like a peer than the wife of a patient. "Strokes are tricky at first, as you probably know. Everything hinges on how long he was out before your daughter found him. When the medical team arrived on the scene, they administered medication that dissolved the clot, but . . ." The doctor trails off and Anna starts twirling her hair around her finger. "Until we can pinpoint exactly *where* in the brain the stroke occurred and how long ago it happened, we won't know about his chances for recovery."

Anna takes a few steps back, as if that's too much for her to take, and I ask her mom if I can take her outside to get some air.

We take the elevator down to the first floor and I steer her toward the entrance. The wind outside blows our hair back, but we huddle close to each other on a cement bench next to a tall ashtray. It smells like fresh rain and stale cigarettes.

"I want to go back." I don't wait for her to answer; I just start running her through the plan I've been concocting since we left the bookstore. "I'll go back to this morning. I'll get Brooke and bring her to your meet, and then I'll tell you what's going to happen with your dad, okay? It'll be fine."

Anna shakes her head. "What about the side effects? Last time you ended up with twenty-two hours you could never account for. What if you try, and instead, we all get knocked back somewhere? Or what if we lose those hours and I don't find my dad when I did? You can't mess with this one, Bennett."

I hear her, but that doesn't stop me from running through the easier scenarios again. If we went back to the bookstore, I don't know what would happen to Anna. If we went back to this morning at the race, I don't know what would happen to Brooke.

"Stop," she says, as if she can tell that I'm still trying to figure out a way to make it work. "Listen. You promised me you'd tell me if you ever lost control. But apparently I need to be the one to tell you." Anna locks her eyes on mine. "You're not in control. You cannot fix this."

My stomach sinks. God, if she only knew how much I want to. That I'd do anything to fix it. But she's right. I can't. There's too much at stake this time. I'm not in control anymore. Not unless I stick to the rules.

Anna presses her lips tightly together and runs her thumb along my cheek. "You aren't supposed to change things, remember?" Then she rests her head on my shoulder. The two of us sit like that for a long time, listening to the sound of the automatic doors sliding open and snapping shut as people pass us on their way in and out of the building.

I tell her I'm sorry a few more times, and she tells me not to be. But I don't tell her what I'm really thinking: If I hadn't come here today, she would have driven home with her dad instead of Brooke and me. She would have had three hours in the car with him. Three hours to notice that something was wrong.

Those three hours should have been his, and I took them away.

Today, after we found her dad in the bookstore, we both went straight to one question: *What if we could do it over?* We never once thought: *What if we hadn't changed anything in the first place?*

⁓

As Justin and I leave the hospital, the wind slaps us hard in the face. We pull our coats tighter around us as we march, heads down, plowing toward the car. He climbs in first and unlocks my door for me.

"You okay to drive in this?"

His shoots me a look and turns the key in the ignition. "Yeah."

And that's the last thing he says for the next twenty miles.

Every time I look over at him, he has this strange look on his face and his fingers are white-knuckled from gripping the steering wheel so hard. We're traveling down Lake Shore Drive, at or just under the speed limit, but the wind packs a wallop. Each time it slams into the side of the car it feels like it's about to wrap its fingers around this lightweight Honda Civic and hurl it straight into Lake Michigan.

I try to make small talk. "I didn't know you had a car."

"I got it over the summer." He turns onto a side street. "It's nice, but it's light. When it starts snowing, I'm going to have to load the trunk with sandbags so I don't skid."

Now that we're off Lake Shore and heading into the wind, the car feels a little less squirrelly. I see Justin's shoulders relax slightly and his fingers uncurl. He takes one hand off the wheel and squeezes the back of his neck.

"I've known him since I was a little kid," Justin says, his voice deeper than usual. "Our parents have played bridge together every other Saturday night for as long as I can remember." He takes a deep breath. "He's so *healthy*, you know? Healthier than my parents. God, he's been trying to get my dad to go running with him for years."

"I know," I say. Of course, I don't know. I've never heard any of this. But I have no idea what to tell him right now.

"This whole thing is just so weird . . ." Justin trails off as he takes another turn, and I resist the urge to say that I'm sure Mr. Greene will be okay, because I have no way of knowing this, and he may not be. The air in the car is thick with tension, and Justin keeps looking at me like it's my turn to talk.

I haven't known Mr. Greene very long. I don't have years of collected stories that substantiate his impact on my life or anything. I just know that I like him, that he's a nice person and a good dad, and that he doesn't deserve to be hooked up to machines right now.

Justin blows a mouthful of air at the windshield. "They say he could be totally fine, and make a full recovery, but I can't help but wonder." When he pulls up to the stoplight, he turns to me. "I mean, I don't know anything about strokes, but it seems pretty far-fetched that there wouldn't be any damage to his brain. He had to have been out for at least . . . what did the doctor think? Twenty . . . twenty-five minutes?"

This is the part I can't think about, let alone talk about. Anna and I were just down the street during those twenty minutes. What if there had been a parking space in front of the bookstore? What if we hadn't stopped for coffee? What if I hadn't come here today?

"I guess we'll know more tomorrow when the test results are back."

"I guess. But man, doesn't it make you wish you had future sight or something? I mean, if we could just *know*, right?"

As the light turns green, he looks away from me, shaking his head as if it's a ridiculous thought.

⌒

The deadbolt clicks open with a loud *thunk*. I tiptoe inside and shut the door behind me, grateful to find the house is silent and dark, save for the glow of the light that Maggie always keeps on over the desk.

My feet drag across the hardwood floor and it takes far too much effort to lug myself up the stairs. My brain is working overtime, but my body can't wait to fall into bed.

I head straight for the bathroom, where I splash cold water on my face and check out my reflection. My skin is pale and my eyes are bloodshot, lids half closed despite the cold jolt I just gave them. I flick off the light and head back to my room.

I should have insisted on staying with Anna at the hospital, even though the look on her mom's face made it pretty clear that she didn't want me there. For the hundredth time tonight, I picture Anna's expression when she told me I couldn't go back, and I wonder if I'm doing the right thing by not even trying. Especially when I remember how Mr. Greene blinked at me.

But of all the things that happened tonight—of all the things that were said—Justin's words are the ones haunting me and keeping me awake.

He said he wished he could see into the future, with absolutely no idea that *I* can.

I can't fight it anymore, so against my better judgment, I dig my heavy boots out from the back of the closet and step into them, and then I zip myself into my black parka and pull my wool cap low to my brow. I fill my backpack with bottled water and a wad of cash.

I'm not changing anything. I'm not manipulating the clock,

and I'm not doing anything over. I'm observing, just like I've always done. This time, I'm not breaking the rules, and when it's over, no one ever has to know what I did.

The doctor said it would take time and patience; that even if he made a full recovery, it would probably take a year or two. With her words in mind, I stand in the center of my room and close my eyes.

I visualize the yellow paint that's chipping and peeling on the side of the Greenes' house, and clear my head of everything but today's date: November 15.

I pick a time I know he'll be home: six thirty A.M.

And I choose a year in my past, but in Anna's future: 1997.

30

I arrive on the side of Anna's house, exactly where I planned to, and slowly peer around the corner. It must have snowed last night, but not hard. I can still see tiny tips of grass poking up through the thin layer of ice covering the lawn. I feel overdressed in my heavy winter gear.

Peering in the window, I find that the kitchen looks exactly the same—same appliances, same bar stools. I can see the coffeepot perfectly, in the same spot it's always been. I look around, waiting for someone to appear and preparing to duck down fast when they do.

By now, Anna must be away at college, but this is a good time to catch Mr. Greene making the morning coffee.

I hear the front door open and peek around the corner just as footsteps land on the porch. The feet look like they belong to a man, but the door is blocking my view and I can't be sure.

The newspaper disappears and the door closes again. I race back to my spot at the window.

Mr. Greene steps into the kitchen and walks straight for the counter. He unfolds the newspaper, removes a section, and tosses the bulk of it onto the kitchen table.

As he steps away from the counter, I notice the slight limp on his right side. Over at the coffeepot, he treats his right hand like it's cumbersome and in his way, and when he tries to use it to open the bag of coffee he quickly gives up and uses his left hand and his teeth instead.

As the coffee brews, he reaches up into the high cabinet above him and pulls down two mugs. He shuffles over to the refrigerator and returns with a carton of milk.

He's about to bring it back where it belongs when Anna comes around the corner. She rests one hand on his shoulder, takes the carton from him, and puts it away. Then she gives him a quick peck on the cheek, and heads over to the counter for her mug.

Her hair is shorter, hanging loose and just brushing her shoulders. She's wearing jeans and a sweatshirt. It takes me a minute to realize that it reads NORTHWESTERN CROSS COUNTRY and to put the pieces together. Anna still lives here.

Mr. Greene starts off for the pile of newspaper again, and Anna speeds past him and grabs it first. She hands him a section and he folds it in half and uses it to smack her on the arm. She laughs, but I can hear him through the glass as he tells her to stop helping him.

A few minutes later, the doorbell rings, and I look around the corner and find Justin standing on the porch. He's wearing a baseball cap and his backpack is slung over one shoulder. The door opens and Anna yells, "Bye, Dad," before stepping out and shutting it behind her. The two of them head down the walkway toward campus.

I've seen all I needed to see. I close my eyes and bring myself back to my room at Maggie's.

My temples are throbbing. I sit down on the floor next to my bed and reach into my backpack for the water. I down both bottles without stopping, and reach for a room-temperature Frappuccino. When the bottle is empty, I let my head fall back onto the bed and I wait to recover.

I'm in pain, but the symptoms feel more like what I'm used to—a fierce headache and a dry mouth—but no nosebleeds, no piercing sounds, and most important, no losing control of my place on the timeline. I've managed to stay in 1995, successfully go to 1997, and return to 1995 unscathed.

I lie there, picturing Mr. Greene moving around the kitchen, the way Anna helped him, and the way he scolded her for doing so. He's okay. He's not back to normal, but he's alive, capable, and obviously in good hands. And while I know that part of him is relieved that Anna's still living at home, I'm sure that a larger part feels guilty, knowing that Northwestern was never her first choice.

My eyelids are heavy and I can't wait to let them close and drift off to sleep. But just as I start to doze off, something the doctor said tonight jolts me awake again. She said it would be a slow recovery. That it might take years. Her comment makes me wonder what I might have seen if I'd gone forward even farther. Maybe I'd have more solid news for Anna tomorrow.

I stand up and return to the center of the room. I stomp hard until the last of the snow has fallen from my boots. I close my eyes and picture a date in the future when I know Anna will no longer live at home, but will certainly be visiting: Christmas Eve, 2005.

I'm at the wrong house.

The driveway is in the right spot. The kitchen window is where it's supposed to be. I walk around to the front of the house and look up toward Anna's window. I'm in the right place, but the house is no longer covered in yellow, peeling paint. It's now painted deep gray with white trim. It looks nice.

It must have been snowing just hours ago because my feet are buried deep in this light, white powder that doesn't look or feel at all like the snow I remember. It covers my jeans, up to my shins, and I can feel my toes turn cold inside my winter boots.

I look through the window. The kitchen looks different too, with fresh paint and new cabinets, new granite countertops and a bunch of new appliances. It could be the work of new owners. But then I notice that the bar stools are exactly the same, and I smile when I think back to the first time I came to Anna's house and perched myself there, carefully studying her for signs of fear as I disappeared before her eyes.

Anna's mom walks in and I duck back down under the windowsill and count to five. Then I peek inside again, studying her as she reaches into the oven and removes a roasting pan. She scurries around the kitchen, stirring pots on the stove and putting rolls in the oven.

I'm starting to get concerned about Anna's dad, when he breezes into the room and sticks his finger into one of the pots. Mrs. Greene slaps his hand with the wooden spoon she just took out of the gravy, and I can practically hear her chide him from here. I can't hear his response, but it makes her throw her head back and laugh.

I watch him walk through the kitchen and into the dining room and notice a slight limp. When he returns he's carrying a silver platter, and he rests it on the countertop. It's hard to see from this vantage point, but his hands appear to be working like they're supposed to.

Then I hear tires slowly crunching their way through the snow. Lights reflect off the snow on the front yard, and I stand still and watch as a car pulls into the driveway. I come out from behind the house and hide behind the large oak tree so I can get a better look. I'm just in time to see Anna step out.

The driver's-side door opens, and someone else comes around the front of the car. The house lights are illuminating Anna's face perfectly, and I'm close enough to see every detail, but he's in shadow, and all I can see is the back of his head.

He casually grabs her hand, like he's done it a million times before. Then he kisses her. He says something that makes her smile at him. My chest constricts and I suck in a breath.

It's a smile I know well. I thought it was the one she reserved for me, but here in 2005, it seems to belong to him.

The two of them walk toward the porch, holding hands. Before they've even hit the first step, Mr. Greene flings the door open wide and scoops Anna up in his arms. She laughs and says, "Hi, Daddy," as she regains her footing.

Mr. Greene turns to the guy and says something I can't hear from this distance. He pulls him in for a fatherly hug, patting him on the back. He releases him but keeps one arm over his shoulder, leading the two of them into the house. The door closes behind them.

I head across the lawn, over to the driveway, and look inside the car for anything that will tell me who he is and where they came from, but the interior is completely clean. I walk around the back of the car and look at the license plate, and spot a sticker from the rental car company in the corner. They flew in from someplace. Or at least he did.

I retrace my footsteps until I've returned to my position under the kitchen window. I must be a glutton for punishment because once I pull myself up into the corner and peek inside, I find myself stuck there. I want to stop watching them, but I can't.

The guy is nowhere to be seen, but I have a perfect view of Anna as she stands in the center of the kitchen, her parents buzzing happily around her. God, she looks incredible. Her hair is long again, and tonight it's pulled back in a clip at the nape of her neck. I can't stop staring.

She's fluttering around the kitchen like she used to, breaking off pieces of bread and dipping her finger into sauces and closing her eyes as the tastes fill her mouth. She turns and says something to her dad, and he starts cracking up.

Suddenly, Anna pivots toward the window and looks right at me. I duck down quickly, out of sight, and everything's quiet for a moment except the sound of my heartbeat, which I'm pretty sure they can hear from inside. I wait for a full minute to pass before I look through the corner of the window again.

Anna's now sitting on the bar stool with her back to me. Mrs. Greene sets a drink on the counter in front of her and I watch Anna bring the glass to her lips.

He's back. The guy she brought home with her returns to the kitchen and walks straight to the refrigerator. Anna's blocking my view of him and I adjust my position, trying to get a better look, but I accidentally tap the windowpane. Anna spins in her seat and I flatten my back against the side of the house.

"I saw it again, Dad." She's far away and muffled, but I can make out her words, and her voice grows louder, clearer, as she cups her hand to the window and speaks. "There's something out there, I swear."

My heart is pounding hard against my rib cage and it takes every ounce of control to remain silent and motionless. She's right there. I want to say something. I want to stand up and look at her face and see how she reacts. There must be something I can say that will make her come outside, put her hands in mine, and let me take her away to a warmer place so we can sit in sand and talk. I need to know who this guy is and what he's doing in her house and why she's looking at him like that. I need to know what happened to us and how we stop it.

I hear her dad's voice, low and clear. "What is it?"

"I don't know, but I swear, I keep seeing something move out there."

"I'm sure it's nothing," he says. "Stay here. I'll go outside and check it out."

I spin in place looking for somewhere to hide, but there's nowhere to go. I hear the front door open and slam closed, followed by soft footsteps on the wooden porch.

I panic and close my eyes.

When I open them, I'm back in my room at Maggie's. I'm sitting on my bed with my head pounding and my stomach sinking, knowing that Mr. Greene found all my footprints, and wondering what happened when he did.

32

The hospital is busier today. I step out of the elevator and into the waiting room, and it takes a full minute for me to spot Anna. I finally see her, sitting in a chair against the far wall, her mom on one side and Justin on the other, holding her hand. Emma is sitting next to him, arms folded across her chest and staring up at the ceiling.

There isn't anywhere for me to sit, but I walk over to them anyway. As soon as I arrive, Justin stands up. "Hey." He gestures toward the seat. "Take mine. I was just leaving anyway." Anna stands up next to him and wraps her arms around his shoulders, and Justin hugs her tightly, eyes closed as he rubs her back. "Call me later, okay? Or even better, come by the store. I'll be there late."

Anna kisses him on the cheek.

"Mrs. Greene?" I hear the voice behind me, and when I turn around I find the doctor from yesterday standing there.

"You and your daughter can see him, but let's keep this visit short."

Anna grabs my hand as she walks past and gives it a squeeze. She and her mom follow the doctor out of the room and I flop down next to Emma. I let my head fall back against the wall. "How's he doing today?"

"Better, it seems. He regained consciousness in the middle of the night. The test results are promising, but he doesn't have any function on his right side." I picture Mr. Greene using his teeth to open a bag of coffee beans. Emma rubs her forehead with her fingertips. "But they think he'll make a full recovery, eventually."

This is good news, but Emma's lower lips quivers and I can tell she's fighting back tears. "Are you okay?" I ask her.

"Me?" She takes a deep breath and brushes her fingers across her cheeks. "I should be asking you that question, Shaggy. You look like hell."

I thought I looked pretty good considering everything I've been through in the last fifteen hours, but then I bring my hands to my face and feel the thick stubble and realize I'm still wearing the same clothes I was wearing yesterday. "I'm okay," I lie.

She takes a deep breath and sits up straight in her chair, looking around the crowded waiting room like she's taking in the ugly furniture and the stacks of magazines piled up on the end tables for the first time. "This is so weird. I've never been in a hospital before. Have you?"

I picture Anna and me sitting in a different waiting room

in a different hospital—one closer to Chicago and the scene of Emma and Justin's car accident—but similarly ugly and equally devoid of anything even remotely cheerful. "Yeah, I've been in a few."

"It's so strange . . . I have this feeling, you know, like I *must* have been inside a hospital at least once, aside from being born in one, but I don't think I ever have. No one in my family has ever been sick and I've never broken a bone or anything . . . Knock wood," she says, bringing her knuckles to the chair's wooden arm. Then she shudders. "This place gives me the creeps."

I never saw Emma after the accident, but Anna told me everything. It's impossible to look at her right now without picturing her in that sterile hospital room, scratched up and stitched together on the outside, broken and still bleeding out on the inside. Emma will never know what I did for her and I'll never want her to.

Emma's eyes dart around the room again and she leans in close. "Can I ask you something?"

"Sure."

She comes in even closer, resting her forearms on my chair. "Do you think Justin has a thing for Anna?"

"Anna?" I don't mean it to come out in such a "*my* Anna" tone of voice, but I think it does. "No. I mean, they're friends. They've known each other all their lives. Anna thinks of him like a brother."

"Oh, yeah . . . of course. I'm not talking about Anna's feelings for *him*—it's all *you* in that department—I'm just referring to his feelings for *her.*" She looks around the waiting room. "Never mind. I shouldn't have even mentioned anything. I've just been curious about your opinion and we're here, just the two of us, stuck in this crappy hospital." She taps her bright pink painted fingernails on her jeans. "It was just the way he hugged her a few minutes ago looked a little bit 'more than friends.'" She says the last part with air quotes. "That, you know, combined with the whole near-kiss thing . . ."

My head falls to the side and I look at her. "What 'near-kiss thing'?"

Her eyebrows furrow as she chooses her words more carefully now. "You know. After you left town last spring." She must be able to tell from the look on my face that I'm hearing this for the first time, because she covers her mouth with her hand and pulls away from me fast. "Anna told me you knew. She made it seem like it was no big deal."

She never told me. And it might not have been a big deal. If this conversation were happening yesterday, I might have just laughed it off, but coming in on the heels of what I saw last night, I might be feeling a little too raw for this.

"Justin got a little bit drunk at my birthday party, and I might have been taking advantage of the situation, because I finally decided to come right out and ask him how he felt about her, you know? Just to see what he'd say." I'm not sure I want to hear this, but she keeps talking and I don't stop her. "At first he swore they were just friends, but then he told me that after you left last spring, they were hanging out at the record store together one day and they almost kissed." She shrugs, as if that will make it seem like she isn't bothered by the whole incident, but I can tell by the look on her face that she is.

"But don't get mad. It wasn't Anna *at all.* Justin tried to kiss her—he made that part crystal clear. I mean, if you weren't in the picture, who knows, but . . ."

I flash back on what I saw last night when I went to 1997. How Justin met Anna at her house, and the two of them walked to school together. And then I think about the guy I saw her with eight years later. The guy she kissed in her driveway. I hadn't even considered the possibility that it could have been Justin, but now I can't get the idea out of my mind. I don't think the guy had red hair, but I never got a very good look either. I remember how Mr. Greene wrapped him up in a fatherly hug and led him into the house.

"The whole thing is totally one-sided . . ." She stops and lets out a cynical laugh. "Which should have been my first clue, right?" She matches my posture, her head against the wall, her legs kicked out in front of her. "I'm not quite sure why I'm waiting around as if I'm perfectly content with being his consolation prize."

She starts to say more. I wish she wouldn't. I don't have the energy to think about any of this right now and I have much bigger things on my mind. Before Emma can speak again, Anna and her mom return to the waiting room and sit down in the chairs across from us.

"Nothing new, I'm afraid," Anna's mom says as she twists her hair around her finger and lets out a heavy breath. Then, without prompting, she launches into a story about a stroke patient she worked with a few years ago. I pretend to listen before I shoot Anna a look and thankfully, she understands.

"We'll be right back, Mom," she says, and she grabs my hand and leads me down the hall toward the vending machines. She digs around in her jeans pocket for change. "Want to split a bag of Doritos?"

She's about to slip a quarter into the slot but I stop her. "Wait. There's a coffee shop across the street."

"Yeah?" She covers her mouth as she yawns. "Actually, that sounds good." She tells me to wait by the elevator while she tells her mom where she's going, and she comes back holding her coat. I help her into it.

The coffeehouse is nothing like the one we're used to, far more institutional than cozy, with metal tables and matching chairs. Anna finds a spot in the corner window while I go to the counter to order. A few minutes later, I return with a bowl of soup, a chunk of bread, and a latte.

Anna picks up the bread and turns it over in her hands. "This reminds me of Paris," she says. She gives me a tired smile before she takes a bite. "Sadly, this tastes nothing like *that* baguette." She stares down at the bread, looking disappointed. "I'm convinced I'll never taste anything that delicious again."

I don't respond. In fact, I hardly say a word as she finishes off her soup. But as she's balling her napkin up and stuffing it into the empty soup container, I can't hold it in any longer.

"I have to tell you something," I practically blurt out, and she looks up at me. I probably should have planned out what I was going to say, but I didn't. Now I'm just making it up as I go along and hoping it will make sense. "Remember last night, when we were sitting outside and you told me I couldn't fix this?"

"Yeah."

"Well, I thought of something else I could do."

She takes a sip of her coffee and waits for me.

"I went forward."

She yawns again. Then she says, "I don't know what you mean."

"I went forward . . . into your future. To see what happens to him."

Her head springs up and she goes to set her coffee cup on the table but she loses her grip and it crashes to the table. Some of the coffee splashes over the side, and Anna reaches for her napkin to wipe up the mess. She suddenly stops and stares at me.

"I don't want to know, do I?"

I nod my head. "You do. It's good news. He's going to be okay."

She lets the napkin drop as she puts her elbows on the table and buries her face in her hands. I can't tell if she's crying or laughing or so overwhelmed, she's doing a combination of the two.

"It will take a while. In a couple of years, he'll still walk with a limp and he won't have full use of his right hand, but eventually, he'll be fine."

"Eventually when?"

I look at her. "I'm sorry, Anna. I wish I could tell you that, but I can't."

"No, of course you can't. Okay." She shakes her head hard, like she's scolding herself for asking in the first place. She comes in even closer. "I still can't believe you did this," she says excitedly. "What else will you tell me?"

She takes a big sip of coffee and licks the froth from her lips and I take a deep breath. "I saw enough to know that my coming here is a mistake." There. I've said it. "I'm not supposed to be here, Anna. It's changing your whole life."

She presses her palms into the table to steady herself. "For the better."

"I'm not so sure anymore."

She looks out the window and doesn't say anything. "What aren't you telling me, Bennett? What did you see?" She gives me a hard look.

"I saw you and your family with a happy future. And if I tell you any more about it, it might not happen that way." That's enough. That's all she gets to know. Anything else and I might change what I saw, and I can't do that.

"Well, it's *my* future. I want you in it." Her eyebrows pinch together. "Don't *you* want to be in it?"

I nod. "But think about it," I say, shaking my head. "If you'd been in the car with your dad yesterday you would have known something was wrong. You would have seen the signs and gotten him to a hospital faster. He might not even be here right now."

"Oh, come on . . . he had a stroke. That would have happened no matter what. You didn't do anything wrong."

"I was *here*, Anna. With you. And I shouldn't have been. If I hadn't been here you would have been with your dad."

I didn't expect to feel this way, but the more I talk to her, the more anger I feel building up inside me. I seem to be livid with everyone right now. With Emma, for telling me about Justin and Anna's near-kiss, because I didn't want to know that, especially today. With Anna, for making me think that do-overs were okay, simply because her best friend's life was at stake. With my dad, for letting me believe I was more powerful than I really am. And with myself, for going forward and opening up a view into a future I never should have seen and certainly don't want to exist.

And it's selfish, but I'm angry because it's starting to seem like every time I do something good for someone else, I'm the one who pays the price.

I take a deep breath and steady myself for my next words, the ones that have been rattling around in my head ever since I returned from her house on Christmas Eve 2005. This is it. If I'm going to guarantee the life I saw for Anna, where she's happy without me, I have say it.

"I'm not coming back anymore."

"What?"

I start to reach for her hands but before I can, she pulls them away and stands up. The metal chair tips over behind her and crashes to the floor, and she looks over her shoulder like she's considering righting it, but she doesn't. She turns on her heel and heads for the door, out into the cold.

By the time I catch up to her she's standing at the edge of the curb, waiting for a break in the traffic. "Anna. Please."

She stops and turns around, arms crossed, tears sliding down her cheeks. "You cannot do this!" she yells as the cars speed past us. "You cannot do this to me. You promised you wouldn't leave . . ." Her whole face is bright red and the tears are coming fast now. She tries to wipe her face dry but she can't keep up.

I grab her by the arm, but she pulls it away. "Go!" she yells. "If that's what you want, just go!"

I feel something in me snap.

"What *I* want?" I yell back at her. "What do you mean what *I* want? When is this ever about what I want? I don't have anything—not one single thing—that *I* want. Don't you get it?" In my mind's eye I see Anna, standing in her driveway, smiling up at this guy who isn't me, and I feel the blood coursing hot through my veins.

"See, I get to have this tiny little taste of all these incredible things but I don't get to *keep* any of them. I get to meet you and be part of your life, and I get to know your family and your friends, but I don't get to hold on to any of it. I can't stay here. This isn't my home. And every time I have go to back, it kills me. Every. Single. Time. And it always will."

"Bennett . . ." Anna steps back onto the sidewalk and pushes me away from the edge.

"No, wait. It gets even better." I let out a sarcastic laugh and bring my hand to my chest. "I finally find something that makes me feel good about this thing I can do. I figure out how to *save* people's lives. I get to give a few deserving people a second chance. And that feels really incredible for, like, twenty minutes . . . right up until the second it starts beating the shit out of me."

I let out another laugh. "Oh wait, and here's the best part. The more good things I do, the more I lose the one thing I promised you I wouldn't lose—control. It's like this infinite, totally screwed up loop," I say, spinning my finger in the air.

Anna takes a deep breath and presses her lips tightly together. She's crying even harder now, which should make me feel horrible but for some reason doesn't.

"Check it out," I say, bringing my hand to my chest. "I don't get to have what I want. Not ever. Because the one thing I want is a normal life. I don't want to be special and different, I just want to wake up and go to school and do homework and ride my skateboard in the park with my friends. I want my dad to be proud of me because I got an A on some stupid paper, not because I saved some kids' lives. I want to stare out a window and think about how cool it would be to be able to travel back in time, but I don't want to actually be able to *do* it. And I want to be in love with a girl I can see every day, not every three weeks."

I've been gesturing wildly with my hands but now that I'm done ranting, I don't know what to do with them. I run my fingers through my hair.

"I have to go. I'm sorry." I head back toward the coffee shop, but before I can reach the door, I feel Anna's grasp, tight on my arm.

"Bennett, I'm sorry . . . I didn't mean—"

"What? Didn't mean to talk me into all of this?" The words just slip out, even though I know they're not true, and I turn around in time to see her face fall. That should be enough to stop me from talking, but it isn't. "If you hadn't made me help Emma, I never would have known what I could do. I could have spent the rest of my life going to concerts and climbing rocks in exotic locations, never caring that I was being selfish with my ability, because you know what, it's *mine*. Not yours. Not my dad's. Mine." I slap my chest.

"I know that . . . I never meant . . ."

"I structured my life around a set of rules, and then I broke them for *you*. And for what? So I could be a better person?" I huff in exasperation. "How is my life better because a stranger never broke his leg and five people are alive who probably shouldn't be?"

"What you did was *really* good. And if you were a normal person, we never would have met."

"Yeah . . . well I think that's how it's supposed to be."

She pulls away and looks at me. "You don't really mean that, do you?"

As hard as it is to do, I nod.

Tears are streaming down her face and I can't look at her. I need to get away from here.

"I need to think, Anna. You need to think."

"I don't need to think."

"Well you should, because this is crazy." I remember the words Mr. Greene said to me at the meet the other day. *This is ridiculous. Do you really think you can keep this up?* "Come on, what were we thinking? We can't do this forever."

She wipes her face dry and stares at me.

"I'm going to go back to my real life for a while, okay? I'll come back at Christmas," I say, as if this will make it better. "Your dad's going to be okay," I say, as if this justifies my leaving.

She finds her voice, but it's low and quiet and I have to strain to hear her. "Please stay."

Before she can say another word, I take two steps back until I feel the corner of the building behind me, and without even caring who might be watching, I close my eyes and disappear.

december 2012

33

san francisco, california

I spent the whole drive over here psyching myself up for my performance, but once I walked through Megan's front door it all sort of clicked on its own. It could have been the loud music or the underlying buzz of conversation that carried from one packed room to the next, but whatever it was, I was grateful. I stood in the entryway, looked around, and sucked in the intoxicating scent of holiday cheer and out-of-town parents. I reminded myself that I didn't have to genuinely enjoy being at this party; I just had to play the part.

Now I'm all smiles and backslaps, quick one-liners and snappy comebacks, acting so out of character of late that when Sam sees me, he shoots me this *Who the hell* are *you right now* look. I may suck as a superhero, but as it turns out, I'm a fairly decent actor.

"You're certainly chipper tonight." Of all people, I would

have expected Brooke to see through me, but she must not, because I can hear the bitterness in her voice.

"I am," I lie. "And I'm going to stay in a good mood because it's Christmas vacation and you're home from school and I'm surrounded by good friends and I'm tired of feeling like shit." I smile and take a sip of my drink. "I'm done. From here on out, I'm living in the moment." I raise my glass in the air, toasting no one in particular.

"You were pretty upset last night." I look around at the guys to be sure no one overheard her, but I realize it's impossible. *I* can barely hear her over the music.

I lean in close. "Well then, last night marked the end of my wallowing."

Brooke looks at me and slowly shakes her head. After my parents and I picked her up from the airport last night, the two of us sat in my room talking for a long time. Then I made the mistake of showing her Anna's photo album. We got about halfway through when I had to leave the room, and while she was flipping through pages, I was in the bathroom trying not to hurl. I returned with my eyes burning and my cheeks feeling hot, took the photo book out of her grasp, and smashed it back in the drawer. She never got to see the last picture.

"No offense," Brooke says as she taps away on her phone, "but I'm not sure how much longer I can stand this high school party. Kathryn just texted me to see if I wanted to do something, but—" She looks up at me and stops talking.

"But?"

"Nothing," she says, shaking her head. "I guess I just

thought you might need me around tonight, but you seem to be doing just fine, so . . ." She trails off, looking around the room. "I'm going to go outside and call her. See what's up."

Brooke walks away and I spot Sam and Lindsey hanging out by the fireplace. I'm just about to head over there when the room goes dark.

"Merry Christmas," a voice whispers in my ear. I pull a pair of hands away from my face and turn around. Megan's standing there wearing a red dress and a big grin. She pops one hip.

"It's about time you made it to one of my parties." She holds her arms out wide, palms up, and looks around the room. "See, now aren't you sorry you didn't get to one of these earlier?"

I smile and give her an exaggerated nod. "Truly devastated. I had no idea what I was missing."

"Right?" She keeps coming in closer, shouting to be heard above the music. "And now your life is complete." She rests her hand on my arm and lets it linger there a little too long. When I instinctively take a step back, she gets the hint and lets it drop.

"So, what are you doing over vacation?"

I shrug. "People keep asking me that, but I don't think I have a very good answer."

She tilts her head to one side. "What's your answer?"

"Hanging out," I say definitively, crossing my arms like I'm proud of myself for being so aimless. Megan shakes her head as if she's actually disappointed in me and I shrug. "See what I mean? I'm not shooting very high."

"No, not so much."

I think about the only plan I have. The one I can't tell her or Sam or Brooke or anyone else about. The plan I do *not* want to think about right now.

"Bennett?" Megan is using a singsong voice, waving her hand back and forth in front of my face. "You still here?" she asks.

I blink fast. "Yeah. I'm sorry. What did you say?"

"I said that I'm just hanging out too." She looks down at the ground for a moment, and locks her eyes on mine. "I said, 'Maybe we could hang out together?'"

I don't say anything at first and Megan stares at me, eyebrows raised, expression hopeful, while I consider her suggestion. It's not like I know her that much better than I did at the end of last summer, but I think back to the words I said to Sam in the park that day and feel a little bad about my response. Megan's nice. She's pretty. And from what I've learned about her over the last few months, she's not at all vacuous. Besides, Lindsey's incredibly cool and *she* likes her. I don't know, maybe it's time for me to find a "four of us" that exists in 2012 and not in 1995.

"Maybe," I tell her.

Then we hear a crash in the distance, coming from the kitchen. "Uh-oh, that did *not* sound good. I'd better go find out what broke." She brushes my arm again and says, "See you," before she heads off, pushing past people, fighting her way out of the room.

As soon as she's gone, my stomach clenches. I don't want Megan and I don't want another *four of us.* I want Anna. Here.

Now. So I don't have to wake up tomorrow morning with my chest hurting and my mind all fuzzy, or go to sleep tonight feeling sick because I can't stop picturing that horrible look on her face the last time I saw her.

"Kathryn's on her way." I look up and see Brooke in front of me, her thumbs still tapping against the glass on her phone. "I think we're going to—" She stops cold when she sees me, hand clenched at my forehead, my face turning redder by the second. "What happened?"

I need to get out of here. I need air.

"Do you want to go?" she asks, looking me square in the eyes, and I nod quickly.

Even though it's winter, I still haven't put the soft top back on the Jeep. I've been driving around a lot this way over the last month: top down, cold wind, tunes loud, heat cranked. I maneuver out of the parking space I found a few blocks from Megan's house and drive away.

"Do you want to talk—" she begins and I cut her off with a curt, "No."

Out of the corner of my eye, I see Brooke's thumbs flying across the screen, and I can only assume she's texting Kathryn with her change of plans. I wonder if she's got a cover story or if she's texting her the truth: *Bro's a wreck. Need to stay.*

Her attention must move from texting to music, because as I crest over the next hill, she asks, "How about Coldplay on random shuffle?" It comes out like it's a question, but when Brooke's in the car, I rarely get any say in the music anyway.

Not that it matters. I couldn't care less what we listen to, as long as it keeps her from feeling like the silence is uncomfortable and it's up to her to fill the void.

"Ooh, good song," she says, cranking up the volume. She reclines the seat back and stares up at the sky. I don't know what it is. I just drive, listening to the lyrics.

Can anybody fly this thing?
Before my head explodes or my head starts to ring.

I can feel Brooke turning her head to look at me every once in a while, but I ignore it, keeping my eyes fixed on the road in front of me, tightening my grip on the steering wheel. Our house is only a block away now. It's early. I'm not at all ready to go home. And this song is right. Anna and I have been living life inside a bubble.

"Mind if I keep driving around for a bit?" I ask her.

She kicks her feet up to the dashboard and reclines back even farther. "I was hoping you would. I like this view," she says as she stares out the open roof, into the sky. Instead of taking a left turn toward our house, I take a right toward the Great Highway.

The Ocean Beach parking lot is dark and empty, and I pull into a spot facing the Pacific. I twist the key backward in the ignition, cutting the engine without killing the music. We're quiet for a long time.

Finally, Brooke speaks. "Why are you doing this, Bennett?"

I lean back against the headrest and let out a heavy exhale. "Please don't . . . Not tonight."

Brooke twists in her seat to face me. "On a completely different timeline that no longer exists, Anna came *looking* for you, remember? Because she felt so strongly that you were supposed to be in her life. Doesn't that mean anything?"

I shrug. "I thought it did, but no . . . apparently it doesn't." I haven't looked at the page in my notebook in months, but I don't need to. I've read those words from her letter so many times I've committed them to memory. *Someday soon, we will meet. And then you will leave for good. But I think I can fix it . . .*"

"You're making this far more complicated than it is, Bennett."

"It's very complicated, Brooke."

"No. You saw her with another guy and you freaked."

"I think there's a little more to it than that."

Brooke stares at me.

I fix my eyes on the sky and comb my hands through my hair. "Look, I know what I saw. She'll have a better life without me. Every time I go back there, I'm just keeping her away from the future she's supposed to have."

"But that's not the future she *wants*." Brooke tucks her hair behind her ears and leans across the console. "Besides, what's to say she won't do it all over again anyway? You saw her happy in two thousand five, but when she gets to two thousand eleven she could make the same decision she made last time—to go back and find you again."

"Why, because we're, like, *destined* to be together or something?"

"I don't know. Maybe. Yeah."

"You're just a romantic."

"Maybe. But I'm also quite logical." I let my head fall to the right and stare at her. "What you saw doesn't matter because that future isn't set in stone and you know it. Everything single decision you've made beyond that moment is changing what you saw."

"Or, it's changing nothing."

"If you're not part of her life, you'll never know." Brooke doesn't take her eyes off me. "Go talk to her."

I know she's right. I went more than a month without speaking to Anna once before, and that was excruciating. I can't believe I'm doing it by choice this time. I rest my elbows on the steering wheel and hold my head in my hands. "I will."

"Hey," she says, and I twist my neck to look at her. "Now."

"I'm not going right now."

She cranks up the heat and rubs her hands together in front of the vent. "I'll be fine here. Come back in twenty minutes or so. I'll wait."

"I'm not going right now," I repeat, this time slowly and with more emphasis on each word, because apparently she didn't hear me the first time.

"Bennett . . ." she says, almost under her breath. "Anna's *stuck* there waiting for you." She gives me this sad look, like she's upset about what happened between the two of us. But then she says, "How could—" and stops without finishing her thought. But she doesn't have to say another word. All I have to do is look at her, and even though I've never seen this expression on her face before, I know exactly what she's thinking. She's ashamed of me. And she should be. She's right. How could I have done that to Anna?

I need to go. Now. Besides, I've been missing her like crazy tonight.

Without giving myself any more time to think about it, I grab my wool coat off the backseat and pull my arms into it. Closing my eyes, I picture the one place I know I'll find Anna completely alone.

34

The sun is barely peeking over the horizon when I arrive at the Northwestern University track. Unlike all the times I was here before, there's just a light dusting of snow on the metal benches, and when I take my hand to brush it clean, it flutters into the wind, flying away in all directions.

I see Anna right away. She's down on the track, speeding around the curves, her legs reaching out in long strides, her arms pumping hard by her sides. I don't know what she's listening to on her Discman but I can see her lips moving and that makes me smile.

She comes around the bend to the long edge of the track, facing me, but her eyes are fixed on the ground like she's lost in thought. I don't move, but something must get her attention, because just as she's about to turn the next bend, she steals a glance into the bleachers.

She spots me, but it takes a few seconds for it to register.

She slows her pace to jog and stops at the base of the stairs, squinting up at me like it's totally possible that her mind is playing tricks on her. I lift my hand and wave.

Anna bolts up the stairs, taking them two at a time, but when she reaches the fourth row, she stops and doesn't come any closer. I can tell from the look on her face I should stay where I am.

"What are you doing here?" She takes her headphones off and wraps them around the back of her neck, never taking her eyes off me. "I thought you were coming for Christmas. That's still four days away." Her voice sounds wobbly and not at all like hers.

"So did I. But . . . this couldn't wait."

Anna looks around the track, then back at me. She presses her lips into a thin line. "What couldn't wait?"

"I owe you a massive apology." I brush the snow off the bench next to me. "Do you want to sit down?"

She walks toward me but stops short. Hugging her arms to her chest, she looks down at the icy bench and shakes her head no.

"I just wanted to say how sorry I am about that day . . . at the hospital . . . I was so . . . I don't know why I got so angry."

She sighs. "I wish you'd let me explain," she says quietly.

It's clear from the determined look on her face that she has something important to tell me, so even though I don't think she owes me an explanation at all, I sit quietly and let her speak.

"I didn't mean to push you so hard to do things over. I was

never trying to get you to change your rules or change . . . anything about who you are. That's the last thing I'd ever want." She plays with her fingernails as she shifts her weight from one leg to the other. "I guess I'm just . . . fascinated. Not just by what you can do, but by . . ." She looks out toward the track and covers her face with her hand. "Wow. I thought I had a few more days to get this speech down. This really isn't coming out the way I thought it would."

It feels strange to be this close and not touch her. I lean forward onto my thighs and smile at her. "I think it's coming out fine." She slides her hand down but keeps her mouth covered. Still, I can tell from her eyes that she's smiling too.

"Go on. . . . You were saying something about being fascinated." I scoot a little closer to her, but she keeps her feet planted in the snow and starts fidgeting with her headphone wires, wrapping and unwrapping the cord around her finger.

And suddenly, she stops moving and looks straight at me. "I'm in love with everything about you."

Her words make me suck in my breath, and when I look into her eyes, I see something I haven't noticed in a while— this look of pure understanding that reminds me why I told her my secret in the first place. That sense of wonder, how she looked at me like she couldn't know me well enough.

I can't take the distance any longer. I scoot over on the bench and the snow collects on my jeans. "Come here." I pull her closer, parting my legs so she can stand in between them, and she rests her forearms on my shoulders and looks down at me.

"I shouldn't have pushed you so hard to do things over again. I mean, I'm glad Emma's okay and I'll always be grateful to you for making that happen, but . . . it was wrong of me to force you to do it."

"You weren't wrong and you certainly didn't force me to do anything." My fingers settle on her hips. "I was as curious as you were, and I knew what I was doing. I *never* should have blamed you. I was just angry."

"At me?" she asks.

"No. At myself."

I grip her hips a little bit tighter and let my head fall forward until it rests against her stomach. "You know what I've been thinking lately?"

"Hmm?" Her fingers find my hair and I close my eyes. I've missed the way she touches me.

"I wish I could fly."

Her stomach rises when she laughs. "You want to fly now too?"

"No," I clarify. "Not in addition to, instead of."

"Why would you want to fly?"

I keep my eyes focused on the ground as my thumbs trace slow circles at her waist. "No one ever said, 'You really shouldn't fly' or 'Think of all the problems you could cause if you could fly,' right? You cruise around, check out the view, and come back down. Great power, none of the responsibility."

"I have a feeling you'd be bored just flying around all the time." I'm still looking down at our feet, but I can hear the smile in her voice.

"Maybe. But I also wouldn't have to worry about inadvertently changing the past. Or accidentally bumping into another *me* and sending the younger one back where he belongs."

She combs her fingers through my hair again. "You liked it, didn't you?" she asks. "The do-overs."

I pull my head away so I can see her face, and her hands settle on my shoulders again. They feel good there too. She takes another small step closer.

"Yeah . . . I did. I liked what you said about second chances. For a while there, it almost felt like I was supposed to do it, you know? It felt . . . almost . . . right." I shake my head. "I'd do it again. I'd go back for Emma and those kids. If I could have helped your dad, I would have."

Anna lifts my chin up and forces me to look at her. "You did help."

I don't say anything.

"Is he the real reason you don't think you should come back here anymore?"

I nod, even though he's only part of it. "I don't think this is right."

"For you or for me?"

"For everyone." I try to block out the vision of her in the driveway ten years from now, looking up at a guy who isn't me but makes her smile the same way I do. "But, I guess, especially for you."

She lets out a heavy sigh. "You seem to think you're somehow responsible for my future." I start to respond but she puts her finger to my lips. "Listen to me. Please, don't say anything. You are not responsible for my future, Bennett."

Sure I am. It would be totally different if I'd never come here.

"It's mine."

Yes, and you deserve a simpler one.

"And I want you in it."

You shouldn't even *know* me.

She looks over my shoulder, staring into the distance. "I don't know what you saw when you went forward, and I have a feeling you're never going to tell me. And that's fine." Now she looks right into my eyes. "Stop coming here if you think it's wrong for you, or for, I don't know, the space-time continuum or something, but don't stop because of me. From the beginning, you've made this all about how you were affecting *my* future. But I'm affecting yours, too. This time it's *your* choice. What do *you* want?"

I say the first thing that pops into my head. "You."

Her eyes light up. "I'm glad to hear that."

"But it's not that simple."

"Why not?"

"Because it's not."

She brushes my hair off my forehead and plants a kiss there. "I want you to be part of my life. When you weren't in it, I went to great lengths to get you back. So here we are." She spreads her arms out to her sides and looks around the track. "But who's to say what happens next? Maybe a year from now, we'll both be off at college and we won't want this anymore. Or after five years of this, we'll get tired of all the distance or the uncertainty . . . you'll get tired of zapping back and forth, or I'll get tired of waiting for you, or maybe the whole thing will become too much to handle. But right now, we both want to be together. Don't you think we should be?"

I stare at her. "I told you, it's not that simple."

"Sure it is." She runs her thumb across my cheek. "In fact, let's make it even simpler. I don't need a calendar. I don't care if you're here for big events or how long you stay each time. I just need to know that you're coming back."

I reach up for one of her curls and wrap it around my finger, thinking about how easy this all seemed back at the beginning of the school year. I remember that day we sat on my bed, surrounded by my new posters in a room that was starting to feel a lot like home, and built a schedule. God, how cocky I was, thinking I had it all figured out and that nothing would stand in the way of us being together as long as that's what both of us wanted.

"Will you think about it?" she asks.

I look away from her and nod.

"Don't do that," Anna says.

"What?"

"I can always tell when you're lying. You don't look at me."

I lock my eyes on hers. "I'll think about it," I say. And I will.

But I know I won't change my mind.

Physically, I'm here in San Francisco. But all morning I've been mentally absent, my thoughts constantly wandering to Christmas 1995. Ever since I saw Anna at the track, I've been trying to bring myself to go back there, but I just couldn't. Now that it's Christmas here, the whole thing feels unavoidable.

Dad reaches under the tree and makes a big production of reading the tag on the last gift. "To Brooke from Bennett," he says, tossing it high in the air.

Brooke catches it with both hands and shakes it hard for clues. She's already grinning as she rips off the paper, but a huge smile spreads across her face when she peeks inside. "No way." She looks up at me and starts pulling out each of the ten "vintage" concert tees, one at a time. In case my parents are getting suspicious as they watch her, I describe how I found them online, but when Brooke looks at me, I shoot her a wink.

She hugs the *Incubus 2007 World Tour* T-shirt to her chest. "I love them," she says. "Thank you."

Mom tries to pass me this plate of sticky-looking pastries for the third time, and once again, I hold my hand up to block them. She tips her chin down and gives me her concerned parent look. I haven't eaten much over the last few days and Mom's starting to notice, so I grab the plainest-looking thing on the plate.

"Well, I think that's everything," Dad says, taking one last look around the base of the tree. He stands up, straightens his back, and transfers the fluffy ball on his Santa hat from one shoulder to the other like it's a mortarboard tassel. "Christmas gift exchange 2012, officially complete," he says with his hands on his hips. Brooke tosses a wrapping paper ball at him and it bounces off his forehead.

"I'm going to go buy some music," I say, holding up my new iTunes gift card as evidence, and Brooke gives me a knowing look. She's already agreed to cover for me if she needs to, but that doesn't mean she's happy about it.

I start gathering up my gifts as Mom heads for the kitchen with a handful of plates and Dad follows her carrying a trash bag filled with used wrapping paper. Out of the corner of my eye, I see Brooke staring at me from the other side of the couch. As soon as I have everything, I head for the staircase. I'm at the first step when I hear her say my name, but I shake my head and keep climbing without turning around. What's the point? She'll just try to talk me out of this again.

When I'm showered and dressed, I dig around in the back of my closet, feeling for my backpack, and do one last round of inventory. There are water bottles, coffee shots, and Red Bulls; Kleenex and a spare T-shirt, just in case; and down on the bottom, Anna's photo album. I pull it out and thumb through it, feeling sick when I think about giving it back to her. But I can't keep it here.

I stuff the album back inside and toss the pack over my shoulders. There's no reason to stall any longer, so I picture the side of Anna's house, where the yellow paint is peeling and flaking off, and I close my eyes. But before I can leave, they spring open again.

And there it is, this ridiculously stupid thought. Not only is it stupid, it's also risky and more than a little bit pathetic. But this is my last trip for who knows how long, and I haven't been able to stop wondering about the guy she was with that night. And knowing who he is might give me some peace. I could use a little peace.

I squeeze my lids tight and before I can talk myself out of it, I open them to a view of a house painted gray with white trim.

After a quick look around to be sure I'm alone, I peer through the kitchen window. Inside, Mrs. Greene is in the exact spot, wearing the exact same thing, making the same meal she was making last time I showed up here in 2005 and shouldn't have.

I'll stay five minutes. Ten tops. Just long enough to catch a glimpse of him.

I check the driveway and find it covered in a layer of snow but otherwise empty. When I return to the window, Anna's mom is still standing at the stove, and I watch as Mr. Greene sneaks up behind her and wraps his arms around her waist. He gives her a quick kiss on the cheek, and she smiles and squirms away, swatting his hand with her wooden spoon. He laughs and kisses her again. Then he walks over to the sink and looks out the window that faces the street, like he's waiting for someone to arrive.

She should be here any second now. I listen to the sounds of the neighborhood, but there's nothing. It's totally silent.

"You need something to do." Unlike last time, the window is open a crack and I can hear everything the two of them are saying. Mrs. Greene walks to the drawer by the refrigerator and removes some silverware. "Here," she says, handing it to him. "Set the table. My goodness, you're like a little kid."

"Leave me alone, I'm excited." He walks into the dining room and he's out of my sight for a good minute or two. He returns empty-handed.

"Did you get the glasses, too?" she asks.

"Not yet, but I will." He pulls four water glasses down from one of the upper cabinets, and returns for four wineglasses. "Don't you think it's fundamentally wrong to have to take a plane to visit your family?"

Anna's mom laughs loudly. "Yeah, you should have thought about that when you hung a map of the world on her wall and gave her a box of pins to mark all the places she'd go." He shrugs and carries the glasses to the table, and I watch Mrs.

Greene stir whatever she's got in the stockpot. "You should have known she'd never stay put," she says, more to herself than to him.

I picture the map that hung on Anna's wall, briefly wonder if it's still there, and before I know it I'm closing my eyes and opening them in her bedroom. Her room is dark and I have to blink a few times as my eyes adjust, but then I spin slowly in place, taking everything in.

The dimensions are the same, but nothing else is. Anna's shelves are gone, and with them, the trophies and CDs they held back in 1995. There are no more race photos or numbers, and no more travel guides peppering the surfaces of her furniture. The map is gone and so is the box of pins. All the things that mattered in Anna's sixteen-year-old life aren't important in her twenty-six-year-old one, at least not in this house.

The bed has been moved to a different wall and it's covered with a different bedspread. I slowly walk over to it and sit down, running my hand across the surface, wondering if they share this room when they visit. He probably doesn't have to sleep on the couch like I did. I bet he gets to linger here with her in the morning, not sneak out before the sun comes up. Do they unpack their clothes and hang them side by side in the closet? Does Mr. Greene pour him coffee in the morning?

Coming to this room was a bad idea.

I stand up and close my eyes, returning to my spot under the kitchen window. I wonder why it's taking so long for them to get here.

As soon as I open them, I hear tires slowly crunching their

way through the snow, so I peek around the corner and then creep over to the tree, just like I did last time.

The headlights are still a few houses away, but Mr. Greene must have heard the car too, because the front door suddenly opens and he steps out onto the porch. He heads down the front stairs and waits at the edge of the driveway, fidgeting with the buttons on his sport coat.

My pulse is racing as the front of the car comes around the hedge and two streams of light illuminate the snow-covered lawn.

I think I yell.

I feel my stomach knot up tight and my head feels like it's going to explode. My eyes are burning, and without even thinking about it, I squeeze them shut. And when I finally peel them open, I'm standing right where I was when I left—smack in the middle of my bedroom in San Francisco.

I stumble over to the bed and sit down. I'm shaking and sweating, but when I look around and realize what just happened, I start laughing loudly and uncontrollably. It makes the headache a hell of a lot worse, but I can't seem to stop.

I'm back.

I'm shaking and sweating and laughing and . . . back.

I stand up, touching my face, my legs. I stomp the Evanston snow off my feet and watch it collect on my San Francisco carpet. I turn a three-sixty in place.

I'm back.

I was *knocked* back.

And there's only one reason that would happen.

Anna is part of my future and I'm part of hers. And that's all I needed to know, even if there are a million big and little things that could go wrong between now and then.

My backpack lands on the bed with a bounce, and I rip open the zipper, down a bottle of water as quickly as I can, and then dig to the bottom. When I find Anna's photo album, I toss it on top of my bedspread where Mom or Dad could easily find it if they happen to come in while I'm gone. There's no reason to hide it because Anna won't be a secret here anymore. I'll keep most of the promises I made to my parents—no more sneaking around, no more lies—but that "no more traveling" one isn't going to stick after all.

The Doubleshot makes me grimace as I gulp it down and I chase it with another bottle of water. I return to the center of the room and shake out my arms. My legs still feel wobbly as I close my eyes.

36

Anna's house is the color it should be in 1995.

Without giving myself time to process any more information than that, I race around the corner, fly up the front steps, and knock hard on her front door. My mouth is still dry and my head is a little foggy. I can feel the sweat on my brow even though my shoes are covered with fresh snow. But when the door swings open and I see Anna standing there, I forget everything else.

My heart is pounding hard in my chest. "Hi," I say, combing my fingers through my hair.

"Hi." She steps onto the porch and pulls the door closed behind her and I take a few steps back to give her room. She stands in front of me, looking confused, like she's trying to register the expression on my face but can't. She wraps one arm across her body and grips her elbow.

I don't know where to start. I have absolutely no idea what

to say right now. All I can think about is that ten years from now, the two of us will be in the same car, driving back here, walking up these steps and onto this porch, together. I look at my feet because I can't look at her and piece the right words together at the same time.

"Please say something," Anna says, letting out a nervous laugh. "You're killing me here." Her voice catches.

I lock my eyes on hers. "I was wrong," I say, and tears start sliding down her cheeks, one after the other. "I was convinced that I wasn't supposed to be part of your future but I think now . . . that I am."

Her lips are pressed tightly together and she nods quickly as she brushes her hands across her face. "Of course you are," she says. And then she looks at me, tears still streaming down her cheeks, and smiles. *That* smile. My smile. It belongs to me again.

I take two steps forward and throw my arms around her neck, lacing my fingers through her curls and breathing into her hair. I feel her bury her face in my T-shirt and wrap her arms around my waist. She squeezes me so tight, pressed in as close me to me as she can get. We stand like that for a long time.

I don't know if I was wrong. I might be wrong now. But my gut feels right for the first time in over a month and apparently I'm going with it, ignoring the risks and the questions and the consequences. Again. How can I *not*?

The wind is biting and when I finally step away from Anna, I discover that her cheeks are as red as the sweater she's wearing. I kiss each one. And then I take her face in my hands.

This kiss feels completely different from all the others. It's not like the one at the track the other day, when I was trying not to give her false hope. And it's nothing like the one when I first came back to town, back when I was all euphoric and full of conviction, certain we could make this work regardless of the considerable odds stacked against us. I'm kissing her like I've just returned from a long trip and I'm deliriously happy to be back home.

I rest my forehead against hers. I can't hold back my smile.

"What made you change your mind?" she asks.

I give her the only answer I have. "You. In a bunch of different ways."

We kiss again, and this one feels a lot more familiar. I picture her room upstairs, looking like it's supposed to, and I can't wait to be alone with her there.

When Anna pulls away, she hardly leaves any distance between us. "It's freezing out here," she says, brushing her lips against mine. "Come inside." Another small kiss. "Besides, you have presents to open."

Presents. Plural. I only brought her one thing. "Presents?" I ask.

She kisses my cheek. "I got you something. My parents got you a couple things too." I pull back a bit more. Her parents? It didn't even occur to me to buy them gifts. "Don't worry," she says, reading my mind. "They don't expect you to get them anything."

Anna moves toward the front door and I trail behind her,

but when she opens it and steps inside, I stop cold.

She turns around and stares at me. God, she looks happy and relieved and beautiful and perfect as she stands there, waiting for me to follow her. I must have a stupid grin on my face or something because she suddenly smiles at me. "What?" she asks.

I shake my head. "Nothing. I was just thinking about the first time I came over here." We'd both cut school. I'd stood on her porch in this exact spot, and Anna stood inside in that exact same one. When she opened the door I'd been expecting her to be afraid of me after I'd inadvertently shown her what I could do, but instead, she was all giddy and curious, eager to hear how I performed the magic that might have saved her life the night before.

But there was something else in her expression that day. She wanted to *know* me—really know me—and I stood frozen in place, realizing that I wanted her to be the person I told all my secrets to.

I knew it wouldn't be simple. That if I walked through that front door and into her world, both of our lives would be changed forever. Still, she seemed worth the risk. Now I know that she is.

So just like I did that day, I take a deep breath and step inside. Anna closes the door behind me.

I'm not supposed to be here.

But I am.

Don't miss Tamara Ireland Stone's
New York Times best-selling novel!

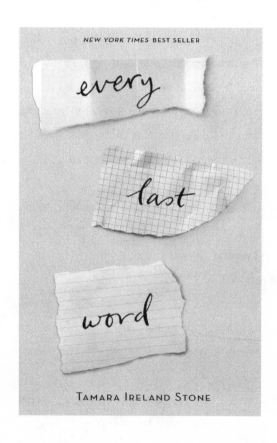

I *shouldn't be reading the notes.*

Hailey trims a rose and passes it to me. As I attach the note to the stem with sparkly pink ribbon, I read it. I can't help it. This one's a little over-the-top, but it's still sweet. I give it to Olivia and she drops it in the classroom-specific bucket.

"No way! You guys . . ." Olivia snorts, laughing hard as she turns the card over in her hand. I guess she's reading them, too. "I can't tell who wrote this but . . . poor boy. This is so cheesy."

Someone's attempt at heartfelt poetry makes its way around the circle. Alexis falls back against my bed in hysterics. Kaitlyn and Hailey double over on my rug. Eventually, I join in.

"This is mean. Let's not read them," I say, hiding the rose in the middle of the bucket, wanting to protect this anonymous guy who put his heart on the line for some girl in his calculus class named Jessica.

Olivia grabs the stack of cards in front of me and starts thumbing through them. "God, who are these people and how do we not know any of them?"

"We're not losers?" Alexis offers.

"It's a big school," Hailey counters.

"Okay, back to work. The flowers are wilting." Kaitlyn's still laughing as she snaps back to her role as the leader of our Valentine's Day fundraiser. "Olivia, since you like the notes so much, switch places with Samantha."

Olivia shakes her head, and her ponytail goes flying. "No way. I like my job."

"I'll switch. My hand's getting tired anyway," Hailey says, and the two of us trade spots.

I grab a rose out of the bucket and pick the scissors up off the floor. The instant I slide my fingers through the handles, this thought hits me out of nowhere, and before I have time to react I feel my brain sink its teeth in and latch on tight, already preparing to fight me for it. My hand starts trembling and my mouth goes dry.

It's just a thought.

I let the scissors fall to the floor and I shake out my hands a few times, looking around the circle to be sure no one's watching me.

I'm in control.

I try again. Rose in one hand, scissors in the other, I squeeze my fingers together, but my palms feel clammy and my fingers are tingling and I can't get a solid grip. I look up at Kaitlyn, sitting directly across from me, watching her face twist and blur as a wave of nausea passes over me.

Breathe. Find a new thought.

If I cut it once, I'll keep going. I know I will. I'll move on to the next rose, and the next one, and I'll keep cutting until there's nothing left but a huge pile of stems, leaves, and petals.

After that, I'll massacre those syrupy sweet, carefully written notes. Every single one of them.

God, that's so twisted.

Then I'll take the scissors to Olivia's ponytail and cut right through that hair tie.

Shit. New thought. New thought.

"I need a glass of water," I say, standing and hoping none of them notice the sweat beading up on my forehead.

"Now?" Kaitlyn asks. "Come on, Samantha, you'll hold everything up."

My legs are wobbly and I'm not sure I can trust them to get me downstairs, but somehow the scissors are gone and the banister is in my hand instead. I head straight into the kitchen and run my hands under the water.

The water is cold. Listen to the water.

"Are you okay?" Paige's voice breaks through the chatter in my head. I hadn't even seen my little sister sitting at the counter, doing her homework. That's when I spot the knife block, full of knives. And a pair of scissors.

I could slice right through her hair.

I take big steps backward until I slam into the refrigerator. My knees give out and I slide down to the floor, gripping the sides of my head, burying my face in my hands to make it dark, repeating the mantras.

"Sam. Open your eyes." Mom's voice sounds far away, but I obey her words, and when I do, the two of us are nose to nose. "Talk to me. Now."

I look over at the staircase, wide-eyed.

"Don't worry," she says. "They won't find out. They're upstairs."

I hear Mom whispering to Paige, telling her to take a bag of chips up to my room and keep my friends distracted.

Then she grabs both of my hands so hard, her wedding ring digs into one of my knuckles. "They're just thoughts," she says calmly. "Say it, please."

"They're just thoughts." I can echo her words but not the steadiness in her voice.

"Good. You're in control." When I look away from her she grips my arms harder.

"I'm in control."

She's wrong. I'm not.

"How many thoughts does the brain automatically deliver in a single day?" Mom moves on to facts to help me center myself.

"Seventy thousand," I whisper as tears splash onto my jeans.

"That's right. Do you *act* on seventy thousand thoughts a day?"

I shake my head.

"Of course you don't. This thought was one in seventy thousand. It's not special."

"It's not special."

"Good." Mom pinches my chin and lifts my head, forcing me to look at her again. "I love you, Sam." She smells like her favorite lavender-scented lotion, and I inhale it, feeling a host of newer, prettier thoughts overpowering the darker, scarier ones. "Whatever you're thinking, it's okay. It doesn't mean *anything* about you. Got it? Now tell me."

The two of us have been here before. It hasn't happened in a long time, not like this, but Mom slips right into her assigned role as if it's second nature. She's well trained.

"Scissors," I whisper, dropping my head to my chest, feeling dirty and sick and humiliated. I hate telling her these awful thoughts, but I hate the thought spiral even more, and this is my ticket out. I'm well trained, too.

"The roses. Olivia's hair and . . . Paige . . ." Mom doesn't make me finish. She wraps her arms around me and I grab ahold of her T-shirt, sobbing into her shoulder, telling her I'm sorry.

"You have nothing to be sorry for." She pulls away and kisses my forehead. "Now stay here. I'll be right back."

"Please don't," I beg, but I know she won't listen. She's

doing what she has to do. I dig my fingernails into the back of my neck three times, over and over again until she returns. When I look up, she's crouched down in front of me again, holding the scissors flat in her hand.

"Take them, please."

I don't want to touch them, but I don't have a choice. My fingertip connects with the cold metal and I let it slide over the blade, lightly, slowly, just tickling the surface. When I feel the handle, I curl my fingers through the holes. Mom's hair is dangling in my face.

I could cut it. But I would never do that.

"Good. It's just a pair of scissors. They triggered a few scary thoughts, but you won't act on them because *you*, Samantha McAllister, are a good person." Her voice sounds closer now.

I drop the scissors on the floor and give them a hard push to get them as far away from me as possible. I throw my arms around Mom's shoulders, hugging her hard, hoping this is the last time we go through this but knowing it isn't. The anxiety attacks are like earthquakes. I'm always relieved when the ground stops shaking, but I know there will be another one eventually, and again, I'll never see it coming.

"What am I going to tell them?"

My friends can't know about my OCD or the debilitating, uncontrollable thoughts, because my friends are normal. And perfect. They pride themselves on normalcy and perfection, and they can't *ever* find out how far I am from those two things.

"Paige is sitting in for you on rose duty. The girls think

you're helping me with something in the kitchen." Mom hands me a dish towel so I can clean myself up. "Go back upstairs whenever you're ready."

I sit alone for a long time, taking deep breaths. I still can't look at the scissors on the far end of the kitchen floor, and I'm pretty sure Mom will hide all the sharp objects for the next few days, but I'm okay now.

Still, I can hear this one thought hiding in the dark corners of my mind. It doesn't attack like the others, but it's frightening in a totally different way. Because it's the one that never leaves. And it's the one that scares me most.

What if I'm crazy?

six months later

more than anything

Lane three. It's always lane number three. My coaches think it's funny. Quirky. A *thing*, like not washing your lucky socks or growing a rally beard. And that's perfect. That's all I want them to know.

I step up to the top of the block and twist at the waist, shaking out my arms and legs. Squeezing my toes tight around the edge, I look down at the water and run both thumbs over the block's scratchy tape three times.

"Swimmers, take your marks." Coach Kevin's voice echoes off the clubhouse walls at the far end of the pool, and when he blows his whistle, my body's response is purely Pavlovian. Palm over hand, my elbows lock as I press my arms into my ears and throw myself forward, stretching and reaching and holding the position until my fingertips slice through the surface.

And then, for ten blissful seconds, there's no noise at all except the sound of water *whoosh*ing past my ears.

I kick hard and lock in my song. The first one that pops into my head is a happy tune with catchy lyrics, so I start my butterfly stroke, throwing both arms over my head in perfect synchronization with the beat. Kick, kick, throw. Kick, kick, throw. One, two, three.

Before I know it I'm touching the opposite end of the pool, doing a tight turn, and pushing hard off the wall. I don't look up or left or right. As coach says, right now, at this moment in the race, no one matters but you.

My head leaves the water every few seconds, and when it does, I can hear the coaches screaming at us to get our chins down or our hips up, to straighten our legs or arch our backs. I don't hear my name, but I check myself anyway. Today, everything feels right. I feel right. And fast. I increase the tempo of the song and kick it into gear for the last few strokes, and when my fingertips connect with the edge of the pool, I pop up and steal a glance at the clock. I shaved four-tenths of a second off my best time.

I'm breathing hard as Cassidy gives me a fist bump from lane four and says, "Damn . . . you're gonna slaughter me at county this weekend." She's won the county championship three years in a row. I'll never beat her, and I know she's just being nice, but it feels good to hear her say it anyway.

The whistle blows again and someone dives off the block

above me, signaling my turn to exit. I pull myself up out of the water, peeling off my swim cap as I head for my towel.

"Whoa! Where on earth did that come from?" When I look up, I'm eye to eye with Brandon. Or, more accurately, eye to *chest* with Brandon. I force myself to keep looking up, past his thin T-shirt and to his eyes, even though the temptation to check out the way his shorts hug his hips is almost more than I can resist.

During my first summer at the club, Brandon was just an older teammate with an insanely fast freestyle who always put up the most points in meets and taught the little kids to swim. But for the last two summers he's returned from college as a junior coach—my coach—and that makes him strictly off-limits. And even hotter.

"Thanks." I'm still trying to catch my breath. "I guess I just found a good rhythm."

Brandon shows me his perfect teeth, and those crinkles next to his eyes are even more pronounced. "Would you do that again at county, please?"

I try to come up with a funny comeback, something that will keep him smiling at me like this, but instead my cheeks get hot while he stares at me, waiting for me to reply. I look at the ground, chastising myself for my lack of creativity while I watch the water drip from my suit, forming a puddle underneath my feet.

Brandon must follow my gaze because he suddenly gestures

at the row of towels strewn across the wall behind him and says, "Stay there. Don't move."

A few seconds later he's back. "Here." He wraps a towel around my shoulders and slides it back and forth a few times, and I wait for him to drop the ends, but he doesn't. I look up at his eyes and realize he's staring at me. Like . . . maybe he wants to kiss me. And I know I'm looking at him like I want him to, because I do. It's all I think about.

His eyes are still locked on mine, but I know he'll never make the first move, so I take one brave step forward, then another, and without overthinking what I'm about to do, I press my dripping wet suit against his T-shirt, feeling the water soak it through to his skin.

He lets out a breath as he balls the ends of the towel in his fists and uses it to pull me even closer. My hands leave his hips and find his back, and I feel his muscles tense beneath my palms as he tips his head down and kisses me. Hard. And then he pulls on my towel again.

His mouth is warm and he parts his lips, and oh my God, this is finally happening, and even though there are people everywhere and I keep hearing the whistle blow and the coaches calling out behind me, I don't care, because right now I just want to—

"Sam? You okay?" I blink fast and shake my head as Brandon releases the towel and I feel it fall slack at my sides. "Where'd you go, kid?"

He's still standing two steps away and not even the slightest bit damp. And I'm not a kid. I'm sixteen. He's only nineteen. It's not that different. He adjusts his baseball cap and gives me that ridiculously adorable smile of his. "I thought I lost you for a second there."

"No." You did the exact opposite of losing me. My chest feels heavy as the fantasy floats up into the air and disappears from sight. "I was just thinking about something."

"I bet I know."

"You do?"

"Yeah. And you have nothing to worry about. Push yourself like *that* at county and keep swimming year-round, and you'll have your choice of college scholarships." He starts to say something else, but Coach Kevin yells for everyone to take a spot on the wall. Brandon gives me a chummy pat on the shoulder. A coachlike pat. "I know how badly you want this, Sam."

"More than you could possibly understand." He's still two steps away. I wonder what would happen if I *really* opened up my towel and wrapped him up in it.

"Sam. Wall!" Coach Kevin yells. He points at the rest of the team, already gathered and staring at me. I squeeze in next to Cassidy, and when Coach is out of earshot, she elbows me and whispers, "Okay, that was cute. That thing with the towel."

"Wasn't it?" I shoot her a surprised look. At the beginning of the summer, Cassidy called him "Coach Crush," but over the last few weeks she's become increasingly irritated with me for not giving up.

"I said it was cute, not that it means anything."

"Maybe it does."

"Sam. Sweetie. Really. It doesn't. He grabbed your towel and dried you off a bit. But that's it. Because he has a girlfriend. In college."

"So?" I lean forward, trying not to make it obvious that I'm looking for him. He's over by the office, drinking a soda and talking with one of the lifeguards.

"So. He has a girlfriend. In *college*," she repeats, stressing the last word. "He talks about her all the time, and it's obvious to everyone except you that he's totally in love with her."

"Ouch."

"Sorry. It had to be done." Cassidy piles her long red hair on top of her head in a messy bun and then grips my arm with both hands. "I'm not telling you anything you don't already know." She comes in closer. "Look around, Sam," she says, gesturing to a long line of our teammates. "There are plenty of fish in the fancy-private-swim-club sea."

I look around and see boys in tight Speedos with solid abs and muscular arms, their skin tanned by the Northern California sun, their bodies lean and solid after three months in the water, but none of them are anywhere near as flawless as Brandon. Even if I did find one of them remotely attractive, what's the point now? Summer's nearly over.

Cassidy tilts her head to one side, pouting dramatically. She brings her fingertip to my nose and sighs. "What am I going to do without you, Sam?"

My stomach clenches into a tight fist as she voices a thought that's been haunting me since the first day of August. Like all my summer friends, Cassidy has never known me outside the pool. She has no idea who I am when I'm not here, so she doesn't know how backward she has it.

"You'll be fine," I say, because it's true. Me? I'm not so sure.

My psychiatrist nailed it back in June, when I practically floated into her office and announced that I'd taken my last final. She strode over to the minifridge, poured sparkling apple cider into two plastic champagne flutes, and said, "To the triumphant return of Summer Sam" as we clinked glasses.

But it's coming to an end. In two weeks, I'll be back in school, Cassidy will be in L.A., and Brandon will be at college. I'll be missing them, along with my early morning dives into lane number three.

I'll be Samantha again. And more than anything, I'll be missing Sam.